Bad Moon Rising

A Parker McLeod Thriller™

By
A. Hardy Roper

West Bay Publishing
Houston, Texas
www.facebook.com/TheGarholeBar

Copyright © 2019: A. Hardy Roper
Cover Graphic by Artist Yue Xiao
Edited by: Chris O'Shea Roper
A Parker McLeod Thriller Series Book Four
All rights reserved

ISBN: 978-0-9840484-8-9

Printed in the United States of America with simultaneous
printings in Australia, Canada, and United Kingdom.

FIRST EDITION
1 2 3 4 5 6 7 8 9 10

Review for: Bad Moon Rising
By: Sharan Zwick
Galveston Bookshop

"A. Hardy Roper, Bad Moon Rising is your best story yet!"

If you have read A. Hardy Roper's three previous thrillers set on Galveston Island, then you know Parker McLeod. The easy-going owner of The Garhole Bar, Parker is at his best with a cold beer in his hand and a beautiful woman at his side. While he never goes out looking for danger, somehow it seems to find him. Bad Moon Rising, Hardy's latest book about this enigmatic but likable character is no exception. Parker's beloved grandfather had used the phrase "bad moon rising" as a warning when a dangerous storm appeared on the horizon. Parker now claims ownership of the expression as the "bad moon" of terrorism comes to the island.

Characters in this fast-paced novel are exquisitely drawn: A beautiful scientist from Germany who is the new Assistant Director of the Gulf Coast Level 4 Biological Lab; the Secretary of Homeland Security, in Galveston for a routine inspection; Islamic terrorists intent on revenge against the Secretary; and Parker—a former Army Intel officer with a personal vendetta against one of the terrorists. Add the FBI, NSA, CIA, Secret Service and local police and the intensity ratchets up with every page. The terrorists will use any means available including kidnapping, coercion and threats, to kill the Secretary. When the first attempt fails, the terrorists devise a scheme to use a deadly pathogen. During a raging winter storm, Parker must race through flooded streets and dark alleyways to try and prevent a cataclysmic event for the usually sun-filled city of Galveston. If you like thrillers, Bad Moon Rising is a must read!

Acknowledgements

What an adventure! It was not the effort but the journey, and now is the time to acknowledge the incredible gifts I received from friends, some new, some longtime. Each of you gave graciously of your time, skills and knowledge. Bad Moon Rising is a testament to your goodwill, and the book would never have been completed without your help. I owe a great deal of gratitude to each of you. I hope you enjoy our collaborative efforts.

I owe special thanks to members of White Oak Writers Group, Anne Sloan and Diane Teichman, both of whom spent many hours reading and digesting chapters and giving me honest critiques. Anne and Diane provided valuable advice and insight into phrasing, plot development, grammar and structure. Diane also developed the "back page wording" when I was stuck and couldn't put it together. Thank you both.

Another big thank you goes to my friend, Jennifer Pinero. Due to her expertise in treating burn victims, Jennifer was able to provide much needed information. I also want to thank Ron Roseman, teacher at Heights High School for his help when I was stuck in Microsoft Word.

Three retired FBI agents provided invaluable assistance, Bob Seale, Senior Resident Agent, Waco, Charlie Rasner, Special Agent, Bomb Technician and Byron Sage, Special Agent. Thanks to each of you for your help. And thank you for your service.

A special appreciation award goes to Bruce Moran, Publisher. Bruce's expertise in formatting the cover and manuscript was a delight to witness. If you need help with a book, Bruce can be reached at totalrecallpress.com.

Thank you, Bruce.

The painting used for the cover was the creation of my friend, Yue Xiao, a very talented artist who offered her time and creative ability as a gift. Thank you, Yue. You are an amazing artist.

I need more than words to express my gratitude to my editor, and author in her own right, Chris O'Shea Roper. Chris you have done it again, providing your invaluable service, stepping up to the plate when I really needed you. I greatly appreciate your indefatigable spirit, editing expertise, and willingness to come to my rescue. Your editing talents always continue to amaze me. For your time and efforts, I offer a most sincere "thank you."

I could never complete a book without the love and support of my lovely bride of twenty-seven years, Dorothy, (Winkie) Roper. Thank you for your patience, dearest. I hope you are not still upset with me for naming a hurricane after you in my first book, *The Garhole Bar*.

Photo credit for the author belongs to John Leech Photographers, Houston.

Chapter One

December 15, 2007
Minneapolis, Minnesota

Every big city has one—that part of town where police don't like to go at night. Minneapolis has one, made up of dozens of blocks where the struggling poor eke out a day-to-day existence on food stamps and welfare checks. Where the unemployed and unemployable gather on street corners hoping for a few hours' work for a contractor who pays off-the-books cash.

The area is an eclectic mix of poor white, black and Hispanic families, struggling at minimum wage jobs and trying desperately to survive. Among the mix are single mothers and their kids who somehow endure, with no help from the deadbeat dads who have already moved on and impregnated another lonely girl.

Of course, the gangs are there too, providing cocaine, meth, heroin and an unlimited supply of opioids.

The city does its best to help, but the struggle continues with no real answer in sight. Minneapolis knows its problems are not unique: Dividing railroad or not, every city has its "other side of the tracks."

The shabby apartment building with its chipped stucco façade, weed-strewn walkway, dirty walls and broken entrance gate stood as a beacon of misery, a daily reminder of its occupants' forlorn lives. People who are just trying to survive pay little attention to their neighbors. And that anonymity, plus the cheap rent, was exactly why Muhammad Rana had picked this rat-invested apartment to create his jihadist cell: No one would notice them, no one would care.

At six-two, Muhammad grudgingly admitted that he had gotten his height from this father. He was also skinny, with a long, thin face and slumped shoulders, which added to his self-consciousness. He didn't like to be stared at.

His seventeen-year-old brother Ratif was short and a little plump, probably from his diet of all-American junk food. Ratif's friend Lutfi, the same age, was also carrying a hefty mid-section. Both of the younger boys had a scattering of teenage acne on their faces. Although Lutfi's was more pronounced, he had managed to grow a scraggly beard to hide the bumps and was highly disappointed when Muhammad told him to shave it. Muhammad had warned the beard might cause undo suspicion around the neighborhood, and they were too close to completing the first phase of their mission for any slip-ups.

The apartment's living area contained a worn couch, coffee table and used chairs they had picked up at garage sales. Two dirty mattresses covered the floor in the tiny bedroom so they could crash after a night of searching the dark web.

A folding table and a couple of chairs were pushed against the wall amidst a tangle of wires running to a computer and printer. A number of bomb manuals they'd found on the internet were printed and stacked by the computer. At the end of the table, two paperbacks lay on top of each other: Islam for Dummies and Quran for Dummies.

The newly-minted amateur jihadists sat hunched over the table drinking Pepsi and eating cold pizza while tinkering with different triggering devices. They finally settled on a simple switch with a battery. They had been up all night and Muhammad decided to give the younger boys a break. He wanted to talk about finalizing the plan.

School would start in a few hours but neither Ratif nor Lutfi would be there. They hadn't attended in several weeks, ever since Muhammad had finally won them over. Although at age twenty-two Muhammad was five years older, they'd all grown up together. Ratif and Lutfi had always idolized Muhammad. Getting them on board had been easy.

After all, they didn't have a chance in this wicked society. Especially since 9/11. The loathing for Muslims across godless America was ubiquitous: hatred for their ways, their customs, all that constant praying and not even to Jesus. The boys couldn't help but be aware of snide looks in their direction, the suspicion in every eye, people distancing themselves in the malls.

Muhammad, older and wiser, had preached that, with the incessant discrimination, good jobs were impossible to get. There was no reprieve for Muslims in America, shuffled to the sidelines of society, marginalized to the edge, isolated within their communities.

Muhammad and Ratif's parents spoke only Punjabi at home, one of the many hundreds of dialects used in Pakistan. So the family's fractured English didn't help. After 9/11, their father's bodega had been vandalized and partially burned. Their mother, who had been a highly educated school teacher in Islamabad, washed neighbors' clothes until he could rebuild the store. Even with this disgrace, his parents had not given up. They wanted to succeed in America and were grateful to be here. The thought of his parents' simple naiveté made

Muhammad want to retch.

A year earlier, Muhammad had finally gotten his driver's license. After a hard search, with many turn-downs, he'd found a part-time job as a short-haul truck driver. A few weeks later, he was arrested for stealing part of a delivery. He'd gotten off with a stern admonition from the judge and deferred adjudication, but privately Muhammad had sneered at the entire system. He'd only stolen because white America wouldn't allow him to succeed.

Totally discouraged, Muhammad had ultimately found solace in his computer. He'd turned to on-line messaging services for support and soon discovered social media sites dedicated to Islamic radicalization. The process went rapidly from there. The Mahdi contacted him and taught him that, in the Islamic faith, Allah had deemed the Mahdi to be the "guided one." His job was to rid the world of evil, but he needed Muhammad's help. The Mahdi directed him to the dark web. He taught him how to encrypt messages using a special key. Muhammad's conversion was rapid, and a few weeks later he recruited his little brother and his friend into the cell. By then, the group's social circle had narrowed to only the three of them. The Mahdi's plan for isolation was complete.

The Mahdi then directed the cell to bomb-making sites and let them know he was an expert: He had constructed and detonated many bombs and had never failed.

He taught them about the wonders of Paradise and how Allah would welcome them as martyrs with open arms, including an unlimited supply of virgins. That sounded really good to Muhammad. He had no idea where the Mahdi lived, but he suspected somewhere in the Middle East because of all the bombings he'd done.

Now sitting around the table amid their bomb-making

materials, Muhammad set the soldering iron down and looked up at his co-conspirators.

"I think this triggering device is good, but we need to test it. We'll break into that hot-rod shop tonight and steal enough high-octane racing fuel to run an experiment out in the woods someplace."

He told the boys that the Mahdi had recommended racing fuel because of its "brisance," whatever that meant. They would use one of the blasting caps they'd stolen at a rock quarry to set it off.

"After that?" asked Ratif, his eyes wide as large plums.

"We pick up four fifty-five-gallon drums, load them into the old pick-up I bought and head south," Muhammad said. "Ratif will go with me and drive the pick-up back. Lutfi, you will stay here and coordinate with us if needed."

Lutfi whined, "I want to go."

Muhammad backed Lutfi down with a stern look. Then he looked back at Ratif and said, "We will take our time in case we run into delays. Just so we're in Houston by late this month."

"And the fertilizer?" Ratif asked.

"There is a feed store in every little bumpkin town in Texas. We'll be a couple of hippies working a farm commune. Pick up small amounts at a time."

Muhammad reached over and removed the paper covering a plastic stick-on sign that read Island Flower Shop. The phone number was, of course, bogus.

"Are four drums enough?" asked Lutfi, his face eager with anticipation. "That McVeigh guy in Oklahoma City used 13."

"Yes, but McVeigh also used one of those large Ryder cargo trucks. A full drum holds 500 pounds. We're using a delivery van. Four drums will be enough. The Mahdi knows what he is doing."

Chapter Two

Friday, January 4th, 2008
The Garhole Bar, Galveston, Texas

Nothing restores the soul like standing at the edge of a deserted beach on a cold winter's evening and witnessing shore birds as they scurry along in tiny flocks and whistle to the sound of their own hearts beating. Hustling for their dinner, they pluck small organisms out of sand and mud that was laid bare by a biting, blue norther which had begun somewhere south of the Arctic Circle and finally pushed down to the coast, driving the surf out from the shoreline. The bleakness of the scene is always faithfully redeemed by the assurance that the water would return after the front passed, covering the sand as before and bringing the comforting joy of rejuvenation. It was a testament to the continuum of life, as though some great architect had planned it that way.

I needed this vision, this restoring virtue—not as much as in 1994 when I'd first returned to West Beach after serving twenty years in the Army, but still I needed it. The scene had always given me a sense of existence, a way forward, a reason to push on.

Thankfully I'd pulled through all the serious health issues I'd developed as a result of my service during the Gulf War. And here I was, standing on the beach, my heartbeat almost back to normal after a five-mile run.

Around me, dark shadows crowded the evening sky. The temperature had fallen ten degrees in the last twenty minutes. The north wind howled like a banshee keening over a grave. I quickly pulled on the sweats I'd left on a piece of driftwood and looked back across the island at the outline of the two-story cedar-planked building I called home.

Galveston Island is shaped like the blade of an irregular prehistoric spear hammered out of a piece of ancient rock, with the larger end owning the city and port and the rest of the island erratically narrowing down to the tip where I live, less than a mile from the island's end at San Luis Pass. My place stands on the edge of West Bay, the body of water that separates the island from the mainland.

At the end of each day, the sun sets far out in the bay, disappearing like butter melting into a skillet. Today, the great ball of light had already sunk below the horizon. I had only minutes to jog back before darkness covered my return path. Among the sand dunes, prickly pear and rattlesnakes claimed the night. I needed to hurry.

Moments later I stopped to jog in place at FM 3005, or San Luis Pass Road, to check the traffic. At twilight, many vehicles had yet to turn on their lights. Better to be safe than sorry. The highway splits the island between the gulf and bay, extending twenty miles from the end of the seawall at the City of Galveston to the bridge over the pass. The bridge connects the island to the mainland and the seaside village of Surfside, twenty miles farther down the coast.

Not seeing any cars approaching, I jogged across the highway and down the sand road to where a lone light bulb, diminished by the howling wind and blowing sand, barely illuminated the hand-painted sign over the door: "The Garhole Bar," my little piece of heaven.

Back when I'd first returned to the island after leaving the

Army, I'd decided to turn the old bait camp into a bar. I stumbled upon a dead, six-foot alligator gar washed up in the marsh. In a moment of inspiration, I cut the behemoth's head off, boiled and bleached the skeleton white, and hung it from the ceiling over the back counter.

When I set out on my jog, I had left the door unlocked with a note on the counter advising any visitors to help themselves and leave the money in the cigar box on the bar. I signed the note "Parker McLeod, Proprietor."

I flipped on the wall-mounted beer signs and eased past the tables I'd gotten at a Salvation Army resale shop. At the rear of the room, two barstools stood in front of the serving counter. Behind the counter were the refrigerator, sink, stovetop and beer cooler. The back door was to the right.

I saw no sign of having had customers, no empty beer bottles and no money in the box: a typical bad weather day at The Garhole. I popped a cold Shiner and, as custom demanded, toasted the gar head hanging from the ceiling, its rows of razor-sharp teeth gleaming in the light and staring down at me.

I had a lot of respect for alligator gars. A creature that had survived thousands of years of evolution virtually unencumbered by climate change, wars, pestilence or the human race's idiotic behavior toward each other. Through it all the lonely gar just kept chugging along, wallowing out a deep hole in the bay somewhere, minding its own business, surfacing only to cruise the canals at night and search for sustenance. I toasted the gar head again and slugged down another swallow of Shiner.

The fast-moving cold front with its punishing gale-force wind had driven the water out of the bay, making fishing pretty much nonexistent for a few days. Even the locals, who occasionally dropped by for a cold beer and bowl of gumbo, rarely ventured out in this kind of weather. This far down the island from the tourist-packed city of Galveston, the livelihood of The Garhole depended on fishing, and fishing depended on the weather, sporadic this time of year at best. But year-round what I made from the bar plus my Army retirement was enough to get by on, and that's all I really cared about.

Out in the bay the howling wind lashed the water with a cruel vengeance, as if the bay was responsible for some great misdeed. After browsing through a fishing magazine and downing a couple more beers, I glanced back at the empty room: silent as a tomb. I decided to call my friend Larry who ran the NOAA station up on the mainland. Larry was a plump fortyish bachelor who liked to drink beer and fish. The calls to Larry cost me an occasional guided fishing trip on the bay, but they were the quickest way to get weather updates. He answered his private line on the first ring.

"So what's the haps for the week," I said. "Am I gonna get any business at all?"

He recognized my voice. "It's gonna be a weird week. This one will blow through and it will warm up tomorrow, but there's another one right behind it, and then thunderstorms and heavy rain at the end of the week. You should see intermittent days of warm and cold and then wet."

"Sounds like I might as well shut down and piss off a little money at the tables in Lake Charles."

"Well, let me know if you decide to go, I might tag along. Either way, you owe me a fishing trip. My cousin's coming in from Kansas and wants to try his hand at it."

"Oh, Jeez, give me a break, Larry. I don't keep any guest rigs anymore. Your last "cousin" tore up my Garcia open-face so badly I had to send it to the shop. Cost me forty bucks."

"I'll pick up a Zebco. He won't know the difference."

I flipped off the beer lights and hustled up the stairs to the deck outside my bedroom. It was too windy and cold to stay out tonight. But on calm nights, my favorite way to pass the evening was to sit in my old Adirondack chair under a full moon and enjoy the peaceful glow spreading across the water. When the night was clear, I could see the red and green lights atop the masts of tugboats pushing barges along the Intracoastal Waterway on the opposite side of the bay.

It had been a while since anything terribly exciting had happened around The Garhole. In fact, after years of running the bar, I hated to admit it but I was getting a little restless. It was after falling asleep on lonesome nights like this that the dream came. The vision was appearing more and more often and was getting more real each time. In it, I sell The Garhole and my grandfather's old ranch that surrounds it, grab a tug down the ICW to Freeport and board a freighter bound for Australia. I then buy a Harley and ride with the wind across the Outback, moving fast, with nothing but desert landscape in front of me on an endless journey into the unknown.

The front was still pushing hard, the wind hurling itself across the bay, the sky a mixture of gray and black. The moon was just coming over the horizon and I wanted a peek before crawling into bed. I pulled the hoodie tight around my cheeks and eased to the dock railing. A full moon with dark, menacing clouds flowing endlessly over its surface stared back at me.

Somewhere, out in the marsh, a lone coyote wailed a forbidding howl. I wondered if the threatening moon provoked the yell or if it was just the canine's innate loneliness that had made him cry. An involuntary shudder rattled my bones as I remembered another night years earlier.

When I was thirteen, my grandfather and I were out in the bay under a full moon, night-fishing for trout. The bay was calm, the sky clear. Suddenly a harsh wind sprang out of nowhere and grayish black clouds like the ones tonight filled the sky and crept across the moon. I still remember the goose-bumps popping across my skin.

My grandfather said, "Reel in your line, son. Crank up the motor, we're going in. I don't like the looks of this...bad moon rising."

Two days later my grandfather, the only person I'd ever really loved, was dead, crushed when his tractor rolled over on him while mowing the levee at the freshwater pond he'd dug for his cattle. I think about the tragedy of the old man's passing and wished he were still here. I loved to ride with him when he rounded up his Brahmas for market, all the while listening to his stories of the old days when there was nothing on the West End but a few scattered truck farms and fishing camps.

My grandfather told me once that everyone has two deaths. The first passing is when your heart stops. The second death is when everyone who has ever known you finally exits from the earth and the memory of you fades into oblivion.

Grandfather hasn't reached that second plateau yet: I think of him daily.

One last glance at the moon and I was inside under a pile of blankets. Late in the night, while in the middle of a new dream, I was awakened by the wind pounding my door. I chased the fading image in the dream, not wanting to lose its meaning. Grandfather and I were fishing, the same moon overhead as tonight. His lips moved without sound, his face twisted and contorted. Was it a message? But what...a warning?

When the lonely wail of the coyote sounded again, the vision plummeted into darkness. And like a ghost disappearing at dawn, the darkness faded into morning.

Chapter Three

Saturday morning
The Garhole Bar

On good fishing days I'd be up early, knowing fishermen would tie up at my dock to use my outdoor cleaning table. But the all-night chop on the bay had turned the water chocolate-brown. Even die-hard anglers stayed home in these conditions. And this was Saturday. If it had been a weekday, wind or not, I would have gotten up early to catch two regular customers who worked the nightshift at one of the chemical plants on the mainland. Billy and Wade were always good for a few morning brews on their way home.

I wanted another hour in the rack, but the annoying leak under the kitchen sink kept gnawing at me, so I rolled out early. I hustled down the stairs rubbing my arms and wishing I'd worn the top to my sweats instead of a T-shirt. The bar, still dark and humid, felt colder than outside. The Garhole's cement floor helped cool the bar during the summer, but the dampness only added to the chill during the winter months.

I rubbed my arms again to try and warm up, turned on the lights, cranked up a small electric floor heater and started the coffee. I fried several strips of bacon and popped two bread slices in the toaster, wishing I'd remembered eggs on my last trip to Red's, the small convenience store down the beach. I had just finished the sandwich and was under the sink with a wrench in my hand and a pain shooting down my back, when the telephone rang.

I scrunched out from beneath the sink, stretched my back and reached for the wall phone wondering who would call me on a day like this. Any fool could see there would be no fishing, and fishermen were about the only calls I got.

I picked up the receiver, "Garhole."

"Parker McLeod, you hunka hunka burning love. How's it hangin'?"

Jeez, Molly Putts. I hadn't heard her bawdy voice in several months, and that hadn't been long enough.

"Hey, Molly."

"Bully wants to talk at you."

Getting involved with Bully Stout was not a pleasant way to start the day. The old geezer had to be at least eighty now. Surprised he was still kicking. Bully was my mother's sister's husband. So that made the old crab my uncle, so to speak, although I never claimed him as such. When my aunt died, Bully had no place to live so, in a weak moment, I'd let him move an old camping trailer behind The Garhole. He was supposed to help out around the bar, but about the only thing he ever did was trap a few crabs for the gumbo. He spent most of his time snatching beers out of my cooler for free, smoking god-awful cigars and harassing me.

Between the aggravating leak under the sink and the sharpness in my spine, I was in no mood for Bully Stout, but then his voice screamed through the line.

"Parker goddamnit, get your forkin' bony ass over here. I need you."

"What's the matter, Bully? Your leg finally too heavy?"

Bully had stepped on a mine two weeks before the Germans capitulated in 1945. The explosion cost him his left leg below the knee, his left eye and two fingers off his left hand. After returning home, he'd carved a wooden leg out of an old piece of driftwood he'd found washed up on the beach. Although the pirate-looking peg leg must weigh twenty pounds, Bully claimed it always fit better than those "damn government legs."

"You shit! You know I'm in a wheelchair. But you ain't called or nothing."

The cantankerous old warrior hadn't changed a bit, still ornery as hell. Harry Stein, my good friend (and lawyer when needed) had called me about a year ago to tell me Bully was hospitalized at the University of Texas Medical Branch (UTMB) in Galveston with a stroke. I didn't know about it because by that time Bully had met Molly Putts and Grumpy had moved in with her. Outside Bully's room at the hospital, I ran headlong into a reunion of the Dead Peckers Club. The club's members were all past eighty and had grown up together on the island. Several of the original members had slipped the earth's bonds and now only three remained: Bully, Harry Stein and Neddie Lemmon. Inside the room, Molly Putts had sat in her wheelchair next to Bully's bed, holding his hand, a tear on her cheek. When the hospital released Bully a week later, he went home in a wheelchair and had been in it ever since joining Molly in hers.

I answered with as much gruff as he'd dished out. "Well I'm talking to you now, Bully, so get over it."

He stammered, mumbled something, and then I heard him spit, probably trying to get a piece of tobacco out of his throat from the ubiquitous cigar always hanging out of his mouth.

"Yeah, well...anyways, this fancy-assed woman showed up. Claims she's my granddaughter and—"

I interrupted, "Damn, Bully. You already forgot about Lisa?"

"It ain't Lisa. Lisa's still up at Austin going to school with all those pinko assholes they got up there."

"Then who—?"

"That's what I'm trying to tell you, damn it. Will you forkin' listen? Says she's from Germany. Something about the war."

"Germany?"

"Get the sand fiddlers outta your ears, damn it. That's what I said."

"Oh hell, Bully. I'm on my way."

I showered and shaved, jumped into jeans and a sweatshirt, and on the way down the stairs realized the wind had quit. The clear sky meant the day would warm quickly. Thinking a customer or two might stumble in, I called the tollbooth at the bridge over San Luis Pass, hoping Neddie Lemmon was working today. I recognized the voice as a sometime customer who occasionally dropped in at The Garhole.

"Hey, Henry, this is Parker McLeod, looking for Neddie. Need him to help out at The Garhole. Is he working today?"

"Yeah, he got off a few minutes ago. Went under the bridge, but he's coming back now. Hold on."

"Under the bridge" meant Neddie was down there checking on the two dozen or so feral cats he gathered every morning.

When Neddie took the phone, I said, "Some local birder's gonna powder your ass with birdshot if you don't stop feeding those damn scavengers. And it may be me. You know most shore birds are ground nesters, and their chicks won't stand a chance this spring against that marauding pack of mini-tigers you harbor."

"Yeah, well it better be my ass 'cause I'll damn sure be looking out front for 'em. Henry said you needed help. I'll be by in a few."

I left Neddie a note and lit out to see Bully, hoping my rust-bucket ten-year-old Chevy pick-up would make it from The Garhole to Molly's house, thirty miles away. The old truck had been a faithful partner, and I didn't see any sense in trading it in since the humidity and salt air of West Beach would immediately begin an assault on a new one.

Twenty minutes later, I reached Seawall Boulevard at the edge of the city. I turned on 61st Street and cut across to Broadway, the wide, flowered boulevard that runs through town to the beach. I turned left on Broadway and hit the six-lane causeway that connected the island to the rest of the world.

Galveston Island is all about tourism, and tourism is about the weather. The traffic on the bridge today seemed exceptionally light, unlike hot summer weekends when cars would crawl bumper to bumper over the causeway on their way to the beaches.

I hadn't been off the island in a year, since my last visit to the VA in Houston. And that was fine with me. Those hurried folks off-island can have all the noise and fast-paced life they can eat.

I came off the causeway, turned right onto Highway 146, and zoomed past the maze of refineries and petrochemical plants that border Texas City. Seeing the huge tangle of valves belching out plumes of supposedly scrubbed toxins sent a wave of nausea through my stomach. I raced on hoping to get past the plants before some noxious fume could invade my car.

A mile past the city limits, I turned onto a short street that dead-ended into a field. A large clapboard house with a wide porch in front stood toward the end of the street. The house needed repairs. Streaks of rust pock-marked the tin roof, some of the sideboards were pulled loose, and there was not a drop of paint left anywhere on the structure. A corroded chain-link fence surrounded the yard.

I pulled beside the silver Lexus SUV parked by the curb. The car was unlocked so I opened the door and peeked in, hoping to find car rental papers. Seeing nothing, I closed the door quietly and entered the front gate.

Molly Putts rolled onto the porch with a blanket across her overly large lap looking the same as I remembered—like she'd ordered a wheelchair two sizes too small. And that was being kind. She spit into a coffee can, wiped a drool of tobacco juice from the corner of her mouth, and moved the binoculars from her lap to her eyes. She pretended to be searching the field beyond my truck, but I knew she was focusing on me. As I closed on the stoop, she lowered the field glasses.

"Damn it, Parker. You ain't changed a bit. Handsome devil. Always loved that coal black hair and those dark wicked eyes. If I was thirty years younger...."

"Molly, cut the crap. What's going on here?"

Molly sighed, "The twit's inside trying to schmooze him."

Molly's obvious sensitivity took me aback. Jealousy at her age? I ignored the comment and entered the front door. A couch and two chairs were covered with sheets to keep the dust off. A whiff of mold left me wondering if they ever opened the windows.

An attractive thirty-something woman stepped out of the kitchen. Tall, five-seven or so, with light brown hair and a slim figure that curved in the right places. Her face was smooth and pretty, with full lips, a cute upturned nose and not much need for makeup. A dark green cashmere sweater and matching wool slacks completed the picture. She moved toward me in a confident stride, extending her hand in greeting. It was then I noticed her hazel eyes, the kind that would change color according to her outfit. Today they appeared more greenish because of the sweater, but tomorrow they could be blue.

"You must be Parker," she said, her voice soft, almost playful.

I hadn't known what to expect when Bully called to say a woman was claiming to be his granddaughter, but I'd learned long ago: Life can be full of surprises. She was a looker. The war had ended sixty years earlier, so if I'd gauged her age correctly, the timing could work.

I took her hand, warm and firm. Before I could answer, she said, "My name is Anna Lang. So glad you could come."

My suspicion antenna shot up. So glad I could come? What the hell was that all about? Spoken as if I was the visitor, not her. An attempt to establish control?

She released my hand, smiling, "Bully tells me you're his nephew. I guess that makes us related."

I tried to ignore her obvious attempt at familiarity, but it was difficult to avoid her piercing gaze. As a result, I may have been the first to blink, not a good response from a former intelligence operative. Trying to recoup the loss of ground, I noted that Anna's English was good, but the accent sounded familiar so I tested it and spoke in German.

"What part of Germany are you from, Anna?"

Her eyes narrowed in surprise that I had spoken in her native language, but she recovered quickly and responded in kind.

"Kaiserslautern. Or what you Americans call K-town. During school I worked part-time in the Post Exchange at Ramstein. Kind of grew up around all those Air Force jockeys."

I had passed through the air base at Ramstein many times. Maybe I'd even met Anna at the PX, who knows? I nodded and reverted to English.

"So you picked up the service slang as well, huh? K-town...jockeys?"

"Couldn't help but get into it," she replied, also switching back to English. "Your German is very good."

"I spent several years in Germany with the Army. Kind of have a knack for languages."

Bully must have managed to fill his weakened lungs because a powerful voice bellowed behind us.

"Don't be talking that Kraut shit, Parker. You know how I feel about them forkin' Nazis. Get this woman outta my house."

Anna smiled and rolled her eyes at Bully's comment. At least she hadn't taken his rant personally. No doubt Nazi sympathizers still existed in the Fatherland, but with no swastika tattoos showing, I didn't figure this sexy interloper to be one of them.

We both looked back and found Bully sitting in his wheelchair at the kitchen doorway. Molly Putts' appearance hadn't changed much, but Bully's sure had. I hardly recognized the tall, strongly built man I'd known for years, his frame much thinner now, his face saggy and gaunt. He still wore a black patch over his left eye, but his wooden leg was off and a towel covered the stump. I didn't have a lump in my throat at the sight of the old coot, but I did feel a slight tug of sadness for the shape he was in.

It was then that a dark thought crossed my mind. Was this a scam? Was Anna Lang a con artist? But then, what would she have to gain? Bully wasn't exactly rich, freeloading off Molly Putts and, before that, living in a camping trailer behind The Garhole. He received a government check each month for his service disability, but that and five dollars would buy a small bag of popcorn at the movies. I shuffled the notion through my brain, wondering why I should even give a damn. So what if Bully had sown wild oats no one knew about. What difference did it make, really? Except that Bully was so damned adamant that Anna was a fraud.

Standing in a dank hallway and hearing Bully rant behind us was no place to learn about Anna and her claim of kinship. When Molly rolled inside to check on Bully, I motioned Anna out to the porch.

"We need to talk," I said. "You like seafood?"

Chapter Four

Saturday afternoon
Galveston

Anna followed me back over the causeway to Galveston. I drove to Gaido's, a famous, old seafood restaurant on the seawall facing the gulf. Gaido's was more wallet-busting than the usual dirty-spoon joints I inhabited on my infrequent trips to the city, but what the hell, this was a classy-looking woman and I thought it best not to start in a one-down position. Besides, January was oyster season.

The hostess seated us by a large picture window that offered a view of tourists strolling on the seawall and the Gulf of Mexico in the distance. I gestured toward a drilling platform a few miles offshore and mentioned something about Texas being an oil state. She feigned interest, her eyes following my lead, but it was plain her thoughts were elsewhere.

A spiffy black waiter wearing a white jacket and bowtie took our drink order, hot tea for the lady and my usual Shiner Bock. While Anna perused the menu, I suggested charcoal-grilled shrimp, the house specialty. When the waiter returned with the drinks, I ordered the shrimp for Anna and a dozen oysters on the half shell for me.

Anna glanced around the room and smiled. "Nice place" she said, her voice as soft as her cotton blouse.

"Old Galveston favorite," I said. "Especially for tourists."

She gazed out the window, the smile dissolving, replaced by a melancholy drop of her eyes.

"You seem far off?" I said.

She turned her eyes to mine. "I was just thinking. Grandfather Bully is a real piece of work, isn't he?"

So was this a rhetorical question or did she want a return comment? Maybe a veiled attempt at sympathy? Army spy school had taught me to gather information from your subjects, let them talk. Ask questions if you need to jump start the conversation, but most people would rattle on about themselves if given the chance. I didn't know if that was the case with Anna, but I was determined to stay disciplined. I was the professional here after all, twenty years of experience investigating East German and Russian spies. Best to answer a question with a question.

"Sounds as if you had expectations?" I asked.

"Well, I did have hopes," she mused. "He's the only grandfather I have. A more civil beginning would have been nice."

"Put yourself in Bully's shoes. Pretty audacious claim, don't you think?"

"But it's true!"

"Still mindboggling."

"You say that without knowing the story. Bully didn't give me the chance to explain. Will you?"

The waiter arrived with our lunch and we settled down to eat, her version of events left hanging for the moment. I mixed enough creamed horseradish into the red sauce to water my eyes. The oysters went down plump and cold, and Anna seemed to enjoy the shrimp. We continued with the meal, chatting back and forth with the usual tedious banalities people use while trying to get to know one another. Married? Children? Read any good books lately? Well, maybe not that one. When the waiter returned, I ordered another Shiner and Anna opted for a glass of chardonnay.

Trying to lighten the conversation, I said, "You're from Germany and you drink wine, not beer. Tsk, tsk."

She seemed to relax. "Just never cared for beer," she said. "If you like the dark kind, do you know about the doppelbocks?"

"Oh, sure," I answered. "A German specialty beer, full bodied, higher alcohol content. So how do you know about doppelbocks?"

"University days," she said and then in German, "Bierhallen und Jungen."

"Beer halls and boys," I repeated in English. I gave her an all-knowing grin. Silence ensued. I waited as she gathered her thoughts. She studied the scene outside the window for a moment, then turned back to me.

"My grandmother was from Belgium. After the war she married a German officer and they moved to Kaiserslautern."

"A German officer? Really? Did they move because she was a collaborator?"

"What?"

"You've seen the newsreels about local women who collaborated with the Germans. The partisans shaved their heads and taunted them in the streets."

She scrunched her eyes, obviously frustrated. "My grandmother was a simple farm girl. She knew nothing of collaboration."

"Come on, Anna. She goes off with a German—be straight with me."

She blinked hard. Her voice went up an octave. "Why are you provoking me? I wanted to meet Bully Stout because he is one of my only living blood relatives."

She threw her napkin on the table and pushed her chair

back to leave.

I put my palms up. "Whoa there, girl. It's not that I don't believe you. It's just that...." I stalled, trying to think of the best way forward. Fortunately, she rescued me. She pulled her chair back and replaced the napkin in her lap.

"Look Parker, you want the story or not? Last chance."

"It's your ballgame, Anna. You're the one struggling for credibility here."

She twisted away and was up from her chair before I could stop her. She quickstepped to the lobby and crashed through the door while I was still fumbling with my billfold. I threw enough cash on the table for the meal and chased after her. Car brakes screeched as her blurred figure dashed across the street to the seawall. She found a stairway to the beach and started running across the sand. She stumbled and fell.

I caught up just as she stood and reached for her shoulders, trying to calm her. She slipped her arms up between mine, flailed at my chest and pushed away.

"Damn you, Parker. Damn you."

If this was all part of an act to win me over, she was a hell of an actress. But my gut screamed it was real. I wanted to hear the story, but first I had to steady her.

"Anna, please, calm down. Tell me...."

Her shoulders dropped, tension easing. We moved to a couple of empty beach chairs under an umbrella and sat facing the surf. The wind had died, and the bright sun was already warming the sand. Anna leaned against the back of the chair and closed her eyes as if willing her breathing to calm. I moved to the edge of my chair and waited while she regained her composure. She removed a tissue from her pants pocket and dabbed her eyes. After a moment she began to speak.

"My grandmother's name was Emma Meier. She lived with her parents on a small farm. She married a local boy named

Heinz Gunther, a school friend. They had grown up together."

"Wait...you said they lived in Belgium and she married a German officer."

I spoke softly so she would have to sit up and look at me to hear my words. When Anna moved to the edge of her chair, our eyes locked.

"Let me explain," she said. "The closest town to the farm was only fifteen miles from the German border. For hundreds of years the region had been part of Prussia. After WWI ended in 1918, the area was ceded to Belgium. Many of the local people still clung to their German roots. They spoke the language and kept their German customs. When war broke out, Heinz Gunther went east and joined the Wehrmacht. He was only eighteen. By the time the war ended, his unit was so badly mauled he had been promoted to *oberleutnant*."

"First lieutenant."

She nodded.

"So what was the name of the town where your grandmother lived?"

"A small village called Malmedy."

Anna dropped her eyes to the sand. Her reaction told me she suspected that I probably knew the Malmedy story. She waited for my response. She seemed relieved when I told her I had studied the tragedy in War College, even visited the area while touring WWII battlefields. Thinking about the murders and the poor bastards lying in the snow sent a shiver down my spine.

"I can only imagine the horror of it," she said. "And it was my countrymen, Germans that...."

She hesitated as if wanting my sympathy, even my forgiveness as an American. But I had studied the massacre too closely and couldn't give it. And then there was the devastation I'd witnessed in Kuwait, the stench of burning bodies, the shear wantonness and futility of combat. I wasn't in a forgiving mood about the horror of war. Suddenly, I knew where this was going. I just didn't know how.

"I get it now," I said. "Bully Stout was one of the American soldiers at the massacre. I knew he'd escaped, but none of the details. Tell me how it all fits."

"I will tell you everything my grandmother Emma told me. But if you know the true story of what happened at the battle that day, please tell me. I need to make more sense of it."

"You really want to hear all of it?"

She nodded.

"Well, okay...but what occurred at the crossroads south of Malmedy wasn't a battle, it was a slaughter."

She winced, but her eyes pleaded for me to go on.

"It was during the Battle of the Bulge, the last great battle for the Americans before the invasion of Germany. The Germans attacked with complete surprise and confusion reigned. Battle lines were unclear, some changing hourly. On December 17, 1944, units of the 1st SS Panzer Division surprised a company of GIs at the crossroads. Outnumbered and outgunned, the Americans surrendered. The Germans lined the disarmed GIs up in a field and opened fire with machine guns. Then they went through the field and shot the wounded men in the head just to be sure. Eighty-four American soldiers were murdered. A few survived by escaping into the woods."

Anna dabbed again at the moisture gathering in her eyes.

"Thank you," she said. "That makes everything easier to understand. Grandfather Heinz told me he was fighting in France at the time. He was wounded and spent six months in the hospital. He returned to Belgium after the war and was shocked to learn of the murders. More than shocked, he was ashamed. He told me this many times. He was never a Nazi, only a loyal German. I think the massacre was probably the reason Grandfather left Malmedy and made a home for Emma and her child in Kaiserslautern."

"Hold it," I said. "Her child?"

"Yes. My mother Johanna was a year old by the time Heinz was repatriated home in 1946."

My head was still spinning from recalling the details of the massacre. Something didn't add up.

"But you said that, when war broke out, Heinz went to Germany and joined the Army. If your mother was a year old in 1946, she was born in 1945. Did Heinz somehow return to Malmedy during the war?"

"No," she answered.

I hesitated, still unclear. "Then...."

Anna reached across her chair and put her hand on mine. "Heinz wasn't my mother's father," she said. "It was Alfred."

"Alfred?"

"Bully."

"Bully's real name is Alfred?"

Anna nodded.

I slipped my hand from Anna's grasp, leaned back against my chair, and blew out all the air from my lungs. A tight grin crossed my lips. The name Alfred was a shocker. Bully was the only name I'd ever heard him called. But with a name like Alfred, no wonder he had stuck with Bully.

When Bully lived at The Garhole he was all of 300 pounds, most of that in a super gut. It was hard to think of him at age eighteen. Then I remembered seeing photos of Bully when he played football for Ball High in Galveston. Lean and powerful.

A few months later, he was storming the beach at Normandy, lucky to have escaped the murderous machine gun fire from the German pillboxes. And then he moved with his unit up through the torturous hedgerow country where camouflaged panzer tanks lay hidden, waiting to open fire.

In December 1944, many thought the Nazis were finished, that it was only a matter of time before the Allies crossed the Rhine and hurtled across Germany to Berlin. Christmas was just around the corner. And then: Blitzkrieg! While Eisenhower played bridge in Paris, thousands of German troops, spearheaded by the Reich's finest panzer divisions, rolled into Belgium and caught the Allies unaware.

Soldiers who endure the worst of war rarely speak afterward of their time in the trenches. And so it was with Bully Stout. I had barely known Bully growing up and had little knowledge of his wartime experiences. I knew he was the most decorated WWII veteran on Galveston island, but I'd never bothered to learn the details.

Anna's piercing hazel eyes had never left mine during the entire conversation. We both knew there was more to come.

I spoke first. "I knew Bully was at the massacre. I also knew he was one of the lucky ones who'd escaped. But I never asked how."

Anna leaned toward me and in a hushed tone, as if sharing a state secret, said, "Bully was wounded in the shoulder, but he managed to get into the woods. He ran and ran, eventually finding Emma's farm. Artillery fire had almost destroyed the house, killing Emma's mother and father. Emma survived in the cellar. Wounded and bleeding, Bully stumbled into the ruins of her house. Emma was so frightened by the sight of an American soldier, she started to flee. But when Bully passed out at her feet in the doorway, she couldn't let him die. She patched his wounds and moved him into the cellar to hide from the German soldiers converging on the area."

Anna paused, searching my eyes. "They were just kids," she said. "Bully nineteen and Emma only seventeen."

Then she grew quiet, maybe wanting me to acknowledge

the innocence of youth, the inevitable plight of wartime desperation. I offered a gentle nod of acceptance.

Anna seemed to understand and continued.

"Emma, a frightened and lonely schoolgirl with her parents dead upstairs, cleaved to Bully for support. One night during another bombardment, when all hell was breaking loose and it seemed they would never see daylight again, it happened. And only that night, according to Emma. When the Americans came through, a passing unit found Bully, and Emma never saw or heard from him again."

Anna sat back, her gaze hard on me.

I didn't know how to respond. Finally I said, "Anna, the story is so surreal, it couldn't have been made up. So you're telling me your grandmother conceived after one night with Bully?"

"Yes," she said. "One night, one time. Of course Bully knew nothing of the pregnancy. Emma told me the night had been so special she hoped and prayed Bully would return to her after the war. But...."

"I think I can explain that part, Anna. His shoulder must have healed quickly, because he rejoined his unit for the final assault across Germany in the spring of '45. At a small town outside of Berlin, Bully's lieutenant wandered into a mine field. Bully went in to save him and stepped on a mine on his way out. The lieutenant received minor injuries but Bully... well, you've seen what happened to him: a missing leg and a patch over his eye. The blast left him unconscious for weeks. After several months in an Army hospital in Germany, they transferred him directly to Walter Reed in Washington D.C. So you see...Bully couldn't have gone back."

"Yes," Anna said her eyes full of hope. "But did he want to?"

Chapter Five

Saturday afternoon
Galveston

The question Anna had asked about Bully stirred my mind. Had Bully wanted to return to Emma? Did he even remember that night after the trauma of seeing his friends massacred and the house where he'd sought refuge bombed continuously? Then later stepping on a mine and nearly killing himself? Had PTSD affected his memory?

We left the beach and climbed the seawall stairs to Anna's Lexus parked at the top. I opened the driver's door and she slid behind the wheel. I hung on the open door and told her I would visit Bully again to get his side of the story.

"What's the name of your hotel?" I asked. "I'll give you a call."

"No hotel, Parker, I live here."

"What?"

"I've been here three months now, with my new job. I'm renting a condo downtown on Mechanic Street across from the Tremont House. It's temporary until I decide where to live. I'm thinking about a beach house on the West End.

"Wait," I said. "You work here? I don't get it."

"Are you going to see Bully now?"

I nodded.

"Great, meet me at the Tremont bar later for a drink and

I'll explain everything." She wrote on a piece of paper and handed it to me. "Here's my cell number. Text me when you leave Molly Putts' house."

"Text? You kidding? I don't have a cell phone."

She laughed. "It's okay to come out of the dark ages, Parker."

"Yeah well, I don't need one of those things growing out of my ear."

"Okay Neanderthal Man, but you'd better call Bully before you go. I went early this morning because Molly said he naps in the afternoon. Want to use my phone?"

Anna dug her cell out of her purse, made the call and handed me the phone. Molly answered and confirmed Bully was sleeping. Then she told me Neddie had called from The Garhole and said Harry Stein wanted me to drop by his house. Harry said my friend Maurice Matthews was in town.

I'd first met Matthews several years earlier when I'd gotten involved in a plot orchestrated by the Castro brothers to assassinate a high-ranking Venezuelan diplomat coming to Galveston on business. At the time, Matthews was the Special Agent-In-Charge (SAC) of the Houston FBI office. Working together, we managed to foil the plot and eliminate the assassin.

If Matthews was in town now, it probably meant he'd just gotten off a cruise. Since retiring and leaving the agency, Matthews spent most of his time as the lead dance host on cruise ships that sailed out of Galveston. He'd become so popular with the ladies, the cruise line advertised his schedule in advance.

I handed the phone back to Anna and told her I'd call her from Harry's house. As she drove off, the Texas license plate on the back of her car reminded me I'd seen nothing indicating that she was driving a rental. I must be slipping: A good investigator wouldn't have missed that.

I fired up the truck, turned left on 21st Street by the Galvez Hotel and pushed the old Chevy through the busy intersection at Broadway. A right turn on Church Street pointed me toward Harry's house.

I'd first met Harry Stein on my sixteenth birthday. My mother had run off to New York with her boyfriend du jour, a museum curator from Houston. She was killed two weeks later by an errant taxi as she stepped off a curb. The court appointed Harry as my guardian, and he had looked after me like the son he never had.

Harry lived in the East End Historical District where stately two-story Victorian homes built in the 19th century were protected by law. Many of the fine old structures had been severely damaged by the ravishing tides and winds of the 1900 hurricane. The storm had claimed 6,000 lives, still the most devastating natural disaster in the nation's history. Harry's 1850 one-story Greek Revival was one of the lucky homes that had survived.

I parked at the curb, my old truck looking a little out of place in the neighborhood. Anyone watching probably thought I was here to repair Harry's plumbing, not knowing I had yet to fix my own. Two rocking chairs sat on a wide porch that stretched across the front of the house. The two bay windows protruding onto the porch contained original hand-blown glass. The cypress-wood siding was painted a pastel green with pink trim, giving the façade a fresh, Caribbean-style appearance. A Texas Historical Commission brass plaque mounted beside his door stated the year the house was constructed and the architect's name.

Harry, only five-six, was well known as the sharpest dresser on the island. He greeted me at the door with a smile, appearing as though he'd just stepped off the cover of GQ magazine. He was decked out in a well-cut navy suit, white shirt, pink tie with a matching breast handkerchief and highly-polished black Oxford wingtips. He combed his stylish silver hair straight back, and kept his Colonel Sanders look-a-like goatee and mustache expertly trimmed. All spiff from head to toe. I draped my arm over his shoulder as he led me to the back kitchen, all the while listening to him babble about his new granite countertop.

Matthews sat at the bar drinking iced tea, his face dark from the Caribbean sun. He wore his gray hair cut short like a football coach and had kept his weight well in line for a sixty-year-old. He looked ready to dance in a blue shirt, red tie and neatly pressed gray suit.

We greeted each other warmly and, with a wry grin, I said, "Enjoying the ladies, Maurice?"

"Yes, I am, Parker. But I am going to have to slow down, too much—"

"Dancing?"

His face flashed red. We both laughed. I glanced back and forth from Harry to Matthews. "You guys are dressed to the nines today. Too early for Mardi Gras, where's the funeral?"

Harry said, "No funeral, Parker. I wish you'd been here earlier. We have to run or we'll be late for the reception."

"Reception?"

"Yes, General Perry, the Secretary of Homeland Security is in town for a routine inspection of the Port of Galveston and the Coast Guard base."

"Really...so his reception is open to the public?"

"Hardly," Matthews replied. "I'm sure you didn't know, but Ronald A. Perry is my cousin. We were close growing up and spent summers together on my grandmother's farm up in Huntsville. I wrangled an invitation for Harry, and he's graciously putting me up here."

"It was the least I could do," Harry chimed in.

"You remember Burney Hebinck?" Matthews asked. "He took my place as SAC in Houston."

"Sure, I remember Burney. Good to hear he got your old job."

"Burney's already at the base along with half the island's police force, agents from his Houston office and a contingent of Secret Service agents. Want to tag along?"

I looked down at my jeans and tennis shoes. "Not really dressed for a party. Besides, it's not my style." I shook hands all around and said, "Come back when you've got some time, Maurice. Bring Burney, we'll catch some fish."

They followed me to the front door. As I stepped onto the porch, the concussion from an enormous explosion threw me against the railing. Harry and Matthews raced past me to the front yard. I gathered myself and followed. The neighborhood roared to life, car alarms blaring, dogs barking, people streaming out of their houses. Somewhere in the distance behind Harry's house, a thick, black column of smoke rose above the trees.

"The port," Harry yelled. "A ship?"

I caught Harry's eye wondering if we were on the same wavelength: the explosion at the Texas City docks in 1947 that killed 700 people. A fire in a ship's hold ignited its cargo of ammonium nitrate fertilizer. Eighteen volunteer firemen fighting the fire on the dock were virtually vaporized. Hundreds of homes and businesses were destroyed.

"It couldn't be like Texas City," Harry said, as if reading my thoughts. "Too many safeguards at the ports now. I'll get my scanner."

Harry's friend, Rory Puryear, the Galveston police chief, had given him a radio so he could listen to emergency calls. He rushed back out, scanner in hand, screaming, "The Coast

Guard base."

"Holy shit," Matthews snapped. "The Secretary."

Harry turned pale from the shock. He stumbled and collapsed into Matthews. "Oh my God," he mumbled, his voice weak, "The police chief, the mayor, police officers...."

I wanted to stay for Harry but this was bigger than both of us. I probably knew people there, too. I ran for my truck, yelling over my shoulder for Matthews to take care of Harry.

He shouted, coming toward me, "Hebinck's there, other friends from Houston, too. I'm coming with you."

Harry collapsed on the grass. I ran back and helped him up. He seemed in a stupor, unable to focus. Matthews saw his condition and stopped. I waited a few seconds to make sure Harry wasn't having a stroke or worse. I caught Matthews' eye and mouthed "Please." Matthews acquiesced and helped Harry into the house.

Two minutes later, I turned off Ferry Road at the intersection to the Coast Guard base and raced up the two-mile long street. One of the first to arrive, I jammed my truck to the side so it wouldn't be in the way of approaching emergency equipment and ran toward the mangled vehicles and dead bodies.

The acrid stench of burned flesh hung in the air. Wounded victims were everywhere on the ground, struggling to get upright. Most were in shock, with blackened faces covered in soot, their clothes shredded. Some were sprawled on the grass outside the area where the incinerated guardhouse once stood, the chain link fence on each side of the gate peeled back.

A man sat bent over in the road, balanced on his right arm, trying desperately to hold himself up, his left arm missing below the elbow, with blood streaming out. I fashioned a tourniquet with my belt around what remained of his left arm, gathered him in a fireman's carry and stumbled to a pick-up that had just arrived from inside the base. Two Coast Guardsmen loaded him in back and squealed off toward the hospital. First responders were arriving now: ambulances, firetrucks, police cars.

Then I noticed the remains of three smoldering vehicles just outside the guard gate. A burned SUV in the middle of the line was the only vehicle not totally destroyed, probably saved by its reinforced door panels and extra thick window glass.

A woman kneeled beside the SUV, checking a man's pulse, her long hair shielding her face. The victim lay naked from the waist up, his face blistered and chest blackened from burns. The woman's profile flashed through my mind.

"He's going into shock," she said without looking up.

I knew the voice. "Anna, Anna. It's me, Parker."

She turned and collapsed into my arms, her heart racing against my chest. She pushed me back and waved to an EMT pushing a gurney.

"Over here, quick," she screamed. "Careful, he has third-degree burns on his chest and at least second on his face. He needs fluids and transport now!"

We loaded the burn victim onto the stretcher and whisked him to the nearby ambulance.

"I'm a doctor," she shouted, pushing the identification card hanging around her neck at the paramedic standing in the truck's rear. "Don't wait on another victim or he won't make it. Drop a burn sheet over him and take off. UTMB burn unit, priority one!"

The medic tossed out an emergency bag stuffed with supplies and slammed the door shut. I grabbed the bag and flung it over my shoulder.

"Let's go," I said.

A man in a suit, gun in hand, yelled, "FBI, ID now!"

Anna stepped in front of me, showing her ID again, shouting, "He's with me. We need to help these people."

The agent hesitated, his job to protect the scene, gather information, talk to witnesses, identify suspects. But his eyes said he had friends injured here, too. Anna pushed me toward another victim. People were shouting all over the scene now, helicopters circling overhead, more police cars and ambulances converging with sirens blaring. Coast Guard petty officers wearing shore-patrol armbands patrolled the perimeter.

A Galveston police officer checked me again and photographed my driver's license with his cell phone. Anna was on the run, splinting a broken leg, bandaging a chest wound, triaging as she went, moving past those too far gone to save. I did what I could, hustling saline bottles from the ambulances and grabbing bandages.

And then, suddenly, an eerie quiet descended, the wounded all evacuated. ATF agents converged on the scene along with more FBI agents. They moved quietly across the carnage, assessing and gathering evidence. The last ambulance departed as twilight crept in, leaving a field of dead bodies for the coroner to investigate.

For the first time since arriving, I slowed to survey the area. Car parts and unidentifiable pieces of metal combined with shards of cinderblock and wood from the guard gate lay strewn about, mixed and tangled together like the ingredients for a giant ghastly stew. Huge portable lights plugged into generators flicked on at dusk, allowing the search for evidence to continue through the night.

Finally, a chance to rest. I snagged two bottles of water from a nearby police car, handed one to Anna and guzzled the other. Anna drank quickly, reviewing the scene and looking for someone else to help. Then realizing her job was over, she leaned into me. I put my arm around her as she closed her eyes for the first time. The charred scent of burned wood and metal permeated her hair.

She had long ago peeled off and discarded her blood-soaked sweater, her simple white blouse now streaked with red. She peeled off her latex gloves and touched her cheek as though thinking about her own appearance for the first time.

"Anna, look at me," I said.

She lifted her eyes, moist with tears. I held her until the sobs subsided. I grabbed another water bottle, moistened some gauze patches, and wiped the dirt and splotches of victims' blood from her cheeks.

"Let's go home," I said.

The neighbor Anna had ridden with was nowhere to be found, so we ducked under the police tape and scooted past the circus of flashing cameras and microphones stuck in our faces. A police officer was bent over the passenger seat of my truck rummaging through the glove box.

"Hey," I yelled. "What the hell are you doing?"

He straightened. "Parker? Is that you?"

It was Derry Jones, an old schoolmate, now a Galveston cop. Back in high school, Derry had gotten the name Tube, because the roll of flab that perpetually circled his abdomen made him look as if someone had shoved an inflated inner tube down over his stomach. I motioned him out the door and helped Anna into the seat. She laid her head back and closed her eyes. I unsnapped her UTMB ID card and pushed it toward Tube.

"See the blood on her shirt? The doctor's tired. Saved a bunch of the guys here today. We're going home."

Tube studied the card and handed it back to me. He glanced at Anna. "The door was open and the keys were in the ignition. Looked suspicious. I had to check."

Minutes later we walked off the elevator to her second-story condo. I guided Anna to the living room couch and found orange juice in the refrigerator to hydrate her. But back in the den she was already asleep, sprawled on the couch. I slipped a cushion under her head and a blanket over her.

I studied her tired face and summed up what I knew so far: Mid-thirties woman from Germany claiming to be Bully Stout's granddaughter, a doctor who worked at UTMB and lived in a rented condo on Mechanic Street. Not much, but more than I had known this morning when I took the call from Molly Putts.

I used her bathroom to wash the smut and grime from my face and spotted a hairbrush on the counter. I removed a few light-brown hairs and wrapped them in a tissue.

Chapter Six

Saturday morning
Coast of Yemen

As dawn broke over the Gulf of Aden, Rashad Zahir set his coffee cup on the table and raised his binoculars to view the boat approaching the beach. From his second-floor veranda, he watched Yasser cut power on the small outboard and expertly guide the twelve-meter *hūrī* onto the shore. Yasser, a third-generation Yemeni fisherman, old-school and proud, maintained one of the few remaining wooden dhows on the coast, built by his grandfather forty years earlier.

As Yasser started for the villa carrying a hemp-woven sack, Rashad hobbled slowly down the narrow stairway, wincing with every step. His once stout, six-foot frame was reduced by the continual pain in his legs, manifested by a slight stoop as he walked. Because of his limp, he had to be careful not to tangle his *thawb*, the white cotton robe that covered his body to his toes. He covered his head with a *keffiyeh*, the cotton and wool scarf traditionally worn by Muslim men.

He entered the courtyard and waited, habitually stroking his long, Osama bin Laden-style beard that extended a full six inches below his chin. He'd never met bin Laden but had trained many of his followers. Rashad was Hezbollah not al Qaeda. Until recently, his family had always been more concerned with the destruction of Israel than America. But that had changed.

Rashad was slightly dismayed at the steady streaks of gray that had recently appeared in his hair and beard. After this jihad was completed, it would definitely be time to quit. The enemy was growing smarter and he had pushed his luck far enough. He had accomplished much in his career and was eagerly anticipating this final act of retribution. At age forty-eight, he was looking forward to a quiet retirement in the mountains of some peaceful country. He just wasn't sure which one.

Rashad's servant, Badih Khoury, opened the thick wooden gate. Badih was a small man in his late seventies, with leathered skin and tired eyes. He averted his gaze as Rashad passed to the outside.

Rashad, fluent in French, English and two Arabic dialects, wished Yasser well using the modern standard Arabic greeting. "As-salaam 'alaykum." Peace be upon you.

"Wa 'alaykum salaam," the old fisherman replied. Upon you peace.

Rashad used standard Arabic when needed, but he preferred the Levantine dialect taught to him by his father Nassim, who had been a distinguished professor of anthropology at the American University in Beirut. His father had studied the Zahir family history going back several generations and had taught Rashad that the family roots were not Arabic but Phoenician, the ancient Mediterranean civilization that originated in the Levant, specifically Lebanon.

Yasser handed the sack to Badih, who took it inside.

"Good fishing, my friend?" Rashad continued.

"With the grace of Allah, your friendship enabled our travel to the Red Sea, where the good fish are more abundant. I have brought you several fine snapper."

A few rials for gas, thought Rashad. Friendship so cheaply purchased. He captured a hundred years of suffering in

Yasser's lined, sun-beaten face as the fisherman dropped his eyes to the sand. The trip around the horn of Yemen and into the Red Sea had taken several days, and Rashad knew Yasser had probably given him the best of his catch. He also knew how hard Yasser struggled each day to support his family.

Rashad suspected Yasser's troubles were the same as thousands of other fishermen on the coast. Since the first Gulf War in 1990, Saudi Arabia had repatriated a million Yemenites to their homeland. Many had come to fish the Gulf of Aden, further exacerbating the already narrowing supply of good fishing grounds. Yasser had told him the gulf was so fished out that only a few shark and mackerel were brought in each day.

When Yasser departed, Rashad lingered outside the villa, taking in several deep breaths of the warm salt air. He was pleased that Yasser had brought the fish. Knowing his brother Abul would arrive in the afternoon, Rashad had instructed his servant to prepare the evening meal for two. As the great ball of light cleared the horizon, tangled thoughts raced through Rashad's mind. Were they prepared? Had they anticipated every possible problem?

Lamenting the unusually warm January day, Rashad wiped his forehead with the sleeve of his robe. He was grateful that at least the *shamai* hadn't started, the relentless desert wind that stirred the sands and harassed the country from March to August. And that it also wasn't summer, when daytime temperatures often soared to fifty-plus degrees Celsius. He didn't think he could take those unmerciful days anymore, and he prayed that, after tonight, he wouldn't have to. If all went as planned, he would soon escape the pervasive poverty, filth and ignorance that filled the forbidding landscape surrounding him.

Rashad backed closer to the compound wall and glanced at the sky, wondering how many American spy satellites were traveling overhead, relentlessly searching every village. And how many drones with attached missiles? He stepped inside the gate and glanced at the tightly woven cloth covering the top of the veranda, a small but vital safeguard for his security and protection from the ubiquitous eyes in the sky. He grimaced, chastising himself for breaking the rule this morning by stepping out to greet Yasser. Never show your body to the heavens. It was said the cameras on the CIA satellites were so powerful they could document the color of one's eyes. He would not make that mistake again.

Rashad had rented the seaside villa as both a sanctuary and a hideaway while he planned his final gift to Allah. He stepped inside the compound feeling the euphoria from his morning pipe of hashish diminishing, the pain in his legs returning. He limped across the open space and went inside to eat.

Rashad smiled as Badih served the morning meal, goat yogurt with dates and *manāqīsh*, the unleavened flatbread, topped with fresh oregano and thyme that had been his family's favorite repast for as long as Rashad could remember. For a fleeting instant, sacrificing etiquette, Rashad and Badih's eyes met. In that moment, Rashad knew Badih was back in Beirut serving Rashad's father. Pleased at the thought, Rashad was grateful that the family's long-time servant had stayed with him following the tragedy.

In his Levantine dialect Rashad said, "Thank you Badih. I must rest now. Please prepare my pipe."

"The pain?"

Rashad nodded, knowing he needed the drug to help him rest during the heat of the day. Praying that the brothers would have much to celebrate, he must be ready for Abul's arrival.

Later into the afternoon hours, Rashad heard the slow,

methodical puttering of his brother's motorbike as it turned off the dirt road. Rashad waited patiently while Abul parked the bike and entered the front door. Rashad shouted down to him in English from the veranda.

"Welcome, my brother. Allah has blessed you with a safe journey. Come let us eat. You must be famished."

"First some of your excellent Yemeni coffee," replied Abul.

Rashad greeted his brother with kisses on both cheeks, then pushed back to study him. He saw a reflection of his father in Abul's square-shaped face, prominent forehead, strong chin, and thick, black hair that started tight at the top of his forehead and went back into a single wave. It was only Abul's lighter skin and deep blue eyes that gave a hint of his American mother's Northern European heritage. Rashad had been nine years old when Abul's mother's left abruptly for the States. Until his father told him years later, Rashad had never known he had a younger brother.

"Five hours on that damned bike and impossible road," Abul said, moving away from the embrace.

"Such language," Rashad replied, chiding his brother.

"Sorry," Abul offered. "One of my bad American habits."

"Your travels went smoothly then?"

"If you mean the forged Jordanian passport, it got me into Oman with no problem. Such names you come up with."

"And the boat from Oman?" Rashad asked, imagining the misery during the trip along the coast from Oman to Yemen on a garbage scow, the secrecy necessary to avoid possible surveillance.

"That shit boat was hotter than Badih's oven," Abul said. "And the food... my God it reeked." He waved a hand below his nose as if fanning away the smell.

"Enough," Rashad barked. "You know better, using Allah's name."

Abul waved off the rebuke

Rashad ran his fingers down his thickly matted cheeks. "So where is your beard?" he asked.

"I am a consulting engineer living in the great midwestern heartland of America. The memory of 9/11 is still fresh for most Americans. The last thing I need is to look like a Muslim."

Rashad nodded, embarrassed that he had asked such a foolish question.

When Badih brought a flask of steaming coffee Abul, speaking in broken Arabic, greeted the long-time family servant with a smile. "So good to see you, my friend."

"And you as well," Badih responded. He quickly served the coffee, bowed to his masters and departed.

Abul sipped the coffee. "Hmmm, an excellent brew," he noted.

"From the small village of Haraaz in the mountains. The world's finest coffee, at least by the price. But nothing is too good for you, my brother."

"Why so expensive?"

"The farmers are growing less, switching their crops to *gat*. Do you know it?"

"Oh, yes," Abul said. "The drug contains amphetamine. They chew the leaves and stay high all day."

Rashad nodded. "The plants thrive in the higher altitudes, competing for space with coffee production. And of course the farmers quadruple their income."

"It is capitalism at work," Abul said.

Rashad frowned at Abul's comment, then turned to him. "Rest now," he said. "Badih will wake you later for prayers."

When Abul went down to his room, Rashad called to Badih for his pipe. Rashad enjoyed the quiet evenings by the Gulf of Aden. He liked to smoke and watch the sea with his binoculars, looking for ships sailing in the distance, the colorful navigation lights a reminder he would soon travel away from this ghastly place. He would never tell Abul, but he envied his brother's secular life, living among the washed and the educated. As he had once lived as well, growing up with his family in Beirut.

To be safe, he knew he would have to stay hidden until he was sure the Americans hadn't connected him to the attack. And then again, perhaps they didn't even know he was still alive.

He closed his eyes, thinking of the scenes he'd witnessed in the last few weeks: women in full burqas scavenging garbage dumps with their children. Yemen, the poorest of the poor of the Arab world. He couldn't wait to leave it.

The only good thing that had ever happened in Yemen was the attack on the American destroyer, *USS Cole*, in October 2000. Al Qaeda thought the attack successful with thirty-nine infidels killed and even more wounded. But Rashad had no doubt that, if he'd been in charge, the entire ship and all aboard would have been destroyed.

Rashad longed to return to Beirut, the "Paris of the East," with its beautiful tree-lined boulevards and international cuisine. Except that he knew better. The old Beirut was gone forever, torn apart by sectarian strife and inundated with foreign workers from Sri Lanka and Bangladesh, people who cluttered the streets with trash and lived like animals. No, the Beirut of his childhood, with the great fruit orchard in his backyard, would live only in his memories.

He had already gathered forged passports for Spain and Portugal. And then he thought, why not Argentina? Following WWII, hundreds of ex-Nazis had quietly slipped into the country and successfully melted into its communities. Rashad figured, with the family's money to help him, his assimilation wouldn't be difficult.

When Badih brought up the tea and fig plate, Rashad

asked him about his family.

Badih bowed slightly. "With the grace of Allah, they are doing well, master. Of course, only my sister and her children are left. The rest are in Paradise."

"And where is your sister?"

"They live In Beirut. She is a nurse."

Rashad noticed an unusual sadness in Badih's eyes as he prepared the pipe. He wondered if Badih was worried that the only family he had left was living in the hellhole of Beirut.

When Badih left, Rashad inhaled a deep puff and held it, allowing the blessed smoke to completely infiltrate his lungs. He exhaled slowly and raised his binoculars to the sea. The Gulf was quiet tonight, no ships in sight. Rashad lowered the glasses and closed his eyes. Memories flooded in: His beautiful little sister Akilah with her shining hair and impish smile. His mother Amal, teaching him to sit properly while eating, to cleanse himself, and to use the ritual greeting he had exchanged with the fisherman this morning.

But then the hashish took over and the dark thoughts came, the noise, the burning and the stench of his own charred flesh. He placed the binoculars on the table and fell asleep.

"Rashad, it is time," Abul said, back from his nap.

Rashad and Abul rolled out their mats and prostrated themselves for the final prayer of the day. When completed, Badih arrived with the freshly baked snapper and their father's favorite side dish of sautéed eggplant and rice. The scintillating aroma of olives, capers and garlic smothered in olive oil wafted across the table. The brothers ate in silence.

After late-night coffee, Rashad glanced at his watch and announced, "Two hours yet...a game of chess?"

Rashad expected no satisfaction in the challenge. He had always beaten his younger brother handily. After the first game, Rashad noted Abul's wrinkled brow and scrunched eyes. He allowed Abul the fleeting satisfaction of winning the second game. He was the smarter one, no reason to humiliate his only sibling.

Abul pushed the board away and noted the time. "Almost 12:00 a.m.," he said, nodding toward the black box in the corner.

Rashad lifted the remote control and clicked on the television. An image of CNN International fluttered onto the screen, the moderator ranting about some new Washington scandal. Rashad pushed the mute button, his eyelids heavy from the mind-numbing babble. At 12:15 a.m. an alert flashed across the screen and a new announcer appeared. The brothers straightened and leaned toward the set, their heightened senses sharp and focused.

"Breaking news. Information is just coming in about an explosion in Galveston, Texas, moments ago. Witnesses reported a car bomb detonated at the entrance to the United States Coast Guard base. No casualty report yet, but we do know the Secretary of Homeland Security, Retired General Ronald Perry, was due at the base for a reception at 3:00 p.m. local time." The camera switched to a clock on the wall. "Just fifteen minutes ago. We will of course break into our regular program to bring you updates on this tragic event as soon as we receive them. Please stay tuned."

The brothers stood and raised their glasses. Rashad spoke in Levantine Arabic, "For our family, my mother, our father and little sister Akilah. As they rest in Allah's arms, may they be rewarded with his grace."

Rashad and Abul ordered more coffee and continued to watch the news station late into the night, waiting for a full report on the deaths and injuries. At 3:00 a.m. the casualty tally stood at eleven dead and thirteen injured. All of the injured were critical. There was no word about Secretary Perry, but someone had sent in a cell phone video of his limousine. Seeing the mangled doors and crushed windows, the reporter noted that although the limo had not been totally destroyed, it seemed doubtful anyone inside could have survived.

"So be it," said Abul.

"But we must be certain," added Rashad. "American authorities never make death announcements until family members have been notified. We will learn nothing more tonight, and I have grown weary. Let us rest and meet at dawn for morning prayers. We will know much more then."

"Can you imagine the alert status?" Abul interjected. "The entire American transportation system locked down. No planes in the sky, no trains or even buses on the roads. The airports shuttered, fighter aircraft patrolling the skies over Washington. The chaos must be equal to 9/11. Missile bases with stepped-up alerts, the American Navy in combat mode. Mass confusion and fear."

"As it should be," Rashad replied. "The whole country running around 'chasing their tails' as the infidels are fond of saying. Not even knowing in which direction to point their missiles. I would love to see their terrified faces. Allah has honored our prayers."

At dawn, fatigued from the late night but filled with a satisfying sense of retribution, Rashad joined Abul for morning prayers on the veranda. They gave thanks to Allah for the success of the strike and moved to the table for their morning meal. The brothers dined without comment, savoring the subtle combination of freshly baked croissants and dried apricots.

When Badih arrived to clear the morning dishes, he said,

"If I may be allowed."

Rashad nodded to him.

"The bouquet of your excellent coffee and the scents of the croissants and fruit remind me of the morning meals at your beloved father's home in Beirut," Badih offered. "Fresh-cut flowers, oranges and grapes from the nearby hills. It is still so real to me." Then Badih paused a moment and said, "May your father rest in Allah's arms."

Rashad said nothing, but he lowered his eyes as if remembering the scene and his father. As Badih bowed and backed away, he reached for the remote and clicked it on. The talking head droned on about a typhoon in Indonesia killing several hundred people. Rashad sneered at the moderator's fake sympathetic voice. Any fool could see the glee flowing from the man's eyes, ecstatic that he was the "chosen one" delivering the news. So pathetic, Rashad thought. What the infidel Americans considered as success.

Rashad started to turn off the TV, but then another moderator broke in with a news flash.

"...the current casualty count at the bombing in Texas is fifteen dead and ten wounded. Two Secret Service agents and one police officer severely burned in the explosion have died in the hospital from their injuries. We now go to a live press conference at the White House."

"Good evening," announced the Press Secretary. "The President will speak following my report on this national tragedy. We have just received an update on General Perry. The Secretary is in critical condition at the University of Texas Medical Branch burn unit in Galveston. Perry was the only survivor in the limousine. Two Secret Service agents and Secretary Perry's personal assistant were killed. Fortunately for the Secretary, a physician responding to the scene found him outside the limousine and was able to perform emergency lifesaving treatment. We will of course keep you updated on the Secretary's condition."

Rashad shot up out of his chair, screaming, "No! No!" He flung the remote at the TV. He pressed his palms against the sides of his head as though fearing his brain would explode. Twisting around, his weakened legs buckling, he grabbed the table for support.

"Something went wrong," Abul said. "The attack was supposed to be inside the base. It...it...makes no sense. Damn it, damn, damn. All the planning, the risk...." He sat down, crossed his arms on the table and dropped his head.

Rashad balled his fist into tight knots and banged the table, his face an angry torrent of red. He kicked the chair away and struggled to the wall overlooking the beach, belting out unintelligible words at the sea as if blaming some great monster in the water.

He turned to his brother, eyes flaring hate. "Look at me, Abul," he screamed. "Look at me."

Abul slowly raised his eyes, saying nothing.

Full of purpose now, Rashad nodded slowly as though confirming his thoughts, his eyes steady on Abul, his voice soft as rain. "This is not over," he whispered. "Not over."

Chapter Seven

Saturday evening/Sunday morning
Galveston

My mind was having difficulty putting the pieces together. The explosion incinerated the terrorist's van and left a six-foot deep hole in the road. ATF and FBI agents investigating the scene would be lucky to find the bastard's big toe, much less identify him. But what if the bomber hadn't acted alone? Maybe a spotter hovered nearby to confirm and report the results of the attack? If more than one terrorist was suspected, that would mean shutting down the island to prevent escape.

Other than a boat, plane or helicopter the only exits from Galveston Island were the ferry to Bolivar Peninsula, the causeway bridge, and the bridge over San Luis Pass. And that meant traffic jams with panicked weekend visitors fleeing to safety. But I knew that if most hardcore B.O.I.s (Born-on-the-Island) residents wouldn't evacuate for a category-four hurricane, it seemed doubtful an explosion would panic them.

After leaving Anna's condo, I planned to circle back and check on Harry at his house. Harry is the same age as Bully, in his early eighties, but in a hell of a lot better condition. He eats healthy, exercises and has never smoked. Still, he collapsed when the explosion happened. I glanced down and knew Harry would freak out if he saw my blood-splattered shirt. I raced around the corner to the Strand.

During the 1870s, when Galveston served as the largest port in Texas, the local newspaper dubbed the Strand the "Wall Street of the Southwest." The Victorian buildings lining the street were filled with banks, wholesale houses, insurance companies and steamship agents. Today, the Strand is the main tourist shopping area, with mostly T-shirt shops and restaurants renting space in the old buildings. Usually packed on weekends, the street now appeared deserted, with most of the stores closed. I ducked into one of the few open shops and bought two T-shirts and a pair of jeans. I slipped into a booth and hurried into the new clothes. I glanced at the mirror, the T-shirt said, "Galveston Island, Fun in the Sun." Not today, I thought.

I wrapped my bloody shirt into the old pair of jeans and dumped the package into a trash receptacle on the street. Back in my truck, overwhelmed with fatigue and nothing to eat in the last eight hours but a few oysters, my head dropped to the steering wheel. Buck up, I told myself. I took a deep breath, reached for a second wind and slapped my face to stay awake. I needed rest, and the vision of my bed at The Garhole entered my head. Then I remembered asking Neddie Lemmon to run the bar for a couple of hours. Now ten hours overdue, I jumped out at a corner payphone to call.

"The Garhole Bar, Neddie Lemmon speaking. How may I assist you?"

"It's me."

"Holy crap, Parker! So glad you're okay. I called Molly Putts. She said you left hours ago."

"It's been a son of a bitch. I went to the scene and—"

"Oh Christ, Parker."

"Shut it down, Neddie. I'll catch up with you tomorrow."

"Can't, the joint is packed."

"What?"

"Folks fed up waiting in line for DPS to open the bridge are streaming in here. Tables are full, people on the back-dock fishing. I've emptied the freezer of gumbo, shrimp, everything I could find. Almost out of beer, too."

I knew Neddie shoved food down the pipe like Popeye's friend Wimpy, the hamburger man. I figured him for a good hunk of the smorgasbord and a healthy portion of the beer. But he was always ready to help when I needed him, so what's a couple of shrimp po'boys and a few bottles of brew in the scheme of things.

"Okay," I said. "I'm on my way."

"Forget it, Parker. Cars lined up for miles out on the highway. No sense getting in that mess. I can handle it."

"Owe you big time, Neddie."

"Free beer for life?" he said, chuckling.

"Like you don't already," I said and hung up.

My mind flashed to the contents of Harry's refrigerator: food and Shiner Bock. The fastest drive from Anna's condo to Harry's house meant taking Harborside Drive, the thoroughfare that ran from the causeway past the Port of Galveston and cruise ship terminals to the hospital. Except that police barricades blocked the entrance. A steady stream of police cars and big, black FBI and Secret Service SUVs raced down the road with sirens blaring. Flashing red and blue lights bounced off the walls of nearby buildings and projected eerie shadows as night fell. Coast Guard and DPS helicopters buzzed overhead. I turned around and cut through the back streets toward Harry's house.

Maurice Matthews stood on the porch, his steeled eyes full of anger yet welled with moisture. I grabbed him in a bear hug. No doubt, as the ex-SAC of the Houston FBI office, Matthews had lost friends in the bombing.

"So sorry," I whispered.

"Two agent friends from Houston that I know of...."

His voice trailed off, his thousand-yard stare into the night saying everything. I let out a big breath and bit my lip. A million needles attacked my lower back, stressed from bending over victims and carrying stretchers.

"What about Hebinck?" I asked.

"He was at the rec hall on the base with the rest of the invitees, waiting for the Secretary." "At least that was good," I said. "How is Harry?"

Matthews sighed. "He's asleep now, finally took a pill and conked out. He was on the phone all afternoon. He eventually got hold of a friend on the force and found out that the chief and mayor are okay. They were waiting at the rec hall, too. But he knew the two motorcycle officers leading the caravan."

Matthews looked away and then seemed to stiffen. He straightened his back and puffed his chest. "Goddamn terrorists...."

"They know anything yet?"

"Said it was a van...blew up right at the guard gate."

"Accomplices?"

"Don't know. Authorities have sealed the island. Gradually letting people off, but checking IDs and photographing license plates. "

"What about Secretary Perry?"

"Still critical. That's all I know."

I had seen burned soldiers during the Gulf War. It wasn't a pretty sight. A vision of Perry lying in the burn unit with his skin peeled back raced through my mind. What misery. No one should have to go through that agony.

Matthews and I went inside to the kitchen. While he sat at the bar sipping a Dr Pepper, I moved anything that looked good in the refrigerator to the counter: pickles, tomatoes, tuna salad, left-over baked chicken.

I grabbed a Shiner and gestured to Matthews, but he waved me off. I devoured a tuna sandwich and a chicken leg, alternating with slugs of beer.

"What's your plan," I asked, my mouth full of chicken.

"I was due at the ship tomorrow for a cruise, but it pulled out right after the explosion. The captain's ten miles offshore waiting for instructions from corporate. I called in and cancelled."

"How did the ship leave? The port's gotta be closed."

"It's emergency procedure for a terrorist attack. We trained for it when I was aboard. The captain pulled lines and hauled ass before the port authorities called the ship. The Coast Guard's pissed that the ship left without clearance. They have a cutter out there getting ready to board her."

I nodded, finished the sandwich, and grabbed a huge pickle and another beer out of the refrigerator.

Matthews' cell phone buzzed. He noted the number and area code. "Washington," he said. He pushed the receive button and answered.

I walked out to the porch to give him privacy. Nine o'clock at night and the neighborhood buzzed with people on the street, talking in small groups, gesturing toward the base. Women held half-full wine glasses while men slugged beer and whiskey. Armchair theorists, full of alcohol and opinions.

I sat in one of Harry's rocking chairs and closed my eyes. Scenes from the afternoon filled my head, with visions of the walking wounded stumbling around in shock. Bodies burned almost beyond recognition. Then I was back in Kuwait with burning oil wells, smoldering Iraqi trucks and fly-covered bodies lying in the sand. I pushed back the acid taste in my mouth.

Matthews stepped out to the porch. "The director wants me back on temporary assignment to assist Hebinck."

I straightened in the chair.

"I was SAC in Houston for ten years and have been out of the loop less than a year. He said I know Houston and Galveston better than anyone they could assign. Burney's sending a car to pick me up. "

"Couldn't find a better man," I said.

"I'll do what I can. Can you stay the night with Harry?"

I nodded, thinking with the highway to San Luis Pass blocked and The Garhole out of food, there was no reason to go home. A black SUV arrived at the curb, lights flashing but sirens quiet. Matthews and I shook hands, and he hustled to the waiting car. An agent opened the back door and he slid in.

Back inside, I peeked into Harry's bedroom and heard a light snoring sound. I retreated to the spare bedroom, steamed myself for ten minutes in a hot shower and collapsed into bed.

Early the next morning from under a pile of blankets, I heard Harry's voice at the bedroom doorway.

"Coffee's on."

I slipped into my pants and shirt and joined Harry in the kitchen. The enticing aroma of fried bacon filled the room. I filled a cup with hot coffee and sat on a stool at the counter.

"Heard anything from Maurice?"

"A text," he said, cracking several eggs into the skillet. "Now that he's back on the team, he can't say much. Over medium okay?"

I nodded and reached for the plate piled high with bacon. I scarfed down several pieces while Harry slipped bread into the toaster.

"Eat all of it," he said, gesturing with the spatula. "I got a pound of the heart stopper for Maurice. You know I don't eat pork."

"Maybe not, but you sure know how to cook it crisp."

He flipped the eggs over and raised his eyes. "I'm barely making it, Parker. Those two motorcycle officers were good friends of mine...."

Harry's shoulders slumped. He leaned into the counter for support. I leaped around the counter and put my arm around his shoulder to steady him.

"Sorry, Harry," I said. "Anything I can do?"

I pulled a stool around. He sat and took several deep breaths trying to calm himself. I picked up the spatula and turned to the skillet, not wanting to see the tears in his eyes. I slid the eggs and toast onto a plate and stood beside Harry, eating in silence and thinking about what to say next. Besides the two motorcycle cops, there were probably others he knew who were at the explosion.

When his breathing normalized, he twisted around. "There is something you can do, if you really want to help."

"Anything," I said.

"A friend of mine called earlier. He set up a food tent for the officers outside the police tape. But his cook didn't show."

After assuring myself that Harry was going to be okay, I drove to the scene. The checkpoint had been moved from the point of explosion to the intersection of Ferry Road and the road to the base. A Galveston police officer standing next to his unit waved me to a stop and examined my driver's license. I explained about the food tent and he waved me through.

The big white tent was set up about twenty yards this side of the police tape. Several agents sat at a table outside the tent drinking coffee, their nylon windbreakers imprinted on the back with glow-in-the-dark FBI and ATF letters. I nodded as I passed by, noticing the pungent smell of burned flesh that still hung in the humid morning air. A touch of acid hit my tongue.

As soon as I entered the tent, the smell changed to the sweet aroma of sautéed peppers and onions. A young Hispanic man stood at the propane burner, scrambling eggs in a large skillet.

He glanced up. "You are the cook, Señor?"

"You're doing fine," I said. "Just here to help. What's your name?"

"Juan. I was hoping someone would come to help. I can only do the eggs."

He gestured toward a stack of tortillas on the counter and nodded toward another burner and skillet. I warmed tortillas as fast as I could while he filled them with eggs and peppers and wrapped them into breakfast tacos. We fed a steady line of officers until we ran out of eggs.

An hour later a seafood truck arrived. I filled a huge fry pot with grease, mixed flour and cornmeal in a bowl, and asked Juan to start breading the shrimp and oysters. The tent filled with the smell of hot grease and fried seafood. Officers and agents with slumped shoulders and tired faces stood patiently in line holding napkins and paper plates. The more we cooked, the longer the line grew.

Two hours later I hung a sign on the tent flap indicating that we were out of food. Not knowing if we were getting more, I thanked Juan with a pat on his shoulder and sent him home to rest.

I wiped sweat from my brow with my arm, stepped to the open flap and surveyed the scene. Inside the police tape, several agents in white coats and green gloves were bent over searching for evidence, examining pieces of twisted metal and unrecognizable hunks of debris. Anything suspect from the panel truck, including pieces of cardboard or metal that might have housed explosives, would be taken from the scene for further study.

A small group of agents clustered around the charred remains of a SUV. I recognized the vehicle as the one next to us when Anna treated that badly burned victim. I choked back a sudden rush of bile as a vision of the man's blistered face and charred midsection surged through my mind.

As the group parted, Anna and Burney Hebinck stepped out from its midst. Anna saw me and quickened her step to the police line.

"Parker!" she shouted, her face grim. She pushed hair back from her face. "What are you doing here?"

"Cooking," I said pointing to the tent. "I guess you're the only one who hasn't eaten."

"Agent Hebinck and I just arrived," she said, pushing Burney toward me as if to introduce him.

Hebinck stepped closer and we shook hands. I hadn't seen Burney in a couple of years, but he looked the same, a fire plug of a man, still solid in his mid-fifties from his daily workout routine. Rather than deal with patchy baldness, he'd elected to shave his head.

I kept a strong grip on his hand and said, "So sorry for you loss, Burney."

His face tightened. "Two dead from my Houston office and two from the Texas City office...."

Anna spoke, her voice soft, "You know each other?"

I nodded.

Anna said, "Agent Hebinck called me to look over the scene where we found Secretary Perry."

"We?" I asked.

"You and me," she said. "Remember the first victim? Burned face and chest?"

"That was Perry?"

Hebinck broke in, searching my face, "You were there, too?"

"Yes," Anna answered before I could say anything. "Parker helped carry the Secretary to the ambulance."

Hebinck frowned, "What the hell were you doing here, Parker?"

"Trying to help, like everyone else. I was at Harry's with Matthews, two minutes away when the bomb went off."

"Doctor Lang gave me a concise report of what she saw at the scene," Hebinck said. "Think you could add anything?"

I shook my head. "Doubt it, but I'll be around if you want to talk."

"Good," he said and turned to Anna. "I'll have a car drop you at your office."

"I'm done here," I said to Anna. "I can take you."

We said goodbye to Agent Hebinck, climbed into my truck and drove away from the scene. Behind the police barricade at Ferry Road, several panel trucks with huge antennas extending high overhead sat in the grass at the side of the road. Newscasters and reporters gathered like flies to meat, jostling for position and interviewing anyone coming from the explosion site who would stop.

As we slipped past the media circus, I said, "So how did you happen to be at the explosion site so quickly?"

"UTMB protocol," she said. "We train for catastrophes. I was off work but the hospital texted an urgent message on my phone."

I nodded, but felt Anna staring at me with anxious eyes as though she wanted to say something more. I kept my eyes on the road.

"When do you plan to see Bully again?" she asked.

And there it was…exhausted from the trauma of the explosion the day before and tired from standing on my feet cooking for several hours, Anna's relationship with Bully wasn't something I wanted to discuss at the moment.

"Too tired to even think about it right now," I said.

"I know a lot's going on, Parker, but I really want to get this settled. I'm going to be here a while and it would be nice to have a grandfather to visit."

"We'll see," I said. Out of the corner of my eye, I could see the scowl building on her face.

"Damn it, Parker. What kind of an answer is that?"

"Look, Anna. Can we talk about his tomorrow? I mean I'm really bushed and—"

"I checked on you," she said. "Twenty years in Army Intelligence, most of that in Germany. You were trained to be suspicious, but—"

"How did—"

"The internet, dummy. National Archives in St. Louis has all service records online."

As I pulled to a stop at Harborside Drive, I felt steam building in my ears. But she wouldn't quit.

"Your background tells me you're going to check me out, so get with it. You'll find I'm legitimate. But if you don't want to help, I'll figure out how to convince Bully on my own. Either way, it's going to happen. He has to admit I'm his granddaughter."

I crossed Harborside and drove slowly into the massive UTMB complex.

"Look, Ms. Lang."

"Dr. Lang to you."

"Whatever," I said, dismissing her comment with a wave. And then I remembered an Army psychologist in a spy training class saying: "Whatever is the most discounting word in the English language. Never use it during an interview. Good way to distance your subject."

But so what, I was pissed.

"Let's get something straight," I continued. "You show up

at Bully's house with this crazy-assed claim that you're his granddaughter. I've known you for what...twenty-four hours? I don't need your grief right now. Get it? So where can I drop you off?"

We continued in silence as I passed the Emergency Room. The Level One Trauma Center provided twenty-four-hour availability of trauma surgeons, specialty trained nurses and X-ray facilities. I thought about the mass hysteria at the explosion and wondered how many of the victims were saved because the ER was so close to the scene.

Anna worked somewhere in this warren of around forty UTMB buildings in the heart of downtown Galveston. But doing what? Her hurried proficiency at the explosion site made me think she was an off-duty surgeon or emergency room physician.

"Which building?" I asked, my tone still at a low boil.

She directed me through the maze of streets and buildings until finally telling me to stop on a corner in the middle of the complex. Before I could say anything, she got out in a huff and strode across a wide tree-covered plaza surrounded by several buildings. I watched her disappear into an eight-story structure tucked away at the far end of the court. The building was too small for a hospital and with no close parking, I doubted it was a facility used by the public. What kind of a doctor practiced in a building like that? And what did she do there?

I pulled away from the curb, unsure what to do next. No doubt Anna Lang was a hell of a woman. She seemed to have it all: looks, brains, accomplishment. But nothing I had seen so far explained why she had come to Galveston. She could be a doctor anywhere. No one moved 5,000 miles just to meet a wannabe grandfather. Did they?

Chapter Eight

Sunday afternoon
Galveston

My confrontation with Anna left us in a standoff and me in a quandary. It appeared neither of us was going to take any lip off the other.

The almost block-long Rosenberg Library sat at the corner of 23rd Street and Sealy Avenue. I parked in the lot across the street and stood at the curb admiring the massive Italian Renaissance-styled building. Henry Rosenberg, a successful merchant and banker and one of Galveston's greatest benefactors, died in 1901, leaving most of his estate to the city with the stipulation that part of his bequest be used to build a grand library for its citizens.

I had learned all of this several years ago when Harry Stein bullied me into attending one of his lectures. As president of the Galveston Historical Foundation, Harry was the resident expert on the island's past. During my Famous Grouse drinking days, eaten up with pain and a bad case of broken wing syndrome, Harry thought just getting me out and away from The Garhole might be a start in my recovery. Socialize and meet new folks, he'd said. A good thought on Harry's part, except I hadn't been ready.

I entered the library through the front doors and hustled up the stairs to the computer area on the second floor. Anna called me Neanderthal Man. Maybe in some respects I was, but it's not that I didn't know better. I'd just chosen to not let technology rule my life. The Army had required computer skills of its intelligence officers, so it didn't take long to reorient myself. During the next hour I waded through several websites, gradually bringing myself up to speed.

The UTMB website included an interactive map naming most of the more important buildings on the campus. The location where I dropped Anna off showed the building but not its name. Interesting. Then I remembered seeing a photograph of the building somewhere. I searched the *Galveston Daily News* website, located the photo, and found several articles about the new Gulf Coast Biological Laboratory. One of the stories contained a statement from Anna about a possible safety breach at the lab:

According to Assistant Director Anna Lang, M.D., a vial of Avian Influenza (Bird Flu) was discovered to be missing last week by a researcher at the Gulf Coast (BSL4) Laboratory. Dr. Lang stated that the vial, less than two inches tall and three-eighths inch in diameter, was normally kept at minus 112F, so cold that it could have unknowingly stuck to a researcher's glove and inadvertently dropped to the floor. Dr. Lang added that it could then have been swept up with the trash, steam sterilized under pressure in an autoclave and then incinerated.

The rest of the article described the elaborate safety measures employed by the lab to prevent any "infectious agents" from leaving the containment areas.

Okay, so Anna was a medical doctor who worked at the lab. Doing what? I ran a search for Anna Lang, M.D. and found several scientific articles written by Anna concerning the nature and spread of rare diseases. Anna's bio stated she received a dual Ph.D. and M.D. degree from Hannover Medical School. According to their website, Hannover was one of the top medical schools in Germany. She followed that with a three-year fellowship in Virology at the University of Munich.

I already knew the woman was no dummy, but wow! I considered my own education: a B.A. from the University of Maryland extension school based in Munich. I was also fluent in German and Spanish and had taken many advanced courses in Intelligence and Psychology at Fort Huachuca in Arizona. Nothing to sneeze at. But why was I suddenly comparing my education to hers? Was it because she was doing something with hers and the best I could do was make gumbo?

After two hours of learning about the bio lab and Anna Lang's background, my back ached, and my eyes needed a rest from the tedium of punching a keyboard and staring at a screen.

According to Neddie Lemmon, The Garhole was out of food and beer. The weekly beer truck was due tomorrow, but I needed to take care of the food myself. My stock of shrimp and crab was usually no problem. I could catch shrimp off my dock with a cast net or buy them directly from a shrimp boat captain who often stopped in for a cold beer. Crabs I got from running Bully's old line of traps. But in the middle of winter, shrimp disappeared from the shallow waters of the bay and most of the crabs were buried in the mud.

I stopped at Walmart on Seawall Boulevard to replenish the basics, like oil, flour and cornmeal. For a brief moment I considered buying some of their frozen shrimp but, in the end, I just couldn't do it. I had never served my customers anything but fresh gulf seafood, and I wasn't ready to start with farm-raised, antibiotic-filled crustaceans now. I spied a payphone and called Neddie.

I thanked him for his help again and said, "I know you do some shrimping in the bay, Neddie. Got any in your freezer I can buy?"

"Sure, Parker. Want some trout, too? I caught some nice ones last week."

"Against the law to sell speckled trout caught in Texas. You know that."

"So give them some exotic name like the restaurants do. No telling what those folks are really serving. Probably some goddamn bottom sucker from China they're passing off as red snapper."

I finished shopping and began the trek out San Luis Pass Road to The Garhole, driving past the various real-estate developments scattered along the route. Thinking of their names, I pictured the developers sitting at a bar somewhere tossing out enticing tags they thought would lure prospective buyers to their new weekend getaways. Between Galveston's storied past of buccaneers and its laidback beach atmosphere, I had to admit some of the names they invented were downright alluring: Pirates Beach, Jamaica Beach, Spanish Grant, Sea Isle, Bay Harbor. Sexy names or not, there was no doubt that the canals dug in developments like these had damaged West Bay's delicate ecosystem. There were some days when I felt every house on West Beach should be swept off with the next storm. Even The Garhole Bar.

Fortunately, there were still a few open spaces between developments. As I drove by them, the fields began at the highway and spread to the marsh bordering West Bay. In one of the fields, a group of Sandhill Cranes picked its way through the salt grass, grazing for seeds and insects, their long necks bobbing as they traveled. Their tall gray stature and red-banded foreheads always made me think of a line of Confederate soldiers marching across a field on their way to battle. Hundreds of the majestic birds had once spent winters on the fields of West Beach, but increased land development over the years had steadily reduced their habitat. I was lucky to see a few dozen on the entire island now.

I read once that the birds work in pairs, male and female, communicating as they move in a deep guttural tone, the female uttering two calls for each one of the male. I chuckled, thinking it sounded about right to me.

I turned down the sand road to The Garhole and found a handwritten note tacked to the door: "Bar closed—out of food and beer." I tore the note off and went inside. The bar felt stuffy with a hint of mildew from the winter dampness. But Neddie had cleaned up well, leaving the place neat and tidy.

When I created The Garhole Bar, I cut out part of the wall at the front of the building and attached ropes and pulleys so I could raise the section and secure it to the inside ceiling. This morning I pulled up the wall and immediately felt the warm breeze off the gulf hit my face. I turned on the ceiling fans over the tables and opened the back door to create a draft. I unloaded and stowed the groceries and checked the beer box: empty for the first time in ten years. Must have been a hell of a night. I glanced up at the gar head smiling down on me.

I smiled back. "Sorry old friend, can't toast you today. The box is empty. But thanks for the company."

After a shower and a fresh pair of shorts and T-shirt, I folded myself into the Adirondack chair on the deck, wishing for a cold Shiner. Winter days in Texas are like hot flashes in women: one minute they're cold, the next they're shedding clothes and wiping perspiration from their foreheads. Two days earlier in Galveston the mercury had dropped to almost freezing and this morning you could water ski.

Seventy-degree days always brought out boaters. A hundred yards out in the bay a forty-foot sloop sailed by on a full reach, its canvas fully billowed from the following wind. Two young girls in bikinis relaxed on the bow, giggling as we exchanged waves. I chastised the girls in my mind for acting so callously only a day after the horrific tragedy of the bombing. But I had witnessed the scene and they hadn't. I decided to give them the benefit of the doubt.

An hour later, Neddie arrived with the frozen shrimp, a six pack of Bud and a wad of folded money from last night's receipts at the bar. As a friend of Bully's and a surviving member of the Dead Peckers' Club, he had to be at least eighty. Neddie was tall but thin as a marsh reed in winter time. When I thought of Neddie and super-gut Bully together, an image of Laurel and Hardy came to mind. Neddie's lined face was as dark as a beer bottle after too many days in the broiling Gulf Coast sun in his sixteen-foot skiff. He covered his naked dome with a baseball cap that read "Fish Whisperer." A too-large T-shirt hung from his thin frame like a dishtowel on a hook. The inscription on the shirt read "Free Mammograms."

I bit my lip and said, "It doesn't take a genius to grab the less-than-subtle meaning behind your T-shirt slogan. Where did you get that?"

He pulled the shirt away from his chest, glanced at it and said, "Had it made. Thought of the words myself." He dropped the shirt back to chest and scrunched his eyes. "I don't know what the hell you meant by what you said."

I leaned in close. "Neddie, some woman's gonna beat the crap beat out of you for wearing a T-shirt like that. And it could be any woman, not even a libber. It's downright insulting."

"Maybe," he said. "But the gamble's worth it if the right chick digs the shirt. Couple of weeks ago a woman came by on a motorcycle while I was wearing it at the tollbooth. Ended up spending two days with her. Kinda plump, but I like 'em that-a-way."

"Two days? What are you, eighty-two?"

"Eighty-three. I know what you're thinking, Parker. But what do you think them little blue pills are for? I get 'em free from a Doc I take fishing."

I turned away and squeezed my eyes trying hard to chase away the vision of Neddie and his new girlfriend together in bed. As a diversion, I popped open two Buds and handed one to him. A long pull from my Bud seemed to work as the picture in my mind went away. After finishing the beers, we packed the goods in the freezer and adjourned to the upper deck for another cold one. While he rambled on about last night's crowd, I slipped a hundred-dollar bill out of the roll of cash he'd given me and shoved it toward him, his eyes lighting up at the sight of the greenback. He started to reach for it, but pulled back and waved his hands.

"Thanks, Parker. But you don't owe me nothing. I got more than that in tips."

I shoved the bill into his hand anyway, thanked him again and said, "So, what are you going to do about those damned cats at the bridge?"

He seemed a bit taken aback by my question but recovered quickly and said, "Parker, I know how you feel about birds, but come on. How much damage can a few house cats do?"

I didn't want to argue with a friend who'd just helped me out of a jam, but I knew the havoc two dozen marauding felines could inflict on ground-nesting birds. I couldn't let the thought of the lurking devastation go, so I thought of a compromise. I grabbed another hundred dollars in twenties out of my pocket and waved the bills in front of him.

"Okay," I said. "How about you take this money and buy some traps? Each time you capture one of the little devastators, take it to the Vet in Jamaica Beach. I'll pay the neutering bill for all you can bring in."

Neddie scrunched his brow, "Male cats too?"

"Of course," I said.

Neddie shook his head and gritted his teeth. "I don't know, Parker. I mean how would you feel if someone held you down and cut your ba—"

"Damn it, Neddie! There're feral, completely wild. Nothing but a bunch of goddam killers plundering the sand dunes."

Startled at my outburst, Neddie sat back, his eyes wide. I had outdone myself. By way of apology, I opened two more beers and handed him one. I knew Neddie loved his cats, but I was at my wit's end. We shared the rest of the six-pack, and then Neddie left without telling me what he planned to do.

I spent the rest of the afternoon tidying up around The Garhole hoping for company besides the gar head, but no one came. Most weekend visitors had fled the island, and my regular customers were probably glued to their TV sets waiting with open mouths for the latest on the injuries from the explosion. As far as I knew, the list of names was still not public, but Galveston was a small enough town that everyone knew at least one cop.

To keep my mind off the tragedy, I snaked a hose around the corner and washed the salt grime off a stack of crab traps, part of a regular routine to keep the rust off. I then turned to the back dock and hosed down the cement. An hour before sunset, I gave up waiting for customers and closed the bar.

I drove down the sand road that led to the pond my grandfather had built for his cattle and parked by the berm. As I crested the levy, a Great Blue Heron rose off the edge of the pond and lumbered toward the setting sun. The majestic raising and lowering of its wings reminded me of the strength and determination so basic to the bird's instinctive quest for survival.

It was easy to envy birds their freedom of flight, the ability to soar above all of life's petty issues and simply appreciate the joy of existence. To live by instinct and not thought, to be ignorant of the trials and complications of the human condition. Life at its simplest: eating, procreating and nourishing young. No egos, jealousies or religion. No difficult relationships. Nothing to stir the pot. No responsibilities at all beyond the day-to-day struggle to survive.

I had studied Abraham Maslow's hierarchy of needs while in the Army. The pyramid structure starts at the bottom with basic needs of food, sleep, clothing and shelter. Next is the need for safety and health, above that social belonging and self-esteem. Finally at the pinnacle, self-actualization. A life plan with a pretty ribbon tied around it. If only life really worked out that way.

I wondered about my own place in the structure. Probably stuck somewhere in the middle, I thought, around social belonging. I pictured the Kemp's Ridley turtles that nested on Galveston's beach, scurrying along the sand to lay their eggs, only sticking their necks out to find their way back to the water.

For the next hour, I trained my binoculars on the oak motte across the pond, a favorite resting spot for songbirds during their annual migration back and forth to Central America. When I was a boy, there were still several mottes like this one on the island, but over the years the expanding developments had wiped out all but this one. A coastal oak motte of stunted live oaks, gnarled and tangled together by years of the prevailing southeast wind, was a true art form all to itself.

Today, in the dead of winter, there were nothing but grackles and mockingbirds in the trees. I couldn't focus on the motte without remembering the many evenings my grandfather and I had spent sitting on the levee counting bird species. We'd catalogued close to a hundred species at this spot alone, everything from a dozen types of Warblers, to

Orioles, Purple Martins and Hummingbirds. We'd even seen an occasional Painted Bunting, the prettiest of them all, the male resplendent in its blue head and cape and red chest. Somehow, sitting on that berm, thinking of the old man, I knew I was never alone.

Realizing I had missed the sunset, I scurried down the levy to my truck and chugged back along the sand road to the bar. The lights were off at The Garhole, the night was quiet, the wind still and the bay calm. Tomorrow morning I would cross the causeway again and confront Bully Stout about Anna.

But tonight the moon was up, waning from its maximum circumference but still full. The clear sky meant no clouds drifting across its surface, no harbinger of ill times to come. Two nights ago, the stormy, dark clouds passing over its surface portended evil. And that curse had come in the form of a devastating explosion and loss of life. It would take a while, but life in Galveston would return to normal with locals going to work and having dinner with their families, tourists enjoying the beach and shopping on the Strand. It had been a most painful few hours, but the island was now due for something good.

Chapter Nine

Sunday evening
Beirut to Paris

Abul felt Allah had smiled upon him. Because of his constant bickering about the disgusting motorbike trip from Oman, Rashad had ordered a private jet which sat at a nearby airport ready for takeoff. Using a fake passport, Abul deplaned in Beirut and had arrived in time to catch the afternoon flight to Paris.

Using his American passport Abul Zahir, now David Arnold boarded the Air France Airbus 318 and settled in for the four-hour flight to Paris. David gazed out the window as the plane flew over the site of the 1983 terrorist bombing that had killed 241 American servicemen.

What a waste, he thought. All those men dead because of America's continued imperialist attitude, always butting into other countries' affairs and pushing their misguided vision of the world. Would they ever learn? President Reagan called it a "despicable act," while Hezbollah, the terrorist group dedicated to the destruction of Israel, rejoiced. Crazy stuff.

As far as David knew, responsibility for the act was never proven, but his mother had always asserted with contempt that his father Nassim probably had a hand in the plot.

Although she was a devout Muslim, he knew his mother could never have been an extremist.

David adjusted his seatback and closed his eyes, reflecting

on the confusing route that had brought him to his current life. He had been only thirteen, and had never met his father, when the so-called "Barracks bombing" occurred. His mother had long forbidden David to visit his father in Lebanon while he was growing up, fearing that Nassim would kidnap her only son and she would never see him again.

But unbeknownst to his mother, David's brother Rashad had visited him several times in America during David's younger years, continually indoctrinating him on why the true believers were against the infidels. Rashad had delivered personal letters to David from their father, urging him to come home to Lebanon and join the battle against the godless ones. Rashad had also given him videos produced by various extremist groups and had taught David how to access more on the dark web.

Rashad had directed him to a specific mosque in David's hometown of St. Louis, Missouri. The imam at the mosque had been purposely brought over from Saudi Arabia to spread Wahhabism, the most fundamental of all Islamic sects and the branch of Islam their father followed. The imam preached that those who do not practice their brand of Islam were heretics and therefore enemies.

At age twenty-one, David spent a semester studying at the University of Paris. One weekend he flew to Beirut and met his father for the first time. Several more trips to Beirut left him more conflicted than ever. Thanks to his mother, David had followed the more peaceful tenets of the Islamic faith, but due to Rashad's continuing influence and the deep respect he had developed for his father, he continued to struggle with his identity.

On the morning of September 11, 2001, at his office in Indianapolis, David had just finished the last *Rakat,* the second of two required recitations of *Fajr,* the morning prayer, when his secretary Mary banged on his locked door, screaming something he couldn't understand. He trusted Mary, but he didn't want her to burst in and catch him prostate on the floor. Neither she nor any of his clients needed to know about his Muslim beliefs.

Growing up he had memorized the recitations of the entire *Sala,* the five daily prayers which were the obligatory religious duty of every devout Muslim. The next prayer in order after *Fajr* would be *Suhr* or midday prayer, followed by the afternoon prayer or *Asr*. Then came the *Maghrib* prayer at sunset and, lastly, the *Isha* or nighttime prayer.

David wasn't a perfect Muslim. Due to his heavy work schedule, he often missed some of the midday prayers, but he at least tried to complete the dawn and nighttime obligations.

David hastily put away the prayer rug and opened the door. Mary rushed by him and flicked on his television set. Smoke billowed out from a hole in the World Trade Center building. Mary began to sob and hurried out of the room. David watched the scene, mesmerized, knowing the jihad against America had begun in earnest.

After an uneventful flight, the airbus lumbered into Charles de Gaulle Airport on time at 4:30 p.m. Because of the close connection between France and Lebanon, David had felt comfortable shuttling between Paris and Beirut. Following the breakup of the Ottoman Empire after WWI, the League of Nations awarded the mandate to govern Lebanon to France. French businesses flooded the country, and their influence continued today, long after France ceded power to Lebanon in 1944. Business travel between the two countries was as natural a relationship as mother and daughter—a little tense at times, but persevering.

David gathered his briefcase out of the overhead bin.

While waiting to deplane, he absently patted the specially designed secret compartment in his briefcase where he hid the forged passport. He worried that he should have destroyed the passport, knowing that if the Customs inspector at either Paris or Chicago discovered the faked document, he would be a terrorist suspect forever.

After casually perusing David's American passport, the French Customs agent studied David's face and said, "Welcome to Paris, Mr. Arnold. Was your business trip successful?"

David saw no mistrust in the agent's eyes as the officer handed back his passport. But then, he thought, maybe the agent was specifically trained not to look suspicious, not wanting to tip David off if he was under surveillance. Damn paranoia.

"Just trying to drum up a little business for my engineering consulting firm back in Indiana," David answered. "I hope I made some good contacts."

David retrieved his passport and proceeded to the UAL first-class lounge to await the next leg of his trip. He couldn't wait to be back in Indianapolis with his hot girlfriend and his newly decorated apartment, styled in the latest contemporary design by the most sought-after designer in town. And not a bad looker herself, he thought. But better than either the girlfriend or the apartment was the new BMW M3 CSL with its 355 HP 3.2 liter, straight-six engine. His dream car.

The United flight left Paris on time at 6:00 p.m. and due to the time difference, the plane arrived at Chicago O'Hare just before 8:00 p.m. the same day. Aware of the National Security Agency's (NSA) ability to track telephone calls, David had purposely not used his cell phone during his time out of the country. As soon as he landed, he powered up the phone for the first time in several days and called his secretary at her home.

"Hi Mary. I just arrived in Chicago. I will be coming in to Indianapolis tonight, but I wanted to call and check before it got too late. Anything going on?"

"Welcome home, Mr. Arnold. Nothing that won't wait until tomorrow. How was your vacation? I've always wanted to visit Paris."

"Still the City of Light," he said. "See you in the morning."

David hung up and called his girlfriend Jennifer Hatton, a twenty-something-year-old flight attendant. Over the years, David's conquests had been so many he couldn't remember their names. But he did have an uncanny ability to recall pet names. Nicknames helped him recall specifics, like peculiar sexual habits, interesting or even challenging positions and preferred methods of climaxing. Being able to recall the details of each past encounter enabled David to continue to hone his own near-perfect technique. He'd given Jennifer the name Snake, for the unique way she could twist her body into the most delightful positions.

"It's me," David said. "I'm back from my trip. Did you miss me?"

"So glad you're home," Jennifer said. "Are you coming over?"

"Well, I'm still in Chicago, but I think I can catch the nine-thirty flight and be at your place by twelve or so. Is that too late?"

"Not for you," she said. "I'll fix a late dinner and have a bottle of wine open and ready. Should I wear clothes?"

"Not for the first hour," David said.

David arrived a little after midnight. They skipped dinner, but it didn't take him the full hour to expend his energies. They lay in bed naked, Jennifer smoking a cigarette, David marveling at the Snake's latest contortions.

"Hate to tell you," Jennifer said, stubbing out the cigarette in the bedside ashtray. "But my roommates are coming in on an early flight in the morning. Sorry you can't spend the night."

"Aww," David moaned in mock disappointment. "What about dinner?" he prompted.

Jennifer smiled and reached down, stroking him. "You just finished it," she said. "Want dessert?"

David gently removed her hand and kissed her cheek. With carnal lust satisfied, he now had more important things on his mind.

Thirty minutes later, David sat in his polished aluminum chair with its linen covering, admiring his newly decorated all-white living room, his computer on his lap and a glass of Malbec at his elbow. Good Muslims were forbidden alcohol, but since his mother had converted to Islam from a Protestant belief and because of his lighter skin and blue eyes, he concluded there was a good chance he was less than fifty percent Middle Eastern descent. David smiled at the thought. He could rationalize anything if it suited him, a trick he'd learned from his mother.

Over the years, his mother had become more and more devout, continually professing her love of the beautifully written and comforting words in the Quran. She'd never regretted her conversion for a moment. After 9/11, she'd proffered that all religions run the risk of perversion by radicals and pointed out how Fundamentalists in America had fostered their own myopic, far-right version of Christianity. David almost laughed out loud when his mother had offered that excuse for jihad. A perfect rationalization, he thought. She was so good at it.

For the next hour, he pulled up several websites about Galveston, Texas, including places to stay and the city's highlights. David had never been to the island, but the websites educated him on Galveston's appeal as a tourist attraction: lots of sun, miles of beaches, seafood restaurants, Victorian homes and a past that included everything from houses of ill repute to big-time gambling and buried pirates' treasure. Much of it was history, but according to what he read, the aura of excitement still lingered on, permeating the city's fabric and enhancing the city's attraction for tourists and convention trade.

All David needed now was a cover, a reason to be there. He reviewed several more websites and found a calendar of events for scheduled meetings on the island. The National Society of Industrial Engineers was having a seminar at the Galveston Convention Center starting in two days. How fortuitous, he thought. He hurriedly found the Society's website and registered for the event.

Now he needed a flight to Houston and a place to stay in Galveston, but more importantly, he needed a plan.

The Galveston explosion had been orchestrated by his brother, Rashad, including seducing the actual bomber, a disaffected Muslim teenager Rashad had found on the internet. It hadn't been difficult for Rashad to groom the boy, even exhorting him to recruit others and form a cell. Over the years, Rashad had successfully recruited several jihadist cells in Germany and one in France. David knew it wasn't difficult to radicalize Muslim youths. Young men suffering from personal trauma and perceived maltreatment who felt marginalized by society were all over social media.

When the mission had failed, Rashad had told David that he wanted to make the next attack himself. But with the heightened security after 9/11, he knew getting into the U.S. would be risky. But as an American citizen, it would be easy for his brother. So the burden of the final operation had fallen to David.

David protested. A damn good way to screw up an idyllic

life, he thought. Still, the Americans had murdered his father and sister. In the end, David knew he had to do it. He just didn't know how.

Chapter Ten

Monday morning and afternoon
The Garhole Bar

After a fitful night of tossing and turning, the squawking outside my bedroom woke me earlier than I'd wanted. I needed more rack time. The stress of the past few days had made my old war pains act up. It was during times like this that the vision of the bottle of Famous Grouse under the counter popped into my head.

I dragged out of bed and opened the door to a bright, sunny morning, the temperature already in the seventies. As I stepped out, two seagulls perched on the deck railing took off and joined the dozen or so in the air. Down below, a school of shad congregating off my dock was bringing the birds in for a feeding frenzy. Normally I wouldn't mind the ruckus, the morning ritual being all part of living on the water. But this morning, I was already tired and the day was just beginning.

I stood in the shower under a hot spray wondering how I got myself into these predicaments. For the past ten years since coming home from the Gulf War, all I had really wanted was to be left in peace and quiet to heal myself. I considered a five-mile run on the beach to loosen things up, but an hour jogging through the sand would put my mind in a trap. I'd probably spend the entire time thinking about the horrific trauma of the bombing. Too much, too early.

And the thought of today's schedule wasn't pleasant either. Confronting Bully would be as much fun as spending a 100-degree day in a tent in the desert interrogating a line of Iraqi prisoners. A bottle of water and a few crackers usually warmed those guys up, but Bully Stout, well...the old coot was as unpredictable as a hurricane's path.

I stumbled into fresh jeans and a golf shirt thinking that the only good news was that the route to see Bully led me past the Waffle House on 61st Street. The optimist in me needed a silver lining for the day and pecan waffles and hot coffee seemed like the ticket. I debated whether or not to call Neddie again to help out at The Garhole, but decided the receipts from the night of the explosion were good enough that I could afford to shut the joint for the day. And then a pang of guilt hit me for making money off a tragedy.

Twenty minutes later I sat at the counter of the Waffle House watching the cook stand over the griddle and listen to the waitresses yelling breakfast orders from all over the kitchen. The chef was acting as if he was not hearing them, while simultaneously cracking eggs and flipping bacon and sausage on the griddle all without missing a beat. A Waffle House cook has a lot of talent and tolerance...mostly tolerance.

The longer I watched the cook the more I realized the traits I needed with Bully: tolerance and patience. Did I have enough of either?

As the early morning crowd departed, the second shift of late-sleeping tourists straggled in. Middle-aged couples with big stomachs and stringy hair pushed into the booths for their usual 3,500-calorie meal. Just because Galveston suffered a devastating terrorist attack was no reason for the few remaining tourists on the island not to enjoy a plate full of artery-clogging hash browns. But who was I to judge? I pinched my midsection and ordered a waffle with whipped butter and imitation maple syrup. I convinced myself that preserving the little day-to-day habits of life was important during times like these. Otherwise, we'd all go nuts worrying about the state of things.

As I waited for my breakfast, an attractive, thirtyish blond waltzed in and seated herself in a booth. She ordered coffee and opened her Day Timer as if checking her appointments for the day. Anna Lang popped into my head. I imagined her in a white lab coat with her hair tucked under a cap, alternating between leaning over a microscope and making notes on a computer. Although Anna and I may not have left one another on the best of terms, I figured a drink or two at the Tremont would square things. As I well knew, alcohol both created and solved a myriad of life's problems.

I was mopping the last bite of waffle in the syrup when Police Officer Jones, AKA the Tube, slid onto the stool next to me wearing the "Galveston uniform:" shorts, T-shirt and flip-flops, with the T-shirt on the outside of his shorts conveniently covering the roll around his midsection.

"Parker McLeod," he said. "High rolling today, huh? Dining out at Galveston's finest?"

I laughed, "You know the good places, too?"

"Best waffles in town." He cocked his head back at an angle. "Sorry about the thing at the scene, going through your truck and all. I didn't know it was yours. We were all on edge."

I put my hand on Tube's shoulder. "No worries, I was shook up myself. Any news on Perry?"

"Critical is all I hear. Place is like Fort Knox, the whole area sealed off with concrete barriers blocking the streets. Galveston PD and FBI have surrounded the hospital, Secret Service on every floor. I feel sorry for the folks trying to see their kin in the hospital with the security checkpoints they gotta go through just to visit. Damn...."

I dropped money on the counter and slid off the stool.

"Hey, my kid's in football," Tube said. "Wants to play quarterback. Think you could show him how to spiral a long pass, maybe teach a few moves?"

"Sure," I said. "Bring your boy and football by The Garhole, we'll toss some. Be safe," I said, catching Tube's eye as I left.

At the payphone on the way out of the restaurant, I called the UTMB main number and asked for Dr. Anna Lang. The operator put me on hold for a full minute, as though she was having a difficult time locating her. Finally, she cut back in, her voice sounding like she was in a barrel.

"Dr. Lang is not available. Would you care to leave a message?"

I hesitated, knowing there was no number where she could reach me and not sure she'd return my call anyway.

"Could you give me her direct line, please?"

"Afraid that's not allowed, sir."

I told the operator I'd call back and hung up. It was time to do something I swore I'd never do. The Neanderthal man was lumbering toward the 21th century. Two blocks up from the Waffle House on 61st Street, I pulled into a strip center and parked in front of a Verizon store. Thirty minutes later including ten minutes for a quick demo, I sat in my truck putting into my contacts' list the only number I knew by heart: The Garhole Bar. It was a start.

The traffic over the causeway appeared back to normal. Life goes on after a terrorist attack. People go to work, kids go to school. I held my breath as I passed the Texas City refineries, still thinking about a possible chemical leak. Ten minutes later I turned onto Molly Putts' street and gazed at the surrounding land, nothing but prairie in all directions. A long way out in the field across from her house, a herd of cattle moved slowly toward a man on horseback. I lowered the window and heard his voice echoing across the prairie as he called the herd toward him. He stood tall in the saddle, wearing one of those old-time wide-brim western hats designed to keep off the sun. He seemed to be looking at me while at the same time calling the cows. I thought Molly owned the fields around her so I made a mental note to ask about him.

Molly sat on the front porch as usual with a coffee can full of tobacco juice in her lap. I parked and strolled toward the house. The way her butt cheeks folded over the sides of the chair made me think she'd make a hell of a soccer goalie, probably take up most of the net. She yelled down at me.

"Hey, hot lips. You miss me?"

"Always," I said. "Bully up?"

"All shucks, it's always Tubby you come to see," Molly said, a fake look of dejection on her face. "How are things in Galveston now? TV's startin' to put out names. Glad I don't know any of 'em."

She spit in the can and raised a pair of binoculars from her lap, searching the field in front of her house. "I got my shotgun out in case any of them terrorist sons of bitches show 'round here."

I followed her line of sight and said, "So who's the man on horseback in your field?"

She lowered the glasses. "Oh, that's old Ernie Deats, last of the old-time cowboys. Runs a pretty big spread, so I hear. He's been leasing my land for grazing ever since Clarence died. What do you think I live on out here, that pissant government disability Tubby gets?"

I found Bully in the kitchen just finishing a bowl of nutritious Fruit Loops, his favorite cereal. He twisted his head as I entered the room, a frown on his face and a spot of leftover milk pasted on his lips.

"What you doing here? I ain't called you."

"Gee, I'm glad to see you too, Bully."

He waved his hand dismissing me, then grabbed a dish towel off the table, dug into his eye socket and pulled out his glass eye.

"Forkin' thing's always itching," he groaned.

He wiped the eyeball clean, opened his socket wide, and pushed the glass eye back in. He slipped the black patch out of his top shirt pocket and positioned it over his bad eye.

"Neddie called, said you were at the explosion."

"Got there just afterwards."

"Damn...."

"Yeah, Harry knew the two motorcycle officers."

"Is Harry okay?"

I nodded.

"Forkin' terrorists. What the hell's this country coming to?"

I moved to the other side of the counter and leaned forward. "Let's talk about Anna Lang," I said.

Bully scrunched his forehead. "Who?"

"Don't give me that innocent bullshit, Bully. You know who I'm talking about. What did she tell you?"

"You mean that witch was here the other day?"

"She's actually a pretty nice woman," I said. "Took her to lunch after we left here."

"So forkin' what?"

"Tell me about the farmhouse you stumbled into after the massacre."

"What?"

"Malmedy."

"Ahh shit, Parker...fifty years...don't remember," he shook his head, mumbling. "All those GIs, the snow...." He moved his hand to his face, shielding his good eye.

"You were wounded, Bully. Bleeding badly. You wouldn't have made it without help."

"They told me a GI patrol picked me up. Saved my life."

I slammed the table with my palm. He dropped his hand.

"No, Bully. The woman in the farmhouse saved your life. What was her name?"

"Woman? I don't...don't...." His voice faded. He raised the eyepatch and rubbed the socket around his glass eye.

"Her name, Bully."

"Krauts shelling...noise...freezing cold, ice, a blanket...."

"The blanket, Bully. Who gave you the blanket?"

He blinked, "Blanket? What blanket?"

Then he looked at me, confusion on his face, squeezing his good eye almost shut, as if the combination of his age and the fog of war hindered his thoughts.

"Blanket, Bully. Where did you get the blanket?"

He looked at me with vacant eyes as though lost somewhere in a confused memory. Was he faking it or truly trying to remember? I couldn't tell and decided to push.

"Bandages, Bully. The bleeding stopped. Where did the bandages come from? Someone helped you in that farmhouse. What was her name?"

"Wha...."

"Come on, Bully. Just say it, say her name."

He dropped his chin to his chest and emitted a low whistling sound as he exhaled. Session ended.

So close, I thought. Damn. Should I wait? Wake him, go at it again?

The sound of Molly's wheelchair groaning across the hardwood floor meant she was coming my way. I slipped into Bully's bathroom, located his electric razor and shook a few cut hairs into the extra baggie I'd brought. I told Molly goodbye on the way out, got into my truck and drove away.

I tossed the baggie with the remnants of Bully's last shave into the glove box and remembered the hair from Anna's brush was also in there. I decided to call my friend Jenny Hillbro to see if she was available for a short visit. Jenny lived on Bolivar Peninsula, which meant a ferry ride in both directions. The trip would take the rest of the afternoon so I didn't want to go over there cold. I hit "O" for operator, was referred to Information, finally got her number and spoke long enough to confirm she'd be home. I ended the call thinking this cell phone thing was really beginning to work out.

The street to the Coast Guard Station that intersected Ferry Road was blocked by a police car and its driver was checking IDs. The acrid scents of burned bodies and car parts still haunted me as I passed by on the way to the ferry. I thought about the remaining wounded being treated at the hospital and hoped they would pull through.

I arrived at the ferry landing to find the line of vehicles waiting to board the boat to Bolivar shorter than usual, the ferry appearing half full. During the summer, the line usually snaked back a mile. But this was a Monday in mid-January when tourists and weekenders were busy making a living somewhere off the peninsula.

The steel loading gates creaked beneath my truck as the workers guided me onto the deck. I put the transmission in park, turned the engine off and listened to a recorded safety announcement from the Ferry's PA system. An air horn blew and the boat moved out into the channel. I rolled the window down and lay my head against the seatback to catch a quick nap during the seventeen-minute trip across the bay. The moist, salt air flowing through the cab brought a steady bouquet of the Gulf Coast: fish, birds, shrimp, wet sand and seaweed all tangled together in a fusion of scents.

The horn jolted me awake as the ferry eased into the landing. Bolivar Peninsula is a thirty-mile stretch of sand filled with beach houses on pilings, real estate agencies, boat storage sheds, beachwear shops and beer joints. Jenny had said that she and Joe Stubbs lived in Holiday Shores, another of those developments probably named in a bar by some scotch-guzzling real estate guru.

Joe and Jenny's success story was partly my doing. They met during high school but lost touch when Joe joined the Army. Joe lost his legs during the Gulf War when his Humvee rolled over an IED. When Colonel Kennon, our mutual VA doctor, called and asked me to check on him, Joe and I became friends. He lived for a while in a trailer behind The Garhole.

About that time, I got involved helping a fifteen-year-old kid, Jake Green, whose Mama was on the run from drug dealers. When Clementine Garza, a PI from San Antonio, came sniffing around to check on Jake's parentage, she asked Jenny to have DNA tests run on the boy. It was during all this that Jenny and Joe hooked up again, and they've been together ever since.

Jenny waved as I pulled to a stop in front of her house. She looked just as I'd remembered: attractive in a plain sort of way, just enough makeup to cover her freckles, light-brown hair pulled back in a ponytail and large, black-rimmed glasses. I put the two baggies in my pocket and stepped out of the truck.

"Hey, girl," I said my arms wide for an embrace.

"Good to see you, Parker," she said, moving in for a hug. "I wish Joe was here."

"Where's he working?"

"His old buddy Teddy O'Rourke, head of the local dockworkers, got him a job shuffling paper. Not his thing, but it'll do until we find something better."

"Teddy's a good man," I said. "Couple of years behind me

at Ball High, but a hell of a halfback. How are Joe's legs?"

"That's the best part," Jenny said, her eyes lighting up. "The implants are holding well. You ought to see him shooting hoops with the guys. Runs the court like Steve Austin, the Bionic Man."

I smiled, knowing Jenny had talked Joe into trying the new titanium inserts the VA had been pushing. The process involved implanting a shaft of titanium into the medullary canal of Joe's upper leg. The bone grows around the implanted shaft. When it's all healed, the prosthesis is screwed to it. Joe resisted the operation for a long time but, with Jenny's encouragement, he finally gave in.

"So what do you hear from Clementine?" Jenny asked, an inquisitive grin on her lips.

"Nothing recently. She's back in San Antonio, probably spying on wayward husbands."

"Too bad," Jenny said, still grinning. "You guys were cute together."

Cute wasn't the best adjective for Clementine, a woman with the body of a goddess who knew more bedroom tricks than Candy Barr, the Texas porn queen during the 1950s.

"What are you doing home on a Monday? They need lawyers on Bolivar more than Galveston?" I asked, shaking off the vision of a naked Clementine.

"Actually I do both," she said. "With a computer and a cell phone I can be anywhere."

We moved to a redwood picnic table underneath the overhang of her beach house. Jenny left and brought back a pitcher of iced tea and two glasses.

"Sorry I don't have any Shiner," she said. "Neither of us drink anymore."

"Good for you," I replied, my mouth watering for a cold beer.

Jenny and Joe lived two blocks from the beach and that close to the water the roar of the surf rolled over us as we talked. With my sleep timer not adjusted since the explosion, the soothing sound from the waves made me want to drive to the beach for a quick nap in the bed of my truck.

Jenny squeezed her eyes into a questioning look as if ready to hear why I'd made the long trek to Bolivar.

"Need your help," I said.

"Anything," she said, her eyes showing concern.

"You still friends with the guy at the crime lab?"

She nodded.

I pulled the baggies out of my pocket and lay them on the table. She glanced down and then back at me.

"Oh Lordy, Parker," she said shaking her head. "What are you mixed up in this time?"

Chapter Eleven

Monday morning and afternoon
Indianapolis, Indiana

David arrived at the office early and checked Galveston weather on his computer. Today would be warm and tonight cool, but the temperature could change quickly because of a severe cold front over the midwest that may or may not make it to the coast with any intensity. He ran through the pile of mail on his desk and wrote out instructions for his secretary on how to handle the necessary replies. When Mary arrived, David explained he'd found an important seminar in Galveston, Texas, and decided on impulse to attend.

"What about your appointments this week?" Mary replied, a concerned look on her face. "You have several on your calendar and Jorge Development is waiting on a signed contract."

David sighed. "This seminar is important. It's a great chance to network and meet new potential clients. The Texas economy is booming and it's time to branch out. Reset the appointments and bring in the Jorge contract. Quickly please, my plane leaves in two hours."

Mary hurried out of his office and returned with the contract. David scanned the document. The proposed fees were lower than his going rate. He didn't like accepting the contract without negotiation but there was no time. He signed the last page and told Mary to fax the contract to Jorge.

As he grabbed his small carry-on and hurried out the door, he considered the perplexed look on his secretary's face. She was obviously confused. He had never done anything like this before. He was always so methodical, kept a meticulous calendar and never missed a meeting. She must be wondering what this sudden departure from the norm was all about. Why was her boss going to a seminar about the safety of offshore drilling platforms, an area totally detached from his usual discipline of the design and efficiency of power grids in buildings? He made a mental note to call her during the meeting and act excited about the growth possibilities of expanding his business. Maybe even mention a raise.

David liked to fly first class. He loved the personalized attention from the flight attendants, wider seats, better food and free-flowing alcohol. He hated to fly Southwest Airlines with its cattle-car atmosphere of unassigned seats and passengers dragging luggage down the aisles, only to clog the bins with oversized baggage. Still, the airline was efficient, herd mentality or not, and Southwest used Hobby Airport which was located in Southeast Houston, much closer to Galveston than George Bush Intercontinental Airport.

The flight arrived on time at 2:00 p.m. and twenty minutes later David stood at the Hertz rental-car desk trying to decide on the type of car he wanted. He liked Hertz because of their new "dream car" selections. His favorite was a Mercedes C63 AMG with its 469 HP and 3.9-second acceleration. But not this trip, he thought. Not the time to flaunt his style. The last thing he needed was to be conspicuous. He agonized a moment longer before finally selecting an all-American, plain-Jane, dark-gray Chevrolet Impala.

David set the car's GPS system and forty-five minutes later

he crossed the Galveston Causeway, feeling the warm breeze off the gulf hit his cheeks as he rolled down the window. He liked the feel of the area, laid back and calm, with fishing boats drifting in the bay and the smell of salt water in the air.

He drove down Broadway, Galveston's main street and turned left on 25th the street that dead ended into the port area. He was immediately transfixed by the towering superstructure of a multi-deck cruise ship moored at its dock. The sight of the ship together with what he'd read on the internet confirmed Galveston's status as a tourist town.

Two blocks this side of the ship, he turned onto Mechanic Street, did a quick U-turn and hopped out in front of The Tremont Hotel, carrying his luggage and leaving the car with an attendant. He strode purposefully up the marbled steps to the reception desk, noting the several-storied atrium marking the center of the hotel. White plastered walls surrounded a seating area interspersed with palm trees in the middle of the room. An old, wooden-framed bar at the opposite end of the atrium caught his eye. He checked in, sent his luggage to his room, went immediately to the bar and ordered a Dewar's on the rocks. The engineer in David made him curious about the hotel's construction.

"This is not a new building is it?" David asked, as the bartender set the Dewar's in front of him.

"First time visitor?"

David nodded and sipped his drink. The bartender's name badge read "Gene." Early twenties, tall and skinny, thin faced, with long, brown hair pulled back into a ponytail and secured with a rubber band. His arms were a mass of tattooed roses and stems.

"The building is original, built in 1879, but converted into the Tremont Hotel back in 1985."

"What about the bar?"

"Beautiful, huh? Carved rosewood," Gene said, gently rubbing the top of the bar with a soft cloth. "Originally built around 1900 for a Galveston hotel. The owner found it in an old saloon here in town, refurbished it and brought it here. The mirrors behind me were added to complete the look."

David finished the scotch and wanted another drink but felt the pressure of developing a plan begin to build inside him. He picked up a complimentary copy of the *Galveston Daily News* and a city street map at the front desk and rode the elevator to his room on the third floor. He checked himself out in the bathroom mirror, ran a brush through his thick, dark hair and patted his face, bringing the blood to the surface and giving his cheeks a healthy pink hue.

"All American boy," he said aloud.

He sat in a desk chair and read the front-page story about Secretary Perry, still listed as critical at UTMB. The article indicated Perry's condition was too serious for him to be moved, even to Houston, much less to Walter Reed Hospital in Washington, D.C. It would be several days, maybe longer, before a transfer date could be determined.

David and his brother had anticipated this and concluded that, no matter what, the best place for another attack would be the Galveston hospital. Getting to Perry once he was back in Washington would be almost impossible.

The article said Perry was in the dedicated burn unit of the hospital, with specialty-trained around-the-clock nursing care. The area was so sterile and its environment so critical that the unit was completely sealed off from the rest of the hospital. The unit even utilized its own self-contained air-conditioning system. David realized the lack of specific references to Perry's condition meant Homeland Security was keeping a tight lid on his status. He wondered if that meant Perry's security team was worried about another attack.

David needed more information. With the heavy competition between television news stations, he figured one would have a talking-head "expert" pontificating about Perry's condition and treatment.

He clicked through a few stations and found a reporter interviewing a specialist from a Chicago area burn unit. The surgeon, dressed in a protective skull cap and gown, appeared as though he'd just left the operating room. David caught the interview midway through.

"...Doctor, tell us the routine."

"There is no routine," the surgeon said, sitting on a stool and surrounded by various pieces of medical equipment. "Each case is different."

The surgeon held up front and back drawings of a human body divided into sections. Each section was assigned a number.

"For a quick assessment, we use the "rule of nines." One simply adds the numbers from the burned areas. For example, the chest and abdomen areas are nine each, arms are four and a half each and legs are nine each. The head is four and a half. The same numbers on the back. They all add to 100. The higher the number, the more serious the situation."

"So what is Secretary Perry's number?"

The surgeon lowered the chart and hesitated. It seemed obvious he didn't want to speculate.

"Early reports indicated that Secretary Perry was burned on his face and midsection. I have seen no other detailed reports. Let's hope that's the extent of it."

The reporter pushed, "And what if it isn't?"

"If you add in additional parts of his body—arms, legs, and anything on the backside—the total could easily reach sixty or seventy percent. And in that case...."

The surgeon shook his head slowly, concern showing in the

creases in his forehead. The reporter waited. The surgeon reached for his pager and studied it for a moment. He stood and looked into the camera with more purpose than he'd shown earlier, trying his best to project optimism.

"The good news is that the University of Texas Medical Branch in Galveston has the finest burn surgeons in the world and their unit is second to none. Secretary Perry is in good hands." The surgeon turned and walked out the door.

David was more confused than before. He turned the set off and stared at the blank screen, trying to reconcile what he'd read in the newspaper and heard on TV. If Homeland Security was purposely withholding Perry's status, that could mean Perry's condition was more critical than he and Rashad had speculated. Maybe he should just wait the situation out? But what if Perry's condition was better than reported and his security team was purposely making it appear worse so they could sneak him out in the middle of the night. Either way, waiting was not an option.

David unfolded the street map noting the location of the hospital and surrounding streets. His watch read 5:00 p.m. He must hurry if he wanted to reconnoiter the hospital, check out security and maybe get an idea on how to get to Perry before dark.

David called for his car and went down to wait in the lobby. As he stepped off the elevator an attractive woman in her mid-thirties with light brown hair came in through the front entrance and strode confidently up the marble steps. David quickened his step. Halfway up the steps, she glanced his way but never broke her stride. He hurried to the steps, wanting to catch up with her, but she had already reached the bar. The bartender set a glass of red wine in front of her as she slid onto a chair. Good, he thought, a regular. He felt his pulse pick up.

Ten minutes later David drove slowly past the front of the

hospital, evaluating the scene. Two police cars blocked the circular drive to the main entrance. A man stood beside a crane on the back of a flatbed truck unloading a series of concrete road blocks. David had seen the same type of blocks protecting the front of government buildings all over the Middle East. The blocks were arranged so that a vehicle with a bomb couldn't get close enough to destroy the hospital.

At this point, David didn't know the location of the burn ward. It could be in the middle of the hospital for all he knew, in an area too isolated for a bomb to be effective. Still, he couldn't totally discount the method of attack. However, if Rashad wanted to use another bomb, he would have to bring in someone new to build and deliver it. And that was okay with David. He could be safely away, maybe even back in Indianapolis.

He pulled to the curb a block from the hospital and looked back at the entrance. Two uniformed police officers and two other men wearing light windbreakers stood at the front door carefully observing the line of people waiting to enter. The two men in jackets were obviously Secret Service or FBI. The visitors at the entrance were removing their shoes. When the door opened, David caught a glimpse of a metal detector. As he turned in his seat to drive off, a police officer came out of nowhere and approached his car. What to do...speed off? Not a good idea. David lowered his window.

"Can I help you, officer?" he said, smiling.

"About to ask you the same thing," the cop said, looking down and checking out the car's interior. "This is a restricted area, no parking."

"Oh, sorry," David said. "Where do visitors park?" he asked, at the same time noticing a dog on a leash sniffing the car's hubcaps.

"The garage," the officer said pointing up the street. "But

admission to the hospital is temporarily off limits except for immediate family members of the patients. Visitation times are tightly enforced and now is not one of them. So move along, please."

David thanked the officer and eased away from the curb. He had never reconnoitered a target before and knew he'd made a mistake. A more astute cop might have asked for identification or at least taken his license number. He had some thinking to do. There would never be a better time or place to kill Perry, and the sooner the better. He would have to risk reporting back to Rashad to give him an update, and see if his brother had any ideas or knew of someone in the U.S. he could contact for help. He considered the remaining members of the Minneapolis cell but didn't know how to contact them. Rashad had set that up.

But for now, his pulse quickened as he thought again about the beautiful woman at the Tremont bar. He hoped she was still there. The image of her full, almost pouty lips filled his head. Her commanding posture and confident walk screamed education and intelligence. The slight upturn of her nose gave her profile an almost regal appearance, like a queen or maybe a princess.

If things worked out like he hoped, he would have to come up with a nickname. But not until he'd experienced her sexual abilities. Maybe she was the uptight kind who only relaxed in bed. Sometimes it could be fascinating to watch one like that unwind into a frenzy of torrid sex. David smiled at the thought.

Chapter Twelve

Monday afternoon and evening
Galveston

Jenny Hillbro told me the time frame for getting DNA results depended on the backlog at the county lab and that the terror attack probably slowed the timetable even more than normal. But she also said she'd done a pro bono will for the tech at the lab and he owed her one. She would ask him to put a rush on it.

The steel gate lowered with a clang and I rolled off the ferry back in Galveston, thinking about what to do next. My watch read almost five o'clock. Across from me, the line of cars waiting to board the ferry back to Bolivar grew long this time of day, as residents finished work in Galveston and rushed home for a cold beer or a glass of wine.

I thought about Anna and decided to drop by the Tremont bar, thinking she might stop in for a drink. I glanced down at my jeans and tennis shoes, wondering about my dress for the upscale hotel. But then I figured: What the hell...it's Galveston...island time.

Pulling up for a valet drop-off in front of the fashionable entrance to the Tremont didn't seem right in my salt-encrusted, beach-worn heap of a pickup, so I found a spot around the corner and hiked to the hotel. I ambled up the steps inside the front entrance noting the potted palm trees with their skinny fronds and drooping arms that separated several seating areas. Two areas were vacant but a thirty-something couple occupied the other.

Anna Lang sat at the bar sipping red wine and schmoozing with the bartender. She looked good in dark pants, a light blue blouse and matching sweater, her hair pushed back over her ears.

I stood behind the chair next to her, smiled and said, "Pardon me, miss. Is this seat taken?" She turned, "Parker! What a nice surprise."

Yesterday we had left each other in a tiff, but now it was as if all past sins were forgiven. It appeared we each harbored our own agenda for keeping the peace. Anna needed me as a pathway to Bully, and I needed more time to figure out her intentions.

She patted the chair next to her and said, "Hop on. What will you have? Gene the Machine can fix anything."

That was the first time I'd really noticed the bartender, a hawk-faced kid in his early twenties with tattoos on his arms. I laid a twenty-dollar bill on the counter and said, "Another wine for the lady and a Shiner Bock for me."

Gene picked up the bill and studied it. Then I realized how strange it must have seemed to have someone actually paying cash at the upscale bar. He brought the drinks with a slight smirk on his face and then moved down the bar to wait on another customer.

I clinked my bottle with Anna's glass and sipped my beer. Then I grinned and said, 'So, any bugs get loose today?"

She almost choked on her wine, but managed to set the glass down without a spill. She squeezed her eyes, peering into mine.

"Doing some snooping, huh? You saw the article about me?"

"Believe it or not, I can actually use a computer. Do you really think what you said in the article about the missing vial is what actually happened? The pathogen was swept up in the trash and burned?"

She sighed heavily and paused for a moment. "Yes, I do," she said. "Security in our lab is at the highest possible level. We deal with the deadliest viruses known on the planet, agents that cause diseases in humans for which there are no known cures."

"You got that spiel down pat," I said.

She laughed, "I've repeated it often enough."

"So what are these horrific bad boys you deal with?"

"Oh, you know, simple ones like those that cause incurable hemorrhagic fevers: Ebola, Dengue and Marburg, plus a few most people have never heard of."

"Hemorrhagic? You mean the victims bleed out?"

"Basically, yes. Eventually the bleeding causes the organs to shut down."

"So how are these diseases transmitted? Insect bites?"

"Marburg is transmitted by the fruit bat. Of course, once the virus is in humans, any bodily fluid contact will transmit it. The same with Ebola, except that was originally transmitted through primates...monkeys. People in Africa eat them, you know."

"You said incurable?"

"So far, that's why we're studying them."

"Holy jeez! I think I need another beer."

"Wimping out? Don't worry. We changed the protocols after the incident you read about. We now put electronic tags on each vial. Sensors read the tags and cause a computer warning to flash if one of the vials is not returned to its case."

"Is that supposed to make me feel safe?"

"We know what we're doing, Parker."

Gene the unfriendly machine stopped by and we ordered more drinks. When her new glass of wine arrived, Anna drained the current one and pushed the empty back. The girl liked her red. But then knowing the pressure of her work environment, I could sympathize. She picked up the glass and sniffed the bouquet.

"A bit of cherry and some other fruit," she said. "Good enough for a bar wine." She glanced at her watch. "Which reminds me, I'm getting hungry."

She exaggerated blinking her eyelids, an expression I read as "Take me to dinner." We finished our drinks and Anna said she wanted to change. She quickly paraded across the lobby and out the front door.

It was then a tall black-haired man, early forties, wearing a brown knit pullover, eased into the chair at the far end of the bar. He ordered a drink, swished the ice in the glass and, without missing a beat, grabbed a quick glance in the mirror toward me. I dropped my eyes, pretending not to notice. The man looked vaguely familiar. Not like someone I knew, but rather like someone I'd once seen.

One of the spy-craft courses I'd taken at Fort Huachuca in Arizona taught how to remember a subject. Each one of us supposedly has seven duplicates among the seven billion people in the world. The instructor lined up photos of celebrities and their look-a-likes. I particularly remember images of Anne Hathaway and Leonardo DiCaprio shown next to their so-called replicas. The comparisons appeared amazingly similar, but the instructor pointed out DiCaprio's lips were fuller and the bridge of his nose was not as wide. With the Hathaway comparison, Anne's eyes weren't as far apart.

Using a combination of eight facial dimensions, the instructor indicated the chances of an exact match were one in a trillion. The purpose of the course was to learn how to remember a face. How to memorize noses, eyes and ears and distinguish among the general face shapes: round, oval, square or oblong.

This man's face was square-shaped, what my instructor would have called strong and masculine with a sturdy jawline and cheekbones. His fair skin and his height, at least six feet, meant he was probably of northern European heritage, German or Scandinavian. Yet his coal-black hair portended something else.

So what was he showing me with that furtive glance? Interest? Suspicion? Or just a simple acknowledgment of another patron at the bar? But if so, why hadn't he simply looked my way with a friendly nod? He wasn't a tourist or he wouldn't be alone. He could have been a local waiting for a guest or a business meeting.

I felt the old habits coming back: observing, calculating and comparing, learned skills I'd not used much in the last few years. No reason to. The clientele at The Garhole was just not that interesting: fishermen, drinkers and bull-shitters all. No spies in that crowd.

Tired of playing the game, I tossed the thoughts aside and started to pay my bill just as Anna waltzed back into the bar, a big smile on her face. She'd changed into jeans and another blue blouse but the same sweater. It appeared tonight that her hazel eyes would radiate blue. Like all women, she'd applied fresh lipgloss and maybe a light dusting of powder on her face.

I pulled out another twenty and asked for the tab. Gene played with the cash register and handed me the check. Two twenties were barely enough to include the tip. I left the bar not exactly thrilled that the Tremont didn't have Happy Hour. I was down to forty dollars cash in my wallet and wondering where we could eat a nice dinner in a tourist town for twenty each including tip and drinks. Even if I laid back on the alcohol, the way Anna inhaled two glasses of wine meant she was probably having more. I don't own a credit card. The things are just too damned invasive, enabling some giant entity to gobble up personal information to use at their discretion. Only thing I could think of was to cruise by Harry's house and bum a few bucks off him.

As we left the bar, my peripheral vision caught the dark-haired man following Anna with his eyes.

We ambled around to my pickup, I opened the door for her like a gentlemen, and she slid in. I went to the driver's side, climbed in and cranked the engine.

"We gotta be in Texas," she said, offering a low chuckle.

"Are you knocking my ride?"

She smiled. "First thing I noticed getting off the plane from Germany—a sea of pickups."

I let the comment pass. "What are you hungry for?"

"A good American hamburger. Know a good spot?"

"That's it," I said. "The Spot."

I sighed, feeling relief coursing out of my lungs. Forty dollars for hamburgers should work, saving me the embarrassment of dropping by Harry's house. I cut over to 33rd St., crossed Broadway Boulevard and stopped at the Seawall.

"There she blows, purported to be the city's finest burger. At least they think so. The joint takes up half a block, including three buildings and five venues. So they say. Take your pick."

We parked, went in through the back and got in line at the counter to order. An attractive brunette, tall and slender, with ruby lips and bright eyes slipped into the line behind us.

When Anna turned to say something to me, she spied the woman. "Hi Iryna. Didn't know you were coming here tonight."

Iryna smiled, then glanced at me and back at Anna.

Anna said, "Oh, excuse me. Iryna, this is Parker McLeod. Parker, meet Iryna Kravets, my co-worker."

Iryna and I shook hands, her eyes appraising me like a future mother-in-law checking out her prospective son-in-law.

Anna said, "Iryna works with me at the lab. We were in school together at the University of Munich. She is a brilliant researcher. I recruited her to join me about a month ago. We were lucky to get her."

"Exciting," I said. "Are you from Germany also?"

"No, the Ukraine. I moved to Germany to study virology."

Her tone was purposeful, full of obvious intelligence, and her English was clear, if a little stilted. About that time the line moved up and Anna turned to the cashier.

I asked Iryna if she'd like to join us for dinner.

"Well, uh, thanks, but no. I'm just getting something to go. Long day."

Anna ordered a cheeseburger and red wine. I opted for a shrimp po'boy and a Shiner. We said goodbye to Iryna and climbed the stairs to the open deck overlooking the Gulf of Mexico. A steady breeze blew in off the beach, dissipating the sticky, humid air. Anna's hair fluttered in the wind. She sat her drink down and pushed her hair back over her ears.

"Nice," she said.

In front of us, couples walked the seawall hand in hand, while kids played Frisbee on the beach. The south wind sent waves scurrying to the shore. We watched the night arrive, shadows lengthening, car lights along the boulevard coming on. Anna crossed her arms and squeezed her shoulders as the evening air cooled the night.

"Wanna go inside?" I asked, noticing her gesture.

"No, this is too beautiful to leave."

Far out in the gulf, colored lights from oil platforms

flickered on. The moon rising off the horizon sent rays of pale light across the water. At that moment it seemed as if the sheer terror and panic gripping Galveston were but a distant memory. But like a dream that vanished upon awakening, I knew better. We'd just endured a terrifying explosion, mangled and burned bodies, streets blocked with barricades, and husbands and fathers gone, lives snuffed out in an instant of unimaginable horror.

Now it seemed that FBI and ATF agents in initialed jackets were everywhere. Galveston cops working overtime flooded the streets. An unrelenting fear stalked deep in peoples' psyche. Little things told the tale, like the furrowed forehead of the young girl at the counter when we ordered. Or the nervous glances of customers flittering around, their eyes narrowed with apprehension, not sure the attack was over. Primal fear was exacerbated by the sound of a siren in the night, people unsure if it was a routine accident or another terrorist strike.

Galvestonians were accustomed to dealing with devastating hurricanes, but this was different. It was like the old days on the island at the turn of the century when the scourge of yellow fever invaded the city and killed hundreds, striking an unrelenting fear and ushering in a terrifying loss of control.

The food came and we ate in silence, each of us absorbed in our own thoughts. I looked out over the tranquil water, trying to push away the dark thoughts of the past few days. When she finished eating, Anna got up and moved to the railing. She lifted her face to the breeze, a vibrant, beautiful woman, alone on a starry night. She turned, smiling, the wind blowing her hair.

"I see why you like it here, Parker. It's lovely. Germany has its mountains and forests and beautiful rivers, but this is different. I'm so glad I took this job."

She moved to her seat and sipped her wine.

"Do you miss Germany?"

"Mostly my mother. She's not doing well. Since my father died, she seems to have lost the joy of living. They were so close…."

Whether consciously or not, she'd sent a clear message— her mother—Bully's daughter.

"So sorry," I said, trying to walk the line between empathy and doubt, but it was not easy.

"When UTMB offered me this position, my emotions went crazy. Stay and take care of my mother, the only family left for me, or embrace a new life in America? But mother pushed. Opportunities don't come often, she said. And then she told me it was Bully's hometown. Maybe he was still alive…."

Her voice drifted off, her eyes damp and misty.

"Tell me more about your mother," I said.

Anna perked up. "Johanna Lang, actually Dr. Lang. My mother is a well-known physician in Kaiserslautern." She paused, dropped her eyes and then opened them again with a playful grin. "But it's Aunt Johanna to you Cousin Parker, or Aunt Jo for short."

Her sudden shift from melancholy to spirited gave me an opening. Hopefully I could challenge her allegation in a way that wouldn't send her fleeing across the beach like the last time.

"Whoa, whoa," I said, smiling, my palms up in front of me. "I understand your need for family. But we're not there yet. I'm not a genealogist, and I don't have a clue as to what our relationship might eventually be. Maybe step-cousin if there is such a thing. Bully was my mother's sister's husband. He may be my uncle by marriage, but there's no blood between us."

"Come on, Parker, lighten up. I know that," she said. "But step-cousin, huh? I think I like that."

She touched the bottom of her wine glass to my Shiner bottle and smiled. We were both quiet for a moment. Out in the Gulf, blue and green phosphorescent colors glimmered on the water.

"Look," she said, pointing at the water along the beach.

"Sea sparkle," I said. "Billions of plankton floating just beneath the surface. Beautiful, isn't it?"

She rose and leaned into the railing, studying the sparkle. Whether the timing was right or not, I couldn't put off telling her any longer. I spoke to her back.

"I have some news, Anna. Probably not what you want to hear."

She turned toward me and leaned back against the railing.

"I saw Bully again today and questioned him pretty good."

Anna's smile dissolved, all playfulness gone. The upturned corners of her mouth shifted back to neutral, her eyes on point, anticipating new information.

"And?"

"I don't know...it's going to take a while. I can't figure if he really doesn't remember or he doesn't want to. Or he does remember and he won't admit it."

"That's really disappointing," she said. "I'd hoped that you could persuade him to open up and admit the truth." She paused for a moment, her face tightening. "But you gave it your best shot. Now it's my turn."

"No, please, let me handle this."

She paused, studying me, her blue eyes boring into mine. Finally, she said, "Okay, one more chance. Then I'm taking over."

She finished her wine, then tilted the glass back and forth, gesturing for a refill. Crisis over, I hoped. I opened my wallet and removed the last bill, a fiver. I held it up to the light as though trying to will it into a twenty.

"That it?" she asked.

"Afraid so. Settle for half a glass?"

She laughed.

"My med-school friend always told me to judge men by the car they drove. I should have known better."

"Sorry, what can I say?"

"No plastic?"

I shook my head.

"Oh, for goodness' sake, what's money among family." She reached into her purse and tossed her Visa card on the table.

Chapter Thirteen

Tuesday morning
Galveston

David awoke early. He peeked out the window, saw that the morning light was beginning to chase away the nighttime shadows and realized the sun would be up soon. He prostrated himself on one of the Tremont towels, his temporary prayer rug, and recited the morning prayer.

He showered and dressed and went down to the Tremont cafe for breakfast. He ordered breakfast and moved to a table with his coffee, thinking about the attractive woman he'd seen at the hotel bar last night. He had hustled back from his scouting trip at the hospital hoping to find her still there, but the only customer had been a dark-haired man dressed in sneakers and jeans. Even now, hours later, David still wasn't sure if the man had been surreptitiously checking him out. Furtive glances or innocent wanderings? David clenched his teeth, thinking he wasn't cut out for this spy stuff. Damned paranoia was getting the best of him.

And then the woman he'd seen at the bar earlier came in and marched straight to the man. After a drink, they had left the hotel together. Disappointed, David had found a restaurant around the corner on the Strand. After mixing in a few more drinks with dinner, he had returned to the Tremont, found the bar empty and gone to his room.

David sipped his morning coffee trying to shake off the thoughts about last night and hoped the pounding in his head would stop. He rubbed the sides of his head, chastising himself. The alcohol had put him in such a stupor he'd failed to recite evening prayers.

He looked up to see a waiter bringing his breakfast. He loved the taste of crisp bacon with his eggs, but the sudden vision of his mother reading the Quran each evening had pushed him to smoked salmon. He'd often gotten the same image of his mother when he drank alcohol, but he'd learned to trick his conscience into dismissing her reproach. He was half-American after all, and alcohol was a legitimate component of the average capitalist's daily routine.

Still, his heart winced each time he remembered the hurt in his mother's voice when he had failed to attend mosque for daily prayers. With America at war with radical Islamists, he had tried his best to convince her it was necessary for his business to keep his faith a secret. Of course, those visions of his mother plaguing him were now in his head, since she'd died of cancer a year after the towers fell.

But the confrontations with his brother had never stopped. Rashad regularly berated him for his non-attendance. David had only managed to hold off Rashad's constant lecturing because they both knew the FBI had infiltrated mosques all across the United States. David convinced Rashad that by keeping his background free of Muslim association, he would be in a better place to help Rashad if he ever needed him in America. As a result, like it or not, David was now in the middle of something he'd neither contemplated nor desired.

Another sip of the Tremont's house coffee brought his thoughts back to his visit with Rashad in Yemen and the fine coffee he and his brother shared on the veranda of the rented seaside hideaway. Then he thought of a scene he'd witnessed while bumping along the dusty road on his motorbike traveling from the port to Rashad's house: hungry, bloated children, their hands held out begging for food. He sighed and chewed his lip.

Yemen, the armpit of the world, where scorpions were as common as horseflies and the entire country was on the verge of starvation. Millions scraped by on a daily income that wouldn't buy a package of cigarettes in the U.S. The World Health Organization, battling Yemen's incessant cholera outbreaks, announced that water shortages were so severe the country could be totally void of the life-sustaining necessity within ten years. David hoped he'd made his last visit to the shithole. He would miss the coffee, but he also knew it was available on the internet for a price.

Still, it had been good to see his brother. David had attended their father and sister's funeral in Beirut a year earlier, and he had been disappointed Rashad wasn't there. Rashad had wanted to come, but he was afraid of another drone strike if the Americans caught him there.

David pulled a photo from his wallet. He had never met his half-sister Akilah, but the picture gave life to a beautiful teenager full of zest, with dark hair and eyes and a radiant yet somehow impish smile.

He finished his meal in a leisurely fashion, glancing around as he ate, hoping the beauty from last night would come in for breakfast. He knew it was a long shot since she lived across the street and probably only frequented the hotel at night. Still....

David charged the tab to his room and walked to the front door of the hotel. He was about to step outside to order his car when he saw her. She stepped off the curb across the street and hurried toward the hotel, exquisite in a navy-blue pantsuit and white blouse, her hair pulled back behind her ears, silver earrings dangling with each step. He quickly turned and backtracked to the hotel coffee shop, reaching the service line as she entered. When she came in behind him, he turned as if suddenly noticing her.

"Oh, hi there," he said, smiling. "I saw you at the bar last night and didn't get a chance to introduce myself. My name is David Arnold."

David hoped he hadn't been too brash. He noticed her quick glance around the room as he waited for her response.

"Sorry if I startled you," David said, moving back a half step. "I just wanted to meet you and well…. Do you have time for a quick cup of coffee?"

David stalled, waiting her out. He knew damn well she was interested. Her glance at him in the Tremont last night told him that.

She checked her watch. "Well, I was planning on a coffee to go. Can't be late for work."

"Another time then?"

She glanced at her watch again, nervously moving it on her wrist. "Well, maybe a quick cup," she said.

They both ordered lattes and moved to a table.

"My name is Anna Lang," she said. "And you are David…?"

"Arnold," he said. "I'm in town for a seminar."

He noted her hazel eyes seemed to be more blue than green against her pantsuit.

"What kind of seminar?" she asked.

"It has to do with offshore drilling technology. Pretty boring stuff, actually."

"Doesn't sound that way to me, but then I really don't know anything about it."

"Well, I could tell you anything you want to know, but it would be more interesting to learn about you. What kind of work do you do?"

"Oh, I work at a lab. Testing things."

"Really," David said.

David got up to get the lattes. When he returned, Anna seemed relaxed, eyes brighter, her shoulders slumped slightly. She wore no ring on her left hand.

"What do you mean by 'testing things'?" David asked.

"Actually, I work at Gulf Coast Laboratory. We study viruses."

"Viruses?"

"Yes, I am a virologist."

"Sounds fascinating. He noticed a slight hesitancy as Anna sipped her coffee. She glanced at her watch again.

"Sorry," she said. "I really must go."

"Of course," David said. "I'd love to hear more about your work. Maybe a drink at the bar tonight?"

Anna picked up her latte and rose from the table. "Well, I usually stop by after work. I love the Hotel's décor, especially the antique bar."

"Hope to see you then," he said. "I'll walk out with you."

David held the door as she exited past him. "Nice to meet you, Anna," he said. He watched her cross the street, thinking tonight should be interesting.

Back in his room, David opened his laptop and googled the website for Gulf Coast Laboratory. He found Anna Lang, M.D. listed as the assistant director. He switched off the GCL site and googled Dr. Lang. Originally from Germany, both a medical doctor and PhD. Impressive, he thought. Not only looks but brains.

He flipped back and read several articles concerning BSL-4 labs and the extraordinary measures that were taken to ensure their safety. One report said:

Biosafety level 4 (BSL-4) provides the highest level of precautions for agents that could easily be aerosol-transmitted within the laboratory. These agents cause severe to fatal disease in humans for which there are no known vaccines or treatments. Safety precautions include: heat, pressure and chemical systems that process or "cook" all liquid and solid wastes completely. High efficiency (HEPA) filters remove any airborne material, making all the liquid and air effluents sterile or safe before they leave the facility. Redundant safety systems within the utility, power and mechanical infrastructure secure the area. If a power failure occurs, regularly tested backup generators immediately go into effect. These facilities are the most safely designed and constructed buildings in the world. In over 80 years of operation, no environmental release from a BSL-4 facility in North America has occurred.

David reread the report several times, focusing on the part about aerosol-transmitted agents. He closed his laptop and called for his car.

Twenty minutes later he found the Gulf Coast Laboratory almost hidden among the maze of UTMB buildings. He parked two blocks away, strolled toward the plaza that fronted the facility, and noted that the laboratory was tucked several hundred feet back from the street. Newly placed concrete barriers like the ones he'd seen at the hospital blocked the entrance to the plaza.

A tent with Homeland Security markings had been erected in front of the building to provide shelter for what appeared to be additional security personnel. He assumed they had been brought in as a result of the attempt on Perry. Two officers with automatic weapons stood outside the tent. He took a chance and walked briskly past the entrance.

With a quick glance through the heavily reinforced glass

front doors, David noted a security desk with two uniformed police officers. Beside the desk was a metal detector similar to those used at airports.

David had seen enough. The security at the laboratory was too tight: no unauthorized person could even get inside the building, much less penetrate the lab. And if someone did get inside, how would they get the pathogen out? He needed more information and Dr. Lang was the obvious ticket. He hoped she'd show at the Tremont bar tonight.

He also needed to contact Rashad and, in case the Americans could somehow track his email, he wanted to be as far away from the hotel as possible. He checked the time: 7:30 a.m. here, so 4:30 p.m. in Yemen. His brother should be up from his afternoon rest. He drove up 25th Street toward the beach and parked on the seawall.

Down on the beach a young couple sat in chairs holding hands beneath a brightly colored umbrella. In front of them, a woman holding a small child's hand strolled close to the water looking for shells. The wind had quit, allowing the surf to become unusually quiet. An often-used expression crossed David's mind, "The calm before the storm."

He had followed Rashad's instructions and purchased a burner phone at the Houston airport. He had tried to convince Rashad that a quick call on a burner phone was safe since no one could trace it back to him. But Rashad told him that the National Security Agency (NSA) electronically monitored millions of telephone calls to and from Muslim countries and could pinpoint the location of a call to someone's living room. So the burner phone was needed just in case someone in the U.S. needed to contact him. Rashad had insisted, instead, on using encrypted emails on the dark web to communicate with each other.

David opened the encryption site, copied his private key

from the note section on the phone and pasted the combination of letters and numbers into the link.

David: *The hospital is very secure. They have banned vehicle access for at least a block away. We will need another method to get to him.*

Rashad: *Are you positive about this?*

David: *Yes, impossible to get close enough.*

Rashad: *Do you have another idea?*

David: *If we could somehow insert a deadly pathogen into Perry's room.*

Rashad: *Excellent! How would we do it?*

David: *There is a bio lab here that studies deadly viruses. But the security is too tight, impossible to breach. I need your help to think the scheme through.*

Rashad: *I have an idea that might work, but time is short. Work on a backup plan using the lab you mentioned and get back to me.*

David signed off, disappointed. He'd intended to give Rashad the idea of using a deadly virus to kill Perry and leave the planning up to him. But Rashad had told him to have a backup plan just in case. Damn. He knew anything he came up with would put him square in the middle of things. A place he didn't want to be.

With FBI and Secret Service agents lurking around every corner, David felt more exposed with each passing hour. Still he had no choice, something had to be done. The more he thought about it, the more he realized he'd have to develop the plan that was cooking in his mind.

Chapter Fourteen

Tuesday morning
The Garhole Bar

The morning sun beat hard against the window, signaling another warm January day on the Gulf Coast. I rolled over to the nightstand and toggled the weather radio. The NOAA broadcaster, droning on in his usual monotone voice, announced today's weather: light southeast wind, high in the low eighties, and a steady barometric pressure of 29.95. I never paid much attention to the barometric reading unless it was hurricane season. Dropping pressure during the season could mean a storm was approaching within the next twenty-four to forty-eight hours. Nothing to mess with when it happened.

On the radio, the announcer was saying that another cold front was approaching and would hit Galveston in the next couple of days, dropping the temperature to the mid-thirties along the coast. Add a big rainstorm due at the end of the week, and it was the same stuff Larry, my fishing buddy at NOAA, had told me earlier.

I sat up on the edge of the bed thinking about yesterday's mixed bag of failures versus successes. The meeting with Bully had gone south quickly, starting with my hard questioning about the farmhouse in Malmedy and ending with him dozing off into a morning nap. Was Bully really that cagey, dodging my questions with a dazed-like attitude? Or was his demeanor real, the fading memories of an old man lost in the confused jumble of an aging mind? I couldn't tell.

In any event, it was time to get back to business. The bar couldn't run itself. Since I hadn't opened yesterday, I needed to make the most of the next two days before the cold snap arrived.

I washed up, jumped into shorts and a T-shirt, and hurried down the stairs to the dock. Out in the bay, two boats sped across the water, charging from one favorite fishing spot to another and trying to locate schools of trout. With any luck, one of the boats would end its day at The Garhole.

Inside the bar, rows of gleaming white teeth glared down at me. With no beer to toast the gar head, I saluted instead. Some days The Garhole was so empty of visitors, I found myself talking to the skeleton. The worst part was when he talked back, telling me how isolated he felt out here at the end of the island. Or at the end of the world, as he put it.

I started coffee, cranked up the ceiling fans and hoisted up and latched the cut-out in the front wall. The breeze off the gulf hit my face, bringing the scent of the wild lantana bushes that mingled among the salt grass and prickly pear. As I breathed in the warm gulf air, the telephone sounded. I hustled to the back and picked up the receiver.

"Garhole."

"Parker, it's Burney Hebinck."

His voice sounded solemn, even grave. I didn't think he was calling about the fishing trip I'd promised.

"Hey, Burney. What's up?"

"We need your help. Can you meet us in an hour? The task force is set up at the Coast Guard base."

"The task force? What are you talking about? I can't add anything to what I told you at the bombing scene."

"Not about that," he said. "Can you come in?"

I couldn't imagine why the FBI wanted me in the loop. "I can't leave The Garhole, Burney...sorry. My coolers are empty and the beer truck is on its way. I've only got two days of good fishing weather before the next cold front moves in. I need to keep the bar open. You want to come out here, I'll make some gumbo?"

Burney's muffled voice sounded as if he'd put his hand over the receiver to talk to someone else. "Matthews gives your gumbo five stars. We're leaving now."

Just as I hung up, the beer truck arrived. I helped the driver unload and offered him a hot meal his next time through if he'd help me stack the cooler. As soon as he left, I dragged out my iron skillet, dumped in some flour and oil and started the roux. Twenty minutes later the mixture turned the dark, rich color I wanted. I did a quickie version of gumbo, tossing in onions, frozen okra and spices, trying to get something ready during the forty minutes it would take Burney's entourage to drive here from the Coast Guard station. When everything was simmering nicely, I dropped in one of Neddie's packages of frozen shrimp. It wasn't my best effort, but I figured Burney was a transplanted Yankee from D.C. and he wouldn't know the difference.

A few minutes later, a boat with two fishermen tied up at the dock. Two Garhole regulars, Larry and Alvin from Houston, stepped out of the boat with a stringer of trout. Larry took the stringer to the cleaning table while Alvin headed for the beer box.

"Hit it lucky today," he said.

I said something like "nice catch" but my attention was focused on Burney Hebinck and Maurice Matthews just coming in the front door. As they entered, another dark SUV slammed to a stop beside theirs. The FBI agents turned back to look at the new arrival. A man I didn't know got out and hustled in the front door.

"Got your message," the man said to Hebinck as he came in.

Hebinck and Matthews were wearing FBI windbreakers. The initials on the new man's jacket read ATF. I stepped out from behind the bar to greet them.

"Parker, meet Jim Mooney, in from Washington," Hebinck said. "Jim is the on-scene ATF agent in charge of the bombing."

Mooney was a six-footer with coal-black hair combed straight back, a square jaw and dark, almost black eyes that took in everything in sight with a piercing scan. We shook hands and I guided the group to a table. Matthews nodded toward the back door.

"How long will your customers be here?"

"About through with cleaning their fish. They'll suck down a couple of beers and a bowl of gumbo, then be gone."

"We don't have a lot of time," Matthews added.

"We'll eat first, then," I said.

Larry and Alvin came in staring at the agents' windbreakers on their way to their table. Normally a couple of magpies bragging about their fishing skills, today the fishermen were as quiet as two sloths making love. Which meant I'd get a phone call later from the boys wanting the scoop.

I served Larry and Alvin first, hoping they'd finish quickly and leave. I dished up more gumbo and took it to Hebinck's group. No one at our table spoke during the meal, not even the obligatory praise for my gumbo. The silence in the room reminded me of a movie scene where prisoners sit at long shiny tables scarfing their food in complete silence, anticipating a rumble where someone would get knifed during the meal. Something about the table full of FBI and ATF agents seemed to make Larry and Alvin rush through their gumbo. As they got up to leave, I mentioned they should fish again tomorrow to beat the cold front coming in.

When Hebinck and his gang pushed their empty bowls away, I sat back, waiting for the mystery meeting to begin. Mooney, the ATF agent, spoke to Hebinck without even acknowledging I was in the room, much less looking at me.

"Before we go any further, we need to discuss McLeod's participation. Your message said you were coming out to meet with him, but I don't understand what he has to do with the investigation. He doesn't have security clearance."

Ignoring the host was not a good way to start a healthy collaboration. I pushed my chair back and started to get up. "Got a bar to run," I said, glancing from Hebinck to Matthews while ignoring Mooney.

"Wait," Hebinck said, putting his hand on my arm. He looked at Mooney. "McLeod has twenty years' experience with Army Intelligence. We are working on updating his security clearance. I would ask you to please bear with me on this."

"Highly unusual," Mooney said.

"I'll take responsibility," Hebinck said.

Mooney sighed and looked away.

Hebinck turned to me. "I need to brief Agent Mooney on some new developments. Can you give us five minutes?"

I ambled out to the dock, cranked up the hose and washed the fish scales off the cleaning table. When I finished, Matthews stood at the back door waving me back in. Mooney sat next to Hebinck at the table, staring out the back wall opening. He seemed even more agitated than before I'd walked out. It was obvious that whatever Matthews told him hadn't set well. The breeze had quit, leaving the bar stuffy in the high humidity. I stood by the cooler and asked, "Anybody want a beer?"

Hebinck and Matthews asked for Cokes while Mooney and

I opted for Shiner Bocks. I grabbed the drinks and moved back to the table.

Hebinck said, "Agent Mooney and his team have been working non-stop on the investigation. They have accumulated valuable information about the bomb, and I have asked him to share it with us."

Mooney fidgeted in his chair. "Okay," he said. "But just so you know, I don't feel comfortable discussing confidential information with someone without security clearance. If there's a leak, it's your baby."

Hebinck nodded.

Mooney slugged a gulp of Shiner and said, "Except for the size, the bomb was almost identical to the one Timothy McVeigh used at the 1995 Oklahoma City explosion. As you know, that piece of dung murdered 168 innocent people including nineteen kids in the building's daycare center. McVeigh's bomb was much larger than this one. He used a Ryder truck where this perp had a van. In both explosions, fifty-five-gallon oil drums were packed with crushed ammonium nitrate fertilizer and diesel fuel. Both also used a booster, nitromethane, better known as racing fuel. All in all, two damn powerful bombs. We fried McVeigh in 2001, but there are still a lot of sickos like him running around this country. In fact, the notoriety he created probably spawned a few. Maybe even this one."

No one spoke. Everyone realized he could be right. Then Matthews said, "Actually, McVeigh was executed by lethal injection."

"Too humane for that bastard," Mooney said, waving Matthews off. "I would have pulled the switch and sucked in the vapors if they still used Old Sparky."

Mooney's comment brought a moment of silence to the table. I didn't like Mooney, but found myself agreeing with his comments about McVeigh's execution.

"Let's focus on Galveston," Matthews said. "McVeigh actually lit a fuse. How did the bomber here set it off?"

"Electronic blasting caps wired to a nine-volt battery," Mooney said. "And a toggle switch probably held in his hand while he was speeding out the gate."

Mooney got up, inhaled the rest of his beer, and set the empty bottle on the table. "That's all I have," he said. "I'm outta here."

Hebinck focused on Mooney. "Sorry I didn't update you before you got here, Jim. Everything was happening so fast I—"

"Sure," Mooney said, interrupting. "Typical inter-agency bullshit. Meanwhile people are getting killed."

Mooney turned and marched out the door. We all sat speechless as he powered up his SUV and spun up the sand road to the highway. Something Mooney had just learned had obviously aggravated him even more than my lack of security clearance.

"Not exactly kumbaya," I said, smirking.

Hebinck sighed, looking totally deflated. "Since we have information that foreign terrorists may be involved, the FBI is now in charge of the investigation, meaning the ATF is out. I didn't get back to Jim with the information until just now. He probably felt like he'd been sandbagged, but we didn't leave him out on purpose. I'll buy him a drink next time I see him. He'll calm down. I really feel badly about it, though. After all the lack of communication between agencies prior to 9/11, we've been trying hard to keep each other informed. We don't need these kinds of screw-ups."

"What do you mean foreign terrorists may be involved?" I demanded.

Hebinck hesitated. He looked back at the parking lot as if

to make sure Mooney was gone and said, "I'm putting my ass on the line here, Parker, trusting you."

"Hey, you called me, remember?"

Hebinck glanced at Matthews and then focused on me. "The rental agent saw the news and called in when the panel truck wasn't returned. The perp used a phony ID to rent the truck, but the dumbass left his prints on the rental form. Lucky for us he'd been arrested for stealing from his employer. Muhammad Rana, age twenty-two, hometown of Minneapolis, Minnesota. We located an apartment in his name. The search warrant produced a computer and a thumb drive. The drive contained videos showing jihadist rhetoric and even one with the beheading of an infidel."

"What about the computer?"

"Our techs broke the password. A lot of emails back and forth between Rana and the other two knuckleheads in his cell, his brother Ratif and another kid named Lutfi. Minneapolis agents rounded them up. Two nitwits about as stupid as we've seen. Ratif and Lutfi actually communicated about the results of the bombing in regular emails."

"So what's the foreign connection?" I asked again, trying to determine what all this had to do with me.

"Our analysts decided the cell members were not smart enough to have pulled this off by themselves. They had to be getting direction from higher up the food chain. Several of the emails referenced someone named the Mahdi.

"And the Mahdi is...?"

"Our best guess? This is the pseudonym for whoever they were getting instructions from: the higher up. Translated, Mahdi means 'guided one.' Many Muslims believe the Mahdi will appear at the end of times to restore righteousness for a short period of time before the end of the world."

"Sounds like their leader picked a good name. Who could

not believe in someone that powerful?"

"So our techs found several instances where Rana, the cell's leader, had accessed the dark web, and after that the regular emails between the Mahdi and Rana stopped."

"Dark web? What the hell is that?"

"A vast underground of encrypted sites that search engines don't reach. Terrorists know the NSA has the ability to intercept phone messages, so encrypted messages on the dark web are now their preferred method of communication. We've teamed with the NSA to try and break the encryption, but it's slow going."

"So the Mahdi taught the cell how to access this dark web?"

Hebinck nodded.

"Okay, so what does this have to do with me?"

"Among the hundreds of emails between Rana and the other cell members, one word stood out." Hebinck paused. Then after a beat he said, "Berlin."

"Oh, Christ." I closed my eyes and looked away.

Hebinck paused. He didn't have to explain about something that still shot a jolt of pain to my heart every day.

February, 1990. My best friend, Lieutenant Montgomery Edwards, and I were celebrating liberty in a Berlin café, a popular hangout for Americans. The blast blew the café apart, killing twelve including Monty and three other U.S. servicemen and women. The dreams of a man not yet thirty years old were snuffed out like a candle. Monty had plans to marry and raise a family with his girlfriend back home in Indiana. A world of hope and love was throttled by a force so dark and evil. It was beyond senseless.

I turned back to Hebinck, a fire burning in my belly. "You're sure it was a reference to the café bombing?"

"Pretty sure. If the cell was getting help from a source on the dark web, in order to trust that source, we think the contact had to provide enough information to convince the cell that he was legitimate. A real bomb expert. He must have mentioned the Berlin bombing."

"Kind of thin," I said.

"Maybe," Hebinck. "But it's what we've got. The director thinks it's good, and we can't afford not to follow the lead."

I dropped my eyes to the table to be alone with my thoughts of Monty Edwards. The joy he would never know of his children laughing and playing, and growing old with his wife. I couldn't remember much for the first few weeks after the explosion, but then images filtered in: smoke, fire, body parts, and the smell of burning flesh.

"So, how about it, Parker?" Hebinck asked. "Are you in?"

"What do you think?"

"We have no photographs," he said. "You are the only person who can possibly identify the bomber."

"Burney, that was a long time ago. I—"

"You told me once you'd never forget the man's face."

"I had only a glimpse...."

I tried to conjure a picture of the man I had seen dropping off the briefcase moments before the explosion. Somewhere in my tired mind, the vision was there. I just needed to dig it out. If there was anything I could do for Monty as well as the victims in Galveston, I'd do it. Plus the FBI wanting me in the loop might be the opportunity I'd dreamed of: revenge, a chance to strangle the bastard who'd killed Monty with my bare hands.

"What can I do?"

"So how about working with a sketch artist? Do the best you can."

Chapter Fifteen

Tuesday afternoon
The Garhole Bar

After Hebinck and Matthews left, my thoughts drifted again to Monty and the horrific explosion that had taken his life. After his death, his finance' and I became long-distance friends. We stayed in contact for a few years consoling each other over Monty's loss, but then she found a new boyfriend and moved on. Shortly after that, I lost track of his mother and father when they sold their farm and moved to an assisted-living complex somewhere in the Midwest.

Monty was one of those rare people who listened rather than running on about himself. It was almost as if he'd taken a relationship course on how to make friends. But I knew it was just Monty, a boy who'd grown up on a farm in Indiana with elderly parents and no siblings or close neighbors his age. I always figured that was the reason he'd become so empathetic. He needed friends as much as friends needed him. Monty knew more than anyone about my failing marriage and my deep feelings about the loss of my grandfather.

I had once asked him how he'd become such a good listener. In his farm-boy drawl he had replied, "Well, I just figure if I rattle on about myself, I'm saying stuff I already know and don't learn anything. I've heard it all before. But if I ask questions, then I grow. Kind of like watering a field of corn."

Monty and I met when he transferred into my unit. Before the fall of the Berlin Wall in 1989, Stasi, the East German intelligence operation, sent dozens of spies over the wall to infiltrate American Army bases. Known as "Romeos," the agents would woo lonely German women who worked at the bases as interpreters and typists, convincing them to copy and pass on sensitive documents. One of the women confessed her collusion during an intense interrogation. Monty and I lured the Stasi spy to her apartment and captured him, but not before the bastard sucker-punched me, breaking my jaw. Monty Edwards saved my life that day.

I read once that if you reach old age and have maintained one or two really good lifelong friends, you've achieved a successful life. So far, I wasn't doing too well. I counted Harry Stein as good a friend as one could have, but he was much older and probably wouldn't be around for my dotage. But Monty and I would have been there for each other if he'd lived. And I wasn't about to let his memory fade.

The roaring sound of a 289 HP V-8 engine brought me back to the present. A 1965, bright-yellow Mustang hatchback screeched to a halt on the oyster-shell driveway outside the open front wall. Damn, I loved those old Mustangs and had always wanted one. That 289 really had some spiff.

The driver fluffed her blond hair in the car's mirror, got out and entered the front door. She seemed vaguely familiar, a tall, graceful woman about five-seven or five-eight in snug jeans that accented a slim figure. She was, maybe, early forties, with high cheekbones and an almost translucent complexion so pale it seemed to glow from the inside. She slipped onto a barstool and pushed her hand across the counter.

"Parker McLeod," she said, smiling. "It's been a while."

"Uh, sorry, I...."

"Oh jeez, I was afraid of that. You don't remember." She squeezed my hand and turned it loose. "Kathy Landry...Nurse Landry," she said. "I was working the ER when Jake's mother came in on an overdose."

"Of course, Kathy. Good to see you again."

When I slid across the Coke that she ordered, she toasted the gar head and sipped from the can. She must have noticed the quizzical look on my face.

"I know the drill," she said. "I've been out here a couple of times on my day off. The peace and quiet soothes my soul after a hard night on the floor. Neddie and I are pals. You must have been out fishing or something."

I took a slug of Shiner, thinking she was one hell of a good-looking woman. It was my loss to have missed her.

"I'm your artist," she said.

"Really?"

"Yep.... Galveston PD doesn't have a full-time sketch artist, so it's my part-time job. I still work the ER at the hospital, too. Agent Hebinck called right after my shift ended at three o'clock. I jumped right on the offer, thinking about that damn gar head hanging over the bar and a cold beer. I'm pretty good at the sketching, so they tell me. Ready to get started?"

"Want a beer first?"

"I'll stay with this for now," she said, holding up the Coke can. "I'm a cheap drunk. One beer will screw up my drawing."

She reached into her briefcase and removed a sketch pad. "How about we move to a table?" She fanned her face with her hand and dotted her forehead with a tissue. "I need the breeze from the ceiling fan."

"Sure," I said. "Guess I'm just used to the humidity."

We moved to a table. She pulled out a pencil and propped the pad on an angle. "Okay, first the basics. Male, right?"

I nodded.

"Race, ethnicity, age?"

"About thirty years old, not Northern European. Maybe Southern Europe or possibly Middle Eastern."

"So he would be about fifty now, right?"

"More or less."

"Since he's a terrorist, everyone wants to assume one of the Muslim countries in the Middle East. But he could be from anywhere, correct? Indonesia, one of the 'stan' countries, North Africa. So on a scale of one to ten, light to dark, what about his complexion?"

"Hey, I got a glimpse, okay? And that was eighteen years ago."

"Relax," Kathy said. "I understand your frustration...losing a friend. I can only imagine your loss." She reached over, put her hand on mine and then quickly took it back. "We're going do the best we can."

"Sorry," I said, exhaling a slow breath. "Maybe his color was a five."

"So medium dark, good," She said.

I looked up at the ceiling fan watching its blades creaking slowly around and hoping I could match its patience. Kathy pulled out a half dozen drawings of face types. I picked the one with the stronger jaw.

"Close your eyes," she said. "Try to visualize his face while I draw a few things in."

I tried but couldn't get much. I opened my eyes to the basic outline of a man's face. She asked about the shape of his eyes and the distance between them. The nose: flat or pointed or rounded. The ears: size and lobes or not. The hairline and hair style. She erased and re-drew as we went, changing features as my memory began to focus better.

We took a break after she completed the first composite,

refreshed our drinks and moved to the outside bench overlooking the bay. The afternoon continued to warm, but the overhead deck provided shade and the slight breeze cooled the dock. Out in the bay, a flock of squawking seagulls were hovering and diving into the water. I pointed at the birds.

"There's a school of fish under those birds. Speckled trout are feeding and pushing shrimp up out of the mud to the surface. The gulls see this and attack the shrimp."

She turned toward me and when our eyes met, she said, "You love it here, don't you, Parker."

I nodded and turned back toward the water. Kathy's deep brown eyes had triggered a memory. Nurse Landry in the ER, her face drawn, shoulders slumped, exhausted from a long stretch in the Intensive Care Unit. She'd performed a difficult task, consoling a fifteen-year-old boy named Jake Green, whose mother was so drugged she'd gone into withdrawal, hallucinating and thrashing about so wildly she had to be tied down and sedated. Jake had witnessed his mother's trauma and was shaken to the core. But Kathy's eyes had flowed with compassion as she found the comforting words and warming touch that calmed him.

Without thinking, I reached over and pushed a loose strand of Kathy's hair away from her cheek. She smiled, turned away and rose from the bench.

"Come on McLeod," she said. "Let's finish this thing."

Another hour of erasing and drawing went by before we both agreed it was the best we could do.

"The next step is to age the suspect," she said. "When I get home, I'll also add a beard on one copy. If he's here in Galveston or coming this way, there's a good chance he lost the beard, but we want to have several versions for folks to consider."

She studied the subject's face again and nodded as if

pleased with her work. She asked me to study the drawing for a final look. I tried, but couldn't come up with any changes. I realized I'd told Hebinck I'd never forget the terrorist's face, but too much time had gone by. Kathy tucked the drawing into her briefcase and got up from the table.

"Hey," I said. "It's been a long day, lots of hard work. How about that beer or a glass of wine?"

"Well, I—"

Just then a dark SUV pulled beside her Mustang and Agent Matthews got out.

"Rain check?" I asked.

"Anytime."

She stopped at the front door, said something to Matthews, then got into her Mustang and roared up the sand road to the highway. Seeing that plume of dust rising behind her car left a hollow place in the pit of my stomach.

I looked at Maurice coming in the door and said, "Really good timing, Maurice. Thanks a lot."

Matthews glanced at the dust swirling off the road. "Sorry to interrupt your love life, Parker. I had barely gotten back to town when Burney asked me to hustle out here with new information."

I nodded and moved back to the counter.

"So how was your recall?" he asked.

"Oh, hell, I don't know. We did the best we could. It's been a long time," I said, still thinking about the rain check idea with Kathy.

Matthews nodded and said, "She mentioned she wanted to work on the sketch some more. I asked her to do the best she could, but to hurry. We need that drawing. Some agencies have gone more to computer-generated composites. They spit out dozens of facial configurations, show them to the witness and gradually narrow down the picture. Personally, I still like the hand drawings. And Ms. Landry is the best artist we have."

Matthews moved to a barstool and lifted a notebook computer to the counter. I popped a Shiner and set a Dr. Pepper down for him. He toasted the gar head overhead and sipped from the can.

"So what's up," I asked.

He slipped off the barstool, went to the back door and looked around the dock.

"Never know when somebody's out there cleaning fish," he said. He glanced at the empty parking lot and regained his perch.

"Our techs found another email address for the bomber, Rana. It hadn't been used in almost a year. Some of the emails were from Yemen. They haven't pinpointed the exact location yet, but they're working on it."

"Anything else new in the emails?"

"Nothing. But at least we may have a start in finding the mastermind. The problem is that Yemen is a hellhole and the FBI doesn't know much about it, we're bringing in the CIA. We're concerned that if the attack on Perry was planned by the "Café Bomber," he may have sent another terrorist to Galveston to finish the job. Or worse, he may be coming here himself."

As much as I hoped he was wrong, part of me hoped he was right. An opportunity to come face to face with Monty's killer.

"We'll have the drawing posted nationwide in the newspapers, on television and at every entry point from Mexico to Canada. At all the airports, arriving ships, you name it."

"Hell, he could come by boat right into Galveston. Wouldn't be difficult."

"Really, Parker. I don't need to hear that."

Maurice straightened on the stool and blew out a big breath, his brow wrinkled in thought, mouth turned down on the sides. His crimson face showed a spike in blood pressure. Not the carefree cruising man I'd seen lately.

I raised a palm. "Sorry, Maurice. Didn't mean to—"

"No, it's okay," he said. "I just need more time to get back into the game. It's been a while."

I nodded and looked away to give him a chance to recoup his composure.

"Agent Hebinck and I agree," he continued. "We have to consider that whoever is behind this will try again here. Secretary Perry is still critical in the burn unit. But if he gets better, they know we will move him to D.C., where security is tighter. We doubt they have another bomb ready to go, so they'll have to build one quickly or take another tack."

"Like what?"

"Wish I knew. We've got the hospital buttoned up tight, but they're creative sons of bitches. It could be anything."

Matthews finished his drink and glanced behind me at the back counter.

"I've got something for you to look at. Got any coffee?"

I put on a fresh pot and thought about another beer for me but passed. Matthews brought his computer to life.

"This is going to take a while," he said. "Photos of all known bomb makers. See if any of these offer the slightest resemblance."

"Oh shit, Maurice."

"I know," he said. "Have some coffee."

Chapter Sixteen

Tuesday afternoon/evening
Galveston

David opened his personal cell phone and googled the offshore technology seminar. Early registration was scheduled all morning so he decided to have an early lunch, hoping to avoid the crowd.

With the flavor of olives and garlic on his tongue, his taste buds suddenly salivated for the eggplant dish Badih had prepared in Yemen. He stopped at a restaurant on the seawall advertising Greek food and settled for moussaka: baked layers of potatoes, ground beef and eggplant, covered with béchamel sauce. Not bad, he thought, but not Badih. After the meal, David ordered a cup of the restaurant's advertised Turkish coffee, thinking the heavy jolt of caffeine would keep him awake during the meeting.

He parked in the garage behind the building and entered the block-long Galveston Convention Center. As he stepped off the elevator on the second level, a twentyish Hispanic woman with a broad smile, dark, long hair and even darker eyes was standing behind a hall table and registering guests.

He glanced at the cleavage peeking out from her low-cut blouse, returned her smile and signed the attendance sheet for the meeting. He slipped quietly into a seat at the rear of the room. It was important to cover his tracks, he thought.

Even if he only stayed a few minutes, at least he had established an attendance record. With his heart pounding through his shirt from the heavy dose of caffeine, he couldn't concentrate on the lecture. Not that he cared. While the speaker droned on about the efficiency of a new type of hydraulic pump, David surveyed the room. Out of about fifty people attending there were four women, none of whom rang his bell. His thoughts went to the girl out front. And then he bit his lip, scolding himself. Get your mind on the mission.

David suffered through fifteen more minutes of the seminar and then slipped out the back of the room. He smiled at the attendance woman, asked directions to the restroom and sneaked down the stairs at the end of the hall.

He drove back to the hotel, left his car with an attendant and stepped out into the street, noticing the sun had passed its zenith. And as Allah had taught Muhammad, it was the beginning time for *Asr*, the afternoon prayer. Back in his room, David performed the daily ritual, giving thanks to Allah for the bounties bestowed upon him.

At six o'clock, he sat at the Tremont bar nursing a Dewar's and water. He bounced off his chair with a smile on his face as Anna approached from the main entrance. She looked harried, lines in her forehead, eyes half open. He motioned her to the seat next to his and climbed back into his chair.

"Tough day?" he asked.

"Do I look that bad?"

"Like you could use a drink," he replied, signaling to the bartender. His comment brought a half smile to her lips as she dropped her shoes to the floor. She rubbed her stocking feet on the bottom rung of her chair.

"I'm okay," she said. "Just tired. Everyone is so damned shook up about all the extra security at the lab."

"Extra? Really?"

Gene sat a glass of red in front of her. She smiled at him, took a sip and then another.

"They brought in all these cement roadblocks. Then the officers with machine guns out front scared the pants off my colleagues. I spent the whole day running around calming everyone. Didn't get a thing done myself."

David knew all this of course, since he'd made a surreptitious run by the building only a few hours earlier. But he knew nothing about the building's interior security. And Anna was the one person who could help him.

"I'm lost," David said. "What does the lab have to do with the explosion?"

Anna sighed. She picked up her glass of wine and took a couple more sips, caressing the stem with a soft touch.

"Forget it," she said. "I shouldn't take out my frustrations on someone I just met." Her lips turned up in a half smile. "I'd rather not talk about it. How was your seminar?"

David realized she'd stopped his inquiry cold. He would have to work into it later. At least she was engaging, asking questions.

"Uninspiring," David responded. "Actually, I just needed a break and heard Galveston was a fun place. It's the dead of winter in Indianapolis. I figured if I could make a couple of contacts at the meeting, it would make the trip worthwhile."

Enough babbling, David thought. The conversation was going nowhere. It was time to make his move.

"The concierge told me about a restaurant I shouldn't miss. Something like Rudi and—"

"Rudi and Paco's," Anna broke in.

"You know it?"

"Sure, excellent choice."

"Care to join me?"

Anna's eyes flickered away from his. Unsure, he thought?

Pushing too much?

"Oh, I don't know," Anna said. "It's been a long day."

"I understand," David said. And then he grew a big smile, his voice teasing, "They're supposed to have an excellent wine selection."

Anna grinned. He waited, sipped the last of his scotch, keeping the smile.

"Oh, why not," she said, finishing the last of her wine. "I am hungry." She slipped her shoes back on and said, "Give me ten minutes to get out of my work clothes."

David walked her to the front door of the hotel and waited just inside while she strode quickly across the street and into her building's entrance. A few minutes later she came out wearing navy blue pants and a matching long-sleeve blouse under a sweater. He crossed the street and met her at the curb. The heat from the day had dissipated into a cool evening.

"Nice night," she said. "Feel like walking a couple of blocks?"

Taking precautions, David thought. Walking was safer than getting into a stranger's car. He knew he had some work to do before she trusted him. They turned on 24th and angled toward Postoffice Street, making small talk as they walked toward the restaurant.

A well-dressed twenty-something hostess with a warm smile greeted David and Anna as they entered the restaurant. David looked over the room. Only a few tables were occupied, but the ambience was right: soft lights and soft jazz playing in the background. Smartly dressed waiters hovered over linen-covered tables and chatted with patrons. The hostess led David and Anna to a quiet table in the rear. A waiter appeared out of nowhere with a wine list and menus. David perused the list and chose a bottle of expensive cabernet.

His pulse raced as he looked into Anna's eyes, her beauty

even more apparent in the ambient light. For a brief moment David's mind slipped from the task at hand. When the waiter poured the wine, David held up his glass for a toast.

"Here's looking at you, kid."

"Humphrey Bogart to Ingrid Bergman in *Casablanca*," Anna replied.

"Movie fan, huh?"

"I grew up watching those old black-and-whites with my mother."

"And where is she?"

"Germany."

"Really? What part?"

"Kaiserslautern. She's a physician, practiced for thirty years. I guess that's what stirred my interest in science. When this job opportunity came up, she encouraged me to take it." Anna lowered her gaze and sipped wine from her glass. She looked up at him and said, "She's not in good health, and I feel really guilty about not being with her. I miss her so much."

David noticed a slight glistening in her eyes, her mood decidedly melancholy. Perfect, he thought, a hint of vulnerability.

When the waiter appeared, Anna ordered the pan-seared sea scallops. David wanted a steak, but decided on Ahi tuna, trying his best to stay in tune with Anna. The waiter nodded and refilled their wine glasses before he left.

David tried hard to get a read on Anna's feelings. If she had been just another of his normal conquests, it would have been easy to fill the evening with meaningless flattery that appealed to her ego. But he quickly surmised she was too wise for his usual approach. The slight welling of her eyes told him how to proceed.

"Anna, uh...when you said you mother encouraged you to take this job, I kind of got the feeling that you weren't sure you'd made the right decision in moving here." David kept his voice soft, his expression concerned.

Anna smiled. "No, no, not at all," she said. "I love my job and I'm beginning to love Galveston, the beach, the laid-back atmosphere. Quite a change for me. People in Germany can be pretty stuffy."

"Touché," David said. He grinned and raised his glass. "I just got here and I already like the feeling of sand in my toes."

The waiter arrived with their entrees and poured the remainder of the wine. He held up the empty bottle and asked if they wanted another.

"Not for me," Anna said. "Tomorrow is a school day."

They each took a few bites of the meal without speaking, enjoying their choices. And then Anna said, "So, tell me about you, David Arnold. What is your life story?"

"Well, not as exciting as yours. I grew up with my mother in St. Louis. Never really knew my father. No brothers or sisters. After graduating from Purdue University, I moved to Indianapolis and over the years I've built a decent one-man engineering practice."

"No marriage in all of that?"

"No. But I'm not opposed to the idea. It's just never happened. How about you, Anna?"

"Marriage? No. Married to my work, maybe."

Perfect, David thought, the opening he needed to get back to her job.

"So, this laboratory where you work. Exactly what do you do there?"

Anna put her fork down. She looked up and said, "We study viruses, but it's not something I can go into a lot of detail about."

"Sounds hazardous," David said.

"Not really," she answered. "As assistant director, I'm also responsible for lab security. We've got backup after backup. It's perfectly safe."

Twenty minutes later David and Anna stood at the entrance to her building.

"I enjoyed the evening," Anna said, extending her hand.

David took her outstretched hand, pulled her close and kissed her cheek. He felt her heart beating against his chest.

"Absolutely lovely," he replied.

She smiled and touched his shoulder. "How much longer is the seminar?"

"Over tomorrow, but I think I'll stay a few days longer."

"Good," she said. Then she turned and went inside.

David wanted more, but he realized the timing wasn't right. Pushing the situation wouldn't have worked. She needed a little more cultivation.

Disappointed, he crossed the street to the Tremont entrance and asked the attendant to bring up his car. He took the elevator to his floor and retrieved his computer. When his car arrived, he drove to the seawall and parked along the boulevard. David's watch said 9:30 p.m. which meant it was early morning in Yemen, the perfect time to contact his brother. Rashad would be sitting on his veranda enjoying coffee and some of Badih's fresh baked pastries. David turned his computer on, accessed the encrypted site, put in the special key and waited.

Rashad had told him to put a backup plan together and get back to him. There was no doubt the deadly toxins at Gulf Coast Laboratory could be the key to finishing the botched attack on Perry. But how to grab them? Security was tight there under normal conditions. Getting in now would be impossible. The only scenario David could think of was to somehow induce Anna to ferret out a vial of one of the deadly viruses. But what would cause her to do that?

And then he remembered the mist in Anna's eyes when she'd talked about her mother. So, kidnap the old woman and put the heat on Anna to comply. Shouldn't be difficult, he thought. Rashad must have contacts in Kaiserslautern, a city close to a huge American base. With Germany's open immigration policy, the country was loaded with jihadists just waiting to be of service to Allah.

When Rashad answered, David messaged his plan about kidnapping Anna's mother. Rashad liked the idea and said he would send a team to reconnoiter her. But when he asked David how he planned to get the pathogen into the burn unit, David confessed he hadn't worked that part out yet.

A long period of silence ensued. David could feel his brother's disappointment in his lack of response, but there was nothing he could do about it. Finally, David asked Rashad if he could help put the second part of the plan together. More time went by. David began to wonder if he would get an answer. Finally, a curt response came through.

"Someone will contact you soon," the message said.

Chapter Seventeen

Wednesday morning
The Garhole Bar

My eyes popped open thinking about sweet, brown-eyed, Kathy Landry. She said she'd be off work at 3:00 p.m. Maybe I'd call and see if she'd finished her drawings. I needed to take one more look just to be sure and, of course, see Kathy.

I flipped on the weather radio and heard the monotone voice of the NOAA forecaster announcing that the expected cold front would arrive later this afternoon, dropping the temperature into the mid-thirties by late evening. I thought it highly unusual that two cold fronts would hit the island only a couple days apart, but as my NOAA contact Larry always said, "If weather was predictable, he wouldn't have a job."

I decided I couldn't put off a run any longer. I jumped into shorts and running shoes, stretched on the deck, drank two glasses of water and walked up the sand road to the highway. Feeling pretty good in the morning sun, I picked up speed at a pace that would take me two and half miles up the beach and back for a five-mile run in about fifty minutes. I'd read in a running magazine that ten-minute miles were average for an old guy. And with the slight bulge around my mid-section, I was feeling pretty average. Not that drinking too much beer had anything to do with it.

By the time I made the turn on the beach, the prevailing

southeast breeze had stilled. It wouldn't be long before the wind began to shift to the north. In front of me, a flock of tiny gray-and-white sanderlings picked its way along the sand, searching for tiny marine worms and mollusks exposed by the retreating surf.

Last night I'd spent several hours reviewing the photos of all known terrorist bombers. None of which reminded me of the man I'd caught a glimpse of at the Berlin café. I finally gave up around eight o'clock and finished the last of the gumbo. I called Anna Lang, got no answer and left a message to call me. When she didn't return my call, I pictured her hanging out at the Tremont bar with her friend Iryna Kravets.

I finished the evening on my upper deck watching a steady line of tugs push barges along the Intracoastal. For some reason, Australia crossed my mind. For the last couple of months the vision of running a bar on an isolated road in the middle of the Outback had appeared more and more often. But by this morning, the image of Kathy Landry and I sitting on the dock looking out over the bay seemed to have pushed the Outback image away.

In an effort to slow my heart rate back to normal at the end of the run, I walked the short distance from San Luis Road down the sand road to The Garhole. As soon as I crossed the highway, I noticed Neddie Lemmon's truck parked in front of the bar. Neddie was leaning over the truck bed moving something around.

"It's too early for a brewski," I said, approaching him. "What are you doing here?"

He looked up. "Just got off work at the toll booth and wanted to get the hell away from there. Somebody squealed about my cats. A reporter was out yesterday, took a picture of me feeding my little buddies. The shit put a big spread in the *Galveston Daily News* this morning. Some crazy-assed birder called the bridge and said he was coming out with a shotgun."

"Yeah, well I hate to be an I-told-you-so."

Neddie shrugged. With the tailgate of Neddie's pickup down, I could see two wire cages with some furry things bouncing around inside.

I stepped closer and gestured toward the cages. "I see you've had some luck with the marauders."

"I took four to the Vet yesterday. On my way to Jamaica Beach to drop these two girls off now. Pretty things. One's a tabby and the white one must have some Persian in it. We got kinda lucky. Turns out the Vet is a bird lover too. But even with him whacking them at cost, it's still expensive. I stopped by to see if you wanted to add to the de-nut fund."

"De-nut? Those are both females. I got a feeling you're trapping the females and letting the toms loose."

He shrugged.

I went inside, took several twenties out of the cigar box under the counter and handed them to Neddie.

He shoved the money into his pants pocket and said, "You gonna need me today?"

"Don't know yet, I'll call you."

I watched Neddie tool off in his truck remembering what he'd said about castrating male cats and knowing damned well what he was doing. Then I thought if he got all the girl cats taken care of, it wouldn't make any difference. Somehow, it didn't seem fair though.

I spent the next couple of hours sweeping out the bar, cleaning the kitchen and hosing down the dock outside. A couple of fishermen parked at the dock and cleaned the trout they'd caught. They drank a few beers and asked about something to eat, but I hadn't prepared anything. They left disappointed.

Just as I was thinking about going up for a nap, the wall

phone rang.

"Parker, it's Henry at the toll booth. Neddie's in trouble. He went down to feed the cats and hasn't come back. I can't leave the bridge, but I slipped to the railing and heard a lot of yelling."

I hung up, realizing that the story about Neddie and his cats in the morning paper had created a stir. I didn't know if they were cat lovers or bird lovers under the bridge but, either way, it was a no-win situation for Neddie.

I approached the bridge to find a line of vehicles parked on both sides of the highway. Just before the toll booth and the entrance to the bridge, a turn-around road goes off to the right. The road circles under the bridge and comes up the other side. I knew Neddie fed the cats on the road as it passed under the bridge. I drove down the turn-around and heard screaming voices through my open window. I left my truck in the middle of the road and hurried under the bridge.

The area served as a convenient dumping ground for trash. Several old tires, a car battery, a soiled mattress and some empty paint cans were strewn along the path. It smelled as though something had died and was tucked into the piles of trash. I wondered if one of the birders had shot a cat and left it to rot.

Neddie stood in the middle of the road with a trap between his legs. Inside the trap was a black feline hunkered down like a lump of coal. Neddie had his palms up trying to hold back the surge of four elderly women in front of him who were wearing T-shirts that read "Save the Pussies."

Behind Neddie was a mixed group of men and women wearing Galveston Featherfest shirts. Between the two groups, it looked like a Mexican stand-off sans the Mexicans. The woman who appeared to be the most elderly member of the cat-lovers' group, probably early eighties, stepped forward and screamed across the road past Neddie at the bird-lovers' group.

"Leave these cats alone. Animals have rights, just as you jerks do."

The leader of the bird group, a tall, thin man holding a placard on a stake that read "Feral cats kill thousands of innocents," yelled back, "So do birds. Galveston is a bird paradise. We're here to stop the wholesale slaughter of innocent chicks."

At that, several people in the bird group gave a hearty "hoorah."

Another of the cat lovers, a short plump woman in her sixties with gray, frizzy hair, picked up a piece of driftwood and started toward the bird leader. The bird guy turned his stake sideways as if to catch the blow from the driftwood. The reporter from the paper doubled as the camera man. With a satisfying smirk on his face, he was busy snapping frames as fast as his automatic camera would work.

I stepped behind the cat woman and grabbed the club. A splinter off the driftwood plunged through the meaty part of my hand between my thumb and forefinger. I yelped and dropped the club. Blood trickled into my palm. The photographer was now snapping away at my hand.

When the bird leader started toward the woman, Neddie stuck his foot out and tripped the big guy. He tumbled hard into a pile of loose sand. He got up with a glob of cat dropping on his palm and yelled a loud expletive. He pulled out a handkerchief and wiped his hand, still cursing. The remaining circle of cat enthusiasts formed a protective circle around the woman who'd dropped the club. Then the lead cat woman saw the poop on the birder's hand and started laughing, holding her stomach. Her teammates joined in.

The bird man, his face turning red, snarled another

obscenity at the cat lovers. The others in his group closed ranks behind him. It looked as if they were going to rush the women. I stepped beside Neddie and extended my arms in both directions like a traffic cop, palms up.

"Hold it," I yelled. "Let Neddie talk." I looked at Neddie. "Tell them what you're doing."

Neddie explained about capturing the cats and having them sterilized.

"That won't cut it," said the bird leader. "There were twenty cats feeding when we got here. Cats in the wild can live fifteen years. Even if they can't reproduce, that's a bunch of dead birds. The National Audubon Society says feral cats kill over a billion birds every year. We're here to do our part to stop the slaughter."

The cat woman looked at Neddie. "You don't own these cats. You don't have the right to interfere with their lives. You're nothing but a cat Nazi."

The confrontation was spiraling out of control. I whispered to Neddie, "We need to defuse this thing quickly, before something serious happens."

"Christ, Parker. I haven't done anything but feed a bunch of starving animals."

"Maybe," I said. "But these people are nuts, and you're too old for a fist fight. Hell, you might even get shot. Here's an idea."

When both groups edged toward each other, Neddie puffed his chest as best he could. He stared down the groups, first the birders and then the cat lovers.

"Both sides are right and both sides are wrong," he said. "So I'm gonna do something I don't want to do—give up my cats. Over the next few weeks, I will trap every feral cat out here. I will have them fixed and take them to the Galveston Humane Society for adoption." He looked at the cat group.

"You know they only keep them so long before they...."

Neddie couldn't finish. He dropped his head and wiped his eye with his hand. The old lady with the cat group stepped up and put her hand on his shoulder.

"Don't worry," she said. "We're a big group. We promise to adopt every kitty you bring in."

Neddie regained his composure and turned to the birders. "The only predators out here will be the natural ones: raccoons, skunks and the occasional coyote. The balance of nature will be restored to the survival of the fittest."

Wow. I felt a jolt of pride filling my gut for the old man. The compromise seemed to work. The tall, thin bird protector and the short, squat cat lover turned to their respective groups for a quick powwow. Looked like Neddie had a deal.

As the protesters drifted up the road toward their vehicles, the photographer was walking backwards in front of them taking shots of each group as they left.

Meanwhile, with my palm throbbing from the splinter, I put my arm around Neddie and said, "Good job."

"Hated to do it," he said, tears building in his eyes. "I'm going to miss my cats."

I sighed, looked away at the sand dunes and turned back to him. "Take a couple home with you."

"Hell, Parker. I've already got three at the house now."

Chapter Eighteen

Wednesday afternoon
The Garhole Bar

I waited at the bridge until all the birders and cat lovers had departed and approached the reporter who was checking his camera.

"I noticed you took a zillion photos. Any of me?"

"Oh, I'm sure," he said. "This will make a great follow up to today's story."

I moved in nose-to-nose to the reporter, my eyes fixed on his, my voice almost a whisper. "Yeah, I'm sure you're really proud of yourself, almost getting folks hurt. You don't have permission to use photographs of me. So leave them out, get it?"

The reporter backed up. "I don't need your permission. First Amendment right, freedom of the press."

"Yeah, well take a good look at me. Cause you're going to see this mug again real close if you print my picture."

"Is that a threat?"

I nodded and turned away. I didn't think my intimidation effort would work, but it was worth a try.

I hadn't been back at The Garhole more than a few minutes when the wall phone rang.

"Parker, it's Maurice," the strained voice announced. "I've

been calling. Your cell phone goes straight to voicemail, but the message says you haven't set it up yet."

I thought about the phone, plugged in beside my bed upstairs. "I got busy and left it upstairs. Anyway, I haven't set up voicemail because I don't know how."

"Find a kid," he said. "Anyway, we're putting together an ad hoc meeting this afternoon. Harry has graciously allowed us to use his home. Burney will be there along with a top NSA man from D.C. and the agent in charge of the Secret Service detail guarding Secretary Perry. We need you in the loop."

"What can I do without security clearance, Harry?"

"That's why the meeting is unofficial, and it's also one of the reasons why we'll be meeting at Harry's. We've put a rush on your clearance, and with any luck it should be in by the time you get here."

Once I committed, I knew my time would be his. But I'd witnessed the horrific scene at the Coast Guard base, the bodies burned beyond recognition and the wounded who, even if they lived, would never be the same. I knew from the beginning of the phone call I would do whatever I could. For better or worse, I was already in the game. I told Maurice I'd be there and asked if he'd seen Kathy Landry's final sketches.

"No, but I'll check with her. We need to get copies out to the public."

"Maybe she could drop the originals by Harry's house. I'd like to take a final peek, see if they trigger any more images of the guy in my tired brain."

I didn't expect many customers today with the next cold front coming in, but I called Neddie Lemmon anyway. He agreed to be here by three o'clock and handle the bar. I told him he could close anytime he wanted, just try not to empty the beer cooler all by himself.

Neddie showed up wearing a T-shirt that read, "Rehab is

For Quitters."

I shook my head. "So tell me. How is that shirt gonna get you laid?"

"You never know," he said. "Just gotta find a woman with the right sense of humor who likes to drink."

I arrived at Harry's house a little before four o'clock and pulled my old rust bucket to the curb behind a sleek, black SUV. Matthews had said one of the reasons we were meeting at Harry's was because the meeting was unofficial since I didn't have security clearance. But then it hit me that the closest FBI office was in Texas City across the causeway, fifteen minutes farther away. In case a quick response was needed, it made sense to stage meetings as close to Secretary Perry as possible. Harry's house was only a couple of minutes from the hospital. It was also a lot more comfortable than the antiseptic smell of a hospital meeting room or some cold office suite.

Agent Hebinck stepped out on the porch to greet me. I followed him down the hallway to the kitchen, nodded to Maurice Matthews, and glanced at a man I didn't know standing at the counter drinking coffee.

Matthews said, "Parker, meet Ellis Roush. General Roush is a retired three-star, now a Deputy Director of the National Security Agency from Washington."

Roush was trim and fit. His ramrod-straight posture and close-cut gray hair confirmed his military background, not unusual for NSA personnel. He looked early sixties, another of those square-jawed-type strangers so common in Galveston since the explosion.

Roush set his coffee cup down on the counter and extended his hand in greeting, his lips upturned into a small smile. I assumed Hebinck had explained my background to him and his reasons for inviting me to the meeting. Roush's demeanor said that he'd accepted Hebinck's judgement.

Roush and I shook hands and I said, "A deputy director, as in several."

Roush chuckled. "Afraid so," he said, a friendly grin on his face. "Deputy Directors at NSA are sort of like bank vice presidents. They give us a title so they don't have to pay as much."

I realized Roush's attempt at levity was classic gallows humor, an effort to break the tension, since the strain of the past few days was evident in the worry lines on the faces standing around the counter. It was as if everyone expected more trouble.

Roush continued. "I hope you know I was just kidding," he said. "It's the only break I get from the pressure. And I mean daily pressure. If you knew some of the conversations we track, you'd move to Australia."

"How did you know?" I asked.

"Know what?"

"About Australia."

"I don't get it," he said.

"Just something I think about sometimes, my fantasy escape destination."

"I hear that," he said, grinning. "Mine is playing in the U.S. Open at Pebble Beach."

A little male bonding never hurt. We all filled our coffee cups and moved to the kitchen table, made from several old solid oak planks. A few years ago, Harry had noticed a tear-down of an old home going on and rescued the wood from the contractor. He'd located some antique chairs and made the table large enough to seat eight. Harry often held meetings of the historical foundation in his home because he liked to show off his cooking skills. I wondered where he was now and Hebinck said he was at the courthouse with a client.

When everyone settled in at the table, Hebinck led the conversation. "Parker, we've got good news. Your security clearance was approved. You're good to go."

He reached across the table and shook my hand. Just as he was about to continue, the doorbell chimed.

"That will be Agent Erwin, the new head of Perry's Secret Service detail. They brought her in from Washington to replace Agent Tolar who was killed in the explosion."

Matthews scurried to the front door and ushered Erwin into the room. Everyone at the table rose and moved around the table to greet the new member of the team.

Hebinck said, "Parker and Ellis meet Special Officer Millicent Erwin."

Erwin shook each of our hands in turn, her grip firm and her dark eyes steady into ours. She was a fortyish, medium height brunette with a short-bobbed hairstyle and an attractive face that would turn heads in any meeting. She wore a dark navy business suit that covered a trim figure with probably well-defined muscles. The lady was all business. When we retook our seats at the table, Erwin sat at the head.

Burney got down to business quickly and said, "Here's what we know. Base security stopped the panel truck at the guard gate to check it out. When the petty officer opened the van's back doors, the area was so stuffed with flowers, some of them tumbled out. The gate guard was so nervous about ruining the flower arrangements, he allowed the van to pass through and move onto the base without a thorough inspection.

"Set up that way," I said. "All part of the plan."

"No doubt," Matthews chimed in.

"Perry was expected to arrive at 2:45 p.m. and speak at the base gymnasium at 3:00 p.m.," Hebinck continued. "We think the terrorist planned to arrive at the gym just before the

Secretary's caravan got there. He would pretend to be unloading flowers and detonate the explosives as Perry got out of his armored limousine. But Perry ran late. The assassin probably thought he'd raise suspicion by parking and waiting, so he drove around the base. Sure enough, Shore Patrol attempted to pull him over. Realizing he was busted, he accelerated and raced back toward the main gate. We think he saw Perry's caravan arriving and, with security hot on his trail, pulled the switch on the explosives right at the guard shack.

"The bomb ripped the shack's concrete blocks into thousands of tiny missiles, instantly killing the two Coast Guardsmen at the gate, plus the two in the chase car and the two Galveston motorcycle cops leading Perry's limo. Perry's personal assistant, who was in the back seat of the limo with him, was also killed. The FBI lost four agents that were in the lead car in front of the Secretary's limo."

"And four Secret Service agents," Erwin broke in, grimacing as she spoke. "Tolar and Johnson in the car with Secretary Perry and two agents in the car behind Perry's limo. Tolar was a personal friend. We joined the service at the same time and went through training together."

As resilient as Erwin appeared, her eyes filled with moisture. Her tone made me think she was on a personal quest as important to her as mine was to me. After she finished, no one spoke. It was almost as if each of us had elected a moment of silence to honor the dead agents and her memory of a friend.

After a moment, Matthews said, "As bad as that was, it could have been worse."

"How?" I asked, giving Maurice a hard stare. "Mangled bodies and cars, the smell of death in the air?"

"The gymnasium was packed with people," he said. "Two

hundred or more."

The room went silent again, each of us immersed in our own field of grief. I felt a surge of righteous anger welling up in my throat at the sick people responsible for this.

"Okay," I said. "What now?"

Matthews cranked up first. "We're convinced they're going to try and hit Secretary Perry again in Galveston," he said to the group. Then he turned to me. "Parker, you know the area better than any of us and have the right background for this kind of thinking. Got any ideas?"

"What makes you so sure they'll try again?" I asked.

Hebinck took over. "It's a rogue operation," he said. "A vendetta against Perry."

"How do you know?" I asked.

"From the beginning, the attack looked personal. Terrorist groups don't normally aim for U.S. officials this high in rank. After our response to 9/11, they know any attempt would bring an unrelenting assault back on them."

"So you don't think it's al Qaeda?"

Hebinck shook his head. "Between Afghanistan and Iraq, we've hit al Qaeda hard, and we're still pounding the bastards whenever we find them. They usually admit responsibility, using the publicity around their participation as a recruiting tool. We've been monitoring their sites, but so far there has been nothing indicating they were involved."

"What about other groups?"

"Hezbollah is based in Lebanon and funded by Iran, but they focus on Israel. To our knowledge, they've never attempted anything in the U.S. Of course, there is a first time for everything. Hamas is a PLO operation that spends most of its energies raining rockets on the Jewish homeland. Their main goal is to destroy Israel and replace it with a Sunni Islamist state. Of course, that just pisses the Israelis off. There are other terrorist organizations, but none that we think are focused enough or have the resources to make this attack. Whoever did this is well-financed with connections in the U.S."

"We're back-checking all threats against the Secretary during the past year," Erwin said. "Haven't found any connection yet."

"You mentioned a personal vendetta," I said. "But Secretary Perry has only been in charge of Homeland Security a few months. What has he done in that short period to bring this down on his head?"

"Nothing that we know of, but prior to this job, Perry was the four-star general in charge of Central Command which, as you know, is responsible for all of the Middle East."

"More than that," Roush added. "CENTCOM's responsibility includes twenty-seven countries using twelve major languages, from Central Asia to the horn of Africa."

"How do you guys at NSA monitor all of that?" I asked, turning to Roush.

Roush shook his head, "Oh hell, Parker. That area is only part of what we do. The world's full of people who hate the U.S."

"Right," Hebinck said. "So let's stay on track. We sent inquiries to contacts who were members of General Perry's staff while he was in charge of CENTCOM, trying to come up with something...anything."

"And?"

"We found the connection. A year ago, Mossad sent the CIA its dossier on a really bad actor, a key figure in Hezbollah named Nassim Zahir. It turns out we'd also been investigating Zahir for years, believing he played a key part in the 1983 Marine barracks bombing in Beirut."

"You just said Hezbollah focused on Israel."

"They do now, but back in 1983 during the Lebanese civil

war, the U.N. authorized a peacekeeping force. The U.S. was a big part of it, but France and Italy also sent troops. Hezbollah wanted control of Lebanon, but they first had to get the foreign troops out."

"So they murdered 241 U.S. Marines and got their way. President Regan pulled the troops out."

Hebinck ignored my sarcasm and continued, "The information from Mossad pointed to Nassim Zahir as one of the main organizers of the attack."

"But what's that got to do with Secretary Perry?"

Hebinck glanced at his watch. "I'm running out of time here," he said. "If you'll just let me finish, we can wrap this up pretty quickly."

"Understood," I said feeling a little chastised. But Hebinck was right: the meeting was mostly for my benefit. I needed to shut up and listen.

He started again. "When Mossad sent Nassim Zahir's dossier a year ago, they had intelligence that Zahir was meeting an Iranian operative in a villa just outside the port city of Aden. The decision was made to use a predator drone strike to take Zahir and the Iranian out, bagging two birds with one stone. Perry objected, concerned about civilian casualties. He wanted to wait and catch the targets out in the open, or at least in a car."

"Good for Perry," I said.

My comment garnered piercing daggers from Hebinck. I'd always been opposed to indiscriminate strikes. We all knew collateral damage created more enemies. An eight-year-old child who witnessed his mother and father destroyed by a bomb from the skies was a confirmed terrorist by the time he was a teenager.

"Perry was overruled from on high," Hebinck continued.

"Politics," I said. "Hell, the decision probably came from

the President himself."

No one spoke. Hebinck dropped his eyes. I'd hit the nail on the head.

Matthews broke the silence. "No one knew Zahir's family was with him. The strike killed Nassim, his wife and their thirteen-year-old daughter."

"Jesus." I averted my eyes and sighed, cursing the futility of war.

"No one excuses the mistake," Matthews continued. "But Nassim was one bad hombre. The President acted on the best information he had at the time. Our assets on the ground reported afterward that five people had entered the villa. Four bodies were pulled from the rubble: Nassim, his wife and child, and the Iranian. The fifth person may or may not have been Rashad, Nassim's son. We don't know for sure."

"What do we know about the son?" I asked, trying to bring myself back from thinking about the loss of innocents.

"Nassim Zahir had significant assets, enough for a vengeful son to fund this scheme and seek retribution. A man was treated for severe injuries at the hospital in Aden right after the attack. Something had fallen and crushed his legs. The patient gave a false name and was spirited away from his bed in the middle of the night. If it was Rashad, there is a good chance he holed up somewhere in Yemen to recuperate."

"And plan this strike," Hebinck added.

"Wait a minute," I said, focusing on Matthews. "You said the FBI located some emails to and from Yemen and the Indianapolis cell that were sent about a year ago."

"Right," Matthews acknowledged. "Another tie to Yemen. We're pretty sure the leader of this pack is there and it's probably Rashad Zahir. Everything fits."

"So how does all this connect to the café bombing in Germany?" I asked.

Hebinck paused. He looked at Matthews and Roush as if getting approval for what he was about to say.

"It turns out that the bombing in the Berlin café wasn't a random act."

"What the hell does that mean?"

"Nassim Zahir learned that two top Mossad agents were tracking a Hezbollah recruitment cell in Germany. The Mossad agents frequented that café."

The news was more than I could handle. I pounded the table with my fist. "Damn it, Burney. How long has the FBI known this?"

"Calm down, Parker. I know what you're thinking. Why haven't we done something about it? Killed this Zahir character before or at least retaliated against Hezbollah? Well, the truth is, we didn't know about the Mossad agents or that Nassim Zahir was responsible until Mossad told us, right before Perry sent in the predator."

"So the Israelis knew all along and didn't tell us."

"Looks like it," Hebinck said.

"Great ally," I said. The sarcasm bounced off my lips like I'd bitten into a lemon. But then I said, "So why not get a photo of Nassim Zahir from Mossad? Why have me try to describe a man I'd seen for half a second more than fifteen years ago?"

"Because the café bomber wasn't Nassim. There are plenty of photos of Nassim. He was a well-known professor at The American University in Beirut, but he disappeared after the Marine barracks bombing."

"How can you be so sure the café bomber wasn't Nassim?"

"Two reasons. Mossad had eyes on Nassim in Beirut when the café bomb exploded and—"

"Hold it," I said, interrupting. "You said Nassim disappeared after the Marine barracks bombing."

"From our radar, not the Israelis'. Remember we didn't get

this info from them until right before the drone attack."

"More petty jealousies between agencies," I said. "Makes me want to barf."

"I get it," Matthews broke in. "But in addition to the Israelis having eyes on him, Nassim's photo was included in the rogues' gallery you reviewed last night. You didn't recognize him.

"Maybe I missed him."

"No, the man you described to Kathy was much younger. The Israelis think the café bomber was Rashad. They suspect he's been responsible for a number of bombings around the Middle East during the past twenty years. That's why they were so adamant about taking both Nassim and Rashad out."

"So," I said. "Rashad survived the predator attack on his family and blames the man who was in charge of CENTCOM, now Secretary of Homeland Security, Ronald A. Perry."

"And that brings us to the present," Hebinck added. "If it is Rashad, and he is planning another attack, we need to be ready."

After a moment Matthews said, "The problem is there are no known photos of Rashad Zahir. He is one illusive son of a bitch. That's why Kathy Landry's sketch is so important."

Roush furrowed his brow. "We monitor thousands of phone calls every day. The computer algorithms do a good job, but unfortunately there is still room for error. We've assigned top priority to this mission and will be watching especially closely for calls to and from Texas to the Middle East."

"I guess all of Galveston hopes that too," I added. "But I thought they weren't using regular phone calls."

"We haven't detected any," Roush said. "But if Rashad is planning another attack on Perry, they may get anxious and slip and use the phone. Who knows?"

"Any news about the encrypted communication on the

dark web?" Hebinck asked.

"The agency hasn't broken the code yet," Roush said. "But we're working on it."

Hebinck looked at Agent Erwin. "What's the status at the hospital?"

"We've brought in another two dozen agents," Erwin said. "We're on every floor of the hospital and at every elevator and stairway. We have enough agents for twenty-four-hour coverage. No goddamn terrorist will get to Perry on my watch."

Chapter Nineteen

Wednesday afternoon
Galveston

The remainder of the conversation at Harry's house centered on when and how we thought the next attempt on Secretary Perry's life would occur. With new alerts sent out to every fertilizer manufacturer plus every wholesale and retail agricultural supply company in the country, it was not likely the terrorists could obtain a significant amount of ammonium nitrate before Perry left the hospital.

General Roush floated the idea that maybe the terrorists had gotten enough from their first purchase to make two bombs. Hebinck concluded that was unlikely because they would have had no reason to suspect the first attempt wouldn't work. And obtaining double the amount of fertilizer would have made their efforts more suspicious. He doubted they would have taken that gamble.

"What if they used the "Mother of Satan" explosive?" I asked.

"Triacetone triperoxide?" Hebinck said, rubbing his chin in thought. "Possible. It's definitely the weapon of choice with the bad guys now. Easy to make with easy-to-find ingredients: a combination of acetone, hydrogen peroxide and sulfuric acid. It's what Richard Reid had in his shoe on that airplane. Only thing that stopped him was a brave airline hostess."

"So if it's so easy to make, why didn't the Galveston bomber use it?" Roush asked.

"TAPT is extremely unstable, where ammonium nitrate is not. And remember, the terrorists in Minneapolis were dumb as a load of bricks. They may have been able to fabricate an ammonium-nitrate device with help from the internet, but TAPT is much trickier. It's easy to blow yourself up in the process of making or transporting that explosive."

"What if they bring in a bomb maker with that expertise?" I asked.

"Unlikely," Hebinck said. "Terrorists have never successfully used TAPT in the states. And even if they built a bomb with the stuff, we don't think they could get it inside the hospital."

"What about outside, like Oklahoma City?"

"Remember, the Oklahoma bomb was huge, filling a Rider truck. We're not allowing trucks of any kind anywhere near the hospital. Not even a pickup. And with the newly installed concrete barriers, it's unlikely they could fit one large enough to penetrate the burn unit in a car. We're also using bomb-sniffing dogs."

"So they could hit him on the way to the airport," Roush said.

"Helicopter on the roof," Hebinck replied.

"A missile?" Roush added.

Hebinck shrugged. "They'd have to steal or buy one," he said. "We're checking the manufacturers and supply depots. Nothing missing so far, but keep thinking. We have to stay a step ahead, keep our minds working and think outside the box."

Everyone seemed to agree, but no one said anything. It was then that Burney took a call on his cell phone. He listened for a moment and terminated the call.

"That was Dr. Lang at Gulf Coast Laboratory. She's on her

way here with some new information."

Good, I thought, a chance to catch up with Anna. While we took a break, I checked the refrigerator for a snack. Always the thoughtful host, Harry had made homemade cinnamon rolls. I stuck a batch in the oven to warm and put on a fresh pot of coffee. Between the additional caffeine and the icing on the rolls, we'd probably soon be bouncing around like a bunch of bobble-headed dolls.

Just as we finished scarfing down a few hundred extra calories, the doorbell rang. Agent Hebinck brought Anna down the hallway. Matthews and Roush straightened as she approached. Even with scrunched eyes showing obvious concern and a tangle of hair hanging over her cheek, her natural good looks radiated in the room. A surprised look spread across her face as she noticed me standing at the counter. And then a smile.

"Parker, I didn't expect to see you here."

"I didn't expect to be here."

She turned to Hebinck. "What I have is confidential."

"It's okay," Hebinck interrupted. "Everyone here has security clearance, including Parker. We're all part of the investigative team. Nothing leaves this room unless it needs to."

Hebinck introduced Anna to Roush, Matthews and Erwin.

"Coffee?" Matthews asked.

"Please," Anna replied.

Matthews filled a cup and pointed her toward the cream and sugar on the counter. She doctored it the way she wanted and took a sip.

"Let's have a seat," Hebinck said, gesturing for Anna to sit at the opposite end of the table from where Erwin had positioned herself.

We filled in on the sides and everyone focused on Anna.

Her eyes swept the room, her face tight with concern.

"I received an urgent email from the CDC in Atlanta. It appears the director of bio research at Louisiana Western University in Lafayette has disappeared, along with a vial of Bacillus anthracis."

"Anthrax!" Hebinck exclaimed. "Please, not another D.C."

"Let's hope not," Anna replied.

"I was in Korea at the time of the D.C. attack with the 2nd Infantry Division," Roush offered. "I remember a little about it, but fill me in."

"I was running the Houston office," Matthews said, glancing around the table. "I can give you the Cliff's Notes version."

When no one spoke, he said "On September 18, 2001, one week after the 9/11 attacks, letters containing anthrax spores were mailed to several news media offices. On October 9, two more letters were mailed to two Democratic senators. In all, five people died and seventeen others were infected."

"Who was the culprit?" Roush asked.

"We identified several suspects. But after one of the most exhaustive investigations in our history, the FBI still hasn't made an arrest."

"The two batches of letters contained different types of anthrax," Hebinck added, taking over from Matthews. "The letters sent to the media contained a brown granular variety identified as cutaneous anthrax. The letter to the senators contained a fine powder, causing the more dangerous form of infection known as inhalational anthrax. Different forms, but not enough to make us think there were two separate perpetrators." Hebinck shifted the attention to Anna. "Your turn, Dr. Lang. Please re-educate us on the seriousness of the threat."

She sat up a little straighter and leaned in. "First, let's talk basics. Anthrax is a potentially fatal disease caused by the bacterium Bacillus anthracis. The bacteria lives in soil. The disease most commonly occurs in cattle, sheep and other plant-eating animals. A person may develop the condition if he or she is exposed to infected animals.

"Now let's talk about the 2001 attack," she continued. "All of the anthrax used in the D.C. cases was derived from a bacterial strain isolated from a cow in Texas in 1981. Known as the Ames strain, the bacterium was eventually distributed to sixteen bio-research laboratories within the U.S. for further study."

Anna shifted her eyes, catching everyone around the table before concluding, "Louisiana Western was one of them."

The room went silent. Worried faces around the table spoke for each of us. We all knew there was more to come.

"Bacillus anthracis is different from many other types of bacteria because it forms spores," she continued. "The missing vial from Louisiana Western could easily contain as much as 100 billion spores."

I blew out a slow whistle. I had no clue as to the damage that many little potential assassins running around could do, but it all sounded damned lethal to me.

"Of course we don't know that the professor took the vial," Anna said. "It could be just a coincidence that both he and the vial were discovered missing at the same time."

"The FBI can't afford to believe in coincidences," Hebinck groused.

"Neither can the Secret Service," Erwin added, shifting around in her chair.

"CDC takes the same approach," Anna added. "The FBI is on scene at the Louisiana Western lab as we speak."

That perked Matthews and Hebinck up even more. Hebinck dug his phone out of his pocket and exited the room.

"I didn't consider the missing vial more than a normal concern," Anna continued. "Until I glanced out my office window at the security in front of the lab. And then it hit me."

"Inhalational anthrax," Matthews blurted out.

"Exactly!" Anna retorted.

"Got it," I said. "We've been wondering how the terrorists would strike again. This may be it."

"Possibly, but let's not jump to conclusions," Matthews threw in. He looked at Anna. "Tell us more about this type of anthrax."

"When the spores are inhaled, they germinate and the bacteria cells infect the lungs. The infected cells then spread to the lymph nodes in the chest. As the bacteria grow, they produce two kinds of deadly toxins. One leads to a fatal buildup of fluid in the cavity surrounding the lungs. Another toxin disrupts cell function."

"What are the symptoms?" I asked.

"Fever, nausea, vomiting, fatigue. It is easily misdiagnosed as the flu."

"Curable?"

"Yes, if caught early and treated with antibiotics."

"That's a relief," Roush said.

"Not in Secretary Perry's case," Anna noted. "Remember, because he was severely burned, his chance of infection is extremely high. Every effort is being made to keep the burn unit sterile: nurses are gowned and gloved, doors are pressurized. Even the catheters are treated with silver oxide. The entire unit is separated from the rest of the patient areas, including having its own air and heating systems." She paused for effect. "But if the terrorists were able to somehow get the anthrax bacteria into the burn unit—"

"Perry wouldn't survive," I said.

Anna nodded, lowered her eyes and sighed heavily. No

one spoke, each of us with our own doomsday thoughts.

Then Anna said, "And it's not only Perry. Everyone in the burn unit could be infected, nurses, doctors, Secret Service agents. The spores could spread throughout the hospital causing real havoc, even panic."

After a moment, Erwin said, "And the terrorists know this?"

"The missing professor certainly does," Anna answered. "And the news has been full of Perry's critical condition."

"So, Dr. Lang," Matthews said. "Walk us through Secretary Perry's treatment and how the burn unit works."

"How much detail do you want?" Anna asked.

"General is okay."

"Wait," Erwin said, holding up a palm. "We're in the hospital now. I need detail."

Anna continued, "I spoke with Dr. Walker, head of the unit. The protocol was to stabilize Perry's vital signs and treat for shock, keep him hydrated with intravenous fluids and—"

Matthews broke in, "How badly was he burned?"

Anna took a breath. "Second and third degree on his chest, and first and second on his face. Dr. Walker said the debridement went well, that's the removal of damaged tissue. They use a water-jet system here. Seventy-five percent of deaths occur in the first five days. Perry is past that now, but still not out of the woods. Of course, he's intubated and on oxygen and morphine for pain. Infection is the main concern."

"So how do they treat for infection?"

"Bandage wraps impregnated with antibiotics are prepared in the hospital pharmacy."

Erwin said, "Let's talk about the anthrax. How would they get the toxin into the hospital?"

"Easiest way would be through one of the burn-unit nurses," Anna replied.

"We'll run them through a gauntlet tighter than a crack a

spider couldn't penetrate." Erwin said. "Doctors, too. Maintenance people, cleanup crew, anyone who enters the burn unit."

"I've got work to do," Roush said, jumping in. "Contact Washington and get them looking at possible contacts between Louisiana and the Middle East, especially Yemen. Give me the professor's name," he said. "We'll zero in on his phones: office, home and cell. If that guy so much as blew smoke rings in that direction, we'll find the contact."

Anna looked at her notes. "Hamid—"

"Turani," Hebinck snapped from the hallway. "Just got off the phone with Quantico. Turani emigrated to the U.S. from Iran in November of '78, during the last days of the Shah's rule. Turani became a U.S. citizen in 1983."

"Lucky for Turani," I said.

"I'm sure it wasn't luck," Hebinck added. "The Shah left Iran for good in January of 1979. Ayatollah Khomeini gained power in February. No doubt Turani read the tea leaves and got the hell out while he could."

"Or maybe he was sent here, a sleeper agent," Roush said

"Possibly," Hebinck said. "Or he could have been recently indoctrinated. There's just no way to know with what we have. Quantico will send more information as they get it."

I spoke up. "Anna, please tell us about the security clearance requirements for your lab and if they would be the same for Louisiana Western."

"Basically the same," Anna replied. "Both labs handle Tier I agents and toxins, the most dangerous pathogens known to scientists. In the rush to protect America after 9/11, Congress passed the Patriot Act. The act established the Federal Select Agents Program, known as FSAP. The program regulates the possession, use and transfer of biological agents and toxins."

I broke in, "Of course, it had to have an acronym. CDC, FBI,

CIA, ATF, FSAP. Seems like the Feds won't be satisfied until they use up the alphabet."

I got a lot of nasty looks on that one. No one appreciated my cynicism. Thankfully, before Hebinck could scold me again, Anna continued.

"FSAP set up the regulations for the agency's Suitability Assessment Program known as SAP."

When she said the initials, Anna looked at me with a smirk, probably waiting for another outburst. I placed both palms up in front of me but didn't utter a peep.

She continued, "The purpose of the SAP program is to determine whether an individual has the appropriate credentials and background to be allowed access to Tier 1 agents. The SAP has two phases, pre-access and ongoing suitability. All applicants for the labs are subjected to vigorous vetting including work history, criminal background and mental health testing, including medications. Sometimes financial background checks and drug screening are included."

"What do you mean by sometimes?" Roush asked.

"The entities have flexibility in setting up their programs."

"Wait," he said. "This Turani suspect is from Iran, for Christ's sake. Didn't his background rate special attention?"

"When the Patriot Act became effective in 2001, individuals who already had approved access to Tier I agents were not required to have a pre-access suitability assessment. Remember Turani entered the U.S. in 1978. By 2001, he was already head of the department at Louisiana Western. He was also a U.S. citizen. And as far as the ongoing assessment, remember that each lab has discretion."

"And Turani, as head of the department, was in charge of the ongoing assessments," I said.

Anna nodded.

"Sounds like a sleeper to me," I threw in.

Anna shrugged. "All we know is he had FSAP security clearance. Same as me." Anna's eyes moved steadily to each of us around the table. "That's all I have," she said.

Everyone rose as she pushed her chair back from the table. She shook hands all around, making sure mine was last.

"Parker, do you have a minute?" she asked.

I followed her out to the front porch. We stood at the railing, the north wind from the arriving cold front sending a chill across the yard. Anna shuddered, placed her arms across her chest and rubbed her shoulders. I knew what was coming: Had I spoken to Bully Stout again?

Thinking about Bully sitting in his wheelchair with tobacco juice on his chin while rubbing his eyeball with a dish towel, I had to wonder how she and Bully could possibly share the same strain of DNA.

Before she spoke, I said, "No, Anna. I haven't spoken with Bully again. I know this is important to you but, as you can see, I've been a little preoccupied."

"You've been preoccupied! A little self-centered, don't you think? You can't imagine the pressure I'm under. If Turani is on his way to Galveston, I...."

She broke off in midsentence and put her hand to her eyes to hide the gathering tears. I reached out for her but she pushed my hand away. She took a moment to steel herself and then turned and strode quickly down the stairs to her car.

I watched her drive away, realizing for the first time the responsibility she must be feeling. Hell, we were all uptight. Were the terrorists really going to try another attempt on Perry's life? We'd only discussed two scenarios so far: another bomber or anthrax. Were there others we weren't seeing?

The issue with Bully seemed a long way off from another terrorist attack in Galveston. Still, it was obviously damned important to Anna. The least I could do was try and get some resolution for her.

Just as Anna pulled away from the curb, Kathy Landry drove up in her bright yellow Mustang. She stepped out with a briefcase in hand. Damn, even in wrinkled scrubs she looked good.

I opened the front door and ushered Kathy down the hallway to the kitchen. She greeted Matthews with a smile and introduced herself to Hebinck. Erwin and Roush were on their phones in separate bedrooms. Kathy opened her briefcase and spread the drawings on the counter. The first depiction was essentially the same as she'd mocked up at The Garhole, a decent semblance of the bomber I'd seen slipping into the café in Germany. The second drawing illustrated the same face aged eighteen years. The third was the same as the second, except that she'd drawn in a full beard.

"Take a look, Parker," she said. "Not too late to make changes."

I studied all three drawings. "Nothing to add," I said. But I did have a brief and fleeting thought that the sketches offered a vague resemblance to someone I'd seen. But who? Where?

Erwin and Roush entered the kitchen at the same time. I introduced Kathy and they immediately hovered over the drawings.

"We'll run facial recognition through the computer just in case something might pop up," Hebinck said, his voice sounding doubtful.

"I'll get these distributed right away," Matthews said. "Television, newspapers. They'll go worldwide by tonight. We'll use the usual 'person of interest' tagline."

Hebinck thanked Kathy. As she turned to leave, I walked her out.

While standing on the porch steps she said, "Why don't you come by my house when the meeting's over?"

"Love to, but I don't have any idea how long it will be."

"No rush," she said. "Call me when you're on the way."

I impulsively pulled her close and held her for a moment. She pushed back without looking at me and hurried to her car. I walked back inside wondering what her quick exit meant. Moving too quickly? Maybe.

I found the rest of the gang back at the table shuffling the drawings around.

Roush said, "I'll have a report on calls to and from the Middle East and Louisiana and Texas by later tonight. Maybe we'll get lucky." He paused and then continued, "The NSA screwed up enough before 9/11. We're damned sure not going to let it happen this time."

Everyone looked at Roush anticipating more.

He got the message and said, "We'd tracked suspicious communications between the hijackers, but failed to alert the CIA. At least we're all in the loop now."

"I know the feeling," Hebinck echoed. "The FBI had information that Khalid al-Mindhar, one of the 9/11 hijackers, was coming to the U.S. But the tip didn't get passed up the chain."

The table went quiet for a moment and then Hebinck said, "I expect an update on Turani tonight. But before we leave, let's make sure we're all on the same page. Let me summarize what we know. See if anyone can add anything.

"According to Mossad, in 1990, Nassim Zahir, a high-ranking Hezbollah agent, sent his son Rashad to murder two Israeli agents by bombing a café in Germany. Because several American service members, including Parker's friend, were also killed, the FBI, along with the Germans, investigated the bombing. But the Israelis never told the FBI that two Mossad agents were killed in that café or who they suspected was behind the bombing.

"Flash forward to a year ago when Ronald Perry, now Secretary of Homeland Security, was the general in charge of CENTCOM. Mossad tipped the U.S. that Zahir was responsible for the café bombing and was meeting his Iranian liaison in a villa outside of Aden, Yemen. Perry, directed by the President, ordered a drone strike, not knowing that Zahir's wife and daughter were with him in the villa. Nassim's son Rashad survived and planned an attack on Perry in Galveston as retribution for the killing of his family. The attack failed, and now we have a missing Iranian professor and a vial of anthrax. Is that about it?"

"That's enough," Matthews said.

Everyone caught the concern in his voice. He turned to me. "How does it feel, Parker, chasing bad guys again?"

I thought about his question and said, "You ever go wade fishing for trout, Maurice? Shuffle your feet along the bottom so as not to step on a stingray?"

Matthews shook his head.

"Well, a stingray has a barb underneath its tail that can be several inches long, its defense against predators. Back in high school I stepped on one and the barb went completely through my calf. I still have the scar. Worst pain I've ever had.

"You asked me how I feel about finding these thugs? It's like wade fishing and seeing patches of mud stirring up, hoping it's flounder moving but knowing it's not. I feel as if I've wandered into a nest of stingrays with no way out. You think that would be fun, Maurice?"

No one spoke. I glanced around the table, all eyes on me. "But," I said, chewing my lip. "There's no sense in letting twenty years of hunting spies go to waste. And besides...this is my island, so...count me in. I'm going to do everything I can to help you stop these bastards."

Chapter Twenty

Wednesday afternoon
Galveston

David left the engineering conference at the lunch break, too nervous about developing a plan to kill Perry to attend the afternoon lectures. Back in his room at the Tremont, he sat in a chair and closed his eyes. He was not used to this kind of stress. He pushed against the sides of his head trying to still his pounding temples. Was he too young for a stroke or an aneurism?

Thinking a drink would help, he poured one of the tiny bottles of scotch in the minibar into a glass. He took a quick sip and sat back, trying to relax.

Both his personal phone and the burner phone were in his briefcase. He took out his personal phone and called his office.

"Arnold Engineering," Mary answered.

Nice and professional, David thought. Well worth the little he paid her. "Hi Mary, just checking in. Anything going on?"

"We got an email from Jorge confirming the new contract."

"Sounds good," David said. "The conference is over this afternoon. I'm excited about a couple of new contacts that should produce some business. I'll bring you up to date when I get back. The weather is so nice I may stay a few days. Call me if I need to talk with anyone."

Lying to his secretary wasn't anything new for David. He'd had to shuffle around the truth many times with her, mostly during the afternoons he'd spent shacked up with any number of hot women. And then the big lie about a Paris vacation when he'd gone to see Rashad in Yemen. He waited for Mary's response, but there was no answer.

"Mary?"

"Uh...oh, okay Mr. Arnold. I will call you."

David heard the hesitancy in her voice. He could almost read her reaction over the phone. So unusual, she was thinking. Not like Mr. Arnold at all.

"Mary, you sound concerned. Is something wrong?"

"No, Mr. Arnold. It's just that...."

"What?"

"Well...I'm just worried about you, taking so much time off. The vacation to Paris and now more time in Galveston. It's not any of my business but...."

David laughed. "Don't worry, Mary. Business is good and I'm fine. Tell you what. Why don't you take Friday off?"

"Oh...well, golly. Thank you, Mr. Arnold."

David hung up satisfied he'd soothed her suspicions. The perk of a day off didn't hurt either. If anything, he figured Mary was just worried about her job especially since her husband had just been laid off at the steel mill.

David felt better after the phone call. The pounding in the sides of his head dissipated. He finished the scotch and thought about his last communication with his brother. Rashad had said someone would contact him soon. What the hell did that mean?

He took another bottle out of the bar and drank half of it in one swallow. He thought about his idea again. He still couldn't come up with a plan to get the pathogen into the hospital.

He checked his watch. It was almost time for the afternoon

prayer. He sipped the scotch and decided to skip the prayer. David didn't have strong feelings about the Muslim faith. He mostly prayed out of a feeling of guilt for his mother. She was a true believer and had spent many hours reciting and interpreting the Quran to him. He loved his mother and often expressed thanks to Allah that she'd escaped from Beirut while pregnant with him. What would his life have been like in a war-torn Middle East?

He'd only gone to Yemen and to Rashad's villa because his brother had demanded he be there when the assassination occurred. David had hated everything about the trip, the long flights and lousy airline food. All along the route from Lebanon to Yemen the smell of the unwashed had hung in the air like a dense fog.

The depressing image of bearded men and fully clothed women in veils was definitely not his part of the world. The males didn't know what they were missing, not seeing the curves in a strange woman's body as she walked and not feeling the joyful titillation of imagining her naked figure in interesting positions of sex.

But when Rashad had called, he'd gone. And that was the part that tugged at his sensibilities: the strange, almost reverent respect he held for the memory of his father and loyalty to his brother, versus his self-acknowledged hedonistic lifestyle. Nothing like the thrill of the hunt for a new woman. Fortunately, he'd also discovered alcohol. A couple of stiff drinks usually abated any residual guilt.

David thought about the cell in Minneapolis that Rashad had recruited. What motivated them: money or belief? If Rashad had used money as the carrot, where did he get it? His brother always seemed to have money. No doubt Rashad had financed the making of the bomb and maybe even provided instructions on how to build it.

He considered his father Nassim, a distinguished professor at the American University in Beirut. His mother had always told him Nassim was rich. But she'd never said how he'd accumulated his wealth. A professor's job in Lebanon couldn't have paid much. But David knew Nassim had also been a top agent with Hezbollah, and Hezbollah was financed by Iran, a country with huge amounts of oil money flowing in.

Then he remembered his brother Rashad showing up unexpectedly on his thirteenth birthday. Rashad had brought a gift from his father: a copy of the Quran with his father's personal, annotated notes explaining his adherence to the Wahhabi sect of beliefs. The puritanical Wahhabi believers were based in Saudi Arabia, home country of fifteen of the nineteen 9/11 hijackers. No doubt there was more wealth in Saudi Arabia than Iran. So which was the connection: Iran or Saudi Arabia? And did it matter?

Rashad was the older brother, so when Nassim had died Rashad had gained control of his father's money. It didn't seem fair, but that's how the primitive system worked. Hell, David thought. Rashad could be worth millions, but he'd never mentioned anything to him about it. Shouldn't he have half? As soon as this was over, he'd confront Rashad and get his share.

David's watch said 5:00 p.m., almost time for a drink at the bar downstairs and hope Anna Lang would come in. He checked the weather on his phone. Dropping temperature and he had nothing warm packed. He showered, combed his hair and brushed his teeth. He flashed his teeth in the mirror, satisfied with the four hundred dollars he'd spent for a whitening treatment. His deep blue eyes stared back at him. He liked what he saw. He put on fresh clothes, and as he started for the door his burner phone buzzed.

A number he'd never seen before. Even the area code was

suspect. Should he answer? Was it a trap? But Rashad had said someone would contact him. David answered.

"Have you been expecting a call?"

"Yes," David said, trying to keep the conversation as brief as possible.

"Tomorrow morning," the voice said. "Be ready. I will call you."

A spasm of relief coursed through his veins. Rashad had done it, found someone more experienced than he was in this kind of subterfuge. The new contact must have a plan. Nothing to do now but wait for tomorrow. Tonight he would enjoy the company of a beautiful woman. See where the evening took him. He checked the weather again and rushed around to a shop on the Strand to buy a jacket.

David was having a drink when Anna Lang waltzed through the front entrance wearing a wool jacket that ended just below her waist. She strode purposely toward him signaling the bartender for her usual glass of wine with her hand. She placed her jacket on top of an empty bar chair and hopped on the one next to David. The turned-down lips and tiny vertical lines between her scrunched eyes made the aggravation in her voice obvious as she spoke.

"That damned Parker McLeod."

"Who?"

"What...oh, never mind. Just talking out loud."

"No, it's okay," David said. "I can see you're frustrated about something."

"You really don't want to hear this," she said.

David cocked his head sideways, a friendly half grin on his face.

"I have days like this too," he said.

Gene set a glass of wine in front of her. She sniffed the bouquet, took a long drink and opened up. During the next few minutes, David heard the entire story of Bully Stout and Emma Meier during the war, including the pregnancy and Bully's stepping on a mine after saving his lieutenant...all of it.

"Wow," he said. "So you really believe Bully Stout is your grandfather?"

"I'm convinced of it. Everything fits."

"Have you considered DNA?"

"Ha," she said, mocking his idea. "I haven't been able to get that close. Bully kicked me out of the house during the first visit, denying everything. Parker promised he would visit Bully again, brace him for the truth and get a confession. But—"

"So who is Parker?"

David held his patience while Anna explained the relationship between Parker and Bully. His eyes widened as she described Parker at the explosion site.

"You were there?"

"Yes, Parker and I got to Secretary Perry first and had him rushed to the hospital."

"Saved his life, huh?"

Anna shrugged.

David turned his head, bit his lip and thought, bitch. He wanted to slap her off the chair. If it hadn't been for Anna Lang and this Parker character, he would be back in Indianapolis with that sweet airline hostess. Damn her to hell. Well, he'd just have to think up a special deliverance for Dr. Lang.

Anna reached into her purse and removed her Visa card. "This round's on me," she said handing the card to the bartender. "Least I can do for boring you with my sad tale."

She slipped down from the chair, donned her jacket and waited while the bartender processed the check.

"What's your hurry?" David asked, trying to hide his disgust from her.

"Screw Parker McLeod," she barked. "I'll handle Bully

myself."

"Whoa," David said. "Not a good idea to rush into a confrontation in your current mood. Let me take you. You're too upset to drive."

Ten minutes later Anna directed David over the causeway toward the mainland. They drove past the Texas City refineries, traveled through the downtown part of the city, passed the city limits and turned onto Molly Putts' street. David slowed and parked in front of the fence. The cold wind whipped across the surrounding fields like a prairie fire. He and Anna got out and put on their jackets. Shivering, Anna pulled the jacket snug around her neck and approached the front steps.

Molly Putts sat on the porch in her wheelchair with a blanket over her shoulders, her large frame bent so far forward it appeared she might tilt the wheelchair over.

"What the hell are you doing here?" she yelled down. "And who is that slick-back you brought with you. Bully ain't gonna talk to you."

Anna stepped back. "Molly, please. Calm down for goodness sake. I just want to ask Bully a couple of questions and we'll be on our way."

"Well you can forget it and haul ass back to Germany for all we give a shit. Bully's on the phone now with Parker. Called him as soon as you pulled up."

Bully rolled out to the porch in his wheelchair and yelled down at them, "I told you not to come back here." He turned to Molly, "Damn it, woman. Go get your shotgun."

Molly rolled her wheelchair to the door, reached inside and grabbed the gun. She wheeled the chair around with the ancient twelve-gauge on her lap. She cranked back both hammers.

"This gun was my grandpappy's. It's old, but good enough

to blow a hole through you."

"Hold it," David jumped in. "No need for that. She's just trying to talk to you."

"Who the hell are you?" Bully yelled.

David didn't answer.

"Don't make no difference who you are," Molly said. "You're both gonna be talkin' to a load of buckshot if you ain't in that car and gone in two seconds."

Anna grabbed her cell phone out of her purse just as a call from Parker was coming in.

Parker's voice screamed through the phone. "Anna, what the hell are you doing out there?"

"That crazy woman Bully lives with has a shotgun. He says she's going to shoot us."

"Who's us?"

"What?"

"You said us."

"David."

"Who's David?"

"Doesn't matter. Quit changing the subject. It's all your fault, you said you would talk to Bully. What are you going to do about this?"

"Damn it, Anna. I promise I'll go tomorrow. Now back off and leave before Molly unloads on you. Bully's already had one stroke and—"

Anna moved the phone from her ear and looked at Bully's face, red as an apple.

"Damn it, Parker. You'd damn well better call me tomorrow."

Anna threw the phone into her purse. She held her palms out, pushing them downward. "Okay, Bully. We're leaving. Calm yourself."

David and Anna backed toward the car. As they drove

away, he glanced through the rear-view mirror. Molly Putts was sitting in her wheelchair with the shotgun on her lap and binoculars glued to her eyes, pointed toward their retreating car.

Chapter Twenty-One

Wednesday evening
Galveston

After the meeting ended, I was sitting in Harry's kitchen, enjoying my second beer and hoping to bum some cash off him when my phone chirped.

"Goddamn it Parker," Bully screamed through the phone. "I told Molly to get her shotgun and shoot 'em. Bunch of forkin' Krauts."

"What?"

"That German woman and some yahoo she picked up. They're standing out in the front yard."

"Whoa, Bully. Jesus, don't do anything stupid. I'll call her."

I terminated the call and found the number Anna had put in my Contacts. We argued back and forth, with me warning her to leave. And who the hell was David? I dropped the phone back in my pocket and slugged down the remainder of the Shiner.

I needed to see Bully soon. Get this thing sorted out one way or the other. But first I needed to check with Jenny Hillbro and see if she had any news on the DNA results. The sooner we knew if Anna was blood kin, the better for all of us. Especially me.

As I was about to call Jenny, Harry came waltzing through the front door, bouncing like he'd just gotten a B12 shot. He wore sharply-creased gray slacks, a perfectly accented mauve golf shirt and matching tennis shoes. The scent of Old Spice wafted by me as he slipped off a gray windbreaker.

"Nasty weather out there. The temperature must have dropped twenty degrees in the last thirty minutes. But like they say, if you don't like the weather in Galveston, wait an hour."

"Yeah, this is killing my business. The north wind drives all the water out of the bay."

Harry pushed back the windblown silver strands of his normally perfectly coiffured hair and reached for the tea kettle.

I looked at this poster boy for fashion and said, "Harry, do you use a hair dryer on that mane?"

He gave me a faked air of disdain and said, "My personal hygiene habits have always been, and will continue to be, none of your damned business. You keep that up and I'll take you off my Christmas list."

"You mean Hanukkah, don't you?"

"Actually, I do both. Good for business."

"That would be a real threat if I had a mailbox. Lost it in the last hurricane."

Harry frowned. "Want some hot tea?"

"Thanks, but no," I said, grinning.

He lit the flame under the kettle, shuttled off to the bathroom and came out complaining. "Damned prostate must be big as a grapefruit. It's hell to get old, Parker." He slipped a tea bag into a cup, poured in hot water and said, "I know you can't discuss details. But was the meeting with the Feds successful?"

I picked up copies of the drawings Matthews had made on Harry's copier and showed them to Harry.

"This face will be all over the news tonight. You get an

early peek."

"Who is this?" he asked.

"As best as I could remember, the man I saw at the café bombing in Germany."

"The explosion that killed your friend Monty? That was twenty years ago."

"Eighteen to be exact."

"And the Galveston connection is...?"

"It's confidential at this point, Harry. If I told you, I'd have to kill you. But keep a lookout for this mug." I pointed to the copy Kathy had aged that showed slightly thinning dark hair with flecks of gray, lines around his eyes and a sun-weathered face.

While he studied the drawing, I said. "Banks are closed. Can you loan me some cash until tomorrow?"

He tweaked his Colonel Sanders' mustache and caught my eye. "How much?"

"A hundred, if you can spare it?"

He opened his wallet and handed me five twenties. "Have you heard about credit cards? They even have something called a debit card. Takes the cash right out of your account."

"Yeah and what if you lose your wallet?"

"Where do you ever go to do that?" he asked, smirking. "If you lost it at The Garhole you'd find it and if you lost it fishing, no one would find it." Harry shook his head. He removed the tea bag, blew on the steaming cup and sipped the hot brew.

Harry was never very subtle about wanting me to join the human race and get on with my life. But he'd always been a good mentor to me, so I took his grief in stride.

"Well, maybe you're right," I said. "If I keep coming to the city on a regular basis, a credit card would help." As I said that the intimacy I'd felt when Kathy and I worked on the sketch sent a warm jolt through my body.

"Coming in on a regular basis?" he asked. "You?" He paused, giving me a quizzical look. "What's her name?"

"I'll let you know if it works out," I said.

Harry sipped his tea and then took a couple of blueberry scones out of the refrigerator and warmed them in his toaster oven. Harry's homemade blueberry muffins were legendary, but scones didn't seem to fit him. He placed the scones on plates and handed one to me.

I couldn't resist and said, "Scones aren't you, Harry. One of the casserole ladies drop by?" I was kidding, but should have known better. Harry was never short of pursuers.

His cheeks reddened. "Two new ones on the block," he said. "June, the younger one across the street, just got divorced. She keeps her eyes peeled for the widow Dorothy down the block. Unfortunately, I get twofers that way. She sees Dorothy bring me something and an hour later I get a frozen casserole from June. Can't eat any of them. I've got four casseroles and a dozen assorted homemade pastries in the freezer. Dorothy's goodies are tolerable, but June's one stop meals are...well, they end up down at the homeless shelter."

We both laughed.

"Why not invite them over. Show them the master at work?"

"You kidding? I'd have to have a referee. And an armed one at that."

"Well, you must like one of them. You've been bleaching your teeth whiter than a flocked Christmas tree."

"I have to look good in court," he said. "I do all the police officers' divorces pro bono. You know cops. The Chief loves me for it. How do you think I got the police scanner?"

I finished my scone and said, "So how was the meeting at the foundation?"

Harry's eyes lit up. Asking about his work at the Galveston

Historical Foundation was like asking a kid if he wanted ice cream.

"Exciting," he said, grinning ear to ear. "We're planning a fundraiser on the Elissa for Presidents' weekend. I'm expecting you to buy a ticket."

"Sure, Harry. How much?"

"One fifty."

I gulped. "Holly mackerel, Harry. The Garhole doesn't gross that in a week this time of year."

He waved me off. "Don't give me that, Parker. Neddie told me about your take the night of the explosion."

His comment slammed me hard. I already felt bad enough about making money off the catastrophe at the Coast Guard station. Harry verbalizing it was more than I needed to hear. But I knew he wasn't trying to shame me so I shrugged off the irritation.

"Least I can do," I said.

"Good," he replied. "I knew you were carrying a load of guilt about making all that money so I just thought I'd tighten the screws."

"You're a mean man, Harry."

I drank another beer while Harry finished his tea. For the next few minutes, we bantered on about the upcoming fundraiser. I knew Elissa's history. Built in Scotland in 1877, the three-masted tall ship hauled cargo on regular routes around Europe until it was finally sold for salvage in a Greek shipyard. The Historical Foundation rescued the ship in 1975 and a group of dedicated volunteers had maintained it through the years.

"They're always looking for folks to help with the ship," Harry said. "Why don't you join them?"

"Hey, I was Army not Navy, Harry. Don't know a thing about rigging sails."

"You could learn."

Good old Harry, I thought. Another stab to get me out of hibernation at The Garhole. When my mind flashed to Kathy Landry again, I thought he may be right. When he went into the bedroom to change clothes, I stepped out on the porch to call Kathy, but the cold wind quickly drove me back inside.

"Meeting all done?" she asked.

"I'm leaving now."

When Harry came out, I asked to borrow a sweater. He took me into a master closet almost as large as his bedroom, upper and lower racks lined with sport coats, shirts and pants. He pointed at a shelf and told me to take my pick among the dozen or so carefully folded sweaters. It seemed like a lot of wool for a city that rarely saw winter temperatures below forty degrees. Then I had to remind myself, it was Harry after all.

I quickly realized the stack containing more colors than a rainbow was not my style. Too preppie. I spied an old Army field jacket hanging at the end of the closet and pulled it off the hanger.

Harry said, "I use that coat once a year for my annual spring birding trip to the Bolivar beach. March winds can be pretty cutting."

It was almost full dark when I stopped in the driveway of a small bungalow on a back street off Avenue L. I was familiar with the neighborhood and knew the house had been built sometime during the 1930s or 40s. The shiplap siding was painted gray with white trim. A flower bed with bright multicolored pansies ran along either side of an unusually small front stoop.

The small front porch was unusual for homes of that era. Before television and air conditioning, people used to sit on their large galleries and watch the world go by. I figured the larger porch must have been enclosed to expand the house to three bedrooms.

I got out and hustled to the front door, shivering from the biting wind with the collar of Harry's field jacket pulled tightly around my cheeks. Kathy opened the door with a smile like a quarter moon. Her alabaster skin sparkled in the porch light. If she was wearing makeup other than lipstick, I couldn't tell it. She looked perfectly comfortable in jeans and a brown sweater that matched her warm eyes.

"Welcome, Parker McLeod. Come in out of the cold," she said, stepping aside. "How about something to warm you up? I've got a half bottle of vodka around here somewhere, leftover from a girlfriend who liked the hard stuff."

An alarm went off in my head. I knew one drink would put me back on a trail I didn't want to travel. I thought back to Harry's porch when she abruptly turned away from me after I impulsively kissed her cheek. I knew a couple of shots of hard booze would bring the courage I needed to deal with the moment, but was I willing to take the risk? Kathy wasn't a sixteen-year-old-virgin, but still....

"Parker?" she asked, looking at me with inquisitive eyes.

"Thanks, but...I can't do that," I said, not willing to open up.

She studied me for a moment. "Beer?" she asked.

"You're after my heart."

We moved through the small living room, warmly appointed with the usual couch, coffee table and wingback chairs. In the kitchen, a fold-out pine breakfast table and four chairs stood against one wall. While Kathy went to the refrigerator, I waited by the counter that separated the kitchen from the breakfast room. She handed me a beer.

"Shiner Bock. Have you been spying on me?"

She laughed. "Neddie told me you liked Shiner so I picked up a six pack on my way home."

I took a deep breath and let it out slowly, trying to calm my racing pulse and hoping she hadn't noticed. What I really wanted was to grab her lithe body and carry it into the bedroom.

Instead I said, "So let's grab some dinner. What's your favorite restaurant?"

"Actually, it's The Garhole Bar. I was hoping we could see the sunset off your dock. But it's too late now."

"Sorry," I said. "I would take you there anyway, but the bar doesn't warm up well in this weather."

She feigned disappointment, then turned her lips into a slight grin. "It's miserable outside. How about I fix something here?"

And I'm thinking, closer to the bedroom here than in a restaurant. She put on a pot of water to cook pasta and began sautéing chicken breasts in olive oil. I sat at the bar while she worked, enjoying her occasional glances my way. I couldn't remember the last time a woman cooked a meal for me. The whole scene felt good, comfy, like an old quilt.

She arranged the chicken over the pasta and whipped up a small salad. I took the plates to the table while she grabbed two more beers out of the fridge. We ate chicken, rolled pasta on our forks, drank beer and talked. The conversation flowed like a soft river.

Several drawings, some black and white and some in color, hung on the light-blue-colored walls. I pointed to a drawing of the Elissa coming in to dock.

"Great drawing," I said, pointing to the ship. Then looked around. "Are all of these yours?"

"Yes," she said. "I also have a few in a gallery on Postoffice Street. I get lucky and sell one once in a while."

"Nice," I said. "How did you get interested in drawing?"

"Well, I was fortunate to have had a wonderful art teacher in high school that convinced a shy, introverted, teenaged girl that she had talent. The next summer I took private lessons from an artist she recommended. It was a great passion, but I was on my own after high school and needed a way to make a living so I decided on nursing."

She paused to take a last bite of chicken and said, "Is that enough about me?"

I pushed my empty plate toward the center and took a sip of beer. "No, you must have had more art training. Somehow you got into working for the police."

"Okay. So I moved to Galveston from Houston for nursing school, met a young med student, got married while we were both still in school. He was the old-fashioned type, wanted me home to cook and clean. I finished nursing school but didn't work for a while. I managed to sneak off during the day to continue drawing. Got into portraits." She paused again, sipped her beer. "Enough yet?"

I shook my head.

"Okay, so I was pregnant when I found out he was running around on me. We divorced after my daughter was born. I got a job nursing at UTMB and continued studying drawing in my spare time."

She paused. "Spare time. That's a laugh, working full time and raising a daughter. Anyway, I had a few dates with a police detective and he got me into suspect drawing. And that's how the chicken crossed the road." She got up and took our plates to the kitchen.

My eyes were drawn to a color drawing of a young girl about ten. It was summer and she was wearing a white sundress, her hair long, below her shoulders. I spent a few moments studying the drawing and felt Kathy's presence behind me.

"My daughter, Margaret. I call her Maggie."

I turned abruptly. "She's beautiful."

"The light of my life. She's on her school's winter break. Her dad took her to see his mom in Dallas. She'll be home Sunday."

"Love to meet her."

"You will," Kathy said, a certainty to her tone.

The rising wind blowing against the kitchen window rattled the shutter. Kathy got up to put on a shawl she'd draped over a barstool. While she was up, she rinsed the dishes and set them aside. I offered to help but she directed me to the couch in the living room. She pulled the shawl tightly around her shoulders, sat beside me and dropped her head on my shoulder.

"So tell me about this West Beach enigma called Parker McLeod," she whispered.

I put my arm around her. "A riddle wrapped in a mystery."

"Winston Churchill."

"You're a student of history?"

"Some," she said.

"Well, the enigma hasn't had that much of a life, I guess, not really."

She raised her head off my shoulder and stared into my eyes. "Something turned you into the Lone Ranger. Neddie told me you were the star quarterback at Ball High. Good enough for a college scholarship. What happened?"

"Prom night," I said.

"An accident?"

"Well, more or less, but not the kind you think."

She straightened on the couch, a puzzled look on her face. I clammed up. Didn't know how to go forward with the story.

Finally, her face lit up, an ah-ha moment. "Oh," she said. "I got it."

"Young love," I said. "I don't regret it. If Jeannie hadn't miscarried, I would have had a daughter."

"Oh, Parker. I'm so sorry." She put her hand on my neck and began to rub with her fingers.

"It's okay," I said. "So, while I was trying to work out the situation, I missed the fall semester of college and got drafted. My friend Harry Stein convinced her mother to let us get married rather than send Jeannie off to a girls' home. I was in boot camp when she lost the baby. Then I was away training at different places and finally landed in Germany. She never lived with me in any of my duty stations. We were only together when I was home on leave. Wasn't much of a marriage."

Then I told her about my struggle with Gulf War Syndrome and drinking a bottle of Scotch every few days to ease the pain. I also shared the story about how Doc Kennon and his holistic treatments got me on the road to recovery. I even told her about the bottle of Famous Grouse that had been sitting on a shelf under the bar, untouched for several years.

"Good for you," she said, still rubbing my neck.

I broke from her and leaned forward. I looked back at her. "This isn't going right," I said. "I got into the 'poor me syndrome' and you followed with a patronizing comment. It's like it was scripted. Like we're playing roles. I'm not that weak, at least I hope I'm not...damn."

Kathy smiled, "Wow, heavy with the psychobabble. I've had a little training in that myself. Should have seen it." She stood, held up her arm and flexed her bicep. "Wanna arm wrestle?"

I laughed, took her arm and pulled her back to the couch. I kissed her and she kissed back. Like on automatic pilot, my hand went to her breast. She didn't move it. Then her hand landed on the inside of my thigh. Oh shit, here we go. In my early days I probably would have slipped my hand to her back and fumbled with the catch on her bra. But hey, we were grownups.

We both came up for air and she said, "I have the three o'clock shift tomorrow afternoon and I don't think you're going to sell any gumbo in this weather. Besides you've had two beers. I wouldn't want you to drive home drunk."

"Two beers?"

"Are you gonna make me work for this?"

"No ma'am."

She took my hand and pulled me off the couch. In the direction that we were going, there was only the bedroom.

Chapter Twenty-Two

Wednesday evening
Galveston

The moment was much more than sex, but with my head swimming in confused euphoria, it was not the time to decipher all that had happened. I lay back on the pillow, staring at the ceiling and enjoying the magic. It was as though I had been lost for an eon in a wasteland of indifference and was suddenly thrust into a nirvana of light.

Kathy reached for the switch on the lamp beside the bed and turned it to low. She laid her hand on my chest.

"Just checking," she said softly, smiling through the words. "Making sure I don't need to call 911. I thought you were going to have a heart attack."

"The dream of every man is to go in the saddle," I said.

The encounter was no doubt frantic and hurried, at least on my part. I reached for her shoulder and pulled her down on top of me. I nuzzled her neck and held her tight. She pulled her head back, her face close on top of me. Deep brown eyes poured into mine as though searching for something.

"What?" I said.

Maybe it was the way the word came out, my tone of voice or the expression on my face. She pulled away and sat on the edge of the bed, her face in her hands, the intimacy between us shattering as quickly as a vase tumbling to a tile floor.

I reached out and touched her. "Kathy, I...."

"No," she said. "It's okay."

I sat up and leaned against the headboard. "No, it's not," I said. "I want this. Maybe I need some help, but I want this."

I was not sure how to move forward. But I knew being adrift is what happens to emotional hermits. Without help we dry up and die. Not dying at the end like other people, but a fraction every day. Even though the heart beats, we are dead. We just don't know it.

She turned and touched my cheek. "Really, Parker, it's okay. I want this, too. Maybe we rushed it. We've both been out in a wilderness of our own making. We just have to find our way back. You're the first man I've really cared about since my divorce. I could feel your hunger. Let's slow down a bit. We've got a long way to go."

The ambient light reflected the moisture in her eyes. My heart thumped. I pulled her to me again and eased my hand to her midsection admiring its taut flatness and the indentations of her hips. We kissed and fell back to the bed, heat rising again. Maybe we needed to slow things down, but not now. Not tonight.

And then a low buzzing sound severed the magic. A pulsating light blinked from inside my pants pocket that I had dropped hastily to the floor in a hurried rush of testosterone and heat. Kathy broke the embrace. I pulled her back.

"Let it go," I said. "More important things going on."

"Better get it. You're on the team now." She straightened again and turned the lamp up to high. She reached to the floor, fished the phone out of my pants pocket and handed it to me.

I reluctantly pushed the send button. "What?" I said, the irritation in my voice obvious. I didn't recognize the number, but it was Matthews' voice.

"We found the bastard. We're forming up now. Want to go?"

"The professor?"

"No, your friend in the drawing."

I gave Kathy a final hug and raced down the stars into the cold night, tugging on Harry's jacket as I ran, wondering if the goose bumps spreading across my skin were from the frigid air or the excitement building in my body. Was the man who'd murdered my friend Monty Edwards eighteen years earlier really here in Galveston? I could only hope. A picture of Monty sitting across from me in the café in Berlin flashed across my mind. Then I smelled the acrid smoke and saw the twisted bodies on the floor. I shook the image away.

My heart pounding, I jumped into my truck and grabbed under the seat for my Colt 911, my Army service weapon. I jacked a cartridge into the barrel and lay the gun on the seat beside me. The terrorist would probably not get past the SWAT team, but part of me wanted him to. And I had one 230-grain hunk of lead in the barrel and six more in the magazine waiting for the opportunity. One shot in the chest should do it.

Developed at the turn of the century for American soldiers fighting tough, hopped-up Moro tribesmen in the Philippines, the big .45 caliber had tremendous stopping power for close-in combat.

I cranked up and hauled off toward the rendezvous, my head in a strange whirl, my thoughts flipping between the softness of the evening with Kathy and my desire to kill someone. One moment my senses captured the scent of the perfume from Kathy's neck, then a second later a whiff of oil from my Colt.

I wheeled through a left turn at the intersection with Broadway and sped north. Broadway turns into I45 and continues over the causeway to Houston. But I wasn't going that far. The staging point was the parking lot of a closed lumber yard on the feeder of I45 just before the intersection with Harborside Drive. Harborside cuts off from the interstate, leading directly to the Port of Galveston. The motel Matthews named was one of the older units on Harborside, a few blocks off the freeway.

I pulled my old clunker into the lumber yard parking lot crowded with black-and-whites, a dark SUV and an armored vehicle belonging to Galveston SWAT. A police officer wearing a bullet proof vest and holding a sawed-off twelve-gauge stepped in front of my car.

"This is off limits," he said, his breath condensing, turning into a light fog as he spoke. "Move along."

Matthews came up, his heavy coat emblazoned with large FBI letters front and back. "It's okay officer, he's with us."

The officer took a hard look at my rusted pickup, shook his head and walked away.

"You almost missed the party. Ride with us," Matthews said, motioning me to his vehicle.

I stuck the .45 in the back of my jeans and hustled to the SUV. I climbed into the back seat behind Agent Hebinck who was riding shotgun. Matthews got in beside me from the other side. Hebinck introduced me to the driver, Agent McElroy.

"Fill me in," I said as the caravan moved onto the feeder road.

"Kathy Landry's drawing went on the air just after seven," Hebinck said, his face half turned toward me. "The local stations interrupted their regular broadcasting and immediately put the picture on the air. They repeated it on the ten o'clock news, too. Galveston PD got a call from the motel manager at 10:08. He swears it's the suspect, checked in about eight tonight. Paid cash for three nights. Signed the registration card as Butch Baristi. He listed a Houston address, but since he paid cash, the clerk didn't bother to check his ID."

"Maybe a little cash also changed hands with the clerk," I added.

"Probably," Hebinck said. "The suspect used a nickname knowing it would hamper a records check. Something's going down with this guy, that's for sure. Of course we ran the name, including known aliases, but nothing turned up. The clerk identified him from the drawing with the beard. Wants the reward."

Two police cars, the SWAT vehicle and our SUV caravanned slowly down the feeder. The lead police car stopped at the intersection and blocked the entrance to Harborside from the freeway. The second unit raced down Harborside and blocked the road from the other direction.

The two-story junker motel sat perpendicular to Harborside going back off the street about a hundred yards. Peeling paint and cracks in the dirty stucco walls showed a building in perpetual decline. A sign read "The Islander Motel" and advertised weekly rentals. A faded "For Sale" sign on the far side of the driveway listed a phone number.

As we approached the entrance, a SWAT member stuck his hand out the window of the armored vehicle and waved us in front. Agent McElroy eased the SUV to a stop near the portico in front of the motel office. Behind us, the SWAT vehicle turned sideways at the entrance blocking the exit. Six SWAT officers got out and waited behind the vehicle, checking their M4, fully automatic carbines with thirty-round clips.

An unmarked police vehicle was parked under the canopy of the motel office. As we got out of the SUV, the wind hit my face, tearing up my eyes. I pulled Harry's jacket tighter around my neck and stuck my hands in my jean pockets.

An officer approached from the SWAT vehicle. He was a large, muscular man decked out in black cargo pants, boots, bulletproof vest, sidearm and helmet. With a face mask, he could have doubled for Darth Vader. His face was pink from the wind. He introduced himself as Lieutenant Koska, commander of the SWAT team. At the same time, an innocuous-looking police detective, wearing jeans, tennis shoes and jacket with "Galveston Police" stenciled in large letters, stepped out of the motel office. He said his name was Stricklin and his partner Barnard was inside with the manager.

"Room 151 at the far end," Stricklin said. "First floor, no lights on in the room."

He pointed to the three vehicles in the parking area. "According to the clerk, the Ford pickup is his own; the Suburban belongs to a family upstairs. The black 1978 Chevrolet Camaro with red stripes belongs to the suspect. Plates are stolen."

Koska nodded. "Are we sure the suspect's still in the room?"

"His car is here," Stricklin answered. "No one else has shown up and the clerk hasn't seen anyone walk by." He checked his watch. "It's almost midnight, no lights in the room. Maybe we get lucky, we catch the suspect sacked out."

"We make our own luck," Koska said, gritting his teeth as he spoke.

Inside the lobby Detective Barnard got up from a chair across from a skinny, fortyish-looking man sitting on a fake-leather couch with large cracks. Barnard said the clerk's name was Harvey Slack. What was left of Slack's stringy red hair was threaded in a weak comb-over, a pitiful attempt to cover his mostly bald head. His hollow face was splotched from too many days in the sun or too much dope or booze, or both, his eyes the color of red grapes. He puffed a cigarette, nervously shifting it back and forth between his lips and an ashtray.

In a low voice, Barnard said, "We ran Slack. Small time stuff, marijuana possession and six months in County for a DUI."

Hebinck nodded and moved to the chair across from Slack. Matthews sat beside him while I stayed back with Koska and the detectives. Hebinck and Matthews flashed their FBI shields. Slack puffed continuously, never saying a word. He glanced through the plate glass window at the armored SWAT vehicle outside and then back at Koska.

Slack butted the cigarette into an ashtray and lit another one using both hands to control the shaking cigarette lighter. A line of sweat broke out on his forehead. As he dabbed his brow with a paper napkin, Hebinck placed three drawings on a coffee table in front of him. The drawings were much clearer than what had appeared on TV.

"Is this the man you saw tonight?" Hebinck asked.

Slack bent forward, studied the drawings. He pointed to the face with the beard. "Yes, no doubt. It's him. Checked in around eight, hasn't left his room."

"Have you ever seen this man before?"

Slack took a drag and quickly blew the smoke out. He shook his head. "No, I'm positive. This is the first time."

"Sit tight," Hebinck said.

He and Matthews got up and motioned the rest of us to move far enough away that Slack couldn't hear us. Hebinck turned to Detective Barnard.

"Have you checked the hotel computer?"

"Can't get it to turn on," Barnard said.

"What about cameras inside and out?"

"We checked. None of them work."

"Has our man in 151 made any calls?"

"Not on the house phone. Probably has a cell."

Hebinck crossed back to Slack. "Take another look," he said. "You better be damn sure."

Slack studied the drawing with the bearded face again. Sweat continued to break out on his forehead. "It's him," he said.

A uniformed officer loaded Slack into a Galveston PD patrol car and drove away. Everyone gathered in a huddle inside the office.

"What do you think?" Hebinck asked, his eyes moving back and forth between the two detectives and the SWAT commander.

Stricklin said, "Don't think we have a choice. The risk is greater if we don't go in. The suspect could disappear tomorrow. Tonight we have him."

Barnard chimed in, "Stolen plates on his Camaro mean something."

Hebinck looked at Stricklin, "Do we have the warrant?"

Stricklin nodded.

Koska surveyed his team standing beside the assault vehicle. With tight lips and a smirk, he said, "We didn't get all dressed up for nothing."

Slack had said the Suburban belonged to a Hispanic family who had just paid for a second week's stay at the motel. Koska radioed to one of his men outside who spoke Spanish. The officer came in and called the room explaining this was not an ICE raid and nothing would happen to the family, but that there was an emergency and he would be up in one minute to escort them to their car.

A rail-thin Hispanic man, his hefty wife and three kids, all under ten, came down the stairs with the officer. The SWAT team driver backed the vehicle from its blocking position and the family drove off in the Suburban. According to the clerk, the motel was now empty except for room 151. Six members of the SWAT team formed up outside the office.

Hebinck said, "I'm not comfortable with a full-on assault. We have no independent verification of this suspect's identity. He may be just Joe Citizen in town for a vacation. We also don't know for sure there aren't more people in that room.

Even kids. Maybe the suspect had someone with him and the clerk didn't notice. The FBI doesn't need another Ruby Ridge."

The room went silent. Everyone knew Hebinck was referring to the 1992 incident in Idaho. Randy Weaver and his wife had dropped out of society and were living on a twenty-acre patch in the mountains planning to homeschool their children. When Weaver failed to appear in court on a weapons charge, U.S. Marshalls went to investigate. A gun fight ensued, during which one of the Marshalls was killed. Weaver's wife Vickie and their son Sammy also died of gunshots. It was a huge fiasco for the FBI, resulting in a Congressional hearing and several lawsuits.

Detective Barnard spoke, his face awash in sarcasm. "That's what we need right now, the FBI getting paranoid. The man does have stolen plates on his vehicle. He ain't no angel."

Matthews broke in, "Maybe not. But the safest way is to call his room and give him a chance to give up."

"Safe for who?" Koska bellowed, his eyes flaring. "Not for my team. No way I'm gonna risk my men's lives when the bastard tosses a bomb or comes out with an automatic weapon and sprays the whole damn parking lot. I don't want this guy to have time to think. We're going to hit him hard, with stealth and power. Lock his ass down before he knows what happened."

"What if we're wrong about the clerk's identification?" Hebinck asked.

"You can knock on his door and get your balls shot off if you want to," Koska said. "If my team goes in, we're going my way."

I didn't say anything, but I agreed with the SWAT commander. These guys do this for a living. There was no reason to risk a cop getting hurt. My lower back where the automatic was wedged against my skin began to itch. I envisioned seven little cartridges trying to get out to do their duty.

The SWAT team crept single file past the first-floor rooms toward the end. The middle two officers carried a forty-inch-long, forty-pound, steel battering ram built for two. Hebinck, Matthews and I followed behind while the two detectives remained at the motel office.

When the team reached Room 151, the largest SWAT officer, at least six-three and 250 pounds, stood in front of the door holding the ram to his side. There would be no warning. The plan was to knock the lock out, crashing the door open. The lead officer would toss in a stun grenade, followed by the second and third officer rushing in to apprehend the dazed suspect. By-the-book training, a routine take down.

The big guy swung the ram twice to create a greater ark and more force. On the third swing, the ram crashed the door open as planned, but just as the next officer tossed the grenade, shots rang out, striking the officer and knocking him backwards. The grenade went off, sending a loud bang throughout the room and out the door. Two officers rushed in, their M4s on full automatic. For the next few seconds, the noise from the room sounded like a firecracker stand exploding.

Chapter Twenty-Three

Early Thursday Morning
Galveston

Police Chief Rory Puryear, wearing a heavy coat and gloves, arrived just as an EMS unit was loading the wounded SWAT officer onto a gurney. Puryear had his hand wrapped around a dog leash. At the opposite end was a large English bulldog, maybe fifty pounds, his mouth dripping saliva. I'd seen photos of the chief and his dog in the newspaper and recognized Colonel Bubbie immediately.

Harry had told me the rumor making its way around the city said that the chief never left the station without the colonel. Tonight, because of the cold, Bubbie was decked out in a body sweater that fit snugly around his thick neck. No way to tell if the dog was happy or not with his sad eyes and turned-down mouth. But he was excited, straining at the leash and sniffing everyone's pant legs he could get close to. As Puryear approached the wounded officer, he unhooked the leash from his hand and gave it to his nearby driver.

With an air of leadership that emanated from the four stars on each collar, Puryear bent over the injured officer. A large compression bandage taped tightly to the side of the officer's neck was seeping blood onto the blanket tucked neatly around his body. An EMT held a saline bottle above the officer's head with a line leading to the plastic tube inserted into his arm.

"You're going to be fine, son," Puryear said. "Just a nick. I'll see you at the hospital as soon as we're done here."

Puryear squeezed the officer's hand as the EMS team loaded the officer into the ambulance. Then Puryear turned and entered the motel room followed by Koska and agents Hebinck and Matthews. They filed out a few minutes later, their faces grim.

Puryear noticed me standing nearby and growled, "Who the hell are you?" The arteries in his neck bulged as he spoke. I wanted to kick him in the balls, but held back.

Matthews spoke up. "This is Parker McLeod, chief. He's part of our team. The body on that bed may be a terrorist who's killed hundreds of innocent people. The problem is there are no known photographs of the suspect. McLeod is the only person who's seen him in the flesh. He needs a quick look to see if he can identify him. If the terrorists are lining up another attack on Perry, we need all the help we can get."

After hearing the barrage of shots, I knew the scene wouldn't be pretty. But if the body was the terrorist, it was worth interrupting my warm snuggle with Kathy Landry and spending time on a cold concrete parking lot next to a rat-infested motel. Attempting to recognize the man I'd only glimpsed eighteen years ago was like trying to buck the odds on a lottery ticket. But like the lottery, the payoff would be huge if the suspect was the winning ticket.

Puryear chewed on his lip. He seemed to be having a difficult time acquiescing to Matthews' request. I suspected his authority had never been challenged in front of his men. I decided to ease the pressure.

"It's okay, chief," I said. "I'll take a look at him in the morgue after he's been cleaned up. I hope your officer will be okay."

Patronizing the chief seemed to work. While continuing to

ignore me, Puryear grudgingly gave permission for me to enter the room as long as Koska accompanied me. I paused in the doorway and took in the scene. The suspect, wearing only bloodied boxer shorts, lay on his back stretched across the mattress, the pillows and sheets a wad of blood-soaked cotton. His head hung over the edge of the bed. The cheap plastic headboard was pocked with bullet holes. A Smith and Wesson revolver lay on the mattress beside his hand.

It appeared the suspect had been sleeping, or at least trying to, and had the gun in bed with him. He must have heard something and managed to get off a shot as the door blew open. The wounded officer had been standing just outside the door as he tossed the stun grenade. A shot from the suspect's thirty-eight had punctured the casing beside the door, splintered the wood and hit the officer in the neck. One hell of an unlucky shot for the cop. As the officer fell, two more SWAT officers rushed in and emptied their magazines before the suspect could recoup from the effects of the flash-bang.

Koska squeezed in behind me. "We need more time on the range," he said, grimacing. "Sixty rounds fired. It's hard to tell how many hit the guy without an examination, and we can't move him until the coroner arrives. My guess is not more than twenty."

I wasn't in the mood for Koska's macho sarcasm but managed to hold my tongue. The victim's face looked as if it had been smashed with a hammer. One round had entered his mouth, leaving an exit hole the size of a small orange in his cheek. Another round had shattered his left eye. Koska said he personally counted thirteen more rounds in his upper torso, making mincemeat of his heart. It was hard to view his bloodied shorts without wincing. At least three rounds had entered the groin area, probably one of the officers trying to shoot his balls off. With his buddy shot in the neck, who could blame him?

The suspect's long black hair hung down toward the floor, his scraggly beard smeared with blood. I stepped carefully around the blood on the floor to avoid contaminating the scene, and studied the victim, trying to compare his battered face with the vision of a man I'd seen for a fleeting moment years earlier. I desperately wanted the corpse to be the terrorist. I needed closure for myself and my friend Monty Edwards, who'd been murdered in the Berlin café. But the suspect was too bloodied to make the judgment now. I would have to wait and see him in the morgue after he was cleaned up.

An officer stuck his head in the door and said, "The chief wants everybody in the motel lobby."

I knew another meeting would be held later, after the autopsy was completed and the investigative team finished their report. Tonight, it was important for everyone to get their stories straight and cover their asses. The meeting was brief, the two SWAT officers justifying the need for quick, decisive action after the first officer had been shot.

Neither Hebinck nor Matthews commented, but the look of resignation on their faces told me what they were thinking. If only they'd been more adamant with Koska about trying to take the suspect alive. If this was the bombing suspect, we'd lost a golden opportunity to interrogate him and learn about the terrorists' plans.

I left the motel office and slipped past the yellow police tape into a herd of reporters standing around their TV trucks, shivering in the wind, waiting patiently for any scrap of news they could report. One of the reporters, an attractive thirtyish brunette, was lightly stamping her feet to keep her circulation going. Lucky for me, Harry's ancient field jacket didn't seem to impress any of them, and I managed to slip by without having my mug on TV.

I bummed a ride back to the lumber yard with a friendly cop, cranked my truck and made a U-turn at Harborside. My watch read 2:30 a.m. This was not the time to have a broken heater, but mine had been out for over a year. I pulled my jacket close.

My gut growled with hunger so I turned right on 61st Street and stopped at the twenty-four-hour Waffle House for the second time in as many days. The inside smelled like stale coffee and burnt grease. A young couple, probably loaded with alcohol after closing some bar, sat red-eyed and giggling in a corner booth.

I grabbed a stool at the counter to save the lone waitress a few steps. She passed me a menu, doing her best to turn her lined face and sagging cheeks into a smile. With stringy gray hair and hunched shoulders, she looked sixty going on eighty. Part of me wanted to ask why she needed to work the dog shift at an all-night restaurant for little more than minimum wage. The woman obviously had her troubles, but who the hell was I to judge? Fifty-three years old and running a dumpy little bar at the west end of nowhere.

I handed the menu back without looking and ordered the breakfast special: two eggs, bacon, toast, hash browns and pancakes. I normally try not to gorge myself with carbs and fat, but what the hell...I'd earned it tonight.

After putting an end to the hunger pangs, I slipped an extra twenty under my coffee cup and slid off the stool. The vision of a cold bed in a damp room atop The Garhole Bar didn't make me want to rush home. I considered cruising by Kathy's house in the hopes of seeing a light in her bedroom window, but as I pulled out of the Waffle House parking lot, my eyes began to droop.

Twenty minutes later, I parked the truck in front of The Garhole and slowly climbed the back stairs. I stood on the top deck and viewed the night sky. A complete cycle of the moon around the earth takes twenty-nine and a half days. The big orange ball overhead was now in its intermediate phase, waning toward the third quarter when only half the moon would be visible with the naked eye.

A light gray cloud cover drifted across its surface, but the sight didn't seem ominous. Not like *the bad moon rising* my grandfather had warned me about two days before he died and the same moon I'd seen the night before the explosion at the Coast Guard base.

I took this as a good sign. Maybe the man lying across the cheap motel mattress was the terrorist. And he'd been unceremoniously dispatched. Could we really be that lucky?

Maybe. But something didn't add up: a renowned university professor was still missing along with a vial of anthrax. It was unknown if the professor had stolen the vial or even if he had been headed this way. But if the professor was part of the plan to assassinate Secretary Perry, why would Rashad Zahir also be on his way here? Was one of these a backup plan in case the other didn't work? Had Rashad been so confident in the first bombing that he didn't have a backup plan and now he knew better? If so, which one was the primary thrust and which one was the backup?

Tossing those thoughts in my tired brain kept me awake until sometime in the early morning. I was still in somewhat of a coma when the sun lit up my room and I realized my cell phone was banging me awake. As I reached for the phone, the battery went dead. I'd forgotten to plug it in. I thought about sticking a pillow over my head and trying for some more snooze time but my taste buds demanded coffee.

I shaved and stood under the shower spray until the hot water ran out, alternating thoughts between calling Kathy and knowing I needed to get to the morgue to identify the dead suspect. Maybe I could do both. I slipped into a reasonably fresh pair of jeans, my only clean sweatshirt and Harry's jacket and maneuvered down the stairs, thinking I would call Neddie Lemmon to work the bar this afternoon.

Neddie must have had telepathic powers because he was standing at the back dock wearing a watch cap and a thick Navy pea coat, while sipping a mug of coffee and looking out at the muddy bay water stirred up by the front. I wondered how Neddie's bony frame had the strength to hold the extra weight of the coat up without causing him to tilt over.

"Must be forty degrees out," he said. "And I wanted to fish today. It's a good thing I brought my heavy coat. It's colder in the bar than out here. You need to get some heat in this joint."

"It might help if you'd eat more than you drink. Put some meat on your bones."

I went inside, poured a cup of coffee out of the electric drip pot and stuck the cup in the microwave for twenty seconds. He followed me in, saw what I was doing and screwed up his face.

"The coffee's hot, Parker. Just made it."

"Those damned drip pots never get it hot enough for me. On days like this I need steam coming off the cup."

I took a sip from the almost boiling coffee, raised the cup and toasted the gar head hanging from the ceiling, wondering if my good buddy was as cold as I was. I thought about wrapping it with a towel.

After the toast I looked at Neddie and said, "So what's the occasion, you coming here at the crack of dawn, standing around, freezing your tits off?"

Neddie pushed the morning paper across the counter top. The headline said: "Cat Fight at San Luis Pass." The accompanying photo showed Neddie standing in the middle between opposing sides as if doing his best to hold them back. I was not in the picture, which told me my little intimidation act with the photographer must have worked. Freedom of the press or not.

I quickly perused the story and said, "How does it feel to be a hero, Neddie, diffusing the showdown?"

"Hell, Parker. I should have let them fight it out. Maybe the cat folks would have won and I'd still have my furry friends under the bridge."

I pulled some bacon out of the refrigerator and had it half cooked when the wall phone rang.

"Garhole."

"Parker, you need a cell phone class. First you don't know how to set up voicemail so I can't leave a message. And now my call went straight to voice mail which you haven't set up which means your battery's down. Cell phones do need to be charged occasionally. They even make chargers for your car."

I recognized Matthews' voice.

"How does that work?"

"You plug it into the cigarette lighter."

"Hell, Maurice, the lighter in my heap hasn't worked in years."

An exasperated sigh came through the phone.

"No need to come to the morgue," he said, his voice sounding tired. "Galveston PD ran the prints on our boy last night. Turns out he was a pusher. Had a suitcase full of everything from dime bags of weed to powder and rock cocaine. A regular cafeteria. Name is Arnie Sledge. He has a sheet as long as a porn star's Johnson. He's only been out of the Huntsville pen for six months. Houston PD had a BOLO out on him as a suspect in a drug deal gone bad. We think he was shifting to Galveston."

"Well, I guess that's bad news for us but good news for Galveston PD."

"How's that?"

"At least Chief Puryear can cover his ass," I said. "The suspect could have been an out-of-town salesman on a low budget for all we knew. Now the chief can tout taking out a bad guy."

"Lucky him," Matthews said. "If the SWAT commander Koska would have listened to me, we could have taken Sledge alive. Maybe turned him and gone up the distribution chain. Now he has nothing but a dead middle man."

"Not your problem," I said.

"We're getting tons of calls from the TV exposure last night and the papers this morning. Seems like everyone has a terrorist in their neighborhood."

"Any good ones specific to Galveston?"

"I'll keep you posted. If we get a hot one, you're going to have to act quick. Charge your damned cell phone."

When Matthews rang off, I hung up the receiver and finished cooking the bacon. I stuck the strips between slices of toasted bread, added mayonnaise and handed one of the sandwiches to Neddie. We ate in silence and then he left for his shift at the bridge. I stepped outside and saw that the wind was still puffing hard and with the bay muddied, I doubted I'd have any customers. Then I thought, maybe Neddie was right about getting some heat in the bar. I looked at the far wall beyond the tables and visualized putting in a brick fireplace. I imagined several old-timers sitting around a roaring fire, eating gumbo, drinking beer and telling sea-stories. Something to think about.

Neddie had said he'd drop by The Garhole after his shift was over and hang around for a while in case a customer dropped by. We both knew that probably wouldn't happen, but it was only going to cost me the few beers he'd drink, so it was worth a try. I checked my watch and decided to call Kathy, hoping she was an early riser.

Chapter Twenty-Four

Thursday morning
Galveston

David awoke early with a pounding headache. What a crazy night. Anna Lang almost got both of them shot. And who were those crazy wheelchair-bound nuts anyway? All David had wanted was an opportunity to get closer to Anna, work his way into a night of torrid sex and learn more about the lab. Instead, when they'd returned to Galveston, she was still so aggravated from her encounter with her grandfather and the old woman, she'd stormed off to her apartment in a huff.

And now he was kicking himself for overdoing the booze, going back and closing the Tremont bar. He had important things happening today and needed a clear head. He showered and went down for breakfast too hungover to worry about the morning prayer. All during the meal he kept checking his burner phone for a message. Nothing. He left the café, picked up a copy of USA Today and moved to one of the big, comfortable chairs in the lobby. He had just finished the financial section when a text appeared on his burner phone.

"Slip 169, Galveston Yacht Basin. Now."

There was no need to respond. David went back to his room, got his jacket and called for his car. Once in his car, he googled the address and punched the location into the GPS system. Five minutes.

As David drove down Harborside toward the yacht basin, he noticed police vehicles blocking the entrance street to the hospital. He passed the hospital and turned left onto Holiday Drive toward the yacht basin. He drove past the empty guard shack and entered the complex. Good, he thought. The hospital was still locked down but the yacht basin was wide open, easy to come and go without anyone checking his credentials.

A large sign pointed to a marina and restaurant. Now he understood. It would be difficult to have a guard at the entrance with so much daily traffic open to the public. Ahead were several long, covered sheds running perpendicular to the parking area. Each shed contained at least a hundred boat slips, fifty on each side. In all, over three hundred yacht, millions of dollars tied up and floating empty.

David cruised slowly, checking the numbers painted at the end of each shed. He stopped at the last shed, parked and walked down the middle pier. A yacht floated in every slip, few of them under forty feet in length.

David didn't know much about boats, but he knew money when he saw it. Yachts with brand names like Sea Ray, Hydra-Sports and Boston Whaler. He remembered seeing the same names when his wealthy lawyer friend invited him up for a cruise on Lake Michigan. His friend kept his fifty-foot Hatteras at the Belmont Marina in the shadow of downtown Chicago. He had told David he'd gotten a super bargain, buying the ten-year-old yacht from a down-and-out bond salesman for a mere $400,000.

When he reached Slip 169, David wondered who owned the yacht and where the money had come from. His brother Rashad? The boat wasn't one of the largest or newest among the yachts in the basin, but he remembered the name Bertram from the marina in Chicago.

David's Chicago friend had told him yachts were of two types: fishing or pleasure. The pleasure yachts were normally larger and more opulent. The fishing boats usually had a large open deck on the stern with chairs mounted outward, where the occupant could match strengths with swordfish and marlin. Tall outrigger poles used to keep the lines untangled during trawling were mounted on either side of the stern. The yacht in Slip 169 was definitely a fishing boat, the wide open stern complete with captain's chairs and outriggers. David judged the boat's length at around thirty-five feet. He walked along the side pier next to the boat, noticing the windows were covered with blinds. He reached a spot even with the end of the cabin and saw no activity. He leaned over and was about to rap on the fiberglass cabin top when the door opened. A man, fiftyish, clean shaven with short-cropped black hair, stood just inside the door frame as though he didn't want to be seen.

David took the man's nod as permission to go aboard. He grabbed the aluminum railing at the top of the cabin, put one foot on the gunnel and swung onto the back deck. The man retreated inside and leaned against a small table next to the bulkhead. Another man, a little older, sat at the captain's console. He had Albert Einstein hair, gray and frizzy, almost as if it had been teased. He was a small man, five six or seven, medium dark, with a long thin face and thin arms. A nine-millimeter automatic sat on the shelf beside him.

The Einstein man said, "Do you know who I am?"

David shook his head.

"My face will be all over the news by tonight."

"Why?" David asked. He had no idea who the man was or what his brother Rashad had planned. His communication with Rashad had been terse and vague for safety reasons.

"The FBI is looking for me. My name is Hamid Turani. I am

a professor at Louisiana Western University in Lafayette, Louisiana. I stole a vial of anthrax out of the university's lab."

David felt a spasm of relief that Rashad had created his own plan using a deadly pathogen to kill Perry. Now he didn't have to worry about using Anna Lang. And more importantly, he didn't have to be personally involved. Perfect, he thought. He had no idea what his brother had cooked up with Turani and he didn't give a damn.

Turani nodded toward the man standing beside him and said, "This is Hussein. We left Lake Charles at midnight so we could transit the Intracoastal Canal in the dark. For six hours we saw nothing but tugs pushing barges."

"Nice boat," David said, because he didn't know what else to say. David was continually amazed at his brother's resourcefulness. Where did he find these people and how did he motivate them?

"Fishing boats don't attract attention," Hussein said. "Look around, this is but one of many moored here. Our escape will be much less conspicuous."

"Our escape?" David asked. "What are you talking about?"

"You are to meet Rashad in Argentina."

David recoiled, a sudden chill crossed his shoulders. What was this? Rashad had said nothing about leaving Yemen, much less traveling to South America. Great, he thought, just what he needed—more conflicting emotions churning his stomach. He had a great reverence for his father and brother as proven by his trip to Yemen and involvement in the plot. But he also had a life at home, a successful business, fast cars and beautiful women.

"Why Argentina?" David asked.

"Your brother is very practical," Turani continued. "It's the perfect escape path. Fugitives from all over the world have been hiding in Argentina for years without detection."

Escape? David was even more confused. Why would Rashad need to escape? And more importantly, why would he have to join him? David didn't like where this was going.

"How do I get there?"

Turani shrugged again. "Why do you think we came in a boat?"

Hussein gestured to a nautical chart on the table. David could see that a red line had been drawn in from Galveston to Panama.

"The route is roughly 2300 nautical miles and should take five to seven days." Hussein explained. "It would be shorter and quicker to cut across the Gulf straight to the Yucatan Peninsula, but we couldn't make it without refueling. The tank holds 495 gallons and burning twenty-seven gallons per hour only gives us a range of about 450 miles.

"The closest Mexican port is Altamira, 521 miles from Galveston. We'll have to refuel in Port Isabel or Brownsville, risky but necessary. After that, we'll hug the Mexican coast then cut around the Yucatan and skirt the coast of Central America: Belize, Honduras, Nicaragua, Costa Rica and finally Panama. We'll refuel four or five more times along the way."

"I have no passport for those stops," David said.

Hussein glanced at Hamid and then back to David. "You won't need one," he said.

David felt a slight tremble in his lips and a knot forming in his stomach. It was obvious Rashad had devised the entire plan without consulting him. Who were these guys?

"When we arrive at our last stop in Colon, you will receive a Panamanian passport which will allow you to fly to Argentina."

David had listened with rapt attention, nodding as Hussein and Turani outlined his future. He needed time to think. He turned to a window and pulled the blinds back to peek out. A large yacht moved out toward the Galveston Ship Channel. David knew it was a short hop from the channel to the jetties and the Gulf of Mexico.

Except that was never part of his plan. When he had received the text from Turani this morning, he thought all was good. He had given Rashad the idea for using a lethal pathogen to kill Perry. His brother had fine-tuned the plan to the point of obtaining anthrax and even getting it to Galveston. Rashad must have also calculated a way to sneak it into the hospital. And now with Turani and Hussein here, none of the rest of the plan should involve him. So why the new passport and why would Rashad need him in Argentina after Turani and his henchman, Hussein finished off Perry?

Whatever the reason, David didn't like it. So far, he had carefully positioned himself as an engineer from Indianapolis attending a seminar on offshore oil rigs. There was no way the authorities could connect him to any of this. He was a legitimate businessman on a legitimate business trip.

"What is your connection to Rashad?" David asked, with urgency to his tone. "And don't shrug off your answer. If you want my cooperation, I need to know more."

Turani and Hussein locked eyes as if trying to decide how to proceed.

"There is much you do not need to know," Turani said. "We only need a little help from you."

"Like what?"

"Simple. To drive me to a meeting with the contact and return here."

"Contact? What contact?"

"Our man in the hospital. How did you think we were going to get the anthrax in?"

David felt a nervous twitch going down his arm into his hand. This wasn't good, he thought. They not only wanted to use his car, they wanted him to drive. And if Turani was all over the news, taking him anywhere would involve risk. He started to ask why they simply didn't have the contact meet them at the yacht basin, but then he realized they didn't want the contact to know about the boat. It was obvious Turani and Hussein's plan was to keep everything on a need-to-know basis.

"If the authorities are looking for you, why not let Hussein meet the contact?"

"Because I am the scientist, not Hussein. I need to be certain our man knows exactly what to do with the anthrax."

The use of his vehicle was David's first real connection to either of the two plots to assassinate Perry. He didn't have anything to do with the explosion at the Coast Guard base, and he'd hoped to stay in the shadows on the next attempt. But they needed a car and driver. Not good.

Turani was a respected professor at a distinguished American university. Yet he'd thrown away everything he'd worked for because of a hurried contact from Rashad citing a desperate plea for help. Why? Since Turani wasn't part of his family, his motivation couldn't be personal.

"Using my vehicle puts me at risk," David said. "And your escape plan to Panama makes me nervous. I need more information—your background, your motivation."

Hussein broke in, "Motivation?" he shouted. His voice blew so loudly it seemed to bounce off the bulkhead walls and reverberate around the small cabin. "These people are godless infidels. Isn't that enough? The Americans murder our brothers all over the world. This man Perry is one of their leaders. The last attempt failed. This one will not."

His face flushed with anger, his mouth frothing, Hussein slammed the top of the navigation table and turned away.

Turani spoke softly. "Hussein and I met at a mosque in

Lafayette. We realized we shared the same hatred for the Jews and their American lackeys. Several years ago during a visit to Mecca, we met Rashad and your father Nassim. When we learned Nassim was a leader of Hezbollah, dedicated to Israel's destruction, we pledged our lives to his service and to Allah's. We were told to wait quietly at our jobs in America until we were needed."

Hussein turned back. "For years we waited patiently for a chance to serve. We were able to help in our own way by raising millions of dollars for Hezbollah. And now, finally, we have an opportunity to wage jihad to avenge Nassim's murder. The Quran says whatever good there is exists because of the power of the sword. We will not fail. Paradise can be opened only for holy warriors."

"Millions," David said. "How have you raised millions?"

"Our friends in Mexico," Hussein said.

"Jihadists?" David said, skeptical that there were that many rich Muslins in Mexico who wanted to spend their money on the cause.

Hussein slowly shook his head. "Cartels."

"They give you money?"

"The cartel bosses may be drug dealers but they are also capitalists. They give us nothing. We make deliveries for them, and they pay us handsomely. Where do you think we got the money for this boat? As we all know, the Americans' taste for drugs is insatiable."

David had no idea which drug cartel Hussein was working with, and he didn't care. They were all the same—ruthless. He saw everything clearly now. He was sure every refueling stop along the entire route from Mexico to Panama had been selected because the local customs officials were on the cartel's payroll. The cartel was probably even providing his new passport. He realized the boat trip would end in Panama because that was where the Mexican cartel's control probably ended.

The cost to provide these conveniences had to be high. Everything was always about money, and whatever Turani and Hussein couldn't provide, there was no doubt Rashad had stepped in. It was becoming more and more obvious to David that his brother had an unlimited supply of funds.

"Rashad only contacted you two days ago," David said, wanting more information. "How could you have a source in the hospital this quickly?"

Turani shrugged.

Of course, David thought: the cartel again. Was there anywhere their tentacles didn't reach? Then he remembered what the police officer at the hospital had said about security. No visitors allowed other than close family members of the patients. Had the cartel gotten to a patient's family member? And if so, how would the suspect get the anthrax into the burn unit. He was sure everyone entering the burn unit would be thoroughly vetted and checked by the myriad of Secret Service agents hovering around Perry.

He considered what he'd read about the pathogens contained in Anna's lab. A person could contract anthrax by several methods, the most damaging of which was inhalation. To keep the rooms sterile, the burn unit utilized a separate air conditioning system. David realized then the contact wasn't a visitor. He was a worker. He was sure of it.

"The cartel has gotten to an employee," David said.

Turani shrugged again.

"Maintenance?"

Turani didn't answer. His condescending smirk made David want to chop his neck.

"You'll see tomorrow," Turani said.

"I want to see the anthrax," David said, an unequivocal

tone to his voice.

Turani scrunched his face. "Not necessary," he answered.

"If you want my help it is."

Turani frowned, nodded to Hussein. Hussein went below and returned with a small container wrapped in a white cloth. Hussein carefully removed the cloth revealing an amber colored vial about two inches long.

David reached for the vial, but Hussein quickly pulled it away.

"Don't touch," Hussein said. "It will stick to your fingers. We keep it in the freezer below."

"It's called a cryovial," Turani said. "Used to protect the anthrax spores for further testing. The spores are mixed with a sterile growth media and kept frozen."

"Growth media?"

"It's a manufactured substance with nutrients necessary to aid in cell production. Helps the anthrax stay alive."

Hussein rewrapped the vial and took it below.

Turani said, "Pick me up here at five in the morning. And don't be late. Everything is planned on a tight schedule. It is imperative you be on time."

Chapter Twenty-Five

Thursday morning
The Garhole Bar

"Kathy," it's me, Parker. Hope I didn't wake you."

"You kidding? I'm a nurse. We're up with the chickens."

"Sorry about last night, having to leave and all."

"I heard about the shoot-out on the TV this morning. They didn't say who the man was."

"Drug dealer. Nothing to do with terrorists. I could have spent the night wrapped up with you."

"Well, it's not too late," she said. "I've got the three o'clock shift today. I need a break. How about a cold beer at The Garhole? Got anything you can whip up for lunch?"

"Absolutely," I said. "Can't wait to see you."

She said she'd be out in an hour. I raced up the stairs, changed the bed linens, and hurried back down to the kitchen. I melted butter in an iron pot, chopped and sautéed onions, celery and a green pepper, then added a can of tomatoes, some crushed garlic and red pepper. I'd add a couple pounds of shrimp when Kathy arrived. I cooked some rice, put it aside and got out a frozen loaf of French bread.

I heard an approaching vehicle and turned to see a pickup I didn't recognize pulling up in front. Kathy shouldn't show for another thirty minutes, so I had time to deal with whoever it was and hope I could get rid of them before she got here.

Tube Jones got out of the driver's side dressed in jeans and a heavy sweatshirt against the chill breeze. A lanky kid with crew-cut blond hair stepped out from the passenger side wearing a Ball High letter jacket. I'd forgotten I'd told Tube to bring his boy out, but there wasn't anything I could do about it now. Tube came in first, his son lagging behind.

"Hey, Parker. Meet my son Travis."

The boy stepped forward and offered his hand. "Heard a lot about you, Mr. McLeod. Thank you for helping me."

The kid was clean cut, with expressive blue eyes and a strong chin. His ears stuck out like Clark Gable's. It didn't seem to affect Gable's standing with the female movie goers, and I suspected it wouldn't bother young Travis' coming legions of hormone-driven teeny boppers either. High school would be fun if you looked like this kid.

Tube said, "Chief Puryear's got us all in panic mode. The whole force is working extra shifts, driving around with a copy of the drawing of the bomber suspect and a photo of the missing professor. I didn't know when I would get another chance to come out here and Travis has been bugging the hell out of me. I gotta work this afternoon and I took the early shift tomorrow for some overtime. I figured with the bay messed up, The Garhole wouldn't be busy, so I pulled Travis out of school for a couple of hours. Hope it's okay."

Tube obviously didn't know about my involvement in the search, and there was no reason to tell him. With Kathy due any minute, their timing was horrible, but seeing the anticipation in Travis' eyes made me step up.

"So you wanna be a quarterback?" I said to the kid.

"Yes sir," he said, showing me the patches on his jacket. "I'm playing baseball and basketball too, trying to letter in three sports. My senior year I want to make it in football. I'm hoping to grow another inch or two. Guess you gotta be pretty tall now."

Travis was thin but well defined, already six feet. His big feet told me he had more to go.

"Let me see your hands," I said.

Travis pushed his hands out and I placed my palm into his. At sixteen, the kid's hand was larger than mine, a good sign for a ball player. Smaller hands had been one of my downsides as a quarterback. Makes it difficult to run and hold onto the ball while scrambling to find a receiver.

"You've got good hands and you're growing," I said. "You'll be fine."

Travis grinned and got a football out of the truck. We tossed a few, and the wobble in his throws told me he was palming the ball. I motioned him up to me.

"First, let's talk about how to hold the ball. The best way to throw a spiral is to place the ring and pinkie fingers of your throwing hand in between the laces, and your thumb underneath them, on the other side of the ball. Arch your knuckles slightly off the ball and hold it with the pads of your fingertips. Don't palm it. Then spin the ball with the release."

I positioned his hand where I wanted it, then told him to back off and throw some more. We stopped after a few tosses so I could show him how to position his arm and shift his weight into the throw.

Tube stood quietly off to the side, beaming with pride at his lanky, awkward son. Tube and I had worked hand and glove our senior year, with Tube snaking his way through the defense, always seeming to find an open spot to catch my throw. Ball High made it to the playoffs that year. Just a bunch of kids who'd grown up together on the beaches of Galveston.

After a few tosses to me, I got Travis to throw to his dad. Soon Tube was running like in the old days, faking and shifting as though he was on the gridiron of Ball High, Travis hitting him with good passes.

I didn't remember Tube's wife Sheryl who was a couple of years behind us in school. But I wanted to meet her. She'd raised a fine, well-mannered boy and seemingly kept Tube in line while doing it. I wanted to see them together, interacting, see what a real marriage was like. I thought about my own and wondered where I'd screwed up. One thing I knew for sure, living alone sucked.

It was then that Kathy's Mustang hatchback rolled down the sand lane. She stopped beside Tube's truck and got out with a big smile, wearing sneakers and a fuzzy orange pullover. She'd pulled her hair back and topped it with a Houston Astros baseball cap.

"Didn't know you were an Astros fan?"

She came close and whispered in my ear, "Lots of things you don't know about me, Parker McLeod."

Tube's eyes hadn't left Kathy since she'd gotten out of the truck. I knew what he was thinking. I made introductions all around and explained why Tube and his son had come out to The Garhole. Tube got the hint.

"Thanks, Parker," he said, winking. "I gotta get Travis back to school. He's played hooky long enough."

I put my arm around the boy's shoulder and walked him to the truck. Told him to work hard and he'd make a fine quarterback. Tube gave me a firm hug and whispered something like good luck in my ear. As they drove up the sand lane, Travis turned in the seat and waved back at us.

Inside the bar, Kathy slid onto a barstool while I heated the creole and dropped in the shrimp. I opened a Shiner and passed it across the counter. She toasted the gar head and took a sip.

"Something smells good," she said.

"Shrimp creole," I said, stirring the pot. "Nice hot dish on a chilly day."

"It didn't feel like you needed anything to warm you up," she said, referring to my hug. She flashed a sexy grin.

When I turned to stir the creole, she said, "Looks as if my drawing got an innocent man killed last night."

I turned and put my hand on hers. "Kathy, look at me. Don't take this on. He wasn't innocent. A drug dealer moving into Galveston? Good riddance. Think about the innocent kids his poison might have reached."

"I know," she said. "I see enough death at the hospital. This time I felt responsible."

I turned back and stirred the pot again, not knowing what else to say. I dished up two bowls of creole, added toasted French bread from the oven and a couple more beers. We moved to a table.

"This is sooo good," Kathy said, finishing a spoonful. "Where did you learn to cook?"

"Mostly piddling around here."

"Neddie showed me your garden. You do anything in the winter?"

"Not really. Mostly summer veggies for the creole and gumbo: onions, tomatoes. Okra likes a really hot summer, which isn't hard to find around here. I grow a lot of it, chop and freeze it." We chatted like that until we finished eating. Kathy got up and went to the back door, the cool breeze hitting her face. She crossed her arms trying to warm herself.

She looked back at me, "You need more heat."

"I've got a blanket upstairs."

Kathy's wry grin was all I needed. I put my arm around her and we climbed the stairs. We fell onto the bed fully clothed. I fumbled with her jeans while she raised my sweatshirt over my head. We went at it like a couple of twenty-year-olds in a dorm room. Afterwards, warm and toasty, and temporarily satisfied, we snuggled under the blanket.

Kathy kissed me on the cheek and put her hand on my chest. She snuggled close to my ear.

"I'm so glad Agent Matthews called me to do the drawing."

"Me too," I said.

"Tell me about you and The Garhole, this land you own, the whole story."

"Well, it goes back a ways. My grandfather bought this ranch during the depression when property out here was cheap. The land was poor, just a bunch of salt grass probably not worth what he paid for it. But he made it work."

"He must have been special to you."

"I spent summers out here helping him work the cattle. After he died, my mother inherited the ranch. She wanted to sell, but I begged her not to. When I was in high school, I talked her into building a bait camp out here. You're in it now. I lived up here and slopped bait early and after school. Mother lived in town. Didn't really see her much."

I could have told Kathy a lot more. About my mother, drunk in a Galveston bar, getting knocked up by the captain of a visiting freighter and producing me nine months later. I could have told her how she continued to shack up with him each time he came to port here, until she found out he had a wife and kids in Denmark. I hated him so much I took my grandfather's name as soon as I was old enough to do it. Maybe that part of the story would all come later. Maybe.

Kathy snuggled closer. "Thanks for sharing about your grandfather and mother, Parker. Put that together with what you told me about your high school sweetheart, and I can see you've had your struggles."

"Oh, I don't know…. My life hasn't been any tougher than a lot of folks. Everyone has their own sack of rocks to carry. But I love this land. It's nothing but weeds really, but I love it."

"Or maybe it's something besides the land," Kathy said.

I scrunched my forehead.

"Memories?" she said.

"Well, maybe. But I'm beginning to realize I can't live here forever. There has to be more to life than cooking gumbo and listening to fishing stories. It was good for me, coming back from the horror of the war. I needed time to adjust. But I'm past that now and...."

Kathy buried her head in my cheek. I felt the warmth from her body flowing into mine.

"You're right, Parker McLeod. There is more," she whispered. "Sounds like you've figured that out."

She kissed me again, long and soft. I caught the flower in her perfume and the scent of her body.

"Yeah...I think I'm beginning to," I said, and buried my face into her neck. We kissed again and I rolled her over on her back. After we finished and cuddled for a while, Kathy looked at her watch and let out a shriek.

"Oh, my God, I'm going to be late for work."

We dressed quickly and scrambled down the stairs, giggling like teenagers who'd just done the forbidden deed. We hugged again and I tucked her into her Mustang. As she drove away, I felt an unsettling mixture of satisfaction and emptiness at the same time. I didn't know where this relationship was going, but I welcomed every moment of it.

Back in the bar, I found a message on my cell phone. I hit the Call Back button.

"We've got new info," Matthews said, his voice a mixture of excitement and anticipation. "We're meeting at Harry's in an hour."

I knew Neddie would be here soon, so I left the cigar box on the counter with a note for payment if anyone showed and headed into the city.

I wondered if Matthews' new information was about the missing professor and anthrax or something new concerning the café bomber. The professor's photo and Kathy's drawing of the bomber were all over the internet and television. Plus, according to Tube, every police officer in Galveston had the photo and drawing plastered to their vehicle dashboards.

During the drive in, I decided to check in with Jenny Hillbro, see if she'd gotten a DNA report back on the hair samples. Luckily, I had powered up my phone and actually remembered to take it with me. No doubt the new me was making progress: the Renaissance Man of West Beach.

Jenny answered on the first ring.

"Parker, glad you called."

"Hey gal, anything for me yet?"

"Just got off the phone with my friend at the lab. Bad news I'm afraid."

"So the two hair specimens I gave you don't match up?"

"Seems as if this DNA profiling is more complicated than I'd thought," she said.

"How is that?"

"You didn't get enough of the hair."

"What?"

"According to my friend, there are two types of DNA, mitochondrial and nuclear. Nuclear is what law enforcement uses for a provable DNA match. The problem is nuclear is found in the root and mitochondrial in the shaft. Sometimes scientists can isolate a small amount of Mitochondrial DNA from the shaft, but in this instance they couldn't."

"So I needed the root?"

"It's called the follicle and appears as a small gray-white ball at the tip of the shaft. How did you get the woman's sample?"

"From her hair brush."

"Hmmm....That's unusual. When a woman brushes her hair, most of the follicles are usually attached to the strands that come out."

I shrugged. "Maybe I just got unlucky and grabbed the wrong ones."

"What about the male hairs?"

"I guess I'll just have to hold Bully down and yank some out. That won't be fun."

"This is Bully Stout we're talking about, your uncle?"

"Yeah, but keep it to yourself. I'll explain later."

"You really get into some weird shit, Parker."

"Tell me about it."

"Anything Joe and I can do to help?"

"Thanks, but I'm gonna have to sort out this can of worms by myself."

It was easy to say that to Jenny, as if I had a plan, knew what I was doing. But in truth, I had put all my eggs into the DNA basket and that basket had come up empty.

But then, a sudden thought: although the first DNA attempt had failed, I now knew what to do. I would just tell Anna I needed a hair sample with a root ball attached. She was a scientist; she'd know about DNA. And I would do the same thing with Bully, just ask him directly. I could tell Bully the DNA comparison would prove Anna wasn't his granddaughter and get her off his back.

While I was thinking all of this, Jenny said, "Okay, if that's want you want, Parker. Call if you need me."

"Thanks, Jenny."

"Oh, and by the way, Joe went fishing with a friend and caught a mess of trout. We're gonna have some folks over for a fry. Want to come?"

"Was he wade fishing?"

"No, in a boat."

"Joe loves to wade fish."

"Maybe he did. But he's afraid spending that much time in salt water would rust his implants. He'd have to have new ones and the procedure might not work the next time."

"Does titanium rust?"

"Who knows?" she said.

"So when is the fry?"

"Saturday."

"Can I bring a friend?"

"Holy cow, Parker. Is Clementine Garza back in town?"

I didn't respond.

"Oh boy, Parker. You've got a new girlfriend. Wait 'til I tell Joe."

Chapter Twenty-Six

Thursday afternoon
Galveston

Galveston had just experienced the worst attack on American soil since 9/11, a horrific bombing that killed fifteen people and wounded ten more. With photos of two suspects all over the media, I couldn't blame the police department for hitting the panic button. It appeared that Chief Puryear had called in help from all over the state. On my way to Harry Stein's house, I passed a dozen or more police vehicles in an area where I might not normally have seen any. Along with Galveston PD, I spied Texas Department of Public Safety officers, several Galveston County Sheriff's vehicles, Justice of the Peace constables and even Texas Rangers.

The wind had quit and the warming sun usually brought people out for morning walks, but because the photos and drawings of the suspects inundated the TV and internet, the seawall sidewalk was almost void of activity. Restaurants appeared close to empty. The tourist trade was definitely at low ebb, with many more open parking spaces along the boulevard than normal.

I rolled slowly down Harry's street, noting two black SUVs parked in front of his house. The FBI vehicles were sandwiched in by a couple of nondescript cars I hadn't seen before. I parked at the curb several cars down from his house.

I hustled to the porch, rapped quickly on the door and went in, not waiting for an acknowledgement. Hebinck greeted me as I entered the kitchen, a smidgeon of blueberry muffin on his lips.

Standing around the counter drinking coffee and eating Harry's fresh baked pastries were Agent Matthews, General Roush, Special Officer Erwin and Chief Puryear with Galveston PD.

Wearing jeans and a light jacket without his gold stars and braided hat, it appeared Puryear was trying to appear incognito. It also appeared he'd left Colonel Bubbie behind. So far, we'd avoided the maze of reporters in town from learning about our meetings at Harry's. Harry didn't allow pets in his house and Colonel Bubbie hanging around outside with the chief's driver would surely have attracted attention. The last thing we needed was a mass of TV trucks parked along the street and reporters hanging around. Of course, the two black SUVs at the curb didn't help, but so far our meeting place had escaped inquisitive eyes.

This was Puryear's first visit to the inner sanctum. I wondered if Hebinck had invited him or if he had learned of our little soirées while snooping around and invited himself. Either way, I was glad he was here. With the safety of the city hanging on his shoulders, he was a hell of a lot more important than me. Plus, rubbing up to him a bit might give me a little insulation against my next speeding ticket.

I nodded to each person in turn and stopped at a face I hadn't seen before. He was a tall, big-chested man with coal black hair and eyes to match. He had a ruddy complexion underneath a heavy beard that covered most of his face.

"Parker, meet Peter Kay," Matthews said. "Pete's the CIA station chief in Jordan. He flew in today with some urgent information."

After Kay and I shook hands, I poured a cup of coffee and grabbed half a banana muffin someone had left on the plate of goodies. We moved to the kitchen table.

Hebinck looked at Kay. "You must be worn out," he said.

Kay took a deep breath and blew it out. "Eighteen hours nonstop from Amman to Ellington. We refueled in the air over the Atlantic. I got a few winks on the plane."

"Well, we're all nervous as hell here," Hebinck said. "Fill us in on what you've got."

"All right," he said. "I'll cut to the chase. The Zahir family has employed a long-time chef and general servant whose name is Badih Khoury. Khoury worked for the family's patriarch Nassim Zahir for many years. He traveled with Nassim and generally looked after his needs as well as managing the household. We know Khoury wasn't in the villa at the time of the drone strike that killed Nassim, but he was either close by or on an errand. Since we think Nassim's son Rashad survived the attack, it makes sense that Khoury now works for him."

Kay stopped and sipped his coffee. The only sound was the quiet hum of Harry's heating unit clicking on. I wondered where they'd shuffled Harry off to this time. Another meeting with the historical foundation? Or was he across the street with June, one of the casserole women?

Kay cleared his throat and continued in the same flat voice. "The servant Khoury has a sister who works as a nurse and lives in Beirut. Mossad has a tap on her phone. They heard nothing of importance until yesterday.

"According to our Israeli friends, the sister received a call from Khoury and they spoke for an hour, catching up on family gossip. The sister never asked Khoury's whereabouts, and he didn't volunteer anything. The long phone call gave Mossad time to track his location. The call came from a villa in Yemen located close to the Gulf of Aden."

"More confirmation about Yemen," Hebinck said. "We're on the right track."

Kay removed several photos from his briefcase and passed them around the table. "These are satellite photos of the villa taken this morning. We're pretty sure Rashad Zahir is in that villa but we haven't verified it."

Matthews broke in. "How do you know Khoury is working for Rashad? Could be a new employer? Have you researched the villa's current owner?"

"Of course," Kay said, frowning at the interruption. "The villa has been owned for a long time by a rich sheik who fled the country when all the sectarian strife started a few years back. He now lives in Qatar with his family, enjoying clean water and vacations in Paris. He rents the villa out. According to our asset in Qatar, the current occupant moved in close to a year ago."

"The timeline fits," Hebinck said. "Whose name is on the lease?"

"A dummy corporation in Lebanon that we're checking for ties to Rashad."

"The link to Lebanon strengthens the case," Matthews said. "Rashad's father Nassim was a professor at the American University in Beirut."

Roush added, "Why not send in a local Yemeni asset to verify the occupants? Maybe get a photo? The strike that killed Rashad's father also killed his thirteen-year-old sister. Lord knows we don't need another mistake like that."

Kay shook his head. "HUMINT is not reliable," he said. "Every other person in Yemen is a spy for someone. It depends on who pays the most. Right now we don't have a trusted asset. If we send in the wrong person and he tips Rashad, our target could disappear before we know it."

When Kay said that, I knew what was coming and wondered if the merry-go-round would ever end. The jihadists murder innocent civilians around the world in the name of religion. We retaliate and kill them with indiscriminate air strikes. Damn.

"So what's your plan?" Hebinck asked.

Kay looked at Hebinck but didn't say anything. I could feel the tension around the table building. Everyone knew what was coming.

Finally, Kay said, "We'll reposition more satellites, get twenty-four-hour coverage and hope we can catch the occupant out in the sunshine. The only other option is to send a drone into the villa and hope for the best."

Bingo! There it was—another drone strike. I couldn't help myself and said, "Do we know there are no children in this villa?"

"We don't," Kay said. "All we know is that neither Rashad Zahir nor his servant is married. We'll do the best we can."

Matthews spoke. "If we can place Rashad in Yemen, it means we at least have eyes on one of the suspects we're tracking."

"Yes. But remember," I said. "Rashad wasn't here when the bomb went off either. That didn't stop him from recruiting that bunch of losers in Minnesota. All it takes is money and he seems to have plenty of that. The question is: If you take out Rashad, will that stop whatever new plan he's come up with? If a new assassin is headed this way, will he quit?"

Matthews looked at the CIA agent. "You know jihadists, Pete. What do you think?"

Kay rubbed his beard as if contemplating the question. He said, "Assuming there is another assailant on the way, the fundamental question is: Is he a dedicated jihadist or a paid assassin?"

"Why is that distinction important?" Puryear asked.

Kay said, "If he is a paid assassin and Rashad is dead, there's a chance he may not continue with the plot. But if he's a dedicated jihadist, well...."

"Which brings this Professor Turani to mind," Hebinck added, his face a mass of wrinkled frowns. "We don't know for sure if this Professor Turani character is headed this way with the missing anthrax. But if so, we can ask the same question: jihadist or professional assassin?"

"Jihadist," Kay said. "Turani had a good-paying job as department head at a high-ranking university. I'm sure he was tenured with a guaranteed income. He was set. Another thing: Turani has to know the FBI is looking for him. He also has to know there is a good chance he won't survive, successful or not."

"Sounds right," Matthews agreed. "So if Turani is a dedicated jihadist, killing Rashad might fire Turani up even more. He'd have a martyr to honor and more incentive to sacrifice himself for the cause. The jihadists are big on that forty virgins in Paradise bullshit."

"On the other hand," I said, "If it's not Turani, and Rashad has sent a paid assassin, it won't be anyone we know about until the attempt is made."

"That's just great," Puryear said.

The table went silent, everyone thinking about what had been kicked around. A lot of heavy sighs, worried frowns and tired faces. The bagged eyes around the table meant sleep was in short supply. I took the opportunity to wolf down the banana muffin and got up to refresh my coffee. Before I could get back, the conversation had started again.

"And we can't totally discount the idea of another bomber," Roush said.

"That'll scare your jockstrap off, just thinking about it," I said, retaking my seat.

"Well," Roush added, "to borrow from what Donald Rumsfeld said after 9/11, 'The problem is that we don't know what we don't know.'"

Chief Puryear stood up. "I need to get back to the station. My officers are worn out working double shifts. We can only go a couple more days like this. We're gonna have to find these sons of bitches."

After Puryear left I turned to Erwin and asked for an update on Perry's condition.

"Still critical," Erwin said, breaking her silence at the table. "I don't think they'll be moving him for a while."

Hebinck looked at Roush. "Anything new from the NSA?"

Roush sighed heavily and shook his head. "We still haven't broken the encrypted emails."

"For God's sake, keep trying," Matthews said. "We're running out of options here."

Hebinck announced we would meet twice daily beginning tomorrow morning. Roush and Kay agreed to stay with the group until the crisis was over. I felt as though I'd contributed all I could and considered bowing out, except that being this close to the action revived my old Army Intel instincts. It looked as if I might have to hire Neddie Lemmon full-time to run the bar, which meant I'd have to order more beer.

When the meeting broke up, I decided to hang around and wait for Harry to return. I checked his refrigerator and munched through a couple pieces of cold fried chicken washed down with a cold Shiner. A picture of Kathy's lithe, naked body curled beneath my sheets flittered across my mind. I found her name among the three or four people in my contact list and punched the phone number.

"Hi, Parker."

"Hey, Kathy. Just wanted to hear your sweet voice."

"Well, not for long. I'm working intensive care until eleven tonight, remember?"

"Oh, that's right. What about tomorrow?"

"Early shift seven to three, intensive care again. Sorry."

"Get some rest," I said. "Dinner tomorrow night, somewhere in the city."

"Sounds good," she said. "It'll give me a chance for a nap tomorrow afternoon."

"Need some company with that?"

"I'm an old woman," she said. "Don't wear me out."

I hung up thinking how tired I was. Time for The Garhole and a nap. I had just pulled away from the curb when my phone chirped.

"Parker, where are you?" Anna demanded, her voice up an octave with excitement.

"Uh, well. I'm in town."

"Meet me at the Tremont in ten minutes. You won't believe what I've got to show you."

Chapter Twenty-Seven

Thursday afternoon
Galveston

Finding a parking spot around the Tremont is like winning at poker. You need a lot of luck. The hotel is one block from the Strand. Even on a chilly January day, there were enough visitors to fill every parking space for several blocks around. I could have used the hotel's valet parking service to park my heap, but that would have cost me a five-dollar tip plus a disapproving stare at my truck from anyone at the entrance, including hotel management, guests or even a bellboy. I don't consider myself cheap, just frugal.

Luckily, I spied a car leaving a spot around the corner. I waited patiently behind the space while the driver maneuvered to get out. Meanwhile, another car, something like a ten-year-old Ford with a battered rear bumper and the trunk tied down with a rope, stopped in front, with the obvious intention of stealing the space from me. As the parked car pulled out, I zoomed up behind the Ford as it tried to back in and blocked its path.

A hefty kid around eighteen, built like a linebacker, got out and stomped toward me, a snarl on his pimpled face. A Ball High football sweatshirt, cut out in wife-beater fashion to show his impressive biceps, hung loosely from his puffed chest. A cute blond opened the passenger door and stood gawking at the anticipated confrontation. He closed within a foot of my door.

"Hey, man. That's my spot. Move your ass out of the way," the linebacker said.

"I don't think so."

When he put his hand on the door handle, I balled my fist and slammed it against his fingers mashing them into the frame. The strike wasn't hard enough to break his fingers, just enough to bring pain. He yelped and yanked his hand back.

While he continued to moan, I said, "You know that group photo in the trophy case of the 1972 football team that went to state?"

"What?"

"You heard me."

"Yeah, the coach makes us look at it before every game. So what?"

"Next time take a good look at the quarterback."

"Why should I?"

A moment of silence passed while he raised his eyes.

"Holy shit! Is that you?"

I nodded. He obviously didn't know my name but at least recognized my worn face. "Now move that piece of shit you're driving, and I won't say anything to your coach about what a dumbass you are."

As the kid slunk away, I hoped he had more brains than he'd shown me. For many high school jocks, whatever success they had in sports remained the highlight of their life. I thought about Tube Jones, a good man who'd never left Galveston. He'd married his high school sweetheart and produced two kids. I hoped Tube wasn't vicariously reliving his high school days through his son. Then I considered my own situation and wondered why I'd brought up the photo to the kid? Was that my high point? I hoped not.

When I reached the hotel entrance, my watch said 5:30 p.m. Assuming that Anna worked until five, she couldn't have been at the bar more than a few minutes when she called me at Harry's.

I was more than a little curious about what she'd found. Surely if it had anything to do with the lab or the missing professor, she would have called Agent Hebinck or Matthews. This had to be something personal. And if it involved me, it must have something to do with Bully Stout. The good part was this would give me a chance to confront Anna about getting legitimate DNA samples.

I hopped up the wide marble steps and turned toward the bar. Anna saw me, grabbed her glass of wine and moved to one of the seating areas. She surprised me with a hug.

"Thank you for coming, Parker."

Between the hug and the nice words, my alert button went off. What was this about? This wasn't the same Anna who'd given me a load of grief twenty-four hours earlier. We sat on the couch. She turned to face me and lightly touched my shoulder.

"I have something to show you."

She pulled a small wooden box from her purse. The box looked old, probably hand-made, a flower carved in the top. When she opened it, something silver flashed in the overhead light. She closed her palm over the object.

"You ready?" she asked.

What else could I do but nod?

She opened her hand, and I immediately recognized the small piece of tin as an Army dog tag stamped with a soldier's name, service ID number, blood type and religion. There was a small hole in one end where the ball chain attached. Soldiers were required to wear the identification tags around their necks. The tags came in pairs. In case of a battlefield death, one tag stayed with the body for identification while a member of his unit collected the other.

A nervous twitch went down my spine. Was this it? Her closing argument, the final proof? Stamped on the tag was Bully's name, Alfred P. Stout, his service number, O-positive blood type and "P" for Protestant. I squeezed my hand around the tag and blew out a long breath.

Anna's soft voice said, "It was in my mail box when I got home today, along with a note from my mother."

"What did the note say?"

"She said she had been going through Grandmother Emma's old trunk when she found the box under her christening gown. The ID tag was the only item in the box. She knew I was trying to connect with Bully so she sent it to me."

This was it, I thought. The DNA sample didn't seem so relevant now. I knew where this was going, but I asked anyway. "What do you want me to do?"

"Don't you see, Parker? Bully can no longer deny this. I want you to go with me to see him. Now."

"Whoa, Anna," I said. "Not so fast."

I stepped to the bar and ordered another wine for Anna and a beer for me, stalling for time and trying to think. Army dog tags were available online. Not real ones, but hell, who could tell the difference?

But to order one, you would have to know a lot of personal information. Anna had looked me up at the National Archives in St. Louis. Could she have done the same for Bully? It didn't seem right. She had found my service record but I doubted she could have accessed my blood type and religious preference. I handed Anna her glass of wine, took a swig of beer and sat down beside her.

"Okay, you've stalled enough," she said. "So how about it, Cousin Parker? Are you coming with me or not?"

She hadn't blinked. She just sat there, a gleam in her eye.

Fifteen minutes later we crossed the causeway, passed the chemical plants and drove through Texas City. After a few minutes, we hit the open fields. By the time we turned down Molly Putts' street, I still had no idea how to approach Bully.

The rusted gate to Molly's yard was open as we slowed to a stop. A man on horseback had gone through the gate and stopped in front of the porch. He was leaning forward in the saddle and talking to Molly in her wheelchair. He seemed tall, with a sun-darkened, handsome face as though chiseled from stone and was outfitted in weather-beaten chaps and a sheepskin coat. He held a ten-gallon Stetson in his right hand. The horse was a tall roan with a shiny coat, maybe sixteen hands high. This had to be Ernie Deats, the man I'd seen in the field across from Molly's house.

As we got out of the car, Deats said something to Molly, pulled up the reins of the roan and walked the horse past us through the gate. He nodded to me and swept his hat in a broad flourish as he passed Anna, showing his long blond hair. Outside the gate, he donned his hat, snapped his spurs into the horse's flanks and galloped away in true showman fashion.

I shouted up to Molly. "Is Deats one of your old boyfriends?"

Molly guffawed, slapped her knee and spit a string of tobacco into the ever-present coffee can in her lap.

"I wish," she said. "He just came by to bring this month's check for the grazing rights I gave him."

We approached the porch and stopped at the bottom step.

Molly rolled her eyes. "I see you've brought that woman again." She pushed the chair to the screen door and hollered inside, "Bully, your kinfolks are back." She grinned and spit into the can again.

Bully pushed the door open with his wheelchair and rolled out to the porch. A black patch covered his right eye and the stub of an unlit cigar was stuck between his lips. He glanced at Anna and then focused his good eye on me.

"What the hell are you doing, bringing that woman back here?"

"I'm not putting up with anymore of your guff, Bully. We've got something to show you. Turn that chair around, we're coming in."

I stepped inside and cranked open a window by the door to let in fresh air. Molly's old double-barreled twelve-gauge leaned against the wall. I picked the shotgun up, broke the breech and stuffed the two double-aught shells in my pocket. Molly rolled in behind us.

"What the hell are you doing with my shotgun, Parker?"

"You threatened to shoot Anna, remember?"

"Aw, shit. I wouldn't 'a done it. I keep that by the door in the day and by the bed at night. We're all alone out here on the prairie, you know."

Anna and I moved to the couch and sat on the sheets I'd noticed from an earlier trip. Bully and Molly positioned their wheelchairs side by side in front of us.

I had warned Anna to let me handle the situation so she remained quiet beside me, her lips turned up into a slight smile. I studied Bully's face. His tight jaw and gritted teeth telling me this wouldn't be easy. I waited but he just sat there chewing on his cigar.

Finally I said, "Bully, we have something to show you."

He seemed to acquiesce, closed his one good eye and breathed out a long sigh. Molly reached over and put her hand on Bully's. He opened his eye. I took the lid off the wooden box and passed it to him. He brought the box close and studied the dog tag without picking it up. He let out another slow breath. He nodded to Molly. She rolled her wheelchair into their bedroom and came back with a shoebox. Bully reached into the shoebox and removed a dog tag on a silver chain. Then he took the other dog tag out of the wooden box and handed both of them to me. Everything matched: name, service number, blood type and religious preference.

He looked at Anna, his eye welling with tears. "How is Emma?" he asked, his voice as soft as a breeze. A tear rolled down his cheek and then another. He closed his eye.

Molly squeezed his hand. "He told me," she said.

We waited silently, tears flowing from everyone now: Anna, Bully and Molly. Everyone but me. A rush of anger welled up inside me. I felt my cheeks redden. All this unmitigated denial, such a waste. Dragging his granddaughter through unnecessary and undeserved mental anguish. Damn him!

Bully raised his arms toward Anna. She got up and bent over into a long embrace with her grandfather. Then she took his hand and sat back on the couch.

"It was a horrible time," he said, almost in a whisper. "Emma's parents dead upstairs. Cannon shells bursting all around us. We were both scared to death. Emma bandaged my wounds. I don't know how long we were in that cellar. I slept on and off while she watched over me. Then an American patrol found me. I gave Emma my dog tag as they loaded me onto a jeep. I'm sorry, Anna. So sorry I didn't tell you. I never forgot her."

"It's okay," she said, squeezing his hand.

"Tell me about Emma," he said. "What happened? You say you are my granddaughter. I don't understand...."

Anna leaned in, spoke softly. "My mother is your daughter, Bully. Her name is Johanna."

Bully closed his eye again. More tears now, streaming

down his cheek.

"Johanna, a beautiful name," he whispered. "I...I had no idea."

"Emma died ten years ago. She married and had a happy life with her husband and raising Johanna. Before she died, she told my mother the story. A few days ago, my mother found the ID tag when she was going through Emma's things and sent it to me."

Molly and I left them to sort through their feelings and went out to the front porch. In the field across the road, the tall cowboy was on his horse working cattle. We sat quietly watching him work the small herd until twilight set in and his figure faded into the shadows.

It was after dark when the screen door opened and Anna pushed Bully out to the porch. Anna and I got into her car and she lowered her window and waved as she drove away. Neither of us spoke: the scene with Bully had said everything. The only sound in the truck was the engine noise and the breeze blowing through the open window.

As we passed through Texas City, I patted my coat pocket. "Aw man, I forgot to give the shotgun shells back to Molly."

"Do you want to go back?"

"Uh...well...no, it's better this way. That crazy old woman might actually shoot somebody."

We drove on. After a few minutes, I said, "Anna, I want to apologize for the rough way I've treated you, and for the doubts. I'm very proud of you for hanging in there. You are one strong woman."

She grinned and said, "How about strong *person*, Parker?"

Oh, shit, I thought. On top of everything else, she's a women's libber, a regular Gloria Steinem. "Strong person then," I said. "Thank you...Cousin Anna."

Her smile broadened across her face, crinkling her eyes.

"You're welcome, Cousin Parker."

At the entrance to the causeway, a Galveston police cruiser sat on the feeder road facing the oncoming traffic. One of the officers held binoculars to his eyes, checking each car as it passed.

"Chief Puryear said he'd have a vehicle at every entrance to the island: the causeway, the ferry and the bridge at San Louis Pass. They're looking for Louisiana license plates in case that missing professor heads this way. A roadblock would slow traffic too much. In the midst of all this threat, Galveston is still a tourist town."

Kathy dropped her eyes and put her hand to her forehead. As the resident expert on the devastation anthrax could cause, she had every right to be concerned. As we topped the causeway, the lights on a tug pushing barges down the Intracoastal Waterway glowed in the soft darkness of the night. The smell of salt water permeated the air. My thoughts went to Kathy and her daughter. Maggie would be back from her trip with her dad on Sunday, and I hoped to meet her. I was still thinking about Kathy and hadn't noticed Anna punching her password into her cell phone.

"One call," she said to herself. She listened intently to the message and then replayed it to listen again.

"Oh, my God," she said. "A message from my aunt in Germany."

"What!"

"The transmission was garbled, but my aunt said something about mother. I'm frightened something has happened."

"Call her back."

Anna checked her watch. "It's late there, after midnight."

"So, call anyway."

Anna pushed the number in, but got a recorded voice. She spoke in German and left her aunt a message saying her phone call wasn't clear and to please call back. Then she did the same on her mother's phone.

"Neither of them have a cell phone. No telling when I'll get a call back."

"Anyone else you can call?"

Anna shook no head. "Something bad has happened, I can feel it. I need to be there."

"Go," I said.

"Oh God, Parker. I want to, need to. But this Professor Turani thing. We still don't know if he's coming here with the anthrax."

"Your mom's more important. Go!"

"I...I can't. I'm in charge here while Dr. Franz, the director, is in Africa fighting an Ebola outbreak. Plus, I did my doctoral thesis on anthrax. I probably know more about it than anyone at the lab."

"Okay," I said. "Let me see if the FBI has an update on the missing professor."

I got Agent Matthews on my cell phone and explained the situation. He called back just as we pulled up in front of Anna's condominium. I listened and terminated the call.

"Nothing new about Turani or the anthrax," I said. "They have no idea where he is. You can't get a flight out tonight anyway. Give it until morning. Decide then."

"That's what I'll have to do," she said. "I'm going over to the Tremont for a nightcap. Interested?"

A beer sounded good, but my eyelids were drooping. "Thanks, but I'm really tired. Call me when you hear back from your aunt."

When she opened the car door to leave, I said, "And Anna...I'm really happy for you and Bully."

She had a nice smile when she wanted to use it.

Chapter Twenty-Eight

Thursday evening/Friday morning
Galveston

David came down from his room after completing the afternoon prayer and headed to the Tremont bar. Gene told him he'd just missed Anna. He described the man she'd left with: six feet, dark hair, casually dressed in jeans and sweatshirt. David remembered he'd seen Anna with a man fitting that description at the bar several nights earlier.

He had a couple of quick drinks at the bar and then a light dinner at the Tremont restaurant. He'd just left the restaurant and settled back at the bar when Anna strolled through the hotel entrance. The bartender saw her and poured a glass of her favorite Bordeaux.

"Just time for one," she said, climbing onto the chair next to David. She sipped her wine. "Long day tomorrow."

"Tired?" David asked, his eyes crinkled with concern.

"Yes and no," she said. "I've had good news and bad."

As Anna turned to thank the bartender, David caught a whiff of her perfume, flowers of some kind. Similar to what his girlfriend used back in Indianapolis. An image of Jennifer stepping out of the shower flashed by, her breasts jiggling as she vigorously rubbed her hair with a towel. Still thinking about Jennifer, he unwittingly glanced at Anna's chest. She self-consciously pulled the top of her blouse together. He thought he'd screwed up. But then, maybe not. She had to know from the dinner at Rudi and Paco's that he was interested.

"Tell me about the bad news first," he said.

"Well...I may fly home tomorrow." She lowered her eyes and sipped more wine. Then she told David about the phone call from her aunt and concern for her mother.

"So sorry," he said. "But you really don't know. She could be okay." He kept his voice as soft and sincere as he could.

"Hopefully," she said. "But it's scary not knowing. I should find out more tonight."

David sipped his drink, thinking that, if Anna was leaving town, it was fortunate Rashad had come up with another way to infiltrate the burn unit.

"A ray of good news, though," she added, and told him about Bully.

"Wow," David said. "So he is your grandfather. I knew it would work out."

David touched his glass to hers in a toast.

"Thanks," she said. "He's the only grandfather I have. I am anxious to get to know him and build a relationship. Beneath that hard exterior, he's a lonely old man. But I saw love in his eyes when he confessed."

David noticed Anna's eyes tearing up. He thought about making a move, but held back. He'd had enough of her problems. If everything went as planned tomorrow, this would be the last time he would see her.

Anna dotted her eyes with a drink napkin. "I am super tired, and whether I go to Germany or not, I've got a full plate." She reached for her purse.

"Let me," David said. It was the least he could do for the woman who'd inadvertently given him the idea for killing Perry. He signed the bill to his room and walked Anna to the hotel entrance.

"Thank you, David. You've been very sweet." She pecked him on the cheek and turned quickly through the door.

Back in his room, he dropped his head against the back of the chair and closed his eyes. He felt a small tick in his left hand. He knew the twinge meant his nerves were shot. He needed sleep, but wanted to run the plan for tomorrow through his mind one more time.

As a security precaution, Turani had insisted on meeting with the contact away from the boat. Having the only transportation available put David square in the middle of the operation. He'd had no personal involvement in the bombing and had hoped to stay clear of the next attempt. But it was too late for that now.

Turani asserted that he had risked everything to steal the anthrax. But he'd also claimed that, no matter what happened, the sacrifice was worth it. Killing the infidel Perry would be his last great gift to Allah.

Good, David thought, a silent smirk on his lips. Maybe the gift would be enough for both of them.

Turani had said he needed a face-to-face with the hospital contact to make sure the man understood the plan. He would give the vial to the contact at the last minute, after he was convinced the man would go through with the plot.

Turani had wanted to meet the contact in a dark parking lot, but David had convinced him to meet in a public place. With all the extra law enforcement patrolling the streets, and with Turani's photo on every squad car's computer, a surreptitious meeting in the shadows would invite automatic suspicion. He'd advised Turani to simply alter his looks as well as he could and find a place open to the public. Hide in plain sight.

He had suggested the Waffle House on 61st Street, an all-night diner that was on the opposite side of town from the hospital. That early in the morning it would still be dark outside and there was a good chance the restaurant would be almost empty.

David considered the newest plan to kill Secretary Perry. It sounded really good because it had been arranged without any additional risk for him. At least until Turani had insisted he needed transportation. If he could just get past the meeting tomorrow morning without any complications, he would be in the clear.

Which brought up another thought. Why should he have to escape Galveston on the boat with Turani and Hussein? He was confident the authorities didn't know he existed. He could be back home by the weekend, making money and enjoying evenings with sweet Jennifer.

The only possible complication would be if the FBI apprehended Turani or his sidekick Hussein alive. They knew his identity. The other risk was going to be the hospital contact. When Turani made contact with him, David would have to make sure the man never saw his face.

And who was this mysterious contact anyway, he wondered. And how was this person going to get the anthrax into the burn unit? In spite of his desire for distance, he decided he needed to know the details of Rashad and Turani's plan. If there were any holes, his analytical mind would see them. Satisfied that he'd thought everything through, David positioned a towel on the floor for *Isha*, the fifth and final prayer of the day.

At 4:00 a.m. the next morning, the alarm on David's phone roused him from a fitful sleep. His nerves were shot. His head felt as if someone was pounding the inside with a sledge hammer. His stomach was in a whirl, causing him to throw up.

He forced himself into the shower and found he had to hold on to the wall to keep from falling. He dressed, feeling warm, like he was running a fever. He wiped a line of sweat off his forehead.

He decided to skip morning prayer; afraid the bending machinations would cause him to vomit again. He slipped the "Privacy Please" sign on the outside of his door and rode the elevator to the lobby. He stepped out into the pre-dawn darkness, surprised by the heavy fog that enveloped the island. Visibility was less than a block. The doorman on duty said something about cool air passing over the warm bay water creating what he called "evaporation fog." The doorman said the sudden fog was not unusual for Galveston and he expected it to dissipate soon after daybreak.

David eased into the heavy mist, thinking Allah had smiled on him again. He couldn't have picked more perfect conditions for the meeting. If everything went on schedule, he would be back in his room at the Tremont before the fog lifted.

The direct route to the yacht basin took him along Harborside Drive past the hospital. Any other route would be considerably longer, especially with the limited visibility. He might even get lost, and Turani had insisted he be on time. He stared nervously into the dense air, hunched over the steering wheel with his stomach roiling.

He worried about the security detail he would have to pass as he neared the UTMB complex. When the flashing strobe lights of two parked police cars penetrated the mist, he knew he'd reached the street by the hospital. He crept along not wanting to cause suspicion, finally passing the two squad cars. He couldn't see the occupants and hoped they couldn't see him.

As he turned down the street to the yacht basin, he straightened in the seat and blew out a slow breath of relief.

This was it, he told himself. In a few hours, he hoped to be on his way to the Houston airport.

He imagined Rashad, relaxing on his veranda on the coast of Yemen 8,000 miles away, sipping afternoon coffee while enjoying a light repast provided by his servant Badih. As far as David knew, Rashad had done nothing for the past year but manage the family's money and plan revenge for his father's murder. David wondered about the size of the estate and hoped his share would be enough to quit working. Or take care of him if something went wrong.

Just before 5:00 a.m. David eased slowly through the yacht basin parking lot and pulled to a stop at the end of the walkway to the boat shed. A ghostly figure crossed in front of his car, giving David a sudden start. Turani yanked open the passenger door.

"This fog has put us behind schedule," Turani growled, climbing into the back seat. "You should have gotten here earlier. Mario must get to work on time. Drive where I tell you."

David turned in the driver's seat. "Before we leave, I want the plan details."

Turani cocked his head, "The less you know the better."

"It was *my* father and sister that Perry murdered. Tell me or the meeting is off. Who is Mario? What is your hold on him? What will he do with the anthrax?"

"We're running out of time."

While Turani fidgeted, David turned off the car's engine and waited.

"Damn you," Turani said.

David said nothing.

"Our Mexican contacts kidnapped Mario's mother and father in Chihuahua with orders to kill them if he doesn't comply."

David shook his head. "They will kill them anyway."

"Not our concern," Turani replied.

"Okay," David said. "So what does Mario do at the hospital that he can get the anthrax into the burn unit? Secret Service agents are probably all over the place, at the elevator, the entrance to the burn unit. There is probably one hovering over Perry's hospital bed."

The corners of Turani's lips turned up into a nasty smirk. "That's the beauty of the plan," he said. "No one needs to enter the burn unit. Mario works in the hospital pharmacy. He prepares the bandages for Perry's burns using an antibiotic cream known as silver sulfadiazine. He will simply spread the anthrax spores onto the bandage along with the antibiotic. The nurses replace the bandages every twelve hours. Because of a shortage of skilled pharmacy technicians, Mario has been voluntarily working twelve-hour shifts. He prepares both daily bandages.

"The biggest threat to a severely burned patient is infection." Hussein cracked the smirk again. "See the irony. The same treatment used to prevent infection will cause it. The anthrax will kill Perry before the hospital knows what happened."

Damn! David thought. So simple and effective he wished he'd thought of it.

"We must hurry now," Turani said. "We have to pick up Mario. He takes the bus to work and has no way to get to the Waffle House."

David hadn't planned on the contact seeing him. If the cops caught Mario, he would be able to identify him. He would just have to do the best he could to hide his face from the man.

He eased out of the yacht basin and drove slowly through the fog. He turned right on Broadway, and a few blocks later he took another right on 37th Street. A couple of blocks later, Turani directed him to stop at a ratty duplex.

Suddenly, out of the pea soup, a figure appeared by the car. David saw a small, thin man, a little over five feet, dark hair cut short, face drawn and tight. He was nicely dressed, wearing cords and a dress shirt, tie and windbreaker. The man bobbed his head side to side trying to get a look inside the car. Turani lowered the passenger window and said, "Mario?"

The man nodded.

"Get in," Turani said.

As Mario opened the back door and climbed in, David kept his eyes straight ahead so the passenger couldn't see his face. He pushed the rear-view mirror up, killing the view from the back seat. No one spoke inside the car.

Ten minutes later, after successfully maneuvering through the dense fog, David stopped just outside the Waffle House parking lot on 61st Street to get a visual of the inside. The place was a beacon of light. Even through the fog, he could clearly see the lone waitress standing behind the counter and staring out at the car. The cook was wiping the grill with a heavy cloth. There were no customers.

He let Turani and Mario out and said he would wait nearby and pick them up as soon as they walked out the door. He drove off, u-turned at Seawall Boulevard, passed the Waffle House again and parked at a spot on the opposite side of the street where he had a good view.

David couldn't sit still. He had to keep moving, to do something to keep from throwing up. He bounced his fingers on the steering wheel as if playing a song on the piano. He couldn't stop the twitch in his hands.

Through the fog he could see the waitress approach Turani and Mario in a booth. Turani had shaved his beard and was wearing a ball cap pulled low over his face. A few moments later, the waitress set two cups of coffee on the table. David could only see the back of Turani's head while, across from him, Mario was talking non-stop, gesturing with his hands. A few moments later, Turani rose and dropped some bills on the table. The waitress said something and Mario gave her a little wave of the hand.

David's watch read 6:00 a.m. There was still time to drop Mario at the bus stop and return Turani to the boat before the fog lifted.

As Turani and Mario cleared the front door, a pickup turned into the parking lot. A police officer dressed in full uniform got out of the truck and walked toward the entrance. Turani lowered his head as the officer passed by.

But then it happened so fast, David couldn't believe what he saw.

The officer turned quickly, got into a firing stance, leveled his gun at Turani and Mario and shouted so loud that David could hear the cop yell from across the street.

"Police, don't move. Hands on your head."

Turani whipped around, gun in hand, and fired twice. The officer fell to the driveway.

As Turani looked around, searching for David's car, the officer fired two shots. Turani collapsed. With both men now on the ground, the officer got off several more shots at Turani's prone figure before the gun fell from his hand and his head dropped to the concrete. The loud popping sounds cut through the dense fog and echoed down the empty street.

Mario seemed frozen in place. Then he suddenly broke and streaked down 61st Street toward Broadway. David figured Mario didn't see him in the fog. He cranked the engine and drove along the street, hoping to spot him before the police converged on the Waffle House.

David's gut was churning along with a racing heartbeat. Finding Mario wasn't his only problem. What if the waitress could identify his car?

He spied Mario two blocks up walking quickly, his head down. David stopped and yelled for him to get in. The whooping sounds of emergency vehicles sliced the through the fog. David's hands tightened on the wheel; his knuckles white. Mario piled into the front seat. Knowing that a cop would be barreling up 61St from Broadway any minute, David hung a right on the first side street. His only chance was to wind through the fog-bound back streets to where Mario could catch the bus.

"What the hell happened?" David barked, staring at the small man hunkering down beside him.

"I...I...don't know," Mario squealed. "The cop said good morning as he passed us. Neither of us answered. Then he yelled, 'Police!' to our backs. Turani turned and shot him. The man went down, but kept firing. I thought he was going to shoot me."

"What about the anthrax?"

"I don't have it. Turani said he would give it to me at the bus stop."

David bit his lip and felt the taste of blood. "Did you see it?"

"I saw a white cloth peeking out of his pocket. I'm sure it was the frozen vial. What should I do now?" Mario asked, tears streaming down his face. "What about my family?"

Good question, David thought. Hell, he didn't even know what he was going to do.

He paused. "Don't panic," he said. "Go to work as usual. The cartel has orders to kill your mother and father if you don't do as you're told."

"Mother of Jesus," Mario said, crossing himself, his eyes wide with fright. "They will hear Turani is dead."

"Don't worry," David said. "I will make sure the cartel knows you are still working with us. Give me your cell number."

With his hands shaking with fear, Mario scratched the number on a shred of paper and handed it to David.

"What can I do without the anthrax?" Mario said. "They will kill my mother and father. Can you get more?"

David didn't answer.

"The nurse collects the bandages for Secretary Perry every twelve hours. We missed the morning run. I must have more anthrax before 7:00 p.m. tonight. It will be our last chance."

After dropping Mario at his bus stop, David turned onto Broadway and headed for the causeway. It was all he could do to keep from smashing the accelerator pedal to the floor. He didn't know what he was going to do about the anthrax. His biggest worry now was wondering if either of the two Waffle House employees could identify him or his car. If so, every cop in Galveston would soon be looking for a dark Chevrolet Impala. Galveston was a relatively small city with a moderate-sized police department. David figured this early in the morning the on-duty police shift would be light. At least until they scrambled more officers. The next few minutes were his best chance to get off the island, drive back to Hobby Airport and switch rental cars. He only hoped the cops hadn't blocked the causeway.

Chapter Twenty-Nine

Friday morning
Galveston

At 7:00 a.m., my cell vibrated on the nightstand. Still groggy from tossing and turning all night, I reached for the phone without looking at the caller ID.

"Yeah."

"Parker, it's Kathy. Get to the hospital quick. Officer Jones has been shot."

"What?"

"They brought him in a few minutes ago. This is the first chance I've had to call you."

"How bad?"

"Bad. That's all I can tell you."

Three minutes later I was racing through a lingering fog toward town. With UTMB more than twenty miles away, I shoved the pedal to the floor and leaned on the horn, passing every vehicle on the road.

I remembered Tube telling me he'd elected to work the early shift this morning to bag some overtime. Damn. My mind flashed to the bombing at the Coast Guard base and Anna and me finding Tube Jones rummaging through the glove compartment of my truck as if it belonged to one of the suspects. Then running into Tube again at the Waffle House when he asked if he could bring his son out to The Garhole.

Damn. Why the Tube?

I thought about the bad moon I'd seen a few nights earlier. A strange feeling hit me. I don't believe in coincidences, but I'd seen Tube three times in the last few days, more than I'd seen him altogether since high school. Nothing good happens in threes.

At the entrance to Seawall Boulevard, I slowed to twenty over the speed limit hoping to pass through town without seeing any cops. I shouldn't have worried. More than a dozen police cruisers, probably half the Galveston force, crowded the street in front of the UTMB Emergency Room entrance. I eased past the scene, squeezed into a not-big-enough parking spot a block away and ran full speed toward the large sliding glass doors.

The morning sun was just breaking through the fog as I neared the entrance. Two Secret Service agents drew their weapons and the lead agent ordered me to stop. In all the rush, I'd forgotten Secretary Perry was also in the hospital.

I raised my hands and shouted, "Officer Jones is a friend of mine. You can verify me with Agent Erwin. Is she here?"

"Keep your hands up," the second agent said. "What's your name?"

I told him and he got on his radio. A minute later the lead agent patted me down and waved me through. I thought every Galveston police officer would be out on the streets searching for the perp who'd shot Jones, but at least a dozen stood in small clusters around the ER, their faces grim but determined.

I hustled to the desk and asked for Nurse Landry. Kathy came out wearing scrubs covered with specks of blood, her face drawn, eyes tired. She motioned me to the side, whispering.

"You know I can't tell you anything. Probably could get

fired for just calling you."

"Just nod if he's alive."

When she dipped her head, a wave of relief coursed through my bones. I took a deep breath and blew it out.

"Where is his family?"

Kathy nodded toward a hallway across the room. Just then her beeper sounded.

"Gotta go," she said and hurried off.

I felt an involuntary shudder, wondering if the call was for Tube or someone else in the ER. I eased to the entrance of the hallway and saw more officers lingering along the walls. Travis Jones stepped out of a room, his shoulders slumped and eyes brimming with tears. He saw me and came forward. I wrapped my arms around him in a bear hug.

In a voice so weak I could barely hear it, he whispered, "Glad you're here."

I edged him to the side for privacy. "How is your dad?"

"They...they won't tell us anything. Come in and meet my mom."

In the middle of the room an attractive blond, maybe five-two, wearing jeans and a wrinkled blouse, was surrounded by three women in consoling mode. The blond, whom I took to be Tube's wife Sheryl saw us enter and stepped forward.

"Mom, this is Parker McLeod, dad's friend we told you about."

Sheryl wiped her eyes with a tissue and put out her hand. Travis walked off to the corner to let us visit.

"Derry told me what you did for Travis. I'm grateful."

I nodded, took her cold hand and smothered it with my other palm trying to comfort her.

"Tube's tough," I said.

"But he's...been in there so long...."

"He's getting the best care available," I said, trying to put a good face on the situation. I'd seen battlefield casualties in Kuwait during the Gulf War and knew survival was often touch and go.

She sighed heavily and dropped her eyes to the floor, worry lines across her forehead. She leaned in and whispered in my ear. "I have friends here." She glanced at Travis standing in the corner with his hand over his eyes.

"But Travis is—"

"Don't worry," I said.

I squeezed Sheryl's hand one last time, then went over to Travis and said, "Walk with me." Thinking the cool morning air might do some good, we sauntered past the anxious eyes of the officers in the ER waiting area, exited through the main doors and sat on a concrete bench outside.

"You been tossing the ball?" I asked.

"Dad and I...."

He put his head in his hands and began to sob. I draped my arm across his shoulders and waited. After a while he raised his head and wiped away the tears on his cheeks with his hands.

"Sorry," he said.

I took my arm away. "It's okay, Travis. I know you want to be brave for your mom. You can do that when you go back inside. But out here, it's just you and me."

Travis seemed to reach down somewhere inside himself to gather strength. He wiped his eyes, straightened upright and pushed his shoulders back.

"Mom and I, we always knew this could happen. Dad's a cop. We didn't talk about it, but we knew...."

"Your dad is doing the job he loves. He wouldn't be happy at anything else."

"He likes to help people," Travis said.

"Your dad's a good man. I know he is very proud of you."

"I...I don't want to disappoint him. Will...will you help me?"

"Of course I will. But making the team is not what I meant when I said your Dad is proud of you. It's because of you, not sports. You're a good person, Travis. Your Dad knows that, and that's what he is most proud of."

A cop came out of the ER door and said to Travis, "Your dad's out of surgery."

Travis looked at me, the beginning of hope in his eyes.

"Go," I said. I stayed on the bench thinking there was nothing I could do now, but not wanting to leave.

Agent Erwin came out and sat beside me. "He made it through the operation. That's all I know."

"How bad was he hit?"

"The one in the chest collapsed his lung. Bled like a swollen creek. Another in the left arm broke his humerus. He's still critical."

"Damn."

"The shooting happened at the Waffle House. The waitress rushed out with a pile of napkins and slowed the blood flow. Probably saved his life. And UTMB has the best trauma surgeons in the area. He's been lucky so far."

"Lucky?"

Erwin sighed. "Well, he's still alive."

The shooting happened around 6:00 a.m., and I'd left the Waffle House around 3:00 a.m. I couldn't help wondering if the waitress was the same woman I'd seen there only three hours earlier.

"So what happened?"

Erwin turned, surprised. "You don't know?"

"Damn it, Millicent. If I knew—"

"Officer Jones killed Turani."

"What? He killed the professor?"

"Jones was going into the Waffle House on 61st Street as

Turani was coming out. We think Jones recognized him from the photo. Turani got off two shots. Jones went down but pumped six rounds into Turani before he passed out."

"Damn."

"The waitress said Turani came in with another man. They drank coffee, talked a while and left. Gave her a crappy tip, she said."

"The other guy was Turani's local contact?"

"That's what we think. The waitress said he was a small man, thin, a little over five feet. Dressed nicely, like he was going to work. When Turani went down, the man took off running down 61st. She and the cook are at the station now looking through mug books."

"Any cameras at the Waffle House?"

"None that worked," Erwin said. "But there is a ray of hope in all this. The good news is the anthrax vial was in Turani's pocket. It's now safely with Dr. Lang at Gulf Coast Laboratory."

"Hell, that's *more* than good news. What do we do now?"

"Well, as Yogi Berri said, 'It ain't over till it's over.' Agent Hebinck has called a meeting at Harry's as soon as we can all get there."

When Erwin went back inside, I checked my watch: eight o'clock. I texted Kathy, asking what time she got off. My phone buzzed.

"So glad you've learned how to text," she said. "You're really moving up."

"Emergencies only. People are going to forget how to talk with each other."

"Parker, you're not the greatest conversationalist."

"I say what I need to, like how about breakfast? I've got a few minutes."

I heard a heavy sigh through the phone. "I normally get off at seven, but when Officer Jones came in it was all hands on deck. I'm dead tired. I need sleep. Call me this afternoon."

I made another quick check on Travis Jones before leaving the hospital knowing that would put me late for the meeting and hoping I wouldn't be the last one to arrive. I found a spot to park two houses down from Harry's house and caught Anna just as she was going up the steps to his porch.

"How is your mother?" I asked.

Her eyes teared. "Oh, Parker...it's so sad. I want to be there, but now with this Turani thing and the possibility of another attack...."

"Tell me," I said.

"Massive stroke. She's conscious, but barely. I hate to leave you guys in the lurch, but—"

"Go," I said.

"I've gotten a flight for tomorrow."

We hugged each other which left me with a tug of sadness, hoping her mother would be okay and Anna would return soon. I still felt a load of guilt for the harsh way I'd treated her. I had some making up to do.

Inside Harry's kitchen, it looked as if Agent Hebinck had rounded up "the usual suspects:" Matthews, Roush and Agent Erwin. Everyone except Chief Puryear, who was at the hospital checking on Officer Jones.

Also at the table was the recently included CIA officer from Jordan, Peter Kay.

Anna and I took our seats and Hebinck spoke. "I just got off the phone with Chief Puryear. Officer Jones is still in Intensive Care of course, but his vital signs are stable. He should be awake in a few hours and hopefully not too groggy for an interview. The problem is, he's intubated, so Puryear doesn't know what we will get from him."

Matthews took over. "Here's where we are," he said. "Turani is dead and we've recovered the anthrax. That's the good news. But we can't be sure these diabolical bastards won't try something else."

His statement begged the obvious question. "Like what?" I asked.

"That's the problem. We can't rule anything out. We don't know when Turani got here or where he was staying. Agents are checking every motel, rooming house and B & B."

"What if he just arrived on the island this morning?" Roush added.

"Possible," Matthews concluded. "What worries us is that we know he had at least two accomplices. The Waffle House waitress said a car stopped on the street and dropped off Turani and the little guy who was with him. She didn't get a look at the driver."

Hebinck broke in, "We think he may have witnessed the shoot-out and took off. Possibly picked up Turani's accomplice as he ran away."

"Think they're still on the island?" Roush asked.

Hebinck shrugged. "No way to know. We have to assume they are." He turned to Anna. "Dr. Lang, what are the chances the terrorists could locate more anthrax or some other deadly pathogen?"

Anna considered the question. "Not likely. All the labs are on high alert. He's sure not going to get into ours. But obtaining another deadly pathogen is not impossible. They could smuggle something in from Mexico."

"Great," I said. "That's all we need."

"Okay. To sum up," Matthews said. "Assuming they haven't fled, we know there are two suspects still on the island. One of whom must have been Turani's contact at the hospital. He's either an employee or someone who has ready access, like a vendor. We took the Waffle House waitress and the cook to the station. They looked through all of Galveston

PD's mugshot books and couldn't identify either suspect."

"What about fingerprints on the coffee cups?" I asked.

"The cups were washed and the table wiped clean before the crime scene techs got there."

Matthews broke in, "Plus the terrorists have to know, with Turani dead and the anthrax recovered, that another attempt using the same method would be suicide."

"They don't mind suicide," I quipped, but no one appreciated my sarcastic barb.

"So have the witnesses checked the photo IDs of UTMB employees?" Roush asked.

"The cook claims he was too busy cleaning the grill to notice Turani and the other man. He bowed out. The waitress fell asleep at the police station and went home to rest. We'll have her at UTMB this afternoon, reviewing picture of employees... all 11,000 of them."

Erwin looked around the table. "We've checked and double checked everyone who crosses the threshold of the burn unit. We even have a masked and gloved agent inside the room at all times."

Hebinck nodded to Erwin then he eyed Roush. "Anything from NSA this morning?"

"Nothing yet, but we're on it like a bird dog on a covey of quail. We're hoping to find some communication between Turani and Yemen."

The table went silent and then Peter Kay said, "I've got news. Last night, which was early morning in Yemen, one of our passing satellites caught who we think is Badih Khoury outside the villa buying bread and vegetables from a local. The bird also got a good image of the figure standing next to Khoury when the man glanced at the sky at the wrong time. The facial recognition is a hundred percent. It was Rashad Zahir."

Hebinck, Matthews and I glanced at one another at the

same time, totally confused.

Kay removed an eight-by-ten image from his briefcase and placed it in the middle of the table.

We all leaned forward for a closer look. The man was dressed Arab style in a white robe and headscarf. The image showed a light-skinned forehead, a large nose, thick eyebrows and a heavy beard.

Matthews spoke first. "There are no known photos of Rashad Zahir. How can you be so sure this is him?"

Kay cocked his head, a surprised look on his face. "We *have* a photo," he said.

"What!" Hebinck barked, his voice up an octave.

Kay removed another eight-by-ten photo from his briefcase and placed it next to the satellite image. The photo was grainy and dark but good enough for a positive comparison.

"Holy crap," I said. "How long have you had this?"

"A while."

"A while?" I said, spewing as much sarcasm as I could muster. I wanted to reach across the table and rip out his larynx.

Kay wrinkled his forehead. "I don't get it," he said. "What's the problem?"

Hebinck bit his lip. "Another SNAFU. I'd hoped the agencies were past this."

"What are you talking about?"

"Petty jealousies."

Matthews jumped in. "Washington asserts there is no known photograph of Rashad. Even the Israelis don't know what he looks like. Parker got a glimpse of him at the 1990 café bombing in Berlin. We had an artist render a drawing and we've distributed it everywhere, even on TV. You must have seen it."

"No, I haven't," growled Kay. "I just got here yesterday,

remember? So don't shoot the messenger."

Hebinck put his palms up and said, "Okay, screw-ups happen. Let's get back on track." He slipped a copy of the drawing out of his briefcase and laid it beside the photos. He looked at me. "Parker, your memory isn't bad, but I'm not sure we would have found Zahir based on the drawing alone...maybe, maybe not."

"Gee, thanks," I said.

Matthews compared the recent satellite photo of Zahir to the other one Kay had pulled out of his briefcase. "Doesn't appear to be much difference in age between the two images. When and where was the earlier one taken?"

"A year ago in Iran," Kay said. "We had an asset who infiltrated one of Hezbollah's bomb-making facilities out in the desert. Over a period of a few months, he surreptitiously photographed every participant who filtered through the factory. Rashad was the instructor, so our asset made sure he got his name and photo."

"And you've had this information how long?" I asked.

"Only about six months. But hey!" Kay snapped, as though on the verge of losing it. "I didn't know he was on anyone's radar."

Hebinck must have noticed the steam coming out of my ears and decided it was a good time to end the meeting before I climbed over the table and shoved my fist down Kay's mouth.

"Okay, that's it for now," Hebinck said. "Another meeting at 3:00 p.m. this afternoon."

Chapter Thirty

Friday morning
Galveston

Abul Zahir, known in the U.S. as David Arnold, principal in Arnold Engineering, Indianapolis, Indiana, slowed to a stop on I45 in the worst stop-and-go traffic he'd ever seen. The morning commute at home was nothing like this. The freeway was completely crammed with mostly single-occupant vehicles headed to the behemoth city of Houston fifty miles to the north. But at least he'd made it off the island without being stopped.

Several times during the painful trudge toward Hobby Airport, he'd considered getting on the first flight available and escaping to any place one of the big silver birds would take him. He knew there were hourly flights to Cancun, the popular Mexican beach resort only a couple of air hours away. He envisioned drowning himself in Tequila amid a bevy of brown ladies eager for American dollars. Sounded good, except he'd left his passport at the office.

At least the thought had given him a temporary diversion from the pounding headache and the constant replay in his mind of the horrific scene at the Waffle House of two men shot and bleeding in front of his eyes.

It was obvious to David that the authorities had connected Turani and the missing vial of anthrax to the plot to kill Perry.

Every cop in Galveston must have had Turani's photo on his car's computer or dashboard. Turani had changed his looks, but not enough to avoid suspicion by a seasoned cop.

David needed to know if Turani was dead or alive. If Turani died at the scene, David thought he was safe. The only witnesses were the waitress and the cook, and they couldn't have seen him through the fog. But if Turani were only wounded, he couldn't be sure the professor wouldn't rat him out.

The authorities had to be wondering how Turani had gotten to Galveston, how long he'd been here and where he had holed up. And what if they found something on Turani's body that would lead them to the boat at the yacht club? Had they already captured Hussein? What would it take for Hussein to identify him as part of the conspiracy? Not much, David thought. Or what if Hussein had already heard about the shootout and headed out to sea? Hell, he could have cranked up the Bertram and cleared the Galveston jetties by now.

And then there was Mario, the pharmacist's technician. David remembered Mario speaking with the waitress. He'd even made eye contact with her, the fool. Mario would be easy to identify: a short, thin, well-dressed Hispanic. The obvious leap for the authorities would be to assume he worked at the hospital. No doubt they would make every effort to identify him. And security at the hospital would be even tighter. Or was it possible that, since the latest attempt failed, the authorities might think whoever was after Perry would give up? If that was the case, they sure didn't know Rashad Zahir.

When the traffic stopped again, David realized he'd gripped the steering wheel so tightly his fingers were numb. He flexed his hands. Was he being paranoid or just super careful? Either way it didn't hurt to think things through.

David finally saw the exit sign for Hobby Airport. At least he'd soon be out of the morning rush. He eased into the exit lane and felt his nerves begin to calm. It suddenly dawned on him to turn on the car radio. A sudden chill ran across his mind that he'd just now thought to get the news. He'd have to do better, think more clearly.

The Waffle House shooting inundated the airwaves. Derry Jones, the wounded officer, had just stopped in for breakfast before reporting to the station when he recognized Turani from the photo. Now Jones was being hailed as a hero, lying critically wounded in the same hospital as Perry. The newscaster reported Hamid Turani, a professor at Louisiana Western University, wanted by the FBI as a person of interest in the bombing at the Coast Guard base, died at the scene. The police were searching for two additional suspects in a dark sedan, the car's make and model unknown. Nothing was said about the anthrax.

A thin smile crossed David's face as he realized a perverted collusion existed between him and the authorities. Neither side wanted the general panic that would ensue if the public knew about the anthrax. David visualized the hospital being completely shut down to visitors, and the locals and visitors making a mad rush for the causeway.

He grabbed the burner phone lying on the seat beside him and called Hussein.

"What happened?" Hussein screamed. A television blared in the background. "The professor's dead. They've said nothing about the anthrax. What about Mario?"

David steadied his voice. "Calm down, Hussein. The cops have the anthrax, but Mario got away. He is at the hospital, trying his best to act normally. Here is what you do now. Call the cartel. Tell them to keep Mario's family alive until they hear from you. Tell them we still need leverage on Mario while we work out a new plan. You got that?"

"Yes, yes, okay." Hussein replied.

David heard the desperation in Hussein's voice and wondered if he could trust him to keep it together. David didn't give a damn about Turani's death except that it had temporarily foiled their plan to get Perry. He cared less for Hussein. But he knew that if the authorities didn't know about the boat, it could still be an escape route.

"Good," David said. "Now. Walk out to the parking area. See if anything looks suspicious. Then call me back."

David exited the interstate and was now only a few minutes from the concession where he could dump the Chevrolet. He glanced around, looking for police cars. The burner phone buzzed.

"It's...it's clear," Hussein said, his voice quaking.

"Sit tight until I get there."

"How long?"

"Maybe an hour."

"Where are you?"

David ended the call without answering. The sign for car-rental returns appeared just ahead. He moved into the lane and threaded his way to the Hertz section. He checked the Chevy in and for a quick moment considered renting the Mercedes he'd considered earlier. But with the Mercedes' power, there was a good chance he'd find himself driving over the speed limit. He couldn't afford to be stopped by some cop lying in ambush just waiting to ticket the driver of a speeding luxury car. He quickly panned the thought and hustled across the parking area to the other car rental facilities.

With long lines in front of Avis and National, David gravitated to the Alamo location. The irony hadn't escaped him. The Alamo: the famous siege of a group of hopeless, embattled fighters struggling against impossible odds for a cause they believed in. And here he was in the same situation, also struggling against a mighty foe. Except this time, regardless of Turani and Hussein's plea about serving Allah, David knew the real cause for Rashad was simple revenge.

David drove out of the Alamo parking area in a new Jeep Grand Cherokee, pleased that the style and light tan color of his new rental was as far removed from a dark sedan as he could find. Riding high in his new vehicle, he felt his self-control returning. He could again concentrate on the task at hand and think with an engineer's mind: linear and focused.

He had to admit that Rashad's idea about using Mario was the perfect plan. Except that Mario was as nervous as a gerbil in a cage. What were the chances he might panic and confess the conspiracy to the authorities? David had seen abject fear in Mario's eyes at the thought of what the cartel would do to his mother and father. In the end, he didn't think Mario would risk his parents' lives by exposing the plan to the cops.

But would Mario be able to control his anxiety at the pharmacy? What if a co-worker became suspicious and reported him? Or what if the authorities had finally considered the pharmacy as a means of getting the anthrax into the burn unit and were closing in on pharmacy employees?

David needed to calm himself. The delivery method to Perry was in place. All he needed to complete the plan was another pathogen. More anthrax or something as deadly. As he approached the interstate heading south, the digital clock on the dashboard read 9:00 a.m. He'd made good time and should be back in Galveston within the hour. When his burner phone buzzed, he was shocked at the caller.

"I just saw the news on CNN International!" Rashad screamed. "Can't you do anything right?"

David's temples flared again. He wanted to heave the phone out the window, but instead worked to calm himself.

"Listen, brother. This was your plan, your people. And now you've put us both in danger by using the phone. What the hell were you thinking?"

"I had no choice, we're out of time. CNN reported Perry may be transferred to Walter Reed in Washington this weekend. They must think keeping him in Galveston is too risky. We have to move fast. I sent several encrypted emails. You never responded."

"Listen to me," David yelled back. "It is time to quit. We are out of time and options."

"No, never," Rashad screamed again. "The cell is ready to move forward with your idea. The target *you* suggested has been under constant surveillance. Our team is on standby. I just need to double check and make sure everything is still a go. I will call you at exactly 1:00 p.m. your time."

The line went dead. David took the next exit and pulled off to the side of the frontage road. He forced himself to take several deep breaths. He regretted ever telling his brother about Anna's mother in Germany. Rashad had set up surveillance and the team was ready to strike. Which meant David would have to handle his end. He had to think about the best way to get to Anna. It wouldn't be easy.

David drove into the yacht basin, parked the Jeep and craned his neck in all directions before getting out. He hurried to the walkway and hustled past the other boats until he got to Slip 169 and the Bertram. He noticed Hussein peeking out through the side curtains. He stepped onto the deck as Hussein opened the cabin door. David pushed Hussein back, entered the cabin and closed the door behind him.

Hussein lowered his head and whispered, "May he be in Paradise."

David ignored Hussein's plea, crawled into the captain's chair and massaged his temples.

"What do we do now?" Hussein asked, his face taut, eyes constricted with angst.

David knew he needed to be the strong one. The dedicated jihadist was collapsing in front of him. What had happened to all that brave machismo?

"We are working on a new plan," David said.

"They are moving Perry this weekend. We don't have time for a new plan. The boat is fueled and ready to go. We can be past the jetties and out in the gulf in twenty minutes."

Hussein unfolded a chart. He pointed to the drawn-in route along the Texas and Mexican coast, around the Yucatan Peninsula and on to Panama. All the fuel stops were noted along with emergency phone numbers in each port.

David moved to the table and studied the chart. Looks simple enough, he thought. "What about money for fuel along the way?"

Hussein ducked into the cabin and returned with a leather satchel. He opened the flap. Banded stacks of twenty- and hundred-dollar bills were stacked neatly to the brim.

"There is $10,000 here," Hussein said. "More than enough."

David realized then how little thought he'd given to using the boat to escape. He remembered Hussein saying Rashad would meet him in Argentina, but David had discounted the idea, always expecting to return to his life in Indianapolis.

The original plan had been free of risk for him: a simple trip to Yemen to sit with his brother on a veranda by the sea, drink fine Yemeni coffee and enjoy Badih's excellent cooking. But the rule of unintended consequences had reared its ugly head. And now he was snared in a web of complicity with a huge vacuum sucking him inevitably toward the center.

David checked his watch: 11:00 a.m. He said to Hussein, "Rashad will call at 1:00 p.m. and tell us if the plan is a go. I am going back to the hotel for a quick rest. You stay vigilant here. Call me if anything suspicious happens. And don't worry. If the police knew about the boat they would have already been here."

David never intended to return to the hotel. He just wanted to get away from the boat on the off-chance that the NSA had captured Rashad's earlier phone call. If they were anxiously waiting for the next one, he didn't want to be at the yacht basin. He felt a lot more confident in his ability to drive around Galveston in the Cherokee and decided to revisit the Greek restaurant on Seawall Boulevard where he'd had lunch before the seminar.

At 11:15 a.m. David ordered the same dish as before, moussaka with béchamel sauce. When the coffee came, his thoughts floated to his father. He had only met Nassim a few times, but he was immediately captivated by his father's stern countenance and dedicated beliefs. He didn't quite understand Nassim's persistent hatred of the Jews, but then he'd been raised in America by a loving mother who'd taught him respect for all races and creeds. David pushed the thoughts away. Because he'd never been able to reconcile the differences, thinking about it only brought frayed nerves and confusion.

He removed the photo of his little sister Akilah from this wallet and studied her profile: the innocence of youth, the quiet intelligence in her eyes, the exuberance for life in her smile. He wished he had known her.

He left the restaurant at half past twelve and drove slowly along the seawall, looking for the best place to stop and receive Rashad's phone call. He found an open space close to the one he'd used before. He glanced up to the cloudless sky and wondered if the clear atmosphere made it easier for the NSA's prying eyes. He had no idea if the National Security

Agency had intercepted the earlier phone call from Rashad, he only knew this call needed to be as quick as possible.

At exactly 1:00 p.m., his phone buzzed. "We have a problem," Rashad said. "The target is unavailable."

"What does that mean?"

"A health issue. I can't say more on the phone. You will have to find another way to put pressure on the source at your end."

David thought for a moment and put it together. Anna had said something had happened to her mother. A heart attack? A stroke? He hoped she wouldn't have to fly home. He needed her. She was his last chance.

Rashad continued, "Everything else is set for afterwards. You will receive final instructions on how and where to meet me."

More silence. David could hear his brother's heavy breathing.

Then Rashad said, "Abul, you are a true brother. Finish this and Allah will bless you. Nassim and Akilah will smile down on you. And I—"

At that moment, a horrific crackling sound reverberated through the phone, followed by an eerie silence.

Chapter Thirty-One

Friday morning/afternoon
Galveston

When the morning meeting ended at Harry's, I wanted to run by Kathy's house on the off chance she was out in her yard tinkering with her flowers. Wishful thinking, and I knew better. She hadn't tried to hide the exhaustion in her voice at the hospital. She'd been the first to attend Tube Jones when the paramedics wheeled him into the ER barely alive, his blood pressure dropping. It wasn't her first shooting victim but it was her first wounded cop. The shooting of a police officer was a rare event in Galveston. As much as I wanted to see her and offer what comfort I could, she needed sleep more.

My stomach was growling so I made a quick detour to a 7-11 and grabbed a bag of beef jerky. I almost picked up a beer for the road, but with the "open container" law in Texas, and the streets loaded with cops, I decided the last thing I needed was to be caught with a brown paper bag at my lips and hauled off to jail.

I trudged through the front door of The Garhole and found Neddie slugging a cold one behind the counter. I considered checking the trash to see how many brews he'd consumed, but then thought what difference did it make, really?

"Nary a customer," Neddie said, draining the last few drops from the can.

His T-shirt of the day was the best one yet, guaranteed to capture the heart of a passing female. The entire front was a life size photo of Elvis in a white jump suit, microphone in hand, crooning a tune.

I leaned in for a closer look and said, "I know you didn't create the Elvis shirt. Did you find it on the Strand?"

"Don't jump to conclusions, Parker. I purchased the photo on line, downloaded it and had the shirt made. Just got it today. I'll wear it at my next shift at the bridge and probably get laid before the weekend is over."

"Well, at least you moved away from provoking half the female universe. You were lucky some libber didn't beat the shit out of you. I can't imagine Elvis pissing anyone off."

He ignored my comment and said, "Are you staying a while or just passing through?"

"My rear is dragging. I'm gonna grab a few Z's and head back to town. How is it going with the cats?"

"I'm on my way to the Vet now with the three I've got in the truck."

"I guess I was too tired to notice them. How many more are still out there?"

"Hard to say. It seems to change every time I feed them. Maybe a dozen or so."

"Yeah, well, don't forget your promise. I don't want to have to come down there and save your ass again."

"Hey," he said. "If I said I'd do it, I'll do it. Don't bug me. But I'm sure gonna miss my little friends." He disposed of the empty and eased another beer out of the box.

"If you can come back after you drop off the cats, I could use your help this afternoon. Between the foul weather and the goings on in town, I need the business. I don't want my few regulars this time of year thinking The Garhole is shutting down."

"Glad to help. Like you said, one of the local alkies may drop in. Make you a buck or two."

Talk about the pot calling the kettle black. I made a quick calculation: If a customer came in and drank a few beers and Neddie matched him, I should at least break even.

On my way up the stairs, Neddie yelled at my back. "I'll probably close early though. NOAA says another front is coming through tonight. A mean one. Rain squalls, a lot of wind, the whole bit."

I was half asleep by the time I reached the top of the stairs. I fell onto the bed fully clothed and conked out. Two hours later I awoke to the sound of nature's alarm clock: a flock of screaming seagulls off my deck.

I splashed water on my face and was thinking about frying up a batch of shrimp for lunch when the thought of my friend Tube fighting for his life in ICU popped into my mind. Maybe the best thing I could do for Tube was to visit his son Travis again and offer what comfort I could. I rummaged beneath some dirty clothes on the top shelf of my closet and found what I wanted for Travis. On the way downstairs, my phone buzzed.

Matthews' voice erupted through the line. "Hebinck wants everyone at Harry's house as soon as possible."

"What's up?"

"New information. It's important."

I parked in the same space as before, two houses down from Harry's house. Everyone had arrived except Erwin and Kay. Anna stood at the bar sipping coffee. She'd developed dark circles under her eyes and an extra crease or two in her forehead. Between worrying about her mother and another possible terrorist attack, she looked ready to collapse.

Hebinck motioned everyone to the kitchen table. "Things

are moving," he said. He nodded to General Roush.

Roush cleared his throat and referred to his notes. "At 9:05 this morning, NSA intercepted a telephone call from a cell phone in Yemen to Houston, Texas. We were able to track the transmitting end to the same seaside villa that the CIA has been monitoring."

"Rashad Zahir?" Puryear asked.

Roush nodded. "The receiving end was traced to an area near Hobby Airport. With Turani dead, we think Rashad brought in another terrorist."

"So soon," I said. "Turani's only been out of the picture a few hours. Maybe we got lucky. Maybe Rashad is done and he ordered the contact to leave."

"We've checked the passenger lists on every arriving and departing flight this morning and can find no one suspicious," Hebinck said.

Matthews said, "CNN reported that Perry may be moved this weekend. It's not true, he is still critical, but the news is out there. If Rashad thinks he has a better chance to kill Perry here than at Walter Reed, it means he hasn't given up. At least we can't afford to assume he has."

"The phone call was fuzzy, but we got most of it," Roush continued. "Rashad told the Houston contact that the target was under surveillance. That the team was ready and on standby."

Puryear groused, "Under surveillance? What the hell is that? Does he mean the hospital is under surveillance or do they have eyes on Perry's room?"

Roush put his palm out to calm Puryear. "Neither," he said. "We think Rashad is referring to someone else entirely. Maybe a potential hostage. Someone the terrorists could grab that could force a situation in the hospital."

"Think about this," I said. "If Rashad had to tell the contact here that the target was under surveillance and the team was ready, then it means the target is not in Galveston."

"Maybe," Hebinck said. "But we can't afford to narrow our focus. I called Agent Erwin with the information," Hebinck said, "She said she'd better skip this meeting and stay at the hospital. Her team is rechecking everyone who has access to Perry: doctors, nurses. They are also contacting their spouses, putting everyone on alert."

"If not here, then where?" Roush said, looking at me.

"I don't know," I answered. "But let's deal with what we do know. There are at least two other suspects involved, the man with Turani at the Waffle House and the driver of the dark sedan. Any news on those two?"

Hebinck shook his head.

"And now we've got a third: the one at the airport."

"How do we know there aren't more?" Puryear asked. "I'm going to ask the governor to call up the National Guard. We're gonna seal off the island."

We all glanced at each other and then focused on Puryear.

"We've been through this before," Matthews said. "First you were going for more state troopers, now it's the National Guard. We've got more FBI and Secret Service agents coming in. They're trained. The National Guard could panic and fire on innocents. You want that for your city?"

Puryear bit his lip.

"We did pick up what we think is a new lead out of the conversation," Roush said. "Rashad called the person he talked to in Houston 'brother.'"

"Could be just an expression," I said. "Like, 'oh, brother.'"

"We checked," Matthews said. "Hard-core jihadists aren't versed in idioms. It's hard to have a sense of humor when all you think about is murdering infidels. None of our information suggests Rashad Zahir has a brother. We've contacted Mossad to see what they have. Should hear back soon."

Roush looked at his watch. "It's 1:30 p.m.," he said. "Rashad told the contact he would call him back at one o'clock. I should be getting the transcript any minute."

"Where is Kay, the CIA officer from Jordan?" I asked.

Hebinck spoke, "He called, said he was running late but to wait for him. Has something good, he said."

We took a break. Hebinck took Anna aside and spoke quietly to her. When he finished, I caught her eye as she refilled her coffee cup and motioned her across the room.

"Have you spoken with Bully since we were at their house yesterday?"

"No, but I wanted to see him again this weekend, maybe go out and clean the house. Both of them in wheelchairs, they can't get around much. But with all this going on and me flying home tomorrow...it will just have to wait."

"Miss Anna, you're going to be a hell of a granddaughter," I said.

She gave a weak smile through tired eyes.

"How are things at the lab?"

"The director is as nervous as a feral cat. He cut his trip to Africa short and is coming in tomorrow. Meanwhile, Agent Hebinck just told me he sent a team of agents to interview everyone in the lab. This news about a possible hostage has us all spooked. After the interviews, I'm going to close the lab for the weekend."

When Peter Kay came in, everyone moved back to their seats at the table. Kay sat at the end and opened his laptop.

"Sorry, I'm late," he said. "But I've been waiting for this. It just came in. I thought you guys would want to see it." He hit the play button and stood to the side so everyone could see. "This video is less than an hour old."

The only sound was the light humming noise of the

computer's fan motor. The screen was black except for the date posted in the upper left corner and the digital clock, the seconds clicking steadily. The date read Friday, January 11, the time read 22:03. It was today's date. The clock posted military time, which equated to 10:03 p.m. or 1:03 p.m. here. If the scene we were about to see was nine hours ahead of Galveston, it had to be Yemen. With a waning moon, the sky there should be very dark.

The video ran for another minute, then Kay said, "Watch closely now."

Grainy black-and-white images of a walled compound came into view, a body of water off to the east, a narrow two-lane highway to the west. The picture continued to zoom until the camera appeared on top of the structure. Still no sound from the video. Nothing moved in the compound.

The camera continued to tighten and focus until I could make out a cloth covering of some type over an open veranda. Without sound, the image was eerie, almost ghostlike. It was as if we were eavesdropping, uninvited into someone's personal space. As an Army Intel officer, I had seen many such scenes taken from satellites and drones. They always left me wondering if our government was watching us from the skies.

I didn't want to take my eyes off the screen for a second, fearing I might miss the hit. But I couldn't help glancing at Anna sitting across from me. She held her hand to her mouth as though expecting the worst.

I never got used to the uneasy anticipation of knowing what was coming: eyes narrowed and straining, mixed feelings of deliverance yet profound sadness, all wrapped in a bundle of controlled emotions.

The entire scene appeared like a supernatural apparition, the digital second hand moving rapidly, the compound still. A sudden, bright-white flash lit up the screen. Then heavy smoke and flames. The angel of death had arrived on the Yemeni coast in the form of a devastating warhead.

The only sound in the room was Anna's gasp as she covered her eyes and left the table. The recording ended and Kay shut the laptop. No one spoke.

"Beautiful, huh," Kay said. "Two Hellfire AGM-114 laser-guided missiles dropped from a Predator drone just vaporized Rashad Zahir. The drone and missiles were under the control of a tech sergeant sitting at a computer console at Clark Air Force Base outside Las Vegas, Nevada. Amazing stuff, huh?"

Kay was the only smiling face at the table. He looked around. "What? We got the bastard."

Hebinck slammed the table with his palm. "Damn it, Kay. When the hell is the CIA going to cooperate?"

"Wha...what do you mean?"

"Rashad was going to call his contact here again at 1:00 our time. According to the time stamp on your computer, it was 1:05 here when the sky lit up. If the missile hit before he made the call, we've lost our best chance to track the contact here."

Kay sighed, averted his eyes. "Nobody told us," he said.

"Good news and bad news," Puryear said. "Good news is the master terrorist Rashad Zahir is dead. Bad news is there are at least three other suspects still in Galveston."

I got up and walked out to Harry's front porch. The last few leaves from the Mexican sycamore tree in Harry's front yard were floating down onto the sidewalk. Fall had arrived late this year in Galveston. I had always loved sycamores, the large crown-shaped leaves that turned yellow and brown as the season changed, the white bark slick, like it had been painted on. Growing up in a rent house on 13th Street, we'd had a large sycamore in our backyard. I'd spent many fall afternoons watching the leaves tumble into the yard, daydreaming about the future, wondering what my life would be like. I could only see one path: my grandfather's ranch. I thought if he could make a living on that hard-scrabble west-end prairie, so could I. I just never considered earning a living on his old ranch meant running a bar.

The United States had just completed its final act of retaliation against the ruthless terrorist who had murdered my friend and a dozen others in a German café. The attack on Secretary Perry and the wanton killing of Secret Service, FBI and Galveston police officers had also been avenged.

I should be feeling nothing but satisfaction and approval, maybe even gloating. But all I could manage was sadness, a hollow, empty feeling in the pit of my stomach. Anna walked out to the porch and stood beside me.

"What the hell has happened to this world?" she asked, staring out at leaves blowing across the yard.

It was a rhetorical question, but I couldn't help myself. "People have been killing each other since the beginning of time," I said. "The Bible is full of death and destruction."

"Damned religion," she said. "From Jesus to the Crusades, the Inquisition, even the Salem witch hunts, and now these idiot Islamic fundamentalists. Will it ever end?"

"Well, I don't profess to be an expert on Islam, but from what I understand, the Quran teaches peace, love and tolerance."

She squeezed her eyes and looked at me like I needed a course in human history.

"Tolerance? I can't believe you said that, Parker. Ask the girls living under Taliban rule who are not allowed to go to school or the women in Saudi Arabia who can't even drive a friggin' car what they think about tolerance."

Anna was right, of course. I thought of the videos of the

madrassas in Pakistan, young boys bobbing back and forth, acquiring xenophobia by rote. It meant we were in for the long haul. I had no doubt the majority of the millions of Muslims in the world were peace loving. But then why did they allow the bad guys to infiltrate their mosques and preach hate?

Matthews came to the door. "Come on back in," he said. "We need to finish."

Everyone except General Roush gathered again at the kitchen table. Roush was over in the corner talking in hushed tones on his cell phone. Faces around the table were grim. We all knew that, if Rashad Zahir had been incinerated in that firestorm, we'd passed a milestone in killing one of the world's most dangerous terrorists. But we also knew there was still a threat to our area, and we were far from done.

Puryear said, "Well, one down and three to go."

"That we know of," Matthews added. "The question is: What will the remaining terrorists do now that their leader has been blown up by a guided missile? Fight or flight?"

"Hey, it's only been an hour," I said. "Do they even know Rashad is dead?"

"Oh, they know," Roush said, coming back to the table. He pulled out a chair and sat down. "I just received the transcription of another phone call. Rashad Zahir was talking on his cell phone with his contact in Galveston when the call abruptly ended with a noise. Our techs think that's when the missile hit."

"Wow," Puryear said, shaking his head.

"What did he say?" Hebinck asked.

"That the target was unavailable."

"Unavailable?"

"Yes, and then he said, 'A health issue. I can't say more on the phone. You will have to improvise on your end.'"

"This is really strange," I said. "Earlier Rashad was talking like he had control of the kidnap team, which indicated the potential target was not in Galveston. Yet this time he told the Galveston contact to handle it."

"So whatever is happening, it will all take place here," Matthews said.

"And there's this," Roush added. "Rashad said everything is set for the next phase, meaning after the final attack. He told the Galveston contact he would be notified on how and where to meet. It's as if Rashad was planning to leave Yemen and they would meet up somewhere."

No one spoke.

"Rashad called the Galveston contact 'Abul'," Roush said. "And said that he was a true 'brother.' Rashad said Nassim and Akilah would smile down on him. That's Rashad's father and sister who were killed in the strike by Perry. That's the second time Rashad has mentioned the word 'brother.' If Rashad has a brother named Abul...and Abul is in Galveston?"

"Son of a bitch," Puryear said.

Hebinck finished with, "All of you stay close. Things are moving fast now. I'm calling another meeting for 5:00 p.m. tonight unless something breaks earlier."

Chapter Thirty-Two

Friday afternoon
Galveston

Back at the boat, the walls of the tight cabin closed in around him. David realized he was on the verge of a panic attack, the sides of his head about to blow out. The pressure growing behind his eyes felt as though strange hands were inside his eye sockets, pushing out his eyeballs. He wiped sweat off his forehead with his hand, turned away from Hussein and gazed out the porthole at the Galveston ship channel. The water looked like a sheet of glass, a stark contrast from the way he felt. He closed his eyes and put his hand against the bulkhead to steady himself. He was losing the ability to reason, to think through a problem.

He heard a voice and realized it was Hussein speaking, but didn't understand what he'd said. Think. Focus.

Realizing he couldn't show weakness in front of Hussein, he toughened, blew out a small breath and forced himself to feel safe in the small confines of the cabin. He began to stabilize, as he put his hand on his wrist and felt his pulse slowing. He heard the voice again.

"Did you talk to Rashad?" Hussein asked.

"Yes," David answered. "But I think something has happened to him."

"What?"

"I heard a crackling noise and the phone went dead. Rashad was always worried about a missile strike...I'm afraid it may have...."

Hussein grabbed the remote and clicked on the television. The commentator was rattling on about the Waffle House shooting.

Hussein muted the volume but kept his eyes on the TV. "Nothing about a strike in Yemen."

"Doesn't mean anything," David said. "The CIA never advertises when they've murdered someone."

"Did you call Rashad back?"

"I tried...no answer."

"What do you think happened?" Hussein asked.

David started to answer when a call came from his office on his personal phone.

"Hi Mary. What's going on?"

"Hello, Mr. Arnold. Uh...a woman called. The connection was not clear, she sounded a long way off. She had some kind of an accent, a little difficult to understand. She mentioned the name Badih and that he wanted you to call him. Here's the number."

David wrote the number down.

"It was a really strange call. Anything I can do, Mr. Arnold?"

David hesitated, thinking. Then he said, "There were several engineers at the seminar from other countries. It was probably one of their secretaries. Maybe my attendance at the seminar is already paying off. I'll handle it. Thanks, Mary."

David pushed End and turned to Hussein. "Not good. Rashad's servant wants me to call him."

"Could be a trap," Hussein said.

"No. Badih has been a faithful servant to the Zahir family for years. He wouldn't betray us. This has something to do with Rashad...I fear the worst."

David's hand began to shake, his eyes hurt. The pain in his temples came back. He winced, turned his head and tried to rub the pain away. He could feel Hussein's eyes on him. He faced Hussein again and said, "It is too risky to call from the boat. Stay here until I get back."

"You are not feeling well," Hussein protested. "I will go with you and drive while you call."

David put his hand on Hussein's chest and pushed him against the cabin wall. "No," he ordered, his face only inches from Hussein's. "We cannot leave the boat unattended. I will be back soon."

David had contacted Rashad several times while parked on the seawall. He decided if the NSA was tracking him, it would be best to change locations. He drove out of the yacht basin, turned left on Harborside and right on Ferry Road. He turned left at the intersection with Seawall Boulevard and drove to where the road stopped at a yellow and black barrier: the end of the island. In front of him a large oil tanker filled with crude rode low in the water, heading out to the jetties and the Gulf of Mexico. Off to the left a car ferry was making a run from Galveston to Bolivar Peninsula.

A station wagon pulled to the barrier several yards away. The man driving glanced suspiciously at David. He said something to the woman beside him, then turned and studied David again. David considered leaving. As he was about to turn on the engine, the man turned to the children in the back seat. Three girls, all under ten years old, piled out of the car, giggling and jostling each other. The man and woman got out, and the man called the children to the barrier and pointed to the tanker cruising slowly out the channel. The older girl handed pieces of bread to the little ones. They rolled the bread into small balls and tossed them up to the hovering seagulls. The sound of clattering gulls intensified with each toss. When the bread ran out, everyone piled back into the station wagon and the man drove away.

David punched Badih's number into his burner phone but hesitated to push the Send button. If the NSA had captured any of the earlier calls, they would surely be listening now. But he was out of time, he had to chance the call. He hit Send. Badih answered on the first buzz.

"Abul, Abul, oh...blessed Allah!"

"Calm down, Badih. What is it?"

"The bomb! The bomb! The villa is gone! I couldn't sleep...went for a walk on the beach. The sky lit up. It was...horrible. Horrible. Nothing left. Rashad is...he is...."

David closed his eyes, visualizing the explosion. He couldn't speak. It was worse than he'd thought. He'd offered a short prayer to Allah when the phone went dead on his earlier call to Rashad, but it had done no good. The last of his family was gone. His father and little sister, now his only brother. Damned Americans!

"How did you find me, Badih?"

"I called my sister in Beirut and told her the name of your company. She called your secretary and left a message for you to call me."

"There is nothing you can do now, Badih. Go to your sister's house."

David terminated the call. He dropped his head to the steering wheel, the pounding in the sides of his head worse than ever, his eyes bulging.

A few minutes later, David sat in the jeep at the yacht basin parking lot trying to calm himself. He couldn't let Hussein see him like this: on the verge of losing it, hands shaking, nerves frayed. His mind flittered back and forth, a jumble of mixed thoughts between his life in Indianapolis and allegiance to his family. Who was he: David Arnold, an American capitalist with a fetish for whiskey, women and fast cars? Or Abul Zahir: a loyal son and brother and, as a result of their murder, a revenge-seeking jihadist.

He removed the faded photo of his little sister from his wallet. Akilah. The innocence in her smile and the hope in her eyes tugged at his heart. A hope she would never see fulfilled. He returned the picture to his wallet.

It came to him then that his whole life was a worthless sham. He was living as a godless infidel. His prayers had been pure rote, memorized though his mother's insistence, with no real meaning for him. Going through the motions seeking her approval. And what had his intransigence gotten him but an empty soul with momentary pleasures of the flesh. Would Allah ever forgive him? Could he redeem himself?

Focus, he kept telling himself. You can do this. For your family, you must do this. Through the darkness of his tormented soul, his father Nassim and his brother Rashad called to him: avenge, avenge. Allah expected it; the Prophet demanded it. Do it. Assuage your misdirected life, your unholy ways. He had no choice now, America had seen to that. He had to kill Perry. The godless Americans had wiped out his entire family. Damn them! Damn them all!

Rashad had said the contact was unavailable, meaning Anna's mother. Maybe she'd died, David thought. But with Rashad dead, it didn't matter. He had no way to contact the German cell anyway. Rashad had handled all that. Kidnapping Anna's mother was not possible. But the idea of forcing Anna to ferret anthrax out of the Gulf Coast Laboratory was a good one. He just needed the right pressure.

Of course...her grandfather Bully. She'd gone on about how much he meant to her. "Her only grandfather" and all that drivel. The old man would be easy. But then he'd also have to deal with that crazy woman with the shotgun. He thought he could pull it off, but he needed Hussein's help.

The day had warmed enough for several of the yacht owners to be working on their boats. David strode casually past a huge yacht and returned the wave from an older couple having lunch on the fantail. The boat reminded him of his friend's Hatteras in Chicago and the good times he'd spent there: the sex and booze. But those days were gone, maybe forever.

Could he kill Perry and still escape? Was it possible? He would also have to kill Bully, the old woman and even Anna. So what? If the cops still didn't know about him, maybe he could disappear. Kill Hussein too, the only other person who could identify him. Except Mario, and he couldn't do anything about him. It just meant he'd be on the run and he had a plan for that, too.

He saw Hussein peeking through the blinds. He slipped down onto the boat and went into the cabin. He told Hussein his plan and Hussein balked.

"They don't even know we exist," David said.

"What are you talking about?" Hussein scoffed, his voice quivering. "It's all over the news." He clicked on the television.

A CNN reporter stood in front of the Waffle House on 61st Street modulating her voice as she had been trained to do as a broadcaster, trying to put as much hype in the report as she could muster.

"...and according to unconfirmed sources in the administration, Secretary Perry will be transferred to Water Reed this weekend." The reporter, an attractive thirtyish woman with long blond hair and perfect makeup and teeth, paused. She then turned sideways and gestured toward the inside of the restaurant.

"The only witness to the officer-involved shooting was the

waitress who worked the night shift. Thanks to her astute observance, authorities are searching for a dark American-made sedan, probably not more than two years old. Due to the heavy fog, she could not describe the driver. But she told police that the man inside the restaurant with Professor Turani was a short, well-dressed Hispanic male in his thirties. If you have any information regarding either the vehicle or the suspect, please contact Galveston police."

"See," David said. "They don't know about you."

"Except that I am short, dark skinned and could easily pass for Hispanic. I'm not going anywhere with you in your rental. We wouldn't make it off the island."

David held the car keys toward Hussein. "I switched. Driving a Jeep Cherokee now." He explained about driving to Houston and changing cars and said, "We must finish this. Allah will bless us."

Hussein gave out a heavy sigh and sat back in a chair. He shook his head. "I mean, well...the cops finding the anthrax on the professor...that changes things. They have to suspect Turani was going to attack Perry with the pathogen. And that leads to someone in the hospital. What if they identify Mario?"

"Mario has never seen you. He's only seen Turani and me. You don't exist. I'm the one who should be worried."

Hussein thought for a moment, chewed his lip and said, "We will need weapons."

He bounded below and came back with two small automatics. He handed one to David. "Nine-millimeter Berettas," he said. "Seventeen-round magazines. I wanted something with punch."

David handled the gun and then glanced at the one in Hussein's hands. "They look the same," he said.

"They are. I got them on the street. Probably boosted from

some gun store."

David held the gun up before his eyes and mumbled a prayer. "For my father and brother and little sister, precious Akilah. For the glory of Allah."

Chapter Thirty-Three

Friday afternoon
Galveston

Hebinck said we'd meet again at 5:00 p.m., or earlier if something popped. I decided this would be a good time to catch Travis and asked Matthews to call Erwin at the hospital and clear me to see Officer Jones. Ten minutes later I parked in the UTMB garage, grabbed the football I'd found in my closet and fast-walked to the ER entrance across the street. I flashed my ID to the agents in front, who waved me through to the Galveston PD officers at the metal detector. Several more cops milling around the waiting area sent suspicious glares as I marched to the admittance desk. The clerk said Tube Jones was still in intensive care. As I turned away, Travis stepped out of the ICU entrance. He saw me and hustled over, his eyes blood red, his face pale. I held the football to my side hoping he wouldn't notice.

"Mr. McLeod, so glad you came back."

We hugged.

"Is your mom here?"

"She went home to check on my little brother. Hope she stays there awhile. She's worn out. Dad's got tubes running into his arm, one down his throat. The nurse said they're keeping him sedated. I...I wanted to hear his voice so bad."

Travis' voice cracked as tears flooded his eyes. He leaned

into me, knees buckling. I helped him to an empty room down the hall and we sat side-by-side on a couch.

"Tell you what," I said. "If you can hang on until later tonight, I'll come back and spell you. When I get here, you go home and take care of your mother and brother."

His eyelids drooped half closed. He put his elbow on the armrest at the end of the couch and propped himself up with his arm. "That's...really nice. But you don't have to—"

I shut him off. "Your dad is a good friend. I'll be here."

Travis managed a half smile and wiped his eyes with his hand. I passed the football to him and pointed to his dad's signature.

"This is the game ball from our last playoff game."

I pointed to the date, December 12, 1972. "Signed by everyone on the team, including the coaches. They gave it to me as quarterback, but your dad was the hero. He made the winning catch, I just threw the ball. He went high in the end zone, caught the pass and came down with two defenders on his back. Held on to the ball somehow. It was...well... miraculous. Nobody knew he could leap like that. The catch is still talked about today."

I paused while Travis examined the other signatures. I laid my hand on his shoulder and said, "Give it to your dad for me, after he gets out of the hospital."

Travis ran his fingers over his dad's signature. A tear dropped onto the ball. I squeezed his shoulder. He closed his eyes, put both hands on the ball and brought it tight to his chest. We both knew the gift was more than a football. If he could give the ball to his dad, it meant his dad would be okay.

I left Travis dozing on the couch and decided to reward myself with a double cheeseburger and chocolate shake. I drove over to the Whataburger on Broadway and went in for a sit-down meal. I'd just unwrapped the burger when my cell phone buzzed.

"Don't forget about the five o'clock meeting," Matthews said, anticipation in his voice. "Hebinck has new information."

I ate half the burger and finished the shake in the truck. I got there early and Harry Stein was walking out the front door when I arrived. As usual, he was a perfect picture of style and grace decked out in brown wool pants with matching suede shoes and belt, a light-green cotton shirt and a checkered green-and-brown cardigan sweater. His perfectly coiffured silver hair was swept tight against his head, and his goatee and mustache appeared waxed and trimmed to perfection.

"I don't mind you guys using my house," he said, a rare frown on his face. "But these last-minute conferences Hebinck calls are a pain in the tookus. Especially when I don't have a meeting of my own to go to."

I shook my head in mock disgust. "Bullshit, Harry. You're dressed like a movie star. You must have something going on. Hot date?"

"I'll be at June's, casserole-number-one's house across the street."

"Mmmm...getting interested, Harry?"

"Don't mess with me, Parker. At my age I'm only interested in eating. And that poor woman should be turned in to the CDC in Atlanta for food poisoning. No wonder her husband left. Her tuna and noodle casserole is straight out of the '50s. Who eats that crap?"

"Harry, such language," I said, grinning.

"Can't help it, she's as boring as grape jelly."

"Grape jelly?"

"Yes. With all the wonderful, even exotic, jams and preserves on the market, why would anyone eat grape? Apricot, peach, maybe. If you want plain jelly at least use wild plum. A blueberry and rhubarb mix is good, but my favorite is a black fig preserves from France. Ooh, la, la. But grape? Really? I feel sorry for them. The same people who prefer grape jelly also like ranch dressing. Might as well use goose droppings. My stomach roils just thinking about it." He dropped his shoulders and sighed, then crossed the street to June's house.

I turned and strode up Harry's porch steps shaking my head, thinking about my occasional late night go to: PB & J.

We were awfully close to putting a ribbon around the terrorist threat. After murdering my friend Monty Edwards and a dozen other innocent people at a Berlin café, Rashad Zahir was now a pile of blackened ash. One more bomb maker gone to his "forty virgins" reward in paradise. Good luck with that, I thought.

On the local scene, my friend Officer Derry Jones had eliminated Professor Turani, and Galveston PD had recovered the deadly pathogen. Professor Turani's co-conspirator at the Waffle House and the driver with the dark sedan were still out there but, with the anthrax recovered, I didn't see them as much of a threat. But then the "Abul problem" raised its ugly head. Was it possible Rashad Zahir had a brother no one knew about?

I was still hungry from eating only half the burger, so since no one else had arrived, I rummaged around in Harry's refrigerator and found two pieces of cheesecake complete with cherry topping. Nothing goes better with cheesecake than a cold beer, so I popped the last Shiner in the box. I had finished the second piece of cheesecake and had the Shiner bottle turned up, sucking out the last drop, when Agents Hebinck and Matthews padded down the hallway.

"Drinking on the job?" Matthews said.

I held the bottle up. "So fire me."

"You won't get severance."

Hebinck growled, "Okay, enough bullshit. This isn't over. We've got at least three suspects still on the ground here. The threat level is high."

I slid the empty beer bottle into the trash. "Hell, Burney. We got the anthrax back. They don't have time to build another bomb, and Plastic Man himself couldn't get into that hospital room."

Hebinck tightened his face, ignoring my jab. "I can't afford your optimism, Parker."

The front door opened and Chief Puryear swaggered up the hallway with General Roush and the CIA man Peter Kay lagging behind. We moved to the now familiar kitchen table. A minute later, Agent Erwin came in.

Hebinck checked his watch. "It's after 5:00 p.m. I'm sure Dr. Lang is on her way, but I don't want to wait any longer. Let's get started."

Matthews cleared his throat. "We think the driver who left the Waffle House scene may be this Abul person. If he is truly Rashad's brother, and if he's as resourceful as Rashad, he may already have a new plan working. The problem is we don't have his description. We're hoping to get a report from Mossad within the hour. Meanwhile, we've got everybody in town looking for the dark sedan."

Chief Puryear broke in, "Our officers have stopped several, but no luck so far."

Roush said, "With Rashid Zahir and Professor Khoury dead, maybe Abul and the rest of the suspects will give up the ghost and sneak out of town."

"I hope not," Matthews replied. "We want to catch the bastards. Besides, if we're right about Rashid Zahir having a vendetta against Secretary Perry for killing his father, Abul could be just as dedicated."

"What about the suspect who was with Turani at the

Waffle House," I asked.

"We still don't know if he is a hospital employee or vendor of some type who has access. Best we can do is work the hospital list," Hebinck said.

Hebinck looked at Erwin.

"UTMB is the largest employer on the island," Erwin said. "We have thousands of profiles to go through. We should know something later tonight."

"And the third suspect at the Houston airport?" I added.

Hebinck grimaced. "Haven't got that figured out yet."

Across from me, Hebinck kept checking his cell phone, waiting for the call from Washington about the report on Abul from Mossad. Kay was lying low, not saying anything. No one was happy about the most recent CIA screw-up by killing Rashad Zahir instead of using him to help the FBI track the rest of the terrorists. If the CIA had waited, the remaining suspects would already have been in custody. No one begrudged sending the missile in, the bastard needed to die. It was just bad timing.

At 5:30 p.m., I said to Hebinck, "What did Anna say when you spoke to her?"

Hebinck glanced at his watch, then scrunched his eyes. "Uh...well, she said our agents were just wrapping up interviewing the lab employees. She was going to send everyone home early and lock up. She said she'd be here by 5:00 p.m."

I fished my phone from my pocket, found Anna's number in my Contacts and pushed Send. "Something's not right," I said.

Chapter Thirty-Four

Friday afternoon
Galveston

David and Hussein drove north over the causeway in the new Jeep Cherokee, passed the chemical plants and downtown Texas City. David checked his watch: 3:30 p.m. Anna usually arrived at the Tremont bar by 5:30 or 6:00 p.m. He would have to intercept her at her condo before she went to the bar, get her to the laboratory, and then to the hospital in time for Mario to doctor Perry's bandage before he went off shift at 7:00 p.m. He didn't have a lot of time to waste capturing Bully.

They stopped at the entrance to Molly Putts' road and surveyed the scene. There were no vehicles on the street and, except for a lone rider on a horse way out in a field, nothing but prairie in all directions surrounding her house. David cruised slowly down the road, studying the house and yard and looking for any signs of movement.

"So far so good," he said to Hussein. "No one on the porch."

"So I hold the old man and woman hostage while you get this Anna woman," Hussein said. "How am I going to get back to the boat?"

"I will bring Anna back here after she gives Mario the anthrax. We will kill all three of them at the same time."

Hussein withdrew the Berretta from the back of his pants

~ 313 ~

and jacked the slide, making sure a bullet was seated in the chamber. David parked fifty feet shy of the house, hoping Bully and the old woman didn't see the jeep. Rather than enter through the front gate and risk being seen, they crept quietly along the side fence, keeping their eyes peeled on the porch. Last thing they needed was for the old woman to suddenly decide to take up her usual perch outside. They hopped the fence and eased onto the porch. Midway to the door, a board underneath Hussein's foot squeaked. They stopped and listened. No movement or noise inside.

David said, "Get on the other side of the door up against the wall. I'll stand in front of the door. When it opens, you rush in."

Hussein held the Berretta by his side and took position. David kept his automatic tucked in the small of his back. He knocked loudly on the frame and waited. Nothing. He knocked again, louder. The door opened. Molly Putts sat in her wheelchair, eyes scrunched, staring at David through the screen door holding the double-barreled twelve-gauge in her lap. Hussein remained unseen.

"What?" she snorted, her voice sassy as ever.

Hussein stepped in front of David, yanked the screen door open and tore the weapon from her hands. David stepped past him and pushed her wheelchair back. He took the shotgun from Hussein and propped it against the wall by the door.

"Where's Bully?" he yelled.

Bully came rolling out of the kitchen, one hand moving the chair wheel, the other swinging a baseball bat. Hussein was facing Molly, his back turned to Bully. Bully slammed the bat into the back of Hussein's knee. Something popped and Hussein crumbled to the floor. The automatic skittered across the plank floor. As Bully drew back for another strike, David stepped forward and grabbed the bat away.

"Don't want to hurt you, old man. Do what you're told and you and the old woman will be okay. Otherwise...."

David glanced at Molly and back at Bully. Hussein got up from the floor rubbing the back of his knee. He limped over, put his hand on the arm of a chair for balance and picked up the automatic. He went back to Bully and slapped him across the face with the gun. Blood spurted from Bully's cheek. He moaned, closed his one good eye and put his hand to the wound.

"Leave him alone," Molly shouted, rolling her wheelchair forward.

Hussein raised the gun to hit her, but David stopped him. Molly pressed a tissue to Bully's cheek. He held it in place to stop the blood flow. Molly grasped his other hand and squeezed.

"What do you sons of bitches want?" she said. "We ain't got no money."

"Pay attention," David said. "I'm leaving. Hussein will stay here to guard you. Try anything stupid and he will shoot you." He looked at the scowl on Hussein's face and then back at Bully and Molly. "You already pissed him off."

The cut on Bully's cheek still oozed blood. He held the tissue to his cheek and moved his jaw around, checking to see if anything was broken. "You gonna leave us here with this forkin' idiot? What's this all about?"

"I will call you and put Anna on the phone. Do as you're told or I will kill her."

"You...you what?" Bully yelled.

"You heard me. You try anything and I will kill Anna and Hussein will shoot your girlfriend. Is that clear?"

As David entered the causeway, he noticed white caps building on West Bay. Gray and black clouds were blowing in from the north, the sky already darkening. Good he thought; the sooner the storm arrives, the better.

He turned the corner onto Mechanic Street at 4:45 p.m. and luckily found a parking spot at the curb just down from the entrance to Anna's building. He turned the engine off and began pressing and releasing the steering wheel with both hands to relieve pressure, trying to control his growing headache. Sweat built across his forehead. He had no experience in this kind of action, but he could do it. He had to. For his family.

He glimpsed Anna approaching on the sidewalk. He knew the routine. She would freshen up in her condo and head across the street to the Tremont bar. Even wearing the long coat pulled tightly against her face, she looked spectacular as she walked, her earrings dangling and hair bouncing at the sides of her neck. A real beauty, he thought. Too bad. He kind of wished he'd made a move on her earlier at Rudi and Paco's restaurant when it might have worked.

The two-story building appeared to have condos on each floor. Not knowing which unit was hers, he would have to risk peeking through the entrance trying to see where she lived. He watched her enter the elevator, ran inside and raced up the stairs. He peered into the corridor and watched Anna open her door. He moved quickly and shoved her into the unit.

She stumbled, but kept her balance and turned, "Whaaat?"

"Shut up," David said. He grabbed her shoulders, pushed her down on the couch and stood over her. She tried to get up. He slapped her across the face. She whimpered in pain and put her hand to her cheek.

He pulled the Beretta out of his back and waved it in front of her. "Shut up and listen and I won't hurt you again. Scream and I'll hit you." He raised the gun high.

She grimaced, touched her swelling lip, then lowered her eyes, trying to steady herself. When she looked up again, David saw a new Anna, her eyes steeled on him, jaw tight.

"You bastard."

He punched a number into his cell phone and spoke into it, "Talk to her." He put the phone on speaker and held it in front of her.

"Hello, Dr. Lang," the voice said. "I have a gun aimed at your grandfather's head. I will not hesitate to shoot him and the old woman. I am putting the phone in front of Bully so he can talk to you. Be careful what you say, old man."

"Don't do it, Anna," Bully screamed. "Whatever they want. Don't do it."

The phone went dead.

"What do you want, you prick!"

David told her.

"Are you crazy? I can't do that. The lab has protocols, everything is secured. The director is out of town. Security is tighter than ever. I have already locked up and sent all the employees home. The guards would be suspicious of me coming back. They wouldn't let me in."

"Bullshit! You're the assistant director. You do what you want. I know the cops probably took the anthrax they found at the Waffle House to your lab. Dangerous stuff, so they would have to. It's probably sitting there in the same vial. You just have to bring it out again. That's all. Simple enough. Bully, or should I say your grandfather, and the old woman will live and you…well…you'll get off. After all, you had no choice."

"You shit. You set me up, manipulated me. Screw you," Anna snarled.

"Not a bad idea," David said, glancing at the bedroom. "I know you wanted me that night at the restaurant. I'm sure all I had to do was ask."

A nasty smirk crowded Anna's face. She averted her eyes and moved her jaw around with her hand. David noticed the mounds on her chest seemed to move with her gesture. He felt himself getting excited. Her scorn just stirred him more. Goddamn, she was a sexy bitch. He glanced at the bedroom again, thinking. He had time. It would only take a few minutes.

But it would be dark soon. Better to wait and take advantage of the night. Just so he got the anthrax to the hospital in time for Mario to slip it on the bandage.

He managed a smile. Maybe? But she was a tigress, would probably fight like hell. Might even get lucky and get the best of him. He couldn't chance losing control this late in the game. Getting to Perry was more important. Way more important. Besides, there were plenty of hot-fleshed Latin women in Argentina. Maybe even in Mexico and the other Central America countries. Life was good. He just had to get past the next hour or two.

He glanced at his watch: 5:30 p.m. Time to go. David grabbed Anna's arm, pulled her up and half dragged her down the hall and into the stairway. Out on the street, a fierce north wind cut across the sidewalk and bit into their faces. Anna still had her heavy coat on, but David was wearing only a thin jacket.

He'd warned her not to scream or try to attract the attention of the valet or hotel patrons that might be entering or leaving the hotel. He needn't have worried. The entire block was empty.

He guided Anna to the passenger side of the Jeep, opened the door and pushed her inside. Then he hustled to the driver's side and slid in, the phone in his hand. He held the text message up for her to see: KILL THEM.

"All I have to do is push Send. That's it, and your grandfather and the old woman are dead." He snapped his fingers. "Just like that," he said. "This phone will never leave my hand."

"I told you I'd do it," Anna said. "Just please don't hurt them."

David's lips peeled back in a sick smirk. He pressed his thumb down outside the phone as though pretending to push the send button and hollered "whoosh," simulating the noise when a message was sent. Then he laid his head back and laughed heartily, his voice shrieking across Anna's ears.

Chapter Thirty-Five

Friday afternoon
Galveston

When my call to Anna went to voicemail, I said, "Anna, it's Parker. We're all at Harry's. Where are you? Call me." I ended the call and looked at Hebinck.

"Well, she did say she was going to run by her condo and change clothes."

"That's five minutes from the lab. She should have been here by now. I'm going to her condo."

Hebinck put his hand on my arm. "Parker, the meeting's not over. Washington will call with the Israeli report on Abul Zahir any minute."

I waved Hebinck off and hurried out to the porch only to find leaves and loose limbs hurtling across the yard. A light rain pelted my truck, but the swirling black clouds overhead told me more was coming.

I cranked the engine and surged toward Mechanic Street and Anna's condo, my mind darting from one scenario to another, none of them good. Car accident? Something happened at the lab? Where the hell was she?

I'd hoped with the anthrax recovered, the terrorists would give up and leave the island. Go back to their worm holes. But Anna's being late turned my stomach in knots. Something wasn't right, I could feel it.

At least two terrorists were still on the loose, maybe three. It made sense that the meeting at the Waffle House was for Turani to pass the anthrax to the hospital contact, maybe give him instructions. But none of us had a clue what he was going to do with the anthrax. The best guess was he would somehow infiltrate the air conditioning system. If that was the case, all he needed was another pathogen. Anna had mentioned they could bring it from Mexico. That wouldn't be difficult, especially if the terrorists had connections with a drug cartel. But it would take time. And if the remaining suspects knew about the attack on Rashad, they might react in panic mode, thinking they would be next and desperate to act quickly.

The Gulf Coast Laboratory was the logical source. The lab contained enough lethal pathogens to wipe out the city of Galveston, if not all of Texas. But the lab was a fortress, its safety protocols unparalleled. And now there was even more security inside and out because of the terrorists' threat. There was no way anyone could break through all those layers of protection. Unless…unless an employee purposely sneaked something out. But the FBI had just vetted everyone again, this time for the possible hostage threat. The lab should be safe. Except for Anna. Damn.

I raced through a red light causing an oncoming driver to slam on his brakes and turn sideways, almost hitting me. I glanced back hoping the driver was okay, but didn't slow down. My watch read 5:35 p.m. I found Hebinck's number in my recent call list and punched his number.

"Burney, call your agent at the Gulf Coast Lab. Find out if your men interviewed Anna about the hostage threat."

Hebinck called back two minutes later. "No, Dr. Lang said she was too busy for an interview."

"Okay, listen. Anna's mother Johanna Lang is a well-known physician in Kaiserslautern, Germany. She's been hospitalized with a stroke. Have someone find her, see if she's in any danger."

"Is she the hostage? Christ, Parker, why didn't you tell us?"

"Just do it," I said.

"It makes sense," Hebinck said. "Rashad Zahir killed your friend in Berlin. There are jihadist cells all over Germany. He could have easily set up a kidnapping."

Three minutes later, I rolled into the tenant parking lot for Anna's condo, a half-block from her building. I slammed my truck into an empty spot, grabbed my .45 out of the glove compartment and jumped out into the pelting rain. The hood of Anna's car was still warm. I stuck the automatic in the back of my pants and ran full speed to the condo entrance.

I raced through the front entrance, barreled up the stairs two at a time and banged on Anna's door. A woman with a familiar face opened the door across the hall. I couldn't place her but should have. She was a looker.

"Hey, what's all the racket? Building on fire?"

"Do you know Anna Lang?" I screamed, panting hard.

"Of course I do. You're Parker McLeod, we met at the Spot."

It was Iryna Kravets, Anna's friend at the lab. "Anna may be in danger, have you seen her?

Iryna's eyes widened. "Danger! What do you mean?"

"I don't have time to explain."

I returned to Anna's door and banged my fist several more times.

"Try this," she said, handing me a key. I opened the door and Iryna swept past me, shouting for Anna. She checked the bedroom and bathroom and hurried back to the living area. "Not here," she said, worry lines creasing her forehead.

"She was due at a meeting an hour ago, said she was coming here first to change."

"There's no sign she's been here," Iryna said. "The bedroom and bathroom are still tidied up the way she leaves them every morning, so I don't think she's been here to change. Have you tried the Tremont bar?"

With Anna due at the meeting, the Tremont didn't make sense, but I decided to check anyway. I gave Iryna my cell number and asked her to call me if she heard from Anna. It was a long shot but a call I hoped to get.

I sprinted toward the Tremont, sloshed through the water building in the street and hustled up the marbled steps. The lobby was alive with folks. Off to my right people crowded around the registration desk, while to the left several more waited for an elevator. Several couples filled the two seating areas amongst the potted palms. Every chair at the bar was full. The bartender Gene, the same long-haired hippy I'd seen earlier, splashed drinks as fast as he could make them. As he rounded the bar headed toward the seating areas with a full tray, I stepped in front of him.

"Hey, man, what's up?" he said, recognizing my face but not my name.

"Has Dr. Lang been in?"

"No she hasn't. And I'm in a hurry. Can I get by, please?"

"You're sure. You haven't seen her in the last hour?"

"I said no."

I didn't have time for attitude. When he attempted to step around me, I grabbed his shoulder and pinched the soft muscle close to his neck. His yelp caught the attention of a couple at the bar. They looked, but didn't say anything.

I spoke softly into his ear, my hand squeezing the muscle. "Listen to me, Gene. She may be in trouble." I took a pen out of his pocket and wrote my name and cell number on a napkin.

"You see her, you call me. Got it?" I squeezed harder.

"Yeah, yeah, sure man," he said. "Easy on the shoulder."

I darted toward the exit, not sure what to do next. My phone buzzed.

"Where are you?" Matthews asked.

"The Tremont."

"I'm on the way," he said. "Our liaison agent in Kaiserslautern said Anna's mother is in intensive care. The local police have cordoned off the entire floor to be safe, but they said there was no way anyone could have kidnapped a patient out of ICU. It was a good idea, Parker, but Rashad must have been referring to someone else."

"Then why is Anna missing?"

"I can't answer that. But there's something else. Mossad's tap on Khoury's sister's phone in Beirut paid off. The sister phoned a company called Arnold Engineering in Indianapolis, owned by David Arnold. She gave the receptionist a phone number and asked her to have Mr. Arnold call. Turns out the number is Badih Khoury's cell phone."

"So Khoury survived the missile attack?"

"Yes, but he had to know Rashad was killed. He wanted David Arnold to know for some reason."

"So who the hell is Arnold?"

"I called Arnold Engineering and spoke to Mary Phillips, Arnold's secretary. I had to brace her with the FBI bit, but she finally confirmed a woman with broken English left a message asking Arnold to call the number. Mary also said her boss was attending a seminar in Galveston. We checked. David Arnold did sign in to a couple of meetings. We found his picture on line. I just sent it to you in a text. We're also running his background. Should have that soon."

David...David...where had I heard that name? I tried to remember but couldn't put it together. I sensed the bitter taste of bile edging up my throat, my heart thumping hard. David...David...where? Then it hit me: the man with Anna when she'd gone to confront Bully. Wait—that meant David knew Bully was Anna's grandfather. He also knew where Bully lived.

"It's Bully Stout," I said.

"Bully Stout? What do you mean, Bully Stout?"

"Bully is the hostage. Rashad must have figured out he couldn't get to Anna's mother so they went to the backup plan and kidnapped Anna's grandfather."

"Your uncle Bully Stout is Anna's grandfather? What the hell are you talking about? That time we went fishing, Bully was living in a camper beside The Garhole. He's Anna's grandfather?"

"I don't have time to explain, Maurice. That was a year ago. Bully now lives with his girlfriend."

"Holy shit! I don't believe it," Matthews snapped. "That cranky old goat has a girlfriend? Who is she and where do they live?"

"A woman named Molly Putts, she lives in Texas City. The local cops must know her. Get somebody to her house now! The kidnappers may have Anna there, too."

I was about to rush out to my truck and head to Bully's house when the photo came through on my phone. Damn! If this was David Arnold, I'd seen him before. But where...? Got it! The first time I'd met Anna at the Tremont bar, the tall, black-headed man at the end. Before Anna arrived, I'd played the spy game, thinking of a course I'd taken on how to remember a suspect by using facial dimensions, memorizing the eyes, ears, nose and face shape: round, oval, square. Arnold's face was square-shaped with a strong jawline. I studied the photo on my phone, wondering how David Arnold, an engineer from Indianapolis, Indiana, was mixed up in the terrorist plot to kill the Secretary of Homeland Security.

And something else: Arnold had followed Anna when she

left the bar, watching as she crossed the street. He knew where she lived.

Gene saw me returning to the bar, a flash of dread in his eyes. I stood at the end and motioned him toward me. He hesitated, but when I stepped behind the bar he moved close.

I pushed my phone to his face. "Recognize this man?"

"Well...I...I."

I grabbed his shoulder again, inched my hand toward his neck.

"Mr. Arnold," he said, his voice breaking. "He's a guest here."

"Room number?"

"I...can't give that to you."

"I told you Dr. Lang is in trouble. The bastard may have kidnapped her."

The glass in his hand started to shake. "She's a nice lady," he said, his mouth quivering. "They've been at the bar together several times. She seemed to like him."

"Room number. Look it up," I said, squeezing the shoulder muscle.

"I don't have to. He's charged drinks to his room all week: Room 369."

"How do I get into the room?"

"You...can't. Have to see Mr. Baker, the manager."

"Come with me." I grabbed his arm and yanked him out from behind the bar and across the lobby to the reception desk. Gene said something to the woman behind the desk. A minute later a tall beanpole of a man with a round face and a gap between his central incisors came out. He looked like a Halloween pumpkin sitting on a stick. He glanced at Gene and then focused on me.

"I'm Dean Baker, the manager here. What's this all about?"

I buzzed Matthews on my cell and handed it to Baker. He

listened intently and handed the phone back to me.

"The FBI is on the way," he said. "We have to wait—"

"There's no time. Give me the pass key!"

"I can't be responsible—"

"Give it to him," Gene said, his voice so forceful it would probably cost him his job.

My buddy Gene coming around, realizing Anna might truly be in danger. We both moved an intimidating step toward Baker.

The elevator door opened and we raced to Arnold's room. When Gene slid the card in the lock, I slammed the door back and went in, crouched over, the .45 in my hand. Nothing but a few clothes hanging in the closet, an overnight bag and the usual toiletries in the bathroom. Then I looked closer at a towel on the floor. Three indentions, one where the head would have been and two for the knees: a makeshift prayer rug. My heart sank. It couldn't have been worse. David Arnold was one of the terrorists involved in the plot to assassinate General Perry. And he'd manipulated Anna in the process.

But something wasn't right. If Arnold had planned to kill Perry, he should have checked out and been ready to escape as soon as the attack went down. Unless he was one of the dedicated suicide types, planning to be a martyr. Then he wouldn't care. Which meant if he had Anna, she was even in more danger.

I ripped down the stairs two at a time and entered the lobby just as Matthews came through the front door.

"Parker," he yelled. "What did you find?"

"A prayer rug."

I slipped past him yelling, "Where is your car?"

"Out front."

"Let's go."

"Where?"

"If Arnold kidnapped Anna, he's on his way to Molly Putts' house. He needs Anna to trick Bully into letting him into his house. He'll threaten to kill Bully and Molly in front of Anna so Anna will get the anthrax out of the lab."

"Wait," Matthews said. "Then how will the hostage thing work? Who is going to guard Bully and Putts?"

"Aw, shit."

"The new suspect at the airport Roush told us about," Matthews added. "Has to be."

Matthews got on his cell phone and called Hebinck. Two minutes later Hebinck called back. Matthews put him on speaker.

"Texas City SWAT is on its way to Molly Putts' house."

Chapter Thirty-Six

Friday evening
Galveston

Bully Stout sat in his wheelchair, his mind churning and thinking about a way out. He hoped Molly felt the same as he did. Their lives spent, confined to wheelchairs, eating mushy food and wearing diapers. Nothing he would confess to anyone. He'd heard someone on TV mention the term "quality of life." Whatever that meant, Bully knew he didn't have any. Even before he and Molly had been taken hostage, he was thinking about Molly's shotgun, sticking the barrel into his mouth and pulling the trigger.

Hell, he was only a burden to Molly, and that wasn't right. Before the stroke and the wheelchair, he could at least take care of her. He was still driving, could go to the store for groceries and even stop to see one of his old high school buddies, Harry Stein or Neddie Lemmon, the three of them the last remaining members of the Dead Peckers' Club. But he couldn't remember the last time Harry had dropped by to check on him. And Neddie had regressed to his teen years, drinking and chasing women. Although what he would do when he caught one, Bully couldn't imagine.

His only visitor now was Anna, and he was embarrassed that she had to see him like this, his once powerful muscles atrophied to limp ropes of sand, a shriveled prune compared to what he used to be.

Molly's life wasn't any better. All her family and friends had gone to the great nowhere. Her last good friend had been Bernice Bentzel, known in the area as the "Turtle Lady" for her devotion to the Kemp's Ridley turtles she rescued every spring on Galveston's beaches. Bernice had lived down the street from Molly and kept a mini-zoo behind her house, home for every injured wild animal or bird that people brought her to rehabilitate.

She'd been a friend to him, as well. In fact, it was while visiting Bernice that he had met Molly. But then that bastard from Cuba, sent by the Castro brothers, had murdered Bernice and set fire to her house. Molly hadn't been the same since. In fact, Bully thought, neither had he.

He and Molly had discussed how miserable their lives had become. If one of them died, they both knew the survivor wouldn't last long, maybe a few months at best. They'd even considered turning out the lights together, hand in hand. Molly had mentioned it again a few nights earlier. Said she could feel herself getting weaker, with no appetite, the will to live slowly fading with the passing of each day.

Why not go out with a bang, Bully thought. Do something good and save his granddaughter.

While Hussein stared out the window, Bully leaned in close and whispered to Molly. She closed her eyes and Bully felt her squeeze his hand. When she opened her eyes, a tear ran down her cheek. She squeezed his hand again and nodded toward the shotgun leaning against the wall, partially hidden by a window curtain.

Why not, he thought? Worth a try. Take this slimy worm out if they could. The shotgun was their only chance. And if Hussein won and shot them both, so what? At least they'd tried to save Anna. Better than just waiting to be killed.

Like those brave souls on that airliner up in Pennsylvania on 9/11 who'd charged the cabin. Everyone died but they'd stopped the attack. And that's what he and Molly could do: stop these bastards. Whatever awaited them on the other side couldn't be any worse than not knowing what new pain or misery they'd wake with each day. Molly had said they were like a couple of old draft horses put out to pasture. Except the old horses still had the freedom to move around.

Bully wasn't stupid. He knew the bastard was going to kill them anyway. He was surprised he hadn't already shot them. Maybe he needed to keep them alive until Anna had done whatever they wanted her to do. And then it hit him. Anna worked at the Gulf Coast Laboratory. They must be forcing her to steal something from the lab, threatening to kill him and Molly if she didn't. It was the only thing that made sense. But he couldn't let Anna sacrifice her career, maybe her life, for him. Not the way he'd treated her, ignoring her plea about Emma when he'd known all along it was the truth. His only chance to save her was to act now. The order to kill them both would come the next time Hussein's phone buzzed. He was out of time.

Hussein peeled the curtain back and stared down the street, wondering how he had let David talk him into this. He could have been several hours down the coast in the Bertram by now with $10,000 in a duffel and a tank full of diesel. No doubt that David was on a suicide mission, forcing Anna Lang to steal anthrax out of her lab and somehow getting her to ferret it into the hospital pharmacy. What if David had overestimated Anna's devotion to her grandfather? Why would she risk her life for these two old windbags, each of them with one foot in the grave?

And what if something went wrong? What if the cops captured or killed David? Even if he escaped their wrath and

Anna got the vial out of the lab, the hospital's security was so tight, David wouldn't be allowed inside. Which meant Anna would have to take it in. And what would keep Anna from screaming for the cops as soon as she was away from him?

Hussein saw nothing down the empty street but a pounding rain and blowing wind. Even the cowboy he'd seen in the pasture across the street was gone. Dark shadows were closing in on the road. Soon he wouldn't be able to see past the fence. He looked back at the old man and woman sitting in the wheelchairs, holding hands with faces contorted in fear, and Bully with a tissue pressed to his cheek.

Hussein checked the street again. Almost totally dark now, the wind stronger, the rain pounding the tin roof overhead. The storm he'd heard about on TV had arrived in full fury. How long would it take David and Anna to get the anthrax out of the lab and get it into the hospital? Would the storm slow them down? He hoped not, he wanted David to hurry and return so they could kill the three of them and get back to the boat. Get the hell out of Galveston.

Maybe David was right, everything would work out okay. Anna Lang steals the anthrax at the lab, Mario slips it onto the bandage. Hussein wanted the scheme to work. He hated Perry as much as David did. The bastard had murdered both his mentor Nassim Zahir and Nassim's son Rashad. And now Professor Turani. The infidels shouldn't get away with killing his brothers in jihad. Someone had to pay.

But then, Hussein thought, if the plan was going so well, why was sweat forming on his forehead? Why was his stomach in a knot? He wiped his forehead with his hand, closed the curtain, and looked back at the old couple again, holding hands, helpless in their wheelchairs. Something had changed. The fear he'd seen in their faces was gone, replaced by a seemingly calm feeling of acceptance. As if waiting for death.

Hell, just shoot the old fools, he told himself. Be done with it. Walk to the highway and thumb a ride. Kill the occupant and steal the car. He could be back at the boat and on his way out the ship channel before David got to the hospital. Screw David. He hardly knew him, didn't owe him anything.

If David's plan worked, fine. David would figure his own way out of the jam. If the plan didn't work, David would probably end up shot to pieces and lying on a concrete parking lot somewhere, like Turani at the Waffle House.

The more Hussein thought about it, the more convinced he became that David wasn't coming back. He would either be captured or killed. Or hell, David could just escape in the boat himself, leaving him holding the bag. He had just about decided to shoot the old geezers and take off when the old woman screamed across the room.

"You know this ain't gonna work, don't you. I can see it in your eyes. You're nervous as a cow in heat waitin' on a big ass bull to mount her."

"Shut up old woman," Hussein yelled back. He paced the floor, swinging the gun with his arm.

Molly droned on, "Best thing you can do is haul ass while you can. Tear out our phone. We don't have no car. We'd be stuck here in these wheelchairs 'till somebody missed us, and there ain't nobody gonna do that. We're pretty much alone in the world. Hell, you could walk to the Houston airport before anyone turned up here."

Hussein stood in front of Molly. "You may be right, old woman. But you better hope I don't decide to take your advice and leave, because I'll shoot you both dead first."

Bully spoke up, "Yeah, you're some kinda tough-ass dude aren't you? Carrying that little pop gun and all." Bully shook his fist at Hussein. "If I could get outta this chair, I'd—"

Hussein raised his hand with the gun in it as though he was

going to hit Bully again, but didn't.

Molly caught the move and said. "You don't really want to hurt us, Mister. Like I done said, if you just leave, we can't do nothing. We can't go nowhere or even call anyone. Let me check the road, see if it's safe for you to go."

Before Hussein could stop her, Molly released Bully's hand and rolled to the window partially blocking the view of the shotgun with her wheelchair. She pushed the curtain back and peeked down the street, the shotgun behind her. Hussein started toward her when Bully yelled as loudly as he could.

"Hey!"

When Hussein turned toward Bully, Molly grabbed the old double barrel and aimed it at Hussein. She pressed the hammers back and pulled the trigger on both barrels. Click...click. She opened the breech and saw the empty chambers. Using her last bit of strength, she raised the shotgun as high as she could and heaved it at Hussein. The effort sapped what little she had left. She dropped her head, almost passing out.

Molly's toss wasn't hard enough and the shotgun bounced on the floor in front of Hussein. He raised the automatic at Molly, but Bully pushed the wheelchair forward and rammed his foot into the back of Hussein's bad knee. Hussein went down but held onto the gun. Molly revived just enough and rolled her 250 pounds over his arm, pinning it to the floor. But it was not the arm with the gun.

As Hussein raised the gun to shoot Bully, a tall man with flowing blond hair, wearing jeans and cowboy boots, burst through the kitchen door and shot Hussein in the chest. Hussein fell back against Molly's wheelchair, the gun still in his hand crashing to the floor, his other arm still pinned by the wheelchair.

When he raised his gun arm, Ernie Deats shot him again.

The bullet from Deats' thirty-eight revolver passed through Hussein's body into the floor beneath the wheelchair, missing Molly's lower half by inches. Molly rolled the chair back and Hussein's head hit the floor with a thud.

Deats stood over the body with his gun pointed at Hussein's head, blood pouring out of Hussein's chest and running across the floor, soaking into an old area rug. Molly rolled to Bully, crying tears of relief. Bully put his arm around her and hugged her tight.

Just then a flash-bang grenade broke through a window and landed close to Hussein's body. Bully pressed his hands to his ears and let out a harrowing scream as the tremendous noise broke what was left of his eardrums.

A battering ram hit the door and a SWAT officer, fully attired in a black helmet, vest and boots, broke through, a Colt M4 carbine with a thirty-round clip in his hands, yelling at Deats to drop his weapon. Deats dropped his gun to the floor and raised his hands. Two more SWAT officers stormed through the door, manhandled Deats against the wall and cuffed him.

"What the hell are you doing," Bully screamed at the officers. "He just saved our asses."

Molly pulled away from Bully yelling, "My rug, my rug. I'll never get that shit's blood outta it. It's all I got left of my Mama. Shit, shit."

Before the SWAT officer could stop her, Molly rolled her wheelchair to Hussein's body and stomped on his chest. As warm blood wicked through her soft-cotton house shoe, Molly cried out to Bully, tears streaming down her cheeks, "Damn it to hell. You gave me these warm bunny shoes for Christmas. They were my favorites, too."

Bully pushed the big wheels of his wheelchair until he was close to her. He reached out with his long arm and wrapped it around her shoulder. "Molly, oh Molly. It's okay, honey. We're back to where we were, Molly. Just you and me, back to where we were."

Chapter Thirty-Seven

Friday evening
Galveston

The storm arrived with full fury, a howling wind and pounding sheets of rain, pushing visibility down to a few car lengths and turning the red-and-blue strobe lights of Matthews' SUV into a ghostly haze.

As Agent Matthews careened onto Harborside and headed toward the causeway, I worried the whoop of the siren was so muted by the wind and rain that drivers would not hear us.

The traffic had slowed to the point that most of the drivers were either listening to loud music or were distracted by texting on their cell phones or both. The red strobe lights on Matthews' Suburban reflected back into the vehicle and matched the color of his face: angry and puffed from his rising blood pressure. He weaved through the slower cars, babbling curses and trying his best not to side-swipe other vehicles. Most of the other drivers were more perturbed than interested.

"Damn it. Don't these drivers know they're supposed to move to the side of the road for emergency vehicles? Where the hell do all these people come from?"

I sat hunched over the dashboard trying to help guide him along. "UTMB folks getting off work. A lot of them live off-island."

When the small Honda in front of us didn't pull over,

Matthews honked and the driver shot the bird. I slammed the dashboard with my palm thinking about Anna and worried we wouldn't make it to Molly's house in time. Every minute counted.

I screamed, "Hit the bastard, Maurice. We've gotta go."

Matthews dropped the gearshift into low, pressed the Suburban to the Honda's rear bumper and jammed the gas pedal. The driver sped up and moved to the side, mouthing curse words and banging the steering wheel as we passed. I returned the same salute he'd offered earlier.

Traffic stalled again in front of the Islander Motel where Galveston SWAT had killed the drug dealer they had mistaken for a terrorist. A dim light showed over the office door and the station wagon belonging to the Mexican family that had been shepherded out of the way for safety sat like a cold witness to the fumbled SWAT mission. Maybe the raid could have been handled better, but the wounded officer was okay and no one was going to miss the slime bag they'd killed.

When Matthews' cell buzzed, he put the phone on speaker.

"Where are you?" Hebinck shouted.

"Just about to get on the causeway," Matthews answered. "Maybe fifteen minutes out from the scene. Anything from Texas City SWAT?"

"They're staging now at the turnoff to Putts' house."

"Staging my ass," I screamed into the phone. "Get them in there now!"

Hebinck yelled, "Shut up and listen, Parker. Matthews needs to hear this. We've got more background on David Arnold."

"Tell me," Matthews shrieked, jamming the brakes and swerving around a car as he spoke.

"His mother Elizabeth Arnold taught English at the American University in Beirut and converted to Islam while she was there. According to Mossad, she had an affair with a married professor, our friend Nassim Zahir. She came back to the states pregnant. Her son David was born in St. Louis. She was a devoted Muslim, a true believer, but never a radical. She raised David in the faith. Margaret died a few years back. David was her only child."

Matthews and I exchanged glances.

Hebinck continued, "David Arnold's Muslim name is Abul Zahir."

"Jesus," Matthews spurted. "Am I hearing you right? David Arnold is Rashad Zahir's half-brother?"

"You got it," Hebinck said.

I gritted my teeth and mumbled, "And all this hell rained down on the peaceful tourist city of Galveston, Texas, on a cold day in January."

"There's more," Hebinck said. "Homeland Security tracked David's U.S. passport. He landed in Beirut the day before the attack on Secretary Perry and left Beirut for the U.S. the day after the attack. We're checking hotels. So far we've found nothing that says David spent the night in Beirut. We think Rashad slipped him across borders and they were together in Yemen when the bomb exploded at the Coast Guard base."

"Celebrating?" I said.

"That's our best guess," Hebinck added. "When the attack failed, we think David returned to the States with orders to finish the job."

"So that's when Abul, AKA David, and Rashad cooked up the anthrax scheme and recruited this Professor Turani character?" Matthews asked.

"That's what we think. Turani was not on our radar. He must have been a sleeper agent."

"So what else do we know about David or Abul, whichever?" I asked.

"Our local agent interviewed David's secretary Mary Phillips at her office after I spoke to her on the phone. Phillips said she had no idea David was Muslim. Claims she wouldn't have worked for him if she'd known. It turns out Phillips attends some fundamentalist sect that meets in one of those old closed-down movie theaters. Our agent said listening to her rant was like listening to Billy Graham on PCP.

"Phillips said she didn't understand how David could be a Muslim with all his drinking and womanizing. She said she would have left the job if it hadn't been for her husband getting laid off. According to her, all the old grouch does now is lie in front of the TV watching *I Love Lucy* reruns, drinking Bud Light and scratching his ass. Her words not mine, the agent said. She also claimed David going to Galveston made no sense. The seminar was not in his field."

"Sounds as if your agent has a new best friend," Matthews said managing a slight grin.

Hebinck said, "Well, he did say she wasn't bad looking for a bible thumper. He thinks with the old man at home, she's probably shagging the preacher."

I broke in. "Enough bullshit, Burney. We're about to hit the causeway. Once we get on, we can't get off. Anything else?"

Hebinck said. "Teams are searching his office and home now. So far they've located a prayer rug in his office closet and one at home, along with a Quran inscribed to him from his mother. He's a weirdo all right: part playboy, part dedicated Muslim and part terrorist. Go figure."

"Not so unusual," I said. "A lot of rich Arabs play the same game. Straight from the mosque in Riyadh to their jets and Monte Carlo. The women have their burqas off and their makeup and gold jewelry on before the plane is wheels up."

"Still, we haven't found anything that suggests David's had terrorist training. Maybe Rashad pressured him into this scheme."

"Good," I said. "If he's not a pro, he may make mistakes."

"Hasn't so far," Hebinck replied. "He's good enough that we're just now finding out about him. Neither one of those yahoos in the Minneapolis cell that bombed Perry has ever heard of David Arnold or Abul Zahir. Hell, those dummies didn't even know Rashad Zahir was their benefactor."

"Right," Matthews broke in. "Remember, Rashad used the name Mahdi, better known in Muslim beliefs as the 'guided one' who will appear at the end of times to restore righteousness before the end of the world."

I managed a chuckle and said, "Yeah, well, I don't know if this is the end of times, but it sure was the end of the Mahdi's world, obliterated under a cloud of dust by a predator drone in the middle of some shithole villa on the coast of the Third World."

Hebinck paused. "Hold it," he said. "I got a call coming in."

Matthews turned right on the feeder road and took the on-ramp to the causeway to find traffic almost completely stopped. With siren blaring, he eased into the far-right emergency lane and crept toward the causeway.

Hebinck came back on the line. "Texas City SWAT says Bully Stout and Molly Putts are safe. Some cowboy broke in the back door before the SWAT team could access the room and shot the terrorist. There're trying to identify the dead guy now."

"What about Anna?" I asked, my pulse racing.

"She's not there."

"What?"

David found a parking place next to the curb a block from the laboratory that had a clear view of the entrance. Two figures in raincoats stood under the temporary tent near the front. He couldn't see inside through the pouring rain, but he knew from his previous surveillance that there would be more security in the lobby manning the metal detector and checking IDs. He held his cell phone in front of Anna so she could see the text again: KILL THEM.

"This is it," he said. "Either you get the anthrax or Bully dies."

David grabbed Anna's arm and jerked her out of the Jeep. She pulled her coat over her head as David searched every direction. He saw no movement in the downpour. They crossed the street, and David guided her to the corner of a building where an overhang gave some relief from the hammering rain and wind. He wiped rain-water from his eyes and peeked around the corner to the lab entrance. The two agents were still huddled under the tent.

"Okay," David said. "Now we walk casually to the entrance. You introduce me as an associate. We go up and I watch you retrieve the vial."

"What!" Anna exclaimed. "That won't work." She pulled a photo ID out of the small purse in her coat pocket and shoved it in front of his face. "You have to have one of these. No one gets in without one."

"You are in charge. Talk your way past the guards."

"They will arrest us both."

David hesitated, not sure what to do.

"You have five minutes," he said. "Or I push Send." He let go of her arm and retrieved the Berretta from his pocket.

Raindrops dripped off the hood of Anna's coat onto her forehead and into an eye. She squinted and wiped the eye with her hand. "Five minutes aren't enough," she said. "I have to go through security, wait on the elevator, unlock the lab. I need more time."

David glanced again at the entrance. He scanned the entire

plaza area as far as he could see, thinking about roving patrols. His watch read 6:00 p.m. Mario had to have the anthrax for the bandage soon. He would have to chance the extra time.

"Okay eight minutes. If I see any unusual movement in front of the building or anyone approaching me here, I push Send. Or if I even see an agent talking on his radio or phone, Bully and Molly Putts are dead."

"What good is the anthrax to you now?" she asked. "Every cop and FBI agent on the island is searching for you. You'll never get into the hospital, much less the burn unit. Think, David. Drop me somewhere, even off the island if you want. You can get away."

"Perry murdered my entire family. He will pay! You have eight minutes starting now."

Anna strode off, sloshing through the ankle-deep water pouring across the plaza. She stopped at the tent and showed her ID to the FBI agents. David watched closely to see if either of the agents glanced his way. They seemed disinterested, just trying to stay out of the cold rain. She went into the building, showed her ID again, passed through the metal detector and entered the elevator.

Seven minutes passed. David scrunched his eyes, straining to see across into the building through the worsening storm. Where the hell was she? In front of the building, the two guards struggled to right the temporary FBI tent blown about by the wind. Wearing only a light jacket and no hat, David was soaked through, chilled to the bone, his body temperature dropping rapidly. He stuck the phone and Berretta back in his pocket and hugged his chest, shivering against the wind.

Inside the entrance, the normally well-lit lobby appeared dull, hazy. David saw movement but couldn't distinguish form. Eight minutes. The entrance door opened and Anna came out with her coat over her head and pulled tightly around her face.

One of the FBI agents seemed to speak to her, but she ignored the gesture and hurried across the flooded plaza.

Knowing that he was in the line of sight from the guards, David stepped back from the corner and waited. When Anna turned the corner, he grasped her arm and pulled her under the overhang.

"Show me," he said.

Anna wiped the rain from her eyes, reached into her purse and pulled out the cryovial wrapped in a white cloth. The cloth seemed the same as what he'd seen on the boat. She opened the cloth. The vial's amber-colored contents shown through the glass. Good, he thought. The bitch came through. Anna rewrapped the vial and started to put it back into her coat pocket. David grabbed her hand and took the vial.

"You get it when we get there," he said. He squeezed her arm at the bicep and guided her toward the rented Jeep Cherokee.

Matthews pulled to a stop in the emergency lane just before the bridge. "Hold it," he said. "I got another call." He hit the Speaker button. The deluge beating on the Suburban's roof made them have to scream to hear each other.

"This is Chief Puryear. Anna just left the Gulf Coast Laboratory. The on-duty officer said Anna was the last one out earlier, but she came back saying she'd left something inside. She was in there maybe ten minutes and left again."

"Anyone with her?"

"No, but she was all nervous and tensed up. Not her usual friendly self."

"Damn. He's got her," Matthews said. "She stole anthrax or something out of the lab and they're headed for the hospital."

"I can't believe she'd do that," I said. "She's a doctor. *First do no harm."*

Puryear, still on the phone, yelled, "I've got every available car searching for that dark sedan with orders to stop them at all costs. We've locked the hospital down tight. Nobody gets in."

When he said that, I thought, why in hell hadn't Hebinck warned the lab? Another inter-agency screw up. Puryear probably thought Hebinck would do it and Hebinck thought the same about Puryear.

Puryear shouted again, "There's a train blocking Harborside. You'll have to take Broadway."

Matthews hit the gas pedal and slid across the grass separating the freeway from the frontage road, spinning mud and slipping sideways in the rain. He gained the pavement and roared wrong-way down the feeder toward the Harborside underpass with siren screaming and lights flashing. With visibility almost zero in the hammering wind and rain, he zipped through the underpass dodging cars and entered the freeway speeding toward Broadway and the hospital.

As Matthews crossed 61st Street and hit Broadway Boulevard, a sudden slump of helplessness grabbed my gut. The Gulf Coast Laboratory stood in the center of the UTMB complex only a few blocks from the hospital. Even with the siren blaring and Matthews' foot heavy on the gas pedal, we were at least five minutes behind them. Five critical minutes. What would happen when David or Abul or whatever his name was realized the hospital was locked down? This was no longer about protecting Secretary Perry. This was all about saving Anna.

The pummeling rain flooded the streets and brought the Friday after-work traffic to a standstill. Matthews tried his best to thread through the vehicles jamming the boulevard, the whooping siren coursing through the storm.

Out of instinct or habit or just plain trepidation, I looked up and scanned the sky overhead, grateful for the pummeling rain that blocked the view. I knew the moon was there, somewhere. It had to be. But something told me it wasn't a good moon.

The University of Texas Medical Branch complex contained more than forty buildings among several square blocks of downtown Galveston. As the medical complex had grown over the years, more buildings had been added, creating a maze that took a map to navigate, streets twisting around, many with no obvious signposts.

David had never approached the hospital from this angle and with visibility down to a car length, he became thoroughly disoriented in the storm.

"Which way?" he yelled at Anna.

Anna looked at him, a confused look on her face. "I...I...don't—"

Traffic was building, people getting off work, trying to get home in the rain. Just then, a police cruiser turned a corner with lights flashing and came right at them. The officer driving stared through the windshield. David turned his head toward Anna. The cruiser slowed, but let them pass. David turned onto the street the cruiser had come from, thinking that might be the way. The curbs were flooded, forcing the jeep to the center of the road. A small car along the edge was stalled in the high water. David chugged through, took the next right and worried about the time. He had to get this done quickly before Mario got off work.

He screamed at Anna, "Recognize these buildings?"

Anna put her hand to her mouth, eyes flashing around. She shook her head, staring into the darkness. She's lying, he thought. She knows the way: She's stalling for time.

At the next intersection another police car had stopped a dark sedan, a man and a woman inside. David eased by. The cop had his gun by his side motioning for the driver to lower the window. Good, David thought. The cops still don't know he'd changed vehicles. He came to Avenue E and remembered Avenue O was close to Seawall Boulevard on the opposite side of the island from the hospital.

"Damn," he cried out to himself. "I turned the wrong way. The hospital is behind us."

He risked a quick glance at this watch: 6:20, almost out of time. He turned left onto Avenue E, looking for a through street back the other way. So much rain water flooded the street under the Jeep, he worried about stalling out. He arrived at 6th Street and looked both ways.

Frantic, he turned to Anna. "Is this it?"

Anna, shaking now from the cold said, "Sorry...I...I'm new to Galveston. The rain, I don't—"

David slammed the steering wheel. No choice now, he had to act. "This feels right," he said. He started to turn onto 6th Street but noticed flashing strobe lights in the next block. He strained through the windshield and saw two police vehicles turned sideways, blocking the intersection. He had no choice but to cross 6th Street and find a way to the hospital around the blockade, maybe a side street ahead.

The traffic on Broadway finally broke. Matthews sped up, yelling above the noise of the rain hitting the roof of the Suburban. "Where should I turn?"

"The next light is 6th Street," I said. "Just before Broadway intercepts Seawall Boulevard. Turn left there, takes you straight into the complex. We should see the hospital."

Matthews' phone buzzed. "What!" he said.

It was Hebinck. "Where are you now?"

"Just turned onto 6th Street headed for the hospital."

"David Arnold changed cars!"

"What?"

"We checked the car rentals at Hobby Airport. Arnold turned in the car we've been looking for, the Chevrolet Impala. He went to Alamo and got a Jeep Cherokee, light tan color. Here's the license plate number." Hebinck read off the number while Matthews and I tried to memorize it. I caught the last few digits, enough for now.

Matthews gripped the steering wheel harder. "Burney! We thought that phone call NSA intercepted at the airport meant Rashad had sent another terrorist. But it was just David Arnold changing cars?"

"Right," Hebinck responded.

"No new terrorist came in. Rashad is dead in Yemen. Turani killed at the Waffle House and the cowboy took out Hussein at Bully's house. Then David Arnold or Abul Zahir, whatever you want to call him, and the contact at the hospital are the only ones left."

"Exactly," Hebinck said. "Agent Erwin and the Secret Service will take care of the hospital contact. You find Arnold!"

"He's had time, must be close to the hospital," I said.

Matthews sped along 6th Street not slowing, the hospital only a few blocks ahead.

At the next street I said, "Flashing lights ahead, a roadblock. They have the hospital totally isolated."

A car zoomed across Ave E a block in front of us. Matthews screamed, "Holy shit, Parker. Did you see that?"

"Jeep Cherokee. Hit it!"

Matthews careened around the corner, the Jeep half a block ahead.

"He's going away from the hospital," Matthews yelled.

"Trying to get around the roadblocks."

The Jeep took the next left too fast, went into a slide and hit a signpost. Matthews slammed the brakes and stopped forty feet short. He jumped out behind the door, trying to get a good visual through the storm. Arnold was out of the Jeep now, behind the driver's door, firing at Matthews.

For some reason, Matthews closed in on the Jeep, firing steadily from his Glock's fifteen-round magazine, with Arnold returning fire. I scrambled out the right side of the Suburban and ran toward Anna in the passenger seat, hoping Matthews was drawing Arnold's attention. Halfway to the Jeep, Matthews went down, hit once, maybe twice.

I reached the back of the Jeep and fired two quick shots over the roof, trying to keep Arnold pinned down, the big .45 bucking in my hand. Five rounds left in my Colt 911 with no backup. I yanked open the passenger door, firing two more shots over the hood. I saw no movement and thought he must be crouched behind the door of the Jeep or maybe working his way along the side in order to get behind me. I yanked Anna out and pushed her toward the Suburban, hollering for her to run. We reached the Suburban as a round shattered the windshield close to my head. I pushed Anna down, turned back and fired three times in quick succession at the ghostly figure crouched behind the Jeep's door. The 911 clicked on empty.

"Stay down," I yelled to Anna and turned toward Matthews sprawled in the street. I hadn't counted Arnold's shots and had no idea how many rounds his weapon held or if he had another clip. But with Matthews lying wounded in the street, I had no choice. I sprinted to Matthews, put him in a fireman's carry over my shoulder and scrambled back toward his SUV, sloshing through the water. I heard two rounds fired from the Jeep and hoped neither had hit Matthews. I laid him down at the back of the Suburban and checked his wounds.

Matthews moaned, bleeding badly through a hole in his chest and a bullet in his leg. I took off my belt and handed it to Anna for a tourniquet on his leg. Then I removed the field jacket I'd borrowed from Harry and pushed it into Matthews' chest to stop the blood flow, all the while hollering for him to stay with us. Knowing the neatnik Harry was, I hated to use his jacket, but there was nothing else. His jacket would be ruined, but at least Harry would be gratified to know that his favorite piece of clothing had saved his friend's life.

I ejected the magazine in my .45 to make sure and found it empty. No idea if I'd hit the bastard. I peeked around the side of the Suburban, expecting Arnold to come toward us and noticed something glistening in the glare from the strobe lights of the Suburban. Matthews' Glock lay in the street, twenty feet away. I could make a dash for it, hope for the best. The gun held fifteen rounds. He'd only fired a few. Had to try. I ran for the Glock, expecting shots. I reached the gun, rolled to the right in the rain, flat on my stomach, a small silhouette hard to hit. I positioned my arm with the Glock in front of me, ready to fire. Nothing. No movement at the Jeep. I waited...and waited...nothing.

Chapter Thirty-Eight

Friday night
Galveston

Anna's voice pierced the storm, screaming that the tourniquet on Matthews' femoral artery wasn't holding, the blast to his chest still pumped red and he was bleeding out. Only minutes left, she yelled. I hurried through a final scan of the Jeep looking for movement. Was he hiding? Waiting for a clear shot?

With both hands on Matthews' Glock, I rubbed rainwater out of my eyes, trying to focus. Matthews had only fired a few rounds. There were enough bullets left in the gun to finish Arnold if I could just find him. What I really wanted to do was get my hands around his throat and finish this thing right.

But behind me, Anna was still screaming for help. She had her arms under Matthews' shoulders trying to lift him into the Suburban. No choice, now. I got to my feet and zigzagged back toward Anna, hoping to avoid a shot in the back. We manhandled Matthews into the cargo bay and Anna climbed in after him. The Emergency Room was less than three blocks away. I shoved the Suburban into drive, turned around and raced toward the roadblock, lights flashing and siren roaring. Abul Zahir, AKA David Arnold, the last remaining terrorist, was someone else's problem now.

An hour later, the worst of the fast-moving storm had blown

through. Although flood waters still inundated some of the main streets, city maintenance trucks were already out clearing debris off the roadways and tow trucks were busy hooking up drowned vehicles.

Anna and I sat huddled under blankets on a couch in a large room off the ER, drinking steaming coffee and listening to Chief Puryear bark orders as he directed the search for David Arnold. Either the hospital had made an exception to its no-pet rules or Puryear ignored them because his English bulldog Colonel Bubbie was sprawled on the floor at his side, slobbering all over a leather bone and oblivious to the dozen or more people crowded in the room. A large coffee urn sat on a folding table that was covered with cold donuts. There weren't enough chairs, but it didn't matter because most folks were standing in small knots around the room. I heard laughter which made me want to get up and slap someone.

It made sense for Puryear to requisition the room as a temporary command center since Secretary Perry was the primary target, and both a wounded Galveston PD officer and an FBI agent were fighting for their lives a few floors up. Heavy radio traffic bounced off the numerous radios and Puryear had to tell everyone to either turn them down or get the hell out.

Agent Hebinck bounded in and out of the room, shuffling between getting regular updates on Matthews' condition and directing his agents in the field who were still searching for Arnold. The Level Four trauma team at UTMB had plugged the holes in Matthews' torso, pumped in several pints of blood and stabilized his blood pressure. The last report indicated he was still in surgery, but holding steady.

With the bombing at the Coast Guard station, a wounded SWAT officer, Tube Jones shot at the Waffle House and now Agent Matthews still in surgery, the trauma team was getting a hell of a workout. Elsewhere in the hospital and under the wary eyes of Secret Service agents, a steady line of concerned Galvestonians packed the blood donation center, offering to help in the only way they knew how.

Agent Erwin entered the crowded room and told us that the mysterious hospital contact had been identified by the Waffle House waitress after searching through thousands of photographs of UTMB employees. Mario Sanchez was now in custody and an elite team from the Mexican National Police was en route to rescue his parents. Hebinck said, at his request, the FBI had authorized a special reward for the waitress in the amount of $100,000.

I smiled when he said that, remembering the tired look on the waitress' face when she'd served me breakfast only a few hours before all the uproar. Good things sometimes happen to good people.

Conspicuously absent was the CIA spook Peter Kay. No one cared, but Hebinck mentioned he was probably already on a private jet on his way back to Jordan.

Chief Puryear barked something into his radio and then motioned me to the corner with Hebinck, Roush and Erwin for a quick update. Anna had fallen asleep and was leaning against my shoulder. I eased her down on the couch, tucked the blanket up to her chin and strode over to Puryear.

He spoke softly, "The entire island is sealed tighter than a gymnast's ass: the causeway, Bolivar ferry and the bridge over San Luis Pass, all closed before Arnold could have possibly reached any of them. The TV stations have the photo of him that we got off the web and are running it nonstop. And it's in every police cruiser."

"Any reports of stolen vehicles?" Roush asked.

Puryear shook his head.

"Could have hijacked a driver," I said. "We wouldn't know."

"Either way, he won't get off the island," Puryear groused.

"He abandoned the jeep two blocks from Ferry Road, but it's more than a mile to the landing. We issued a shelter-in-place alert via the emergency telephone response plan the county devised to warn of an approaching hurricane. We're doing a door-to-door of every house and apartment unit along the route. The road to the Coast Guard base intersects Ferry Road and that section is being searched by Shore Patrol."

He paused, then continued, "Our suspect has seemingly vanished into the thick, muggy atmosphere of Galveston Island. But he's out there somewhere and we're not going to quit until we find the bastard."

"What about the yacht basin?" I asked. "It's maybe three or four blocks from the Jeep, a lot closer than the ferry landing."

"The man's from Indianapolis," Puryear huffed. "What the hell does he know about boats?"

I glanced back at the couch and noticed Anna had disappeared. She came back a few minutes later with her hair combed, a touch of gloss on her lips and fresh makeup under her eyes to mask her weariness. She was beginning to look like her old radiant self.

Chief Puryear approached her and said, "The City of Galveston and the country owe you a great debt of gratitude, Dr. Lang. I understand the President may call later. You placed Secretary Perry's safety above your own. Extraordinary selflessness."

Anna spoke so softy, Puryear had to bend down to hear her.

"Please don't make a big deal of this, chief. It's really quite simple. I had no choice. I am a scientist and a medical doctor. I never intended to deliver the anthrax to that madman. It was easy enough to give him a vial of simple growth medium. I even used the same white cloth."

"Nevertheless," Puryear said. "It was a brave gesture on your part. What was his plan?"

"He knew he couldn't get into the hospital himself so he thought his threat against my grandfather would pressure me to deliver the anthrax."

"What were you planning to do once you got into the hospital?"

"I hadn't gotten that far. But what I really wanted to do was go back out there and scratch his eyes out."

Puryear winced. "Well, you did put your life in danger."

"Danger?" Anna said. She started to tell him to come spend a day with her in the laboratory testing the world's most dangerous pathogens, but caught herself in time and said nothing.

I slipped away to the elevator for a quick visit to Tube Jones. He had been hit once in the right chest, but was now stable and in a private room. Puryear said that he could be rotated back to the force after a long convalescent period.

When I entered the room, Travis was leaning over the bed going over the signatures on the football with his dad. Tube was moving his finger from one signature to the next, explaining as he went. Tube's wife Sheryl came forward with a big hug. She thanked me for offering to stay the night, but was firm on being there with her husband. Travis and I hugged, and I stepped close to the bed and squeezed Tube's hand. He was groggy from the meds but the painful smile on his face said enough.

Back in the temporary command center, Chief Puryear still towered over everyone in the room, barking orders to anyone who would listen. Colonel Bubbie must have been out for a walk with his handler. I thought about sticking around to see how the search for David Arnold progressed, but decided they had enough conflicting advice between the difference agencies. Besides who was I representing, The Garhole Bar?

Agent Erwin had left to check on her agents. With David Arnold still on the loose the Secret Service couldn't be too careful. General Roush stood in the corner showing something on his phone to a knot of FBI agents and cops. I cornered Roush to say goodbye, but before I could make my exit he flashed the phone at me with a vacation photo of his beautiful wife and grandkids, the teenage girl on a horse complete with helmet and a small boy with a golf club in his hand. Then he slid to a photo of his new home on a golf course. Retiring next year, he said. Life was good.

I found Agent Hebinck in the hallway and told him I'd call later to check on Agent Matthews. We talked about a fishing trip in the spring when he could take a few days off and Matthews was back from a cruise.

Chief Puryear assigned a patrol car to take me to Harry's house to get my truck and Anna to her condo. When the cops dropped me at Harry's, I immediately jumped into my heap and followed the squad car. The officers commandeered a spot directly in front of Anna's building and I was lucky to find a space two doors down. We escorted Anna to her condo and made a quick check inside. Anna's friend and neighbor Iryna Kravets brought over a tureen of hot chicken soup with a mound of fresh fruit on the side. I gave Anna a big hug and welcomed my new step-cousin to the family.

She said her mother was doing better and she'd changed her flight home to Monday so she'd have time to confer with her boss and bring him up to speed. That would give her a day of rest tomorrow, but I figured she'd be over checking on Bully by breakfast time. The two cops said Galveston PD would be stationed in front of the building all night and tomorrow, if necessary. At least until David Arnold was caught, or hopefully killed. Their words, not mine.

I left the hospital and realized that if the wind laid, tomorrow should be clear and warming. Even in January, a bright sun would bring families to the beaches and tourists to the restaurants. The peaceful, fun-filled part of Galveston life would return. In February, huge crowds would invade the island for the annual Mardi Gras celebration, and in late April hundreds of oleander bushes along Broadway Boulevard would spring forth in beautiful white, pink and red-flowered blossoms, all offering a cheery welcome to visitors. Of course, the island would also be alive with stories about the terrorist attacks, some real some not, but all of them exciting. Every local would have his or her own version straight from the mouth of a friend or relative who claimed to have witnessed some part of the saga.

Chapter Thirty-Nine

Friday night
Galveston

For the past twenty years, the Kiwanis Club of Galveston had sponsored the annual catch-and-release "Race for the Big Game Fish" tournament that provides thousands of dollars in prizes and prestige for the winners, all for charity. More than forty boats leave the Galveston Yacht Club and spend two days offshore searching for Yellow Fin Tuna, Swordfish and the elusive Blue Marlin.

The contest would officially begin at sunrise tomorrow, but the best fishing grounds were as far as 100 miles offshore. Most of the boats traditionally left early the night before to be in position when the great ball of light broke the horizon.

Tonight, the yacht basin was a beehive of activity with fishermen fueling their boats, testing the engines and packing ice and bait for the trip. Many contestants had already pulled out.

No one noticed a bedraggled man in a wet coat slowly plodding along the pier toward slip 169. Ten minutes later the engine on the thirty-five-foot Bertram rumbled to life. The boat backed out of the slip and followed another rig out of the marina. Thirty minutes later, the Bertram rounded the jetties, entered the Gulf of Mexico and turned south along the coast.

Chapter Forty

Friday night/Saturday morning
Galveston

During the past week, I'd had enough drama to last a lifetime. A hot shower and a cold beer at The Garhole Bar sounded pretty good, but not better than Kathy Landry's arms wrapped around me. She answered her phone on the first buzz.

"You okay?" she asked.

"Well, just a wee-bit tired."

"How about a hot bath, back rub and a cold beer?

"In that order?"

"If you have something else in mind, you better hurry. I have to be at work by eleven o'clock tomorrow night."

She delivered the hot bath and rubdown, as promised. Along with a six pack of Shiner Bock, she'd whipped up a pot of beef stew with onions and mushrooms, and topped it off with homemade jalapeno cornbread, perfect for a dreary winter's night. I chowed down, thinking I could get used to this.

We ended the night and early morning in bed wrapped up together like a candy cane. I didn't want it to end. Eventually, the aroma of fresh brewed coffee drew me into the kitchen. With sleep in our eyes, we sat at the kitchen table quietly enjoying each other's company like old-time married folks who didn't need to say a lot, just trusting the feeling was there. The world outside seemed a long way away; the horrendous tragedies of the last few days were already beginning to pass into the foggy bottom of my memory bank.

It was then that my phone buzzed. I would have let it go to voicemail, but noticed it was Harry Stein calling, probably my best friend in the world.

"Morning, Parker. I just got back from the hospital visiting Maurice Matthews. He's doing so well he was on the phone with the cruise line. With all the publicity from the attacks, they want him back on the dance floor. Women are calling from all over the country. They're talking about lining up a special seven-day trip."

"Well, I'll be switched. How did he take it?"

Harry chuckled, "Well, he's still high on drugs, but he managed to grin and move his hands in some kind of a twirling motion."

"Maybe you ought to get some dance lessons from him. Might help you with the casserole ladies."

"Oh, please."

"How about Secretary Perry?"

"Matthews said he got a report that Perry was coming along. He'll still be hospitalized a while, of course. The word is the President is coming down to see him."

"Sounds like our President. Anything for a photo op: gowned and gloved with a face mask. Front page stuff."

"Maybe I'll invite the President over for one of June's tuna-noodle casseroles."

We both laughed harder than we had in a long time, a sign life was returning to normal. It felt good.

Harry said, "When the Secretary gets out, Matthews wants to take him by the old Perry homestead outside of Huntsville."

"Does the family still own it?"

"No, but with Perry's Secret Service escort, Matthews says

it won't be a problem. It's enough to intimidate anyone."

"I can only imagine. Thanks for the update, Harry."

"Okay. Hey…wait. Turn on your TV quick. You won't want to miss this."

The scene was Molly's house in Texas City, cameras rolling. Molly and Bully sat in their wheelchairs on the front gallery, the shotgun leaning against the wall behind her, the coffee can full of spit in her lap, and Bully beside her complete with the black eyepatch over his eye and the stub of last night's stogie in his mouth.

While Molly was rattling on about how they took out the bad guy, Bully removed his glass eye, wiped it with a handkerchief and slipped it back in, all on camera for the world to see. The reporter asked about the cowboy hero who'd appeared in the nick of time, but Molly said her friend was the quiet type who preferred to be left alone to tend to his cattle.

The camera closed in on Molly's face. The white patches and brown spots reminded me of the old hand-made quilt my grandmother had fashioned from discarded colored cloths.

The reporter asked, "Don't you get a little fearful out here all alone on the prairie?"

Molly scrunched her eyes, as if not believing the question. She reached for the shotgun and set it across her lap. "I been here goin' on forty years. We take care of ourselves." She spit into the can and slid her hand into Bully's.

Coming through the gate behind the cameraman and reporter was a tall brunette wearing tennis shoes, jeans and an old gray sweatshirt. She trudged up the path, shoulders slumped, carrying a mop and a pail full of cleaning supplies. A ponytail flowed from beneath a no-named ball cap pulled low over her eyes. A closer look revealed a light dusting of makeup and lip gloss, but no one noticed. Bully's good eye lit up as she approached, but he managed to turn off the smile forming on his lips before the camera man caught him. She climbed the steps and opened the screen door.

"Morning, Missy," he said.

"Morning Mr. Bully, Miss Molly," she answered. "I'll be starting in the kitchen."

The reporter said, "I see your housekeeper has arrived. We'll let you get back to your routine. Thank you for the interview."

Bully took the stogie from his mouth and pointed it at the camera. "That weren't no housekeeper. She's my granddaughter. Ain't she beautiful?"

I clicked off the TV and Kathy and I had a good laugh. I sipped more coffee and found her searching my eyes, waiting, drawing me in.

"Well...Kathy...I've been thinking. I'm not sure I want to spend the rest of my days slopping gumbo and beer at The Garhole. I mean, I love the land, the water. It's what I know. Still...."

She thought a minute and said, "I think you're a hopeless romantic, Parker. Hiding out beneath the skeleton of a gar head in a lonely bar."

"Wow, that's kind of rough, Kathy. Hiding out, huh?"

"Lost in the forest."

"Or maybe the prickly pear and cord grass of West Beach."

"Even better. Do you see a way out?"

I caught her eye, a reservoir of deep brown that seemed to go on forever. "I've been thinking...."

"You said that already." She smiled and reached across the table and put her hand on mine.

"I occasionally play poker with a bunch of Galveston guys. One of them owns a seafood restaurant on Avenue O between Broadway and the seawall."

"I know it," she said. "Fish and Stuff. The locals love it."

"He's mentioned a couple of times he'd like to retire, do more fishing."

"What would you do with The Garhole Bar?"

"Neddie could run it."

She rolled her eyes.

"I know, I know. I'd be lucky to break even."

"Do you have the money to buy Fish and Stuff?"

"I could sell the beach frontage. It would bring enough, but—"

"A developer would build a line of three-story condos there in a heartbeat."

"Right, and I can't handle that. A few years back, the Audubon Society wanted to buy the bird pond and a few surrounding acres."

"What's wrong with that?" she asked.

"They would put in a parking lot at the highway with a trail to the pond. Can you imagine the weekend crowd?"

Kathy took her hand back and straightened in her chair.

"So, you can't handle that either, huh, Parker McLeod? Sounds like you're not too serious about the restaurant idea. You'd actually have to get off your butt and make a decision."

"What does that mean?"

"Come on. You're just not ready. Probably need another fifteen years. You'd be, what, sixty-eight or so then. Sounds about right."

She got up and moved to the kitchen, got the coffee pot, refilled our cups and sat back down, leaving the pot on the table.

"Parker, you just risked your life saving Anna. Yet you can't make a simple decision to buy a friggin' restaurant."

We locked eyes for a long time. I blinked first and said, "Maybe he'd consider owner financing."

She smiled again and put her hand back on mine. "So, are

you finished with all the Gulf War aches and pains?"

"No pills or hard booze. Only an occasional beer."

"Occasional?"

"Well...."

"You know how important Maggie is to me, Parker." Kathy's eyes sparkled as she spoke. "Think you can handle that?"

"I can't wait to meet her. When is she coming home?"

"Tomorrow afternoon. She wants to learn how to fish."

"I can do that."

"She's also talking football."

"That, too."

"She's crazy about her dad. He's a good man. He has her alternate weekends, teaches her about the science of medicine, exposing her to the possible. But she could always use another friend."

"I could, too," I said.

"That leaves us with every other weekend. And if we're going to be spending a few mornings together, I really need to ask a serious question."

"Anything."

She got up, topped off our coffee and reached for a skillet.

"How do you like your eggs?"

Bad Moon Rising

About the Author
A. Hardy Roper

As a fourth generation Texan and Galveston resident, A. Hardy Roper writes from a wealth of knowledge about the island's storied past and vibrant present. Mr. Roper's great grandparents arrived from Germany in the 1852 and entered through the Port of Galveston, at the time, second only to New York for immigrant destination.

Today's Galveston is an eclectic mixture of 'old money' and Victorian mansions checkered among indigent neighborhoods of African Americans and Hispanics, all weaved tightly together, as if huddled against the onslaught of the next storm like the epic 1900 hurricane that claimed 6,000 lives.

From its 19th Century past of pirates and buried treasures, to its 20th Century lifestyle of bootlegging, bawdy houses and gambling, Galveston Island offers an endless setting for mystery and intrigue.

A. Hardy Roper has studied its culture and its history. His Parker McLeod thrillers weave an intricate path of deceit and mayhem as the city struggles to balance its colorful past with the inevitable collision of sleepy 'island life' and the hurried weekend rush as the playground of Houston's wealthy baby-boomers.

Contact Hardy on Facebook
www.facebook.com/TheGarholeBar

Other Books by the author:

The Garhole Bar™

Assassination in Galveston™

Saving Jake™

Reviews for *The Garhole Bar*   November 4, 2007

The Garhole Bar

A Parker McLeod Thriller by
A. Hardy Roper

From the *Galveston Daily News*
Captivating and Engrossing,

by Margaret C. Barno "story weaver"
(Pflugerville, TX)

How long has it been since you've stayed up to the wee hours of the night so engrossed in a book so that you could read just one more page? It happened to me last night, or rather, this morning.

The Garhole Bar is a thriller, full of suspense, unexpected turns and many of these events unfold on the West End of Galveston Island. Its author, A. Hardy Roper, who called that location home for over twenty years, sets the novel, his first, at a bar owned by Parker McLeod. Named after the skeleton of an alligator gar jaw he had found and pried open, it is displayed prominently, hanging from the ceiling behind the bar counter.

The story's plot is complex; depth of character development, covering a sixty-year time frame. The scenes initially shift from Germany and Galveston, eventually covering three continents.

Parker McLeod, a 19-year veteran, is struggling to get his life back together. While attempting to help an old friend and his granddaughter, Parker discovers skills learned during his military service come in handy in his new career as owner of a small bar on the west end of an island in the Gulf of Mexico off the coast of Texas.

The story is well presented and kept my heart thumping to the last page. I hope that next thriller involving Parker McLeod is ready for press soon. My hunch is that A. Hardy Roper has a new venture as author that will keep him busy and his books in demand for years to come.

Review Written by wilhelmlette (Houston, TX USA)
Well done...had my interest from start to finish!
December 11, 2007
Having been to Galveston Island many times, this book was especially fun to read. This novel will clearly be just as much of a page turner for those who don't know the island at all. A. Hardy Roper does a nice job of character development and successfully weaves the various storylines into a truly entertaining novel of intrigue. The book was an easy and entertaining read.

Review for *"Assassination in Galveston"*   **Dec. 3, 2011**

From the *Galveston Daily News*

by Margaret C. Barno, story creator
"Island thriller is a page-turner."

Military veteran and former spy Parker McLeod had all intentions of settling in Galveston's West End to fish and run a quiet restaurant, *The Garhole Bar*, after his medical retirement resulting from the Gulf War.

Those plans have been only partially realized. He has gotten involved in solving crimes. This book is another of those unanticipated adventures when a dear friend and lover Of Kemp's ridley sea turtles is murdered and her home set ablaze. The plot is multi layered, involving assassinations initiated and orchestrated by Fidel and Raul Castro, of Cuba. The long-range goal is instigating an uprising in Venezuela, resulting in a coup in which a friend and ally hopefully will become ruler, enabling the flow of much-needed oil to go to the desperately impoverished nation of Cuba.

Where there's life and danger, there's usually romantic intrigue. The author has placed a realistic variety of such interludes throughout the book. The scenes are descriptive yet not graphic. For that I was grateful.

It's another page-turner that, on a couple of evenings, I set a chapter limit to read no further before going to bed. Roper's characters are well-developed, like the "bad guys" to the folks at the VA hospital and residents on Bolivar Peninsula and Galveston's West End. Perhaps the best descriptions were the Galveston landmarks, particularly the areas around the ferry landing. I could hear the waves hitting the boat, the ever-hungry gull cries and occasionally see the dolphins racing the ferry no matter who was going where for whatever reason.

I've deliberately not mentioned the ending. If Ii had, you'd not read the book. You'd miss a thriller by doing so. I'm going back to read it again to see what I missed during the first time through.

Review by Saucer

This is another of the Parker McLeod thriller series I couldn't put down until finished. The author's descriptive writing style puts you right in the Texas Gulf Coast area. The beaches, seasonal storms, old restored homes, and other sites bring Galveston alive, right at the seaside.

The protagonist, Parker McLeod, is an ex-army Intel officer who inadvertently gets involved in a plot to murder a South American presidential candidate. When a good friend of Parker's is murdered, he begins his own investigation and meets a cast of nefarious characters and a beautiful Cuban ex-patriot who he teams with to attempt to solve the mystery.

Review for Saving Jake – 4.9 out of 5 stars!   Nov. 3, 2015

From the *Galveston Daily News*

by Margaret C. Barno, story creator

The book begins with the simple act of picking up a boy and woman at a stop in Lake Charles, La. Both look emaciated. The woman only asks to be driven west. One of the few bits of information former Army Intel officer, Parker McLeod, gets is their names, Jake, a boy about 14 and his mother, Joy. The way Joy clutches a duffel, Parker suspects there is more than clothes in the bag. He drops them off just east of the bar he owns at the far western end of Galveston Island. The more Parker learns, the more he is determined to save Jake from the life he has been forced into by his mother's habits as a junkie. Things go from bad to worse when the people who own the bag of drugs Joy has stolen arrive in Galveston. Meanwhile a very wealthy man in Boston has hired a P.I. to learn the truth behind the death of his son. Where there is fire, gun smoke that is, there will be killings and severe injuries, often involving innocent people who are hospitalized unable to talk. That means the only person who knows the location of the drugs is Jake, and he's disappeared. What happens next will keep you, the reader on the edge of your seat. You may even forget to eat, as I did, more than one meal. There's much more, I've not mentioned. You'll need to find those events and personalities when you read the book. If you like thrillers, this is one you can't miss reading.

Format: Kindle Edition, verified purchase

"Saving Jake" is an excellent read! As soon as I finished the book, I immediately bought the other two books by this author. Extremely readable and filled with the sights and feel of Galveston.

Amazon: verified purchase

"Saving Jake" is a great story. I finished the book in two evenings. This is the third book by Hardy Roper that I have read. His knowledge of Galveston is amazing and his other experience makes him a must-read author.

Format: Kindle Edition, verified purchase

Exciting. Interesting character development. Great Plot.
January 14, 2016

Format: Paperback – verified purchase

Hardy Roper's stories get better and better. This is the best writing he's published. Exciting. Interesting character development. Great plot. And I love the setting of this and all his books, the west end of Galveston island. People often say that the first few words of a book are important. I was caught in the story from the first few paragraphs of this book:

www.ingramcontent.com/pod-product-compliance
Lightning Source LLC
Chambersburg PA
CBHW020654110726
47901CB00001B/186